THE MAGPIE'S RETURN

CURTIS SMITH

NO LONGER PROPERTY OF
ANYTHINK LIBRARIES/
RANGEVIEW LIBRARY DISTRICT

D0973757

The Magpie's Return
Text Copyright © 2020 Curtis Smith
All rights reserved.

Published in North America and Europe by Running Wild Press. Visit Running Wild Press at www.runningwildpress.com Educators, librarians, book clubs (as well as the eternally curious), go to www.runningwildpress.com for teaching tools.

ISBN (pbk) 978-1-947041-61-5
ISBN (ebook) 978-1-947041-62-2

One for sorrow,
Two for joy,
Three for a girl,
Four for a boy,
Five for silver,
Six for gold,
Seven for a secret,
Never to be told,
Eight for a wish,
Nine for a kiss,
Ten for a bird,
You must not miss.

— *ONE FOR SORROW,*
CHILDREN'S NURSERY RHYME

To my grandparents, who lifted me up before they knew my name.

I.

* * *

I've been called a genius. The school psychologist in second grade, a parade of others through the years. Men and women with calm voices and busy pens. I solved their puzzles, repeated their ever-lengthening alphanumeric daisy chains both forward and back. When I grew bored, I questioned my evaluators. Did they enjoy their work? Did they have children of their own? What were their names? The testings took place in universities and hospitals, rooms made familiar by their sterile whiteness, their hidden microphones and two-way mirrors. Papers have been published about some of those sessions, journal articles heavy with footnotes and graphs. I don't mention these things to my teachers and classmates, but the whispers swirl in my wake, a layer of distance I have cursed and embraced, depending upon my mood. And while I'm sympathetic to the vagaries of language and to the human desire to categorize, I'm not entirely comfortable with my label. My condition has less to do with intelligence than vision, for I see the world in layers, in ever-evolving webs of connection. *A* may well lead to *B* ninety-nine percent of the time, but given a twist, it might jump to *C* or *H* or crossover to delta or mu or a hieroglyphic character culled from a pharaoh's tomb. Imagine a summer night streaked by branching lightning. That's the slide show in my skull, all day, every day. A thousand burning paths lighting the dark.

And for every light, there is a shadow. My shadow is no darker or wider than yours, but the same lightning that illuminates my outward gaze can't help but splash back inside, and I am left with a more acute awareness of my shadow's depth than most. This, too, is a gift, albeit a somewhat melancholy one. *Gnothi seauton*, Plato urged. *Know thyself*, a laudable goal of

3

those fun-loving Stoics, although I must believe truly knowing one's self isn't a task for the faint of heart. My mother, the poet, strives to capture natural moments both mundane and telling, so allow me, her left-brained daughter, to begin with this image. A solitary girl, her face long, a reluctant, shuffling stride as she crosses her school's campus beneath a leaden November sky.

Every third period I attend honors AP Calculus 2 at the high school. Calc is the highlight of my day, an immersion in concepts and theories and an escape from the junior high circus of selfies and status and warring cliques. Every fourth period, I return. There are numerous theories of time beyond its lockstep march through linear awareness, and allow this trudge across the school's playing field to be my exhibit A in the argument that the second hand sags beneath the weight of dread. I keep my head down, not to avoid the cutting breeze but to save myself the horizon's rise of my school, yet even with a diverted gaze, each step melds the building's brick and steel deeper into my bones. My pace slows as I kick a forgotten field hockey ball. The field's chalked lines have faded, these hard-frost nights. Echoes sprint past, the warmth of early September, my strides across the grass, and the thwack of wood and rubber resonates in my hands. Another kick, and I estimate the ball's circumference and velocity and its travels across an X-axis, its distance impacted by variables of cleat ruts and the gouges cut into the rubber by the groundskeeper's mower. The numbers' dance leads to new numbers, other variables, and for a moment, my anxiety fades until the ball rolls onto the parking lot macadam.

The crows perched atop the lot's light poles aim their beaks at me. One caws, and the others respond. The Stoics had their omens, and I'm not so grounded in the logical that I'm deaf to the birds' warnings. I cross into the school's shadow, a soft eclipse, and with the deeper chill, I pause and lean against a car. I have my calming techniques—belly breaths, positive visualization—but these are my parents' soft skills, which might be nice in the adult world but which broker little sway in the weirdness of junior high. I'm weary and raw—this Thursday in a week when yesterday felt like Friday. My period with its bad electricity and evil thoughts. The Rudolph-pimple on my nose.

Breathe, and I hold in the sobering cold. My reflection stares back from a minivan window. A curved face, a cloud-choked sky. Beneath my reflection, a still life under glass. A coffee cup and a Cheerio-littered child's seat. A gym bag and sneakers. Envelopes waiting to be mailed. A picture of a life lived, but beyond the moment's breathing fulcrum wait a thousand quantum possibilities, a horizon of futures, fragmented and radiating and infinite. Futures benign. Beautiful. Horrific. All plausible. All perhaps real. I close my eyes and imagine a future where I simply keep walking. The school dwindles and the gray weight slips from my shoulders. A smile on my face and not a glimpse back.

The outside bell rings. My daydream evaporates, and I surrender to the only future available to a rule-following, professor's daughter. A warm burst greets me inside the tech wing doors. I pass woodshop, its aromas of sawdust and the alcohol-sting of fresh shellac, its whir of powering-down drills and saws. Teen movies could lull adults into the false memory that high school hallways allow for leisurely milling and civil banter, but let me assure you that is not the case. The corridor floods, the shoulder-to-shoulder maw the fodder of an agora-phobic's nightmare, the assault of voices disorienting after my walk's hush. Conversations overlap, their coherence and meaning muddled. I squeeze my way into the flow and shuffle forward.

Confession number one: for the past year, I've worked on what I privately refer to as my "Invisibility Campaign." It's a kind of subtraction, a math with rules both simple and as intricate as Euclidean vectors. I raise my hand in calc but nowhere else, the remainder of my day dedicated to window views and notebook doodles. It's not laziness; it's more a willful abandonment, my daydreams more entertaining than the swirling rumors of the previous weekend's escapades of who got drunk and who got naked and who got arrested. I hunker in silence, comforted by the quiet's warmth and dulled rhythms, distant but not oblivious because I always keep an eye on the herd, wary of its unpredictability, its desire to turn upon its weakest. I think of the nature shows I grew up watching and how I'd sob when predators picked off the young and stragglers. I've grown up a bit, my tears more guarded, but those images and their truths remain.

I disengage myself from the current and pull up to my locker. A cackle pierces the din, and I'm thankful for the boy with blue hair and enormous headphones who shields me from Missy Blough. An unfortunate synchronicity crosses Missy's path with mine every day. I shrug off my pack and take out my calc text, hoping the blue-haired boy will save me from Missy's gum-cracking comments. As usual, she's holding court. As usual, she broadcasts her opinions loudly and freely, a delivery of judgment and ridicule and venom. Her world's simple division—her home girls and the school's remaining multitudes of losers. She's the unofficial leader of the Wolf Pack, an all-female clan familiar with the principal's office and detention hall. Girls dropped off late to school from muffler-rumbling cars, sloppy last kisses given by the kind of high school boys I don't find in calc. The Wolf Pack's allegiance signified by their fondness for fighting and the red bandannas they knot around their necks.

I keep my eyes down. Deep breaths and I'm encouraged by the blue-haired boy's dawdling, his head-bobbing techno-trance. I shift my books to my left hand and rub my nose against my sleeve. My lock spins, my fingers numb. *Breathe* and maybe today I'll escape being noticed, a win for the invisibility campaign. The universe and fractured realities of quantum mechanics owe me as much. Just for today. Just until I can shake this threadbare weariness. Three other Wolf Packers surround Missy. The girls loud. Curses and sharp-toothed laughs, their collective scents of cigarettes and dime-store perfume.

During this year's shared moments of locker time, Missy has managed to spew her dim observations about my flatness and outbreaks and flyaway hair. She's noted my wardrobe's muted palate and questioned the sexual preferences of field hockey players. I pretend not to hear, another component of my invisibility. I grit my teeth and remind myself her jibes are the overflow of a shallow mind, utterances no doubt forgotten by the end of lunch's free-for-all, yet irony awaits in the fact that I, the supposed smart one, allow myself to be haunted by her insults, the sting carried through my day, the replayed scenes knotting my gut as my bedside clock ticks away the sleepless hours. The blue-haired boy slides on his backpack. New voices join the hallway's mix, the chaperoned line of the life-skills class, a parade of untied sneakers and broad faces. A boy I've known since first grade calls my name and offers a high five. We slap palms, mine still cold, his damp. The girl behind him raises her hand too, a smack harder and wetter.

Theories of time part two: the notion that the moment is all that is real, a knife's edge of action and consequence, our futures unknowable, our pasts set in stone, but with a snuck glance, I flip the quantum lens and consider the tides that have brought Missy to this moment. Her frustrations and uncertainties, the whispers I've heard, a father both absent and criminal, a mother who showed up drunk for an elementary school open house. My heart softens, and I see her as less a rival than a fellow traveler. Both of us stumbling to define ourselves and to carry our burdens with a bit of grace. Lost in thought, I pass my combination's second number. I curse under my breath, spin the dial, and start again.

"What's wrong there, Kayla?" Missy speaks through a wad of chewed gum. A thinned rock beat plays from her dangling earbuds. She ducks, checking her hair in the mirror she's hung inside her locker door. "Thought you were supposed to be freaking Einstein or something." A pink bubble appears between her glossed lips then pops with her laugh. Her red bandanna tied around her upper arm, no doubt to display her neck's half-dollar sized hickey. The other Wolf Pack girls smirk. "Shit, even those fucking retards can remember their combinations."

My hand slows, and I'm cast adrift in an expansive moment. The last of the life skills class shuffles past. The click of passed numbers lingers on my fingertips. *Breathe* but my rawness flares, a fire along my spine that consumes any compassion I had for imagining this stupid girl's past. I seethe at enduring another inane slight, a greater anger for the ease with which she slips into petty cruelty, unfazed by who she might hurt. I open my locker and unzip my coat. "Shut up for once, Missy."

The Wolf Pack chatter falls silent. Missy's gum-chewing jaw slack. "What did you say?"

I crouch and retrieve my books from the locker's bottom. I should be afraid, Missy's tough-girl reputation cemented last spring in a cafeteria brawl where she ripped a fistful of hair from Amy Gray's scalp—but something has broken in me, a filament of caring, the desire to seek the high road or turn the proverbial cheek. I zip my backpack and slam my locker with a force that causes the nearest Wolf Packer to flinch.

"You hear me, girl?" Missy asks.

I secure my long hair into a ponytail. I will not go down like Amy Gray. "Unfortunately, I did."

Missy pushes aside one of her girls. "Sounds like you have something to say, smartass, so why don't you go ahead and spill?"

The hallway traffic slows, the lure of spectacle, a very public crash and burn for my invisibility campaign. I let the backpack drop. I'd always envisioned myself paralyzed in this kind of moment, but that's not the case. "Every day you talk. You say shit. Sometimes it's obvious shit. Mostly it's stupid shit. But it's always shit." The words, bottled up these past months, flow, and although I've never sipped the cherry vodka or smoked the joints Missy and her gang like to whisper about, I can't imagine their effects are any headier than the swell between my ears. The intoxication isn't a blur, quite the contrary, my focus is scintillating and bright. "You and your crew are welcome to say all the shit you want, but I'm tired of hearing it."

"You've got a big mouth all of a sudden, girl." Missy unhooks her silver hoop earrings and hands them to the girl beside her. The hallway a standstill. Murmurs, goadings, the jockeying for a better view. "Get the bitch," one of the Wolf Pack girls hisses. Cellphones appear, the scene recorded from a dozen different angles. Missy steps forward, and with her first hard push, I rock back onto my heels.

I'm neither the fastest nor the most technically sound player on my field hockey team, but last year, I led the squad in takeaways. My secret—the understanding that the ball is nothing more than a magician's prop, a distraction. Truth waits in the body, and the grids I lose myself within during calc appear before me, and a sprinting wing dissolves into a fluid collage, a shifting collection of boxes on a coordinate plane. With a turn of my hips, I herd my mark toward the sideline, and if I've positioned myself right and my thoughts are clear, I recognize the impulse lurking in a shoulder's dip or a wrist's curve. When I'm close enough to hear my opponent breathe, a first step is all I need.

"What's the matter, bitch?" The voices and gathered faces fade, only Missy in focus. "The smart girl's got nothing to say now?"

Another push, and I stumble over my dropped pack. A guttural chorus rises, the anticipation of violence and blood. The grid appears and Missy melts into a jumble of squares and rectangles, her jaw stretched into a snarling, funhouse distortion. A target that expands until it accumulates its own gravity. Her mouth opens, a maw of teeth and gum and a waggling serpent's tongue, her threats cut short by the fist that swings so fast it hardly seems to belong to me.

I climb from my father's pickup. The breeze stiffens, and I tuck my chin beneath the scarf my mother and I knitted last winter. My hands buried in my pockets, my right further buried beneath bandages and gauze, my knuckles less swollen but still carrying the crescent scar from Missy's front teeth. My father stands beside me and sets down our dog Chestnut. Wooden stakes mark the empty lot, and atop the stakes, red plastic strips, a host of fluttering tongues. At the lot's far end, just before the macadam alleyway, stands a fifty-foot oak. Around the oak's base, a moat of yellow and brown. The breeze musty with the leaves' decay, and the scent reminds me of my parents' study, their books and paper stacks and leather chairs. I consider the oak's laddered limbs and imagine how far I could climb.

In my clinical interviews, I've explained my ability to think ahead, a chess player's imagining of steps and outcomes, the calculations of combinations and probabilities. Add this sense of future time to my grid, a Z-axis that stretches into the mist of what could be, an axis I found myself rocketing along as my fist neared Missy's mouth. The moment expanded, and I envisioned the talks with my parents, not the words so much as their tones, my father's calm understanding and his hopes I'd learn from the experience, my mother's nodding approval when she realized what a bitch Missy had been. I imagined the solitary days of my suspension, the boredom of daytime TV and the expanse of hours I'd have to replay the incident, for better or worse.

And just as my fist met Missy's lip, her gum dislodged, the left side of her face buckling, I imagined a moment like this. Not physically—I'm not a psychic—but this dynamic, my father and I in a quiet moment, our long talks behind us, the return to a more nuanced normal. "Shall we?" he asks.

"It's what we came for," I say, and together we step onto the lawn.

My Z-axis flickers, this time in reverse, the memory of how easily I once reached for his hand, a reflex, an anchoring, and the axis dissolves because I can't decide if the distance between today and then is a lifetime or a nanosecond. Instead, I lift my hands to the clouds and cast myself into a cartwheel, only considering my bandages when they meet the soggy earth. My boots kick up, and my hair falls across my face. I right myself and tuck my hair back beneath my scarf.

"Bravo," my father says. I wipe my palms against my jeans. Chestnut barks in approval.

We walk on, my footing bothered by the remnants of furrowed garden rows. I step on a crumpled flier. Red and white, the Reform Party's colors. *McNally's the One*. Arthur McNally, the founder of the Reform Party, his weekly vodcasts a cocktail of nationalistic Christianity, anti-intellectualism, and thinly veiled racism. Every week it seems I find one of his fliers in our mailbox or under our car's wiper. "Idiots," my mother says, the paper tossed into the nearest trashcan. My father does the same, but not before taking a moment to read them. A slight shake of his head, a heavy sigh. The papers balled in his hands. The election almost a year away.

Our plot strikes a sour note in the neighborhood's harmony of ranches and split-levels. A history lesson from my father—the double lot purchased by one of the development's original owners. His home next door and the adjoining field claimed by the garden whose dimensions and maintenance mimicked the trajectory of his health. Tomatoes and watermelons. Zucchini. Strawberries, peppers, cauliflower, and pumpkins. A wooden bench by the sidewalk and his surplus free. Then a small stroke and, a year later, a larger one. The garden neglected these past three growing seasons. Its neat rows ragged with weeds and rabbit holes. Yellow jackets in the beds' rotted wood beams. His sons placed their father in a nursing home and put the house up for sale. The property lingered for over a year until the Realtor suggested subdividing. The forty-three-year-old split-level picked up by a local bureaucrat. The once-garden purchased by my parents.

A moving van sits in front of the split-level. Men in blue jumpsuits wrangle a sofa through the front door, and their voices drift across the open lot. Beneath my boots, a suction-kiss, these last three days of rain and the river out of its banks. Chestnut lopes ahead, his short legs lost in the grass. Chestnut, named for his red-brown coat, is our glorious mutt, his hiccup-ping limp and fur-hidden scars carriers of a secret history. He's my first dog, and I recently admitted to my mother that I'd had no idea how much I'd love him. "How could you not?" My mother tussled the dog's head. "Remember that."

"What?"

"Love has a way of surprising us."

I lift my chin and watch my breath mesh into the gray. I imagine the changes to come. The trucks of my uncles' construction company, my father their gofer laborer, just as he'd been through high school and as an undergrad. My uncles with their callused hands and rough manners and practical knowl-edge; my father the little brother they both teased and protected, a botany major, doctoral fellowships in England and France and the author of a pair of books unread by anyone outside his field. My father is the youngest department chair at the local university he'd attended as an undergrad, his home-town returned to in order to marry the high school sweetheart he'd never stopped loving. He ambles through the weeds, stork legs and wide feet. His hands clasped behind his back. His gaze upon the ground and his thoughts snared in his world of grasses and insects. Each, he's fond of telling his only child, unique. Each a miracle.

I pause beside one of the stakes planted at the lot's center. I brush back the windswept strands that have escaped my ponytail. Chestnut circles back, and I crouch and stroke his head. "Good boy." I wrangle my chin from my scarf's folds and plant a kiss behind his ear, not minding the stink of wet fur. I've seen the blueprints, and as the chill sinks into my lungs, the house rises from the empty space. Rooms and steps and windows. Toilets and sinks. The kitchen. My bedroom. The home where I'll grow up. The home I'll leave only to return to again and again. A college student. A wife. A mother. The years stretch ahead of me, a corridor of shadows and blinding light.

I join my father by the tall oak. "Can we keep the tree?" My boot's toe traces a shallow root.

"Do you know what kind it is?"

"Are you serious?"

"I wouldn't bet against you, but still."

"Oak."

"More specific?"

"Pin."

"Would you like to keep it?"

"Unless there's a good reason to get rid of it. Give me a boost."

He bends his knees, hands cupped and fingers laced. I place a foot into the cradle and he lifts. I scramble onto the lowest branch and sit. I consider him, this higher perch, the perspective of a parent looking upon their child. How vulnerable he seems in this framing, as if he were falling away, shrinking, the way he and mother often do in my dreams. Confession number two: in my school days' invisibility daydreams, I occasionally picture a world without my parents. I guess this is common, a combination of budding independence and my greatest fear. Sometimes one is gone (cancer, a car wreck—but I can't, not even in a daydream, picture them divorced); sometimes both (plague, a natural gas explosion), and there are times I become so swept up that I begin to weep, my chest and throat tight, my reality overwhelmed by the nightmares of my imagination.

I gaze up and plan my route. My thoughts leapfrog—the next step and the five after that. The first reaches easy, the branches solid and wide. I've always had a knack for climbing—trees, jungle gyms, rainspouts. "My little monkey," a nickname given by my mother after I mastered escaping my crib. The branches around me a puzzle, an arrangement of pieces, another testing of grids and boxes and waiting steps. My father and Chestnut below, a straining of necks.

"Careful," he says. He brushes away the bark I kicked onto his jacket.

"What?" I sway, a wavering of hips, my free hand clawing the empty air.

"Please don't kid," he says. Chestnut barks.

I contemplate my next move and grasp a branch. "One should always have a plan," I say. I can't see his face, but I imagine his grin, my words an echo of his favorite advice. I hoist myself to the next perch and welcome the horizon of rooftops and power lines. The breeze colder here. The gray above splintered by thinning branches. I consider the earth below. The branches would slow my fall, a few broken bones, but probably not death. Then another thought, and I remove my scarf. An allegiance to possibilities, the kind of morbid scenarios that keep me up at night. The magicians who accidently hanged themselves. Poor Isadora Duncan.

Chestnut charges, disappearing then emerging from the ruts and weeds. Hackles raised and frenzied barks. Our protector, fearless and loyal and ignorant of his size. The approaching man with a thinning comb over and a self-important stride. Shorter than my father but thick in the chest and waist. He stops and plants his fists against his hips. He forsakes hello for a questioning of what my father's doing. A tone reminiscent of my gym teacher or the sour woman who weighs my mother's mailings at the post office. The man glances up, and I pause my descent. Chestnut's yelps abandoned in favor of sniffing the man's pant cuff.

His name is Slater, and a brief exchange establishes him as the new occupant of the original owner's house. I sit on the lowest branch. My sneakers dangle above the dropped leaves. Slater offers a grudging "Welcome" before diving into his interrogation. The size of the house we're planning. How early the crew will start. Do we have plans for a pool. Do we own more dogs. My father's attempts at humor and connection unacknowledged. I listen, present yet wandering into another future, the day's promise dimmed by the notion of living with this man's scowls. I take a breath and remind myself that first impressions can be misleading, a pep talk that fades the longer our new neighbor prattles on.

The conversation between my father and Slater ends with a stiff handshake. Slater marches off, a retreat marred by his stumble over a stake among the weeds. He looks down then glares back at us.

"I'm not passing judgment," I say. "At least not yet."

"Thank you."

"But he does seem super pleasant, and I think he forgot to ask you a few questions. Like what church we go to and who we're voting for and whether or not we think the moon landing was a fake, which I'm pretty sure he does."

"Give him time."

"What choice do we have?"

"Exactly." He reaches up, an invitation. A pose he's struck a hundred times. A game of leap and catch we won't be able to play much longer. "Come on, monkey. Let's go see your mother."

"Dad?"

"Yes?"

"I don't think I want to be called monkey anymore."

He nods. "Fair enough."

* * *

Midsummer, the morning already prickly and thick. Thunderstorms earlier, but now the sun blazes, the wet lawns and shrubs offering a scent tropical and green, and I bike through a dreamy mist. School's out, and I relish the break from junior high idiocy, relish the season's late, lazy nights and the mornings' luxury of closing my eyes and chasing my dreams back into sleep. I'm taking an online statistics course through my father's university, and truth be told, I'm enjoying it more than I thought I would, its parallel realms, its calculations of what the next breath might hold. I crest a small hill, and as I coast down the other side, the breeze cools my sweat. Overhead, the hiss of sagging electrical wires. The call of cicadas hidden in the trees.

Let me fill in a few gaps along my narrative's Z-axis. Our club hockey team stumbled through a 0-8-2 spring season, a record my father suggested might build more character than a championship. Unfortunately, he offered this advice on our way home from our last game, and I'll stick with my contention that my response of "Fuck the fuck off" was, given his timing, appropriate and syntactically creative, if not actually correct. My invisibility campaign went through its own fade, an unspectacular evolution of feeling more comfortable in my own skin. There was a brief flare up on the Missy Blough front, an incident that may or may not have involved me placing a wad of watermelon gum on her locker dial. There were other developments—the parties and dances I wasn't invited to, our high school math quiz club that took first place at State. My mother signed her second poetry collection. My father published a paper on phosphate runoffs and algae blooms. The three of us spent hours surfing decorating sites and noting the designs that struck us, storm doors and medicine cabinets and light fixtures, our new house unbuilt yet becoming more real with each click.

I pedal on. The beachy scent of sunscreen rises from my neck. My long braid sways between my shoulders. Heat lifts from the macadam, from the metal and glass of parked cars. Two miles separate our apartment from the lot. A pair of facts —the average female skull is 7.1 mm thick and kinetic energy equals one half mass times velocity squared. Of course I wear a helmet.

I stop and straddle my bike at my route's busiest intersection. "Promise you'll walk your bike across," my parents ask, and I usually do. The traffic whips along this stretch, people trying to beat the light, half-thinking turns in and out of gas stations and strip malls, the world and its hurry, its ringing phones and crying children, places to be and the clock always ticking. A deeper concern waits in my parents' goodbye stares and last-minute urgings to *Be safe . . . please,* their apprehensions shifting from distracted drivers to their distracted daughter. *I will,* I answer, but sometimes I worry myself. My daydreams. My drownings in thought. There have been mornings where I've surfaced with a sleepwalker's jolt. A turn missed. A surfacing onto an unfamiliar street and my bike's wobbling stop as I blink away the cobwebs.

I press the crossing button. A summer's experiment—the altering of my thumb's rhythm, the seconds counted between pushes. My theory—a rapid cadence would indicate a single, impatient pedestrian while random pulses might suggest an ever-growing crowd who'd be rewarded with a quicker crossing. My hypothesis so far unproven, yet I'm not so cynical as to believe the button is merely a placebo to soothe an agitated populace. Somewhere tucked within the system, a pulse must await, and when I discover the pattern, I'll share it with my parents and statistics teacher.

Delivery trucks buzz through the intersection. A gutter tide of windswept papers and coffee cups tumble around my tires. The evaporating haze dreary and flecked with grit. In the lot beside me, an inflatable tube man dances. Flailing arms and tasseled hair, a permanent smile. The hum of the tube man's blower and the plastic's ruffle resonates in my handlebars. The dancing shadow falls over me, the flicker of sun and shade, movements I visualize on an undulating graph, another rhythm waiting to be understood.

A barking voice breaks my drift. A black pickup and a sedan at the red light, the pickup's engine running, its driver's-side door flung open. A man clambers out, a muscled torso and tight T-shirt. The sun glistens on his sunglasses and shaved head. The pickup's bumper plastered with red-and-white stickers, a red-lettered decal on the cab's rear window—*Holy America. One America.* The sedan's driver remains in his car, and on his bumper, a different vein of stickers, none of them red and white. The bald man shouts, his arms flung in wild gestures before ramming his fist into the driver's side window. With the third blow, the glass shatters. The light turns green, but the bald man is lost in his rage, deaf to the angry horns. The opposite lanes slow. Drivers and passengers stare, the adults no better than the junior high mobs anticipating a fight's first punch. The bald man yanks at the door, cursing and growling, more animal than human. I freeze, stunned by the first-person witnessing of this summer's violence, the ugly manifestations of McNally's ever-more-rabid calls for a new order, righteous and lean, a nation singular and God-fearing. The cellphone videos replayed on the nightly news. Bus stop beatings. Horrible words exchanged in supermarket aisles. Rampaging gangs, their faces masked by bandannas. The cruelty repulsive both on the surface yet also deeper, its flicker burning in my gut and sinew, the recalled shock of my fist meeting Missy's mouth.

The bald man reaches inside the broken window but then steps back. He holds out his hands, a begging wave, his knuckles streaked with blood. A pistol in the hand that emerges from the shattered window. The honking of the nearest cars falls silent. The sedan's tires squeal, a shower of pebbled glass, a charge through a light just turned red.

From a distance, it's hard telling my father apart from his brothers. All of them ropy, sawdust in their black curls. All of them gangly yet deft afoot, the sidestepping of cords, the ducking beneath beams, the heel-toe crossings of planks laid across the mud. The haze lingers beneath the spreading oak, a parcel of mist stirred as I prop my bike against the trunk. Only from this distance do the brothers' differences announce themselves. My uncles' necks browner, the crow's feet etched by sun and cold, the hitch in the backs knotted from years of labor.

High in the oak, the rustle of leaves, the squirrels' acrobatics. I cross the yard, the sun so bright I'm forced to hold a hand above my eyes. Chlorine on the breeze, the backyards of fence-hidden pools, the carry of voices and splashes. I swat away the gnats' tumbling clouds. The house's foundation already poured, and the wall beams frame the trees and street beyond. The nail gun's sigh and spit punctuate the birds' songs. The house strikes me as a living thing. Its activity and daily growth, its wooden skeleton and waiting arteries of conduit and wire and pipe. I climb the short set of concrete steps and cross the back's doorless threshold. Shade here, the second story's new subfloor, and above, the echo of heavy boots. My sneakers whisper across the sawdust. I pick up a pencil and etch the date and my initials on a beam, a daily ritual, each a whisper waiting the burial of sheetrock.

I climb the open stairwell and emerge back into the

sunlight. Above, the roof's slanting beams and a sky of blue and white. I cross the floor to the corner where my bedroom will be. The open air all around and the earth below.

"Howdy, girl." My Uncle Bill takes off his gloves. "I'm thinking it's a good time for a break. How about you?"

My father greets me with a kiss that smells of sawdust and sweat. Last night, we sat here in the dark, our fingers sticky with our ice cream cones' melt, his hand panning the heavens as he shared the stories of Pegasus and Hercules and Draco. Uncle Alex unplugs his circular saw and wraps the cord. I go downstairs to fetch our drinks, my hand numbed in the cooler's puddling ice. Ninety-plus again today, the eighth day in a row, but I don't mind. It's good to be outside, my hands active, my focus beyond my own stewing thoughts. We sit around the stairwell's opening. My face in the sun, my legs dangling in the shadows. I sip and allow the moment to engulf me. The smiles of my uncles. My father's face masked behind his brow-wiping bandanna. The hot breeze, a cardinal's brief perch atop a roof beam. The scene soothes the nerves left smoldering by the intersection's violence, a witnessing I decide to keep to myself, my parents already worried about my daily ride.

Plans are made—my uncles headed to the lumberyard. Lunchtime calls to subcontractors and wives. My uncles tease me. I'm the youngest of the brothers' children, a baby's baby. My cousins in college, others with careers and marriages. Uncle Alex set to be a grandfather in October. Uncle Bill in December.

"Who's your boyfriend this week?" Uncle Alex asks.

"Same as last week," I say.

"I forget his name." Uncle Bill squints. "Herman? Bruce?"

"You're getting close."

"Really?"

"No."

Uncle Alex taps a hammer in his callused palm. "Let young Herman know your family has high standards for any and all suitors."

Uncle Bill leans forward. "There's an initiation, you know."

Uncle Alex: "Many are called but few are chosen."

I take their empty bottles. I make a point of always working at the site—sweeping, wrapping cords, collecting garbage—my belief that a bit of hustle will ensure my keep. I pause halfway down the steps. "I'll give Herman a heads up, but don't be too rough on him."

My uncles take the truck to the lumberyard. My father leaves to caulk the basement windows. Alone on the second floor's open perch, I stoop and pick up nails. The open walls remind me of the doll's house I'd played with as a child. The unblocked sun falls warm on my shoulders, the breeze sweet with honeysuckle. On the patio next door, Slater leashes his pug. Slater bends as he adjusts the clasp, but his eyes remain fixed on our house. When my uncles learned Slater occupied a desk in the county supervisor's office, they understood the odd attention heaped upon their latest project. Agents from zoning and ordinance pay regular visits. They hold levels over the floors, check permits, measure the inches between beams and the feet from sidewalk to the front stoop. The inspectors are old friends, and they part with handshakes and shrugs that express their powerlessness in the matter. At our property's edge, a new line of stakes, a boundary marking the privacy fence Slater has planned. Beyond the stakes, a growing cluster of red and white yard signs. *McNally for America* and *One America—Holy America*. The dog's leash secure, Slater stands and his gaze lifts to me. I imagine myself from his perspective, a doll in a doll-house, a girl set against the clouds. I don't wave and neither does he. With a flick of my broom, I send a sawdust plume over the floor's edge.

My father advocates patience with our neighbor. Some people need time, he says, and what seems like indifference might actually be a shield. "All of us have been hurt," he said the other night over dinner. "All deal with it in their own way."

"If all of us have been hurt, then there are some who've done their fair share of the hurting." I stuck a forkful of chicken into my mouth. "It's only logical. Law of averages and everything. I'd be glad to show you some statistical models."

"She has a point," my mother said.

"Indulge me, please." My father smiled. When I think of my father, I see this smile first, a welcome for me, an embrace of the world. "It's a small favor for the greater good."

I'm gathering another sawdust pile when a woman's voice calls. "Hey up there."

The woman on the sidewalk holds a hand above her eyes, her other hand resting on her belly's pregnant curve. "Hey, Dr. Klein," I say.

"Doesn't seem right they have you working all alone."

"Dad's in the basement." My voice lifts above the cicadas' thrum. Phyllis Klein is our across-the-street neighbor and a professor in my father's department. She's already recruited me for babysitting, a task which I've never done and am secretly afraid I'll be terrible at, my life without the sibling I once secretly pined for, my inexperience certain to lead to fumbling. A child so fragile and me so naïve and clumsy.

Dr. Klein moves aside as Slater and his pug approach. At the lot's edge, the dog lifts his leg and pisses on a woodpile. Slater stares, a gaze simple and unapologetic. He gives the leash a yank, and the pug yelps. They waddle a retreat, the dog's gait an echo of its owner's. I pick nails from the sawdust and sweep the pile over the floor's lip. In me, a balancing. My sneakers at the floor's edge. My father's advice. The unkind words simmering in my gut.

* * *

Our official move-in day falls on Trick-or-Treat night, and despite the fact that our gas line has yet to be hooked up and nearly all of what we own remains in boxes, my parents make a twilight trip to the store for candy. I was never much for Halloween, its ghouls and costumes a bit silly for a logic-grounded child. The heat may not work but the doorbell does, and Chestnut barks with each ring. Between handing out chocolates, I sit by the window and study the lit cone beneath the opposite curb's streetlight. A cowboy appears. A robot. A soldier and a squad of cheerleaders. Their passings temporary, glimpses before they cross back into the dark.

The traffic increases and so does Chestnut's frenzy, and when the barking becomes too much, I take the candy bowl and sit on the front stoop where I discover a forgotten mask. The mask is simple and black, an oval to cover the eyes and nose, the kind of getup worn by bank robbers in old movies. I test the elastic's anchoring staples and imagine the mask's journey. An excited child, a costume unraveling an item at a time. I slide on the mask. The elastic band pinches my hair, my vision narrowed. Inside, my parents smile, yet when I check the foyer mirror, the mask makes me feel as if I've stepped back, a receding into someone myself yet not. I surprise both my parents and myself when I ask, "Is it OK if I go out, just to walk around?"

My mother fashions a blue sheet into a cape, a knot around my throat and a satisfying flutter as I walk. The night cool, a tingle on my bare skin, the faintest parcel of breath as I cross the streetlight's shine. I'm fourteen—and nothing irritates me more than being treated like a child—but then come moments like this when I yearn for nothing more than childhood's diversions of simplicity and belonging. So I walk, a secret child for the next half hour. I return the stares of jack-o-lanterns and bed-sheet ghosts. I'm bag-less—my desire not for sweets but to observe. Nearly all my fellow travelers are smaller than me, and I'm surrounded by an undercurrent of murmurs and rustling footsteps. A boy dressed like a dog, a rope leash around his neck, bumps my side, his focus on his open bag and the take waiting inside. The children reckless, costumed dashes across empty streets. On the lawns, candy wrappers, testaments to impatience and illicit thrills. I, too, am thrilled, or at least intrigued. This pointless parade, a sugar-driven folly. This chance to walk amid a childhood I'd once believed too frivolous but for which I have a sudden yearning, an appreciation just as my time to be part of it fades.

I return to the smell of fresh paint and Chinese takeout. My father places a log in the fireplace. There's dirt under his fingernails, the day spent readying his garden before the frost, his meticulously arranged pteridophytes and angiosperms, lineages dating back before the time of men. What his beds will lack in blooms they'll atone for in texture and in stories my father, if asked, would be happy to share.

He steps back, and I set a match to the kindling, my cape still on, my mask pulled atop my forehead. I sit close, drawn to the fire's crackle and warmth. Bach on the stereo. My mother with a red pen and proof pages, her collection going to print after Christmas. My father with his head on her lap. This communal gathering rare, my father's fall split between campus lectures and evenings working alongside his brothers, my ninth-grade year already a quarter done, my evenings' homework, my afternoons spent at practices and games. We're in the season's last weeks, our team's derailing self-sabotages less frequent, a recent winning streak and the possibility of a .500 record. I turn another page in my text. Differential equations and linear algebra—an independent study with the chair of the high school math department, a course where I'm the teacher as often as I'm the student. My daily trips to the high school now last period, a release into the sun and the welcomed escape of not having to return to the Wolf Pack's waiting stares. I enjoy reading ahead in my texts, the connecting of the present to what waits, units on improper integrals and first-order equations.

I study the flames, and the grid returns to my thoughts, and on it, waves as beautiful as the notes from Bach's harpsichord. I pull back the fireplace's screen and poke a log veined in orange. Sparks climb the flue. My father can diagram the formula for combustion, the fuel waiting for the spark, the fire's need to breathe. My mother could write a poem about warmth and consumption. Let me cast my meridians and parallels upon the flames. Behind their gasping dance, I imagine parabolas and undulations. An underpinning of logic. A whispered secret I lean close to hear.

The radio plays the top-of-the-hour news report. This bloody marathon of an election nearing its end, halleluiah and amen. McNally in a do-or-die barnstorm across the rust belt and heartland, and the report plays highlights from his Toledo speech. A hoarse tirade, his dust and gravel buzzwords lifted by his followers: *One America. Holy America.* McNally mentions his opponent, the name spat from his tongue. The crowd cries in return—curses and threats and the promise to take to the streets should their man lose. My eyes glaze over, their focus lost in the flames. McNally rails. The media. The elites. The multiculturalists. All traitors against a once-great nation. Another report from outside the rally. Clashing mobs and the wail of sirens. I close my eyes and see it all. Confession number three: the anxiety that I'm slowly losing my mind, the lightning out of control, a storm of figures and ideas and theories and a hundred thousand scenarios, an internal thicket which I fear I will one day enter and never leave. There are nights I don't sleep, my eyes dry and bloodshot, and in dawn's lifting gray, I think of the insomnia of Edison and Newton and Shakespeare, and I know for each of these there waits a multitude of van Goghs driven mad by a brain on fire. Tonight, I listen to the radio, and I think perhaps the madness isn't within me—it's all around, waiting to drown us all.

I turn and the fire warms my back. My father asleep, and I speak softly. "You know his winning isn't impossible."

"It's closer than I'd like." My mother props her glasses atop her head. "But I've got to believe the basic goodness of people will win out."

"Now you sound like Dad. Only you sound like you're trying to talk yourself into believing it."

"Perhaps forced optimism is better than the alternative."

"Sometimes I think he should spend a day with me in school." A pop from the fire, a knot in the wood. I lower the mask over my eyes, and my mother smiles. "There have been studies that indicate one's moral and ethical selves don't change too much after the age of twelve."

"I can see that."

"In which case, the percentage of the population who're dim or boneheads or assholes should be enough to have us all be nervous come Tuesday."

She straightens one of my father's curls and lets go. "Let's bank on the other percentage being a little higher. At least until this time next week."

Chestnut patters in and settles in my lap. "How do you think Slater will take it?" In the past weeks, his yard has grown choked with McNally signs, the sea of red and white overtaking the grass and dropped leaves. "He's rather invested."

"How do your junior high friends act when they don't get their way?"

"It's not always pretty." I turn back to the fire. The flames' dance reminds me of the tube man I saw on a hazy summer morning. "Not pretty at all."

* * *

History is a study of survival. The histories of nations—and, on a smaller and more poignant scale, the histories of individuals. Consider the woman who swims twenty miles from shipwreck to shore; the man given up for dead who staggers, bearded and skeletal, out of the wilderness. I imagine such scenarios involve a series of self-struck bargains, the choosing between the agony of survival and surrender's bliss. The body, despite its dominance in the physical world, bows to the will.

I have never endured that scale of pain and deprivation, and I wonder, if tested, how strong my will would be. Yet I can appreciate the act's mechanics of mind over body for I've trained myself to wake throughout the night and write in my dream journal. In the dark, I push to the surface, forcing back sleep's weight, my pen scribbling, my words lifting and bunching as I wrestle the fading images. The more disciplined I've become, the more I remember, and I have some entries that stretch, epic and surreal, for pages. Perhaps these fragmented narratives are simply the sputterings of an uncoupled mind. Or perhaps they're invitations from another dimension, one of truth and chaos and encoded in symbols I'll never understand. This morning, the first of a new year, I wake in ashy light, the room's chill on my nose. My scratching pen hustles to keep pace—a room like my bedroom yet not, a flashing blue light, my unexplained paralysis, and in the room's center, a monkey with white eyes and backwards feet, my hockey stick clutched in its paw. The beast utters an indecipherable yet human language as it shuffles toward me. Or is it away?

Chestnut shakes himself from the blankets. He leans forward, paws outstretched, head low and rear held high. His black snout twitches, and he licks my hand as I write. I rub the smooth spot beneath his chin, and the dog answers with moans, his eyes closed. My family and I greeted midnight with noise-makers and banging pots. Accompanying us, a house of half-drunk professors—chemists, biologists, physicists. The writers of reports and books. Most carrying the scars of their teen-selves, the wallflowers and late bloomers (a side joke I shared with my father—the mix of botany and teen angst). Most still hampered by awkwardness, the vexing soup of human interac-tion, and in me, a sympathetic kinship, the seeing of myself in their self-consciousness and staked distances. All of us ques-tion-askers, a step removed from trends and fashion. I studied the ones flitting along the edges or alone in corners. Our neighbor Dr. Klein, her five-month old sleeping in her arms. Dr. Lowden, who'd first introduced me to the slippery realm of quantum mechanics on the sidelines of a faculty softball game. Dr. Hamill with her child's whisper of a voice and her recogni-tions from Guggenheim and the Royal Academy. Dr. Lowden, or at least this world's version of him, slipped out unnoticed an hour before midnight. Dr. Hamill surprised us all with her raucous, arm-flailing charades performance. Then midnight with its hugs and kisses. The chemistry department whipped up a fireworks display from cleaning products and ash from the fire pit. They twisted newspaper funnels and stuck fuses in punctured tennis balls. The explosions colored the dark, and Chestnut ran looping circles across the yard before becoming the first to pass out. A celebration, yes, but the beneath the revelry, a sober, ever-more-real truth. The seven-week election hangover, McNally's narrow victory, and the night's conversa-tions interspersed with hushed exchanges. The fire-bombings of mosques and synagogues. McNally's continued attacks on the elites he blamed for the nation's abandonment of God.

I pull back the covers. My thick socks glide over the hardwood, and my body remembers the days before a roof and how I'd shuffled on sawdust. Chestnut in my arms, and his tongue laps my fingers, the thump of his heart against mine. On the stairs, I pass through a moment, a summer day, the slant of blazing sun, my father and uncles, our legs dangling over the stairs as we sipped cold drinks. Ghosts all around, and the July sun and my uncles' voices give way to the dim living room. The lights shine on the Christmas tree, a straggly thing cut from the riverbank. I'd worked the saw, the sap on my gloves and my father's contention that the tree's imperfections gave it a personality one couldn't buy on a lot. His smile obscured by the steam from his mouth, and me doubtful at first but then won over. The tree full of spaces and our ornaments adrift in the emptiness. The branches shining in a light unknown along the river. Yes, I have to admit, it is beautiful.

I've slept in. A growing habit, my lethargy on unclaimed mornings, later than last year, later still than the year before. Weekdays, I rise with my alarm. I mutter curses until I become human under the shower's splash. On weekends, I can doze until noon, Technicolor dreams and my journal filling. The sleep of teenagers, my father says. The replenishment of bone and muscle. The capillaries struggling to keep pace. A brain alight with new chemicals.

I set Chestnut down on the landing. Beer bottles crowd the coffee table. Glasses puddled with melted ice, rims red with lipstick, and the alcohol mingles with the pine's scent. A littering of folded paper scraps—last night's charade answers. I pick up the nearest. *Santa's Workshop,* my mother's neat script. I'd expected good smells from the kitchen. French toast and cinnamon, my mother's strong coffee. I listen for my father's jazz, the clatter of skillets, but hear only low voices from the

TV and the click of Chestnut's nails. I pause at the kitchen entrance. "Mom?"

My mother emerges from the family room. The hair that had once been as long as mine now trimmed above her shoulders, a framing for her pretty face. Still in her robe, she shares no greeting or morning smile, her eyes puffy. All of it odd—my mother the early riser, the completer of chores, her quiet morning hour at her writing desk, even on a holiday. Her expression hollow as we embrace. Her robe soft against my cheek. Her hand lotion's flowered scent. She offers a lingering kiss for my forehead.

Chestnut brushes against my shins, and I step back. My mother's bloodshot eyes remind me of the call that brought news of my grandfather's death, how I knew something terrible, something destined to change us, had happened even before she'd hung up. "What's wrong?"

Her arm around my shoulder, she guides me to the family room. My father in his pajama bottoms and sweatshirt. The remote in hand and the TV muted. He pulls Chestnut onto the couch. The TV light blue on his glasses. I sit beside him, the silence and incongruity making me feel like I'm still dreaming, and I say nothing, not wanting to break the spell and set the terrible thing I feel hovering over us in motion. He hugs me then turns back to the TV. My mother sits on my other side. My chest tightens, the sensation of being underwater.

My father clicks the remote. The news on every channel. Shaky cell phone footage, horizons of mushroom clouds. Talking heads and streaming banners. Heaven's view from a satellite, blossomings almost beautiful. Governments that no longer exist. First India and Pakistan, the border simmering for generations. Pride and territorial claims. Water rights and snow-capped mountains, a disputed region ninety percent of my classmates would be hard pressed to find on the map. Different Gods, different tongues, but their bread made the same. The same fruits ripened on the trees. Each loved their children. The war spread in minutes, China then Russia, North Korea. Aggressions and accidents and failed brinksmanship. A thousand cities reduced to carbon. Numbers I can comprehend, a toll I can not. Computer models predict the fallout's spread. Clouds destined to fatten and circle the world.

My parents dress, but I remain on the couch. I overhear their plans, my focus on the TV. The next six hours see them coming and going, the cold carried on their passing hugs. They return laden with shopping bags, and in the kitchen and dining room, a growing array of boxes and cartons, vitamins, bandages, ointments and tampons, soap and detergent and toothpaste. Cans of soup and vegetables and fruit, powdered milk, crackers, more. The front door opens and shuts, the rattle of my father's truck pulling into the driveway then backing out—movements like a time-lapse film. Their frenzy accentuated by my stillness, my body numb. My father returns from his last trip without his hat and his jacket sleeve torn, stories of supermarket bedlam as the shelves emptied. Outside, sirens and a stiffening wind. We sit close on the couch, the TV still on. All of us witnesses.

We eat hours later, remembering ourselves and our hunger. Our New Year's feast—black-eyed peas and cornbread, pork and sauerkraut—traditions of luck, a superstition that today leaves me hollow and shaken. A report from the local news—a supermarket shooting and a twilight curfew. A special report is broadcast from the White House. The President urges calm, an assurance order will be maintained and that the transition of power won't be halted. My mother and I bundle up and walk Chestnut. We turn up our collars against the cold, and my eyes water in the breeze. The sky blue and white and veined by branches, and I imagine a current of human smoke circling the earth. My thoughts clearer but still muddied, the logic to tie it all together missing. We pass Dr. Klein pushing a stroller. We exchange hugs and ask if the other is all right. My hand reaches for my mother's. Chestnut sniffs a dropped branch.

The leash limp in my grasp and Chestnut lifts his leg. "What's going to happen?"

"I wish I could say, baby." Her voice thin. Steam from her lips. "But as long as we're together, it'll be all right."

* * *

"The Great Shut-In." Shut windows. Shut doors. Not even Chestnut is immune, the five-by-ten-foot enclosure my father's erected off the back stoop, a wooden frame and a tarp that snaps in the wind, dead grass and the stench of urine. Another scent inside our house, the odors of meals and bodies and uncirculated breath. In a few weeks, the war's shock ebbs into melancholy. Dates lose their meaning. Weeks blur. I reset my bedroom clock after each rolling blackout until the afternoon I curse the blinking 12:00 and pull the plug, the time from then on marked only by my state of mind. Clingy days. Days I cry. Days I bitch and snarl, a sister of the Wolf Pack. Days I barely get out of bed. The walls upon me, and beyond, the promise of a greater smothering. A diseased sky. The horribleness of my kind. A memory—I am four, the darkened bedroom of our old house. I hold a flashlight and, in the beam, my father displays a tennis ball. He moves the ball, explaining shadows and moon phases. Now I see the ball again and think of half a world in darkness, and I wonder why I was allowed to stay in the light.

There's a theory in the field of problem solving which proposes even the most complex decisions contain at their heart a binary Ur, a yes-or-no which has the power to trigger an all-changing chain reaction. And if I can burrow to my core, I must believe the Shut-In has left me with a pair of default filters. One is a dread I am loathe to voice, the fear that speaking the horror's name will feed it, and that soon, it will outgrow its cage. The other is boredom, a lesser evil, the Shut-In's white noise, a restless note lurking in every frequency. I've never been bored before—I had parents keen to rescue me with hikes or excursions to the river, I had my imaginings of parallel and

36

hidden planes—but the Shut-In has changed that. The itch burrows deep in my spine, a parasite to my host, and the contagion seeps out until its static reaches my head and the shrinking space I fight to keep as my own. These same rooms. The same faces, none more galling than the one waiting in the mirror. The girl with sallow skin and searching eyes. The one so weak she's discovered new realms of self-pity. The stillness all around encountered by the upheaval within, the swelling in my hips and breasts. The tedium of unchanging window views and a sunless sky. The sting of recognizing my pettiness in this time of want, my gifts of food and shelter, a family I love more than myself but who are also conspirators in my suffocation. A thousand alternate realities crowd under our roof, and on the days I find myself suffocating beneath the press of my parents' bodies and stories, I lock my bedroom door and curse myself and my fate. I plead, scream into my pillow, hold planks until I collapse, my arms too jellied to wipe my brow's sweat. When the itch redlines, I storm my room's cramped space. My hands punch the air, the tears hot on my cheeks. Then, in time, acceptance— or surrender—I can't say which. Decompression, and the bands across my chest loosen, and my march slows. I rub my eyes, and as fatigue descends, I collapse onto my bed. Spent. Hollow. The sleep that follows deep and black. Naps that steal hours in a room where time no longer matters. Narcotic dreams, and half paralyzed, I struggle to call out—but my lips have turned to stone, my mouth stuffed with feathers, with rocks and dirt. The pages of my dream journal fill.

After, I drag myself downstairs, sluggish yet my senses on fire, everything too dim or too bright, too quiet or too loud. I lash out. My parents—who else do I have? Their kind words and suffocating questions. Their worry written in every glance. I accuse them of complicity in their generation's sins. The blinders they've accepted. Their allegiances to a corrupt system's profits and wealth and power, the currencies of fear and war. Then the personal attacks. A sharing of pain. The hurt in their eyes proof I'm alive, that I still have a say in this asylum. My words honed, arrows aimed at their most tender spots. My mother's clutter. The inane pop songs she loves. The poems no one reads. My father's fey obsession with plants while the world burns.

In time, the haze lifts, and with it, a boomerang pain. Acceptance, surrender—again, I can't choose—and with it, a plummet back to my parents' orbit. The ensuing days where their absences trigger panic. Where I'm underfoot more than Chestnut. I curl next to my father on the sofa, not caring what we listen to or talk about. I beg my mother to brush and braid my hair. Anything to be near. Anything not to be alone. The TV off or else I'll cry.

Weeks of this. Months.

* * *

I'm doing pushups in the family room. I've already washed the breakfast dishes and completed my online assignments. Math concepts I mastered in third grade. A paragraph response I doubt will ever be read. My mother dozes, Chestnut on her lap. The Civil Defense Network on TV, a tutorial on indoor games for preschoolers, the instructor's perky chatter, a tone that belongs to a different world than the headlines running across the screen's bottom. Food riots in Cairo and Madrid. The local RAD count. Another pushup, a challenge I give myself, one more and one more after that, and with each rep, I play through the alternate scenarios I might find myself in when I talk with my father.

He finally enters, truck keys in hand. I squeeze out a last rep then kneel on the floor. "It's yellow," I say.

"Yellow's not green."

"It's not a bad yellow. See?" Catching my breath, I point to the screen, the latest RAD count for our sector.

"It's medium yellow."

"It's not high."

He considers his sleeping wife. "It's really cold."

"I'll have an excuse to wear my new jacket."

He sighs. "Come on."

Our back porch mudroom has become a portal between in and out. The mudroom windows locked then sealed with plastic and a new caulk border. Hooks for our goggles and masks, our rubber boots lined by the door—father, mother, daughter—and I smile again at my mother's Goldilocks joke. Jackets then the hooded raincoats we rub with bleach after each return. I lose myself beneath the layers, the raincoat and mask, the goggles' warped view.

Out the back door, and we stoop, our shoulders scraping the tarp of Chestnut's shelter, the space's shade and urine stench, our slouch staying with us as we hurry-step across the lawn's snow. A thud in my chest, the thrill of anticipation for my first trip to the distribution center. Even beneath my mask, I hold my breath. The fear of poison all around, and even if the count is low, no one knows when an inhaled microbe could implant itself, a time bomb's first tick, and perhaps the cells are already dividing beneath my skin. McNally's new administration has temporarily suspended the Fourth and Sixth Amendments and commandeered the airwaves, but the Internet has proven harder to restrict, its mingling of distortions and lies and truths. Radioactive rain and miscarriages. Epidemics. Irradiated crops and looming famine. Rivers thick with dead fish. The rich sitting comfortably, their hoarded goods and country estates, their hired mercenaries better armed than the police. The hinterlands controlled by ragtag militias who promise rebellion if the authorities confiscate a single gun. The National Guard patrolling the cities, tanks and armored vehicles. Reports of looters shot on sight. For a moment, I question my decision to come, the world so changed, our house cold and claustrophobic but at least knowable. My misgivings countered by the thrill of escape, by the deeper breathing possible amid the landscape's expanse. I pause before climbing into the truck. My eyes vexed by so many places to focus. The oak's bare branches clatter. The wind swirls beneath my coat, and with it, a bitter touch, the spasm of muscles. I climb into the cab and shut the door.

"Can I take the helm?" Last summer, my father let me drive down a riverside dirt road. The seat pulled up and the gearshift wrestled, a series of bucks and stalls, curses under my breath.

He smiles. "You'll be back behind the wheel soon enough."

The truck's rattle paints a blurred edge around all I see.

The shaking born in the engine mounts my father was going to repair before the Shut-In, and the vibrations intensify my shivering. Every other Tuesday is our sector's supply pickup day, and early on, I wrangled a standing promise to join my father if the RAD count was green. Today's yellow concession a small victory in a time when victories are rare. The streets narrow, plowed paths, and along the curb, the vague outlines of snow-buried cars. A ten-minute drive and we park outside the makeshift center that's been set up in the gym of my old elementary school.

The outside guard beetle-like beneath his body armor, an M-16 held across his chest. Our ration card disappears in his gloved hand. He waves a metal detector over my outstretched arms, and my reflection stares back from his curved mask. He raises a hand, and the door opens behind him. A second guard pats us down after we remove our masks and goggles. My body stiffens as his hand roams over my belly and legs.

I follow my father down a hallway lined with low-hanging artwork. Watercolors and crayons, ill-proportioned people, swollen heads and feet lifted from the ground. In each, a sense of stalled time, the weeks before Christmas break and the excitement of children, the past a dream for them and for me, a reality I wish I could wake to. How easy it had all been and how much I'd taken for granted. I peek into a classroom. The lights off, an array of tiny desks and neatly shelved bins. The calendar waiting to be turned to January. Nametags hung over the coatrack's empty hooks, and what, I wonder, will they make of all this when they return.

We enter the gym, and the push of memories slows my steps. A high ceiling and thinned acoustics, voices that rise and thin and then fall back like a lazy snow. Cages for the windows and lights, and across the floor, multi-colored tape patterns—kickball bases, dodge ball's no-man's land. I was a child here

41

but now I understand that even in the quantum world, life is full of boundaries that can never be re-crossed. Tables command the perimeter, and for each, a waiting line. Lines for toiletries. Lines for canned goods. Lines for rice and pasta and cereal. I divide the gym into quadrants, make a count and multiply by four, an estimate of a hundred twenty or so, a crowd but not crowded. I spot my health teacher and old bus driver. A pair of sisters from my team. The rest strangers. I wave, say hello, but I stay by my father's side. I overhear snippets of small talk and gossip. My father asks if I'd like to talk with my teammates, but I say no. It's enough to be standing in a different space, to breathe new scents. To look into new faces and contemplate lives that aren't my own.

Slater scurries by. His gaze down, figures scribbled on his clipboard. I tug my father's sleeve and whisper, "Is he the boss here?"

My father grins. "I don't think so."

I can tell by his tone that my father is being kind, an attempt to not voice the obvious—that Slater's regalia of a policeman's hat and epaulets and a braided shoulder cord make him look like a buffoon. I think of Missy Blough and the Wolf Pack's red bandannas and the need of some to belong and command. Slater's shoes click across the hardwood, his gait a battle between his thick middle and thrown-back shoulders. His commands strain against the gym's acoustics. Orders for straight lines and for all to keep moving, even if moving means a single, shuffling step. He grunts a distracted "Hello" as he punches our ration cards, an exchange cut short by a whisper from one of the machine-gun-carrying guards.

We reach the last station. In my hands, a cardboard box, a wedging of cans and bottles and boxes. Another quick calculation figures the probability of our exact combination of goods to be around one in three hundred thousand. The guard walks off, and Slater beckons a bald man I recognize as the school custodian. Slater talks, gesturing to the hallway, but the custodian shakes his head. Slater's volume and vehemence flare as the custodian turns his back. Slater abandoned with his anger at center court.

Our boxes at our feet, my father and I don our coats in the main hallway. Slater brushes past. In one hand, he carries a toilet plunger, the other steering a mop and rolling bucket with a wheel that twists and shrieks and requires continual redirecting nudges. Backing up, he pushes open the boys' restroom door, the wafting stink cut short as I don my mask.

* * *

My mother hums along to a radio song from her youth. She takes my hands and swivels her hips and shoulders, but I remain still. The beat is catchy, but the lyrics might as well be a communiqué from another planet. My mother drops my hands and pouts. "You're no fun." She turns back to her mixing bowl. "This was a big hit when I was your age."

I scour the silverware drawer. Both of us in sweatshirts, the floor cold through my double socks. The thermostat at fifty, the new decrees rationing gas and heating oil. "Sounds like a lot of partying and groping and shallow rebellion."

"And your point is?"

I retrieve the long chef's knife and shut the drawer with a nudge of my hip. "Just wonder when someone will feel like writing a song like that again."

I lean into the knife and cut slivers from the hard block of cheese, another casserole, potatoes and tinned meats. This past week of red days, announcements after every other song. The proper ways to seal doors and windows. The maintenance of one's government-issued respirator. The punishments awaiting black-marketeers. But last night brought a shift in the jet stream. The poisons pushed south and the weatherman predicting wind chills near zero.

I set the pan in the oven. A new song plays, a girl going to a party in a new dress, the boy she hopes to dance with. *Yes,* I promise my mother, I'll go right to Fran's and return before dinner. *No,* I won't call and beg to stay the night. Fran my backfield line-mate and best, perhaps only true, friend. My mother follows me into the mudroom, Chestnut between us, looking up, hopeful. I zip my long raincoat over my parka. My mother hands over my goggles and a book for Fran's mother.

44

A joke about deep-sea divers and kiss before I adjust my mask.

"There and back, OK? And keep your gear on, no matter what."

I salute, my voice muffled. "Aye-aye, captain."

I step outside. The touch of my skin buried, my vision warped by my goggles, my mother's sea-diver comment no longer a joke. I walk slowly and take nothing for granted. My grid fades beneath the day's panorama. The stretching clouds. Gutter icicles as long as my arm. The snow less white than it used to be. An openness that makes me feel as if I've been cast adrift upon the ocean.

I shed my raincoat and boots and mask on Fran's back porch. A glimpse through the window, and Fran pogoes on the balls of her feet, waving for me to hurry. The purple streak in her blond bangs has faded since my last visit. Fran is rarely allowed to go out, even on green days, her father's belief in the Internet's conspiracies. Gene mutations. New cancers. The RAD counts higher than the government is willing to admit. A plot to thin the population. The waiting future of scant supplies.

Hugs inside and the oven's warmth. The book handed to Fran's mother. Fran's cat sniffs my feet. Fran and I talk in bursts, laughter as we run up the stairs and the bedroom door slammed behind us. This little space. A nation of two, if only until dusk. We sit facing each other on Fran's bed, hands held, a crisscrossed, two-handed grip. Confessions and complaints and the relief of abandoning the filters we have to wear around our parents. We curse our boredom. Curse the world. We surf YouTube for music videos and skateboard fails, but our chatter stops after we click into drone footage of a smoldering city. The scene paused when we spot a lone figure in the mist. Fran turns the computer off.

She grabs her hockey stick and takes a ball from her shelf. A date and a score written in black Sharpie, a hot September afternoon when we shared the field. My toes curl with the memory of standing on grass. Fran balances the ball on the flat heel. The ball rolls, hiccups Fran counters with shifts of her wrists, her gaze intent. "Is it weird I'm more afraid of when this all ends?"

"No."

"It's like I don't know what's normal anymore. Maybe this is normal. Now. Maybe before was the weird part and we just didn't realize it."

My gaze upon the ball. A world balanced. "Maybe. But maybe normal is just living. Getting through."

"My dad's so freaked."

"Everyone's freaked."

"Not like him."

"He's just worried about you and your mom."

"Is your dad like that?"

"No, but they're different, you know? They were different before. But I think both are coming from the same place. The same priorities and everything."

The ball drops, a thud dulled by the carpet. She hands me the stick, but I shake my head and stand. "I've been practicing. Ready?"

"Am I bracing myself for amazement?"

I step back until my shoulders touch the far wall and tuck my hair beneath my collar. "Amazement might be a reach." I put my hands down and lift my legs. My raised toe taps the wall, a testing of my center before I stride forward. My arms shake, and with the first shifting of weight from one hand to the other, my hair escapes, a cascade that flows to the floor.

Fran's disembodied voice enters my upside-down world: "Total and complete amazement, sister."

I make my way across the carpet. My shoulders strong, these weeks of pushups and planks, set after bored set. Blood runs to my head, pressure in my ears, and in my chest, the struggles of muscle and balance. Perhaps Fran is my best friend because I can do a handstand in front of her and feel like a normal girl doing a silly stunt and not like a math prodigy stepping out of her role. Another lurch, then another before I tumble just short of the bed. I sit, splayed and flushed. I push the hair from my eyes. "I wish I could stay the night."

"I could ask. It would be great."

"Told my mom I'd be back. She doesn't want me overstaying."

"She never minded before. How many nights have I crashed at your place?

"It's different now."

"I can at least plant a seed. We'll get my mom to agree to the next green day."

I smile. "Yeah. I think we can make that happen."

Bundled beneath my layers, I turn once in the backyard. Fran in the window, the curtain pushed aside and a final wave. I walk, the deep-sea diver's bundled strides. Above, a few milky stars, another night falling. The stale, waiting hours stretch before me. I think of my mother's casserole and the games we might play after dinner. I think of her oldies station, the kind of songs that won't be written again until we all understand a new normal. I don't turn when I reach my corner. A government truck passes, its headlights on. Then silence. The neighborhood's gardens and flowerbeds dormant until the thaw, and no one's certain this spring's blooms will be the same. I pull back my hood, a promise broken. I listen to my boots' crunch over the snow. I lower my mask then lift my goggles and rest them atop my forehead. The cold a balm on my sweating cheeks. Water in my eyes, a sensation bracing and clear. The wind's bite a luxury in my throat. My breath a cloud beneath the first flickering streetlight. A woman pulls aside a curtain and stares, and I think of the video Fran and I watched, a shadow lost in the wasteland. I pull the cold deep into my lungs. Another block, I tell myself. My mask and goggles kept off until I loop back to my street and see my porch light's waiting shine.

*　*　*

My days become a series of grays. Gray skies, gray tastes, the gray of indoor lights and the deeper gray of what I'd first thought of as boredom but now recognize as a fatigue of spirit and soul. I eat my oatmeal (unsweetened, sugar now a luxury), the TV tuned to a Civil Defense channel of no faces, no voices, just a banner of running script and a hypnotic pan of gauges and screens. Temperature. Radar. Wind speed and direction. The RAD needle, the world's scientists flummoxed by the count that keeps exceeding their models. Our pantry with its boxes of stale cereal, the nationwide fear of irradiated milk, rumors of poisoned herds and bonfires of meat beneath the prairie skies. The C.D. anchors urge reason and caution and civic responsibility. Red days like today relegated to level-one activities—the military and basic public services. Repeat non-level-one wanderers subjected to fines and the pulling of ration cards.

Morning, and I have an essay to type, an online response to a documentary on prohibition I watched with my father. Both of us in heavy sweaters, our woodpile running low, Chestnut burrowed deep beneath the afghan. Our post-viewing discussion centers on social movements, their often pure births, their complicated lives.

"They're part of the beauty of a democracy. The will of the people and such."

"Churchill is rumored to have said the best argument against democracy is a five-minute conversation with the average voter."

"I believe Winston enjoyed playing the role of curmudgeon." He rubs his chin, his stubble now a thick beard. Fran's father has razor blades, a connection in his downtown office, the price of a single blade higher than four, pre-Shut-In packs.

I turn on the laptop. "Should I remind you of the last election?"

"And your alternative is?"

I take off my gloves and begin to type. "Let me get back to you on that."

Afternoon. My report submitted, my work time doubled by Chestnut's invitations to wrestle with a length of rope my father knotted for him. The dog now back on the couch, his nose sticking out of his afghan cocoon. The living room chairs pushed aside, and my mother and I roll our mats over the hardwood. A DVD plays, a blissful instructor, a sunset beach backed by wide mountains and towering palms. An island paradise that might no longer exist. I lift and contract and struggle to find peace in my breathing, in the release that sometimes comes with a stretch's last squeezed centimeter. But today, peace eludes me, my self-consciousness too keen. The gray of isolation and the sting of my own fragility. Half the world in darkness, and here I am, alive and aware, and what, exactly, am I expected to do with this gift?

Later, we return to our week-long Monopoly game. My mother the car. My father the boot. The iron for me. Hotels and houses on every property. Fortunes won and lost with a roll of the dice. My thoughts wander. Odds and scenarios. The game's underlying network of permutations. Another drift and thoughts of decomposition, the clockwork of radioactive half-lives. The more fickle organic world. Cavemen entombed in glacier ice and mummified pharaohs. The wet and heat that can strip a water buffalo to bones in weeks. The burned bones of cattle on the plains.

My mother's voice: "Kay?"

I blink. The board surfaces. The images in my head fade. My father hands me the dice. "Your turn, Sweet Pea."

I shake. The dice rattle in my cupped palm. *Bones*, gambler's lingo, a word my mother taught me. *Bones. Sweet Pea. Bones.* Fucking bones. Mountains of bones. Continents of smoldering bones. A phantom in the mist. My hand sinks into my lap. My head hung. The tears come with my father's voice, his hand on my shoulder. "Kay? Honey?"

Evening. The Monopoly board set aside, and over dinner, I offer apologies and assurances. Hollow phrasings, excuses that mean little because I don't understand what to apologize for, my break a reflex, a drowning in a tide that runs deeper than logic. I help with the dishes then retreat to the basement where I clear a path around the perimeter, a side-to-side just long enough to claim a breath of momentum on my roller blades. My strides awkward at first, but by my third lap, form finds me, then speed, and I slash across the concrete for thirty minutes. An hour. Until my body glows with the rush of escaping inertia. I pick up my old hockey stick, and on my path's long stretches, I close my eyes for a stride or two. With the stick held tight, I plant myself back on the open field. The turf rolls beneath me. An open sky above.

I rest on my father's weight bench. A flush, my sweat and thirst despite the cold. Beside me, a duffle bag, the clothes I brought down to throw in the wash. I nudge the bag with my stick. The canvas gives, a smiling dimple. I poke again, harder. I empty the bag, the pile soft around my feet, jeans and sweat-shirts and socks. I place a twenty-five-pound weight at the bag's bottom and return the clothes. Wavering atop my skates, I sling a chain over the ceiling's I-beam and secure the duffle.

I skate, and with each lap, my stick taps the bag. The skates' echoes a seashell hum. Another jab, and the bag twists, its bottom weighted and sluggish. The chain clanks.

I move faster. Around me, a blur of boxes and shelves, the furnace and washer and dryer. The bag's shadow sways over the concrete. The stick an extension of my skeleton, my knuckles bloodless and pale. A blow for the fucked reality of New Year's morning. A chop for the sickness of men. A slash for my frustrations and weakness. Another rumor, articles online and whispers at the distribution center—the skyrocketing suicide rate. Individuals, sometimes groups of a dozen or more. On the nights I can't sleep, I think of them. The faces and the acts' mechanics beyond me, but I can see them alone, their bare feet toeing the abyss. I would never—not in a thousand years—but I understand, coolly and deeply and with the certain truth of a balanced equation.

A strike. The bag dances. The slash of my skates and the chain's rattle telegraphed upwards, notes trumpeted through the metal and plaster and wood. A signal of my own, angry and defiant, my offering to another diseased night. Faster, and my only focus belongs to the bag. All else melts. My next blow crumples the canvas, and in me, the imagining of a blow this hard meeting flesh and bone.

"Kay? Honey?" My mother at the top of the cellar stairs, her voice rises and falls in my swirl. "What're you doing?"

* * *

The Shut-In's third month. The snow stubborn, the shadowed nooks surrounding houses and trees. The RAD count orange, another inside day. I exhale onto my bedroom window, my lips close enough to feel the cold, then wipe away the fog. Below, the back yard, and the plants of my father's garden stir beneath the soil. The first buds in the oak, and in its branches, my ghost-self, a girl not so lonely or unsure. This morning's news brought stories from neighboring states, roaming mobs, public hangings of murderers and profiteers. I think of my father, a tennis ball and flashlight, half a world in darkness. I think of the moment's veneer and the hidden forces churning, and I see another darkness beneath this world. A ping on my computer, and I turn from the window. An email from Fran, and I click the YouTube link.

The video features a girl not much older than me. She fumbles with the camera before settling onto her bed. A guitar balanced on her lap and a bashful wave, her hair pulled back and a halting introduction. Her hometown deep on the Saskatchewan plane. Books on the shelves, dolls she'd no doubt outgrown. An Edmonton Oilers poster. She reminds me of a girl who might sit at my lunch table, a girl who does her homework, reserved yet quick to smile. Her first words barely rise above her strummed chords. Then a swell, the courage of simply pressing on. The song is full of lulls that feel like invitations. I listen twice then three more times with my mother. "What do you think?"

"It's nice," she says. She tucks a strand of my hair behind my ear. "Maybe this is the kind of song that was waiting to be written."

"Doesn't sound like yours yet."

"Maybe it shouldn't." We sit shoulder-to-shoulder on the couch, and I catch her humming along. *"What's done won't consume us / won't define us. / This dream will end / and we'll walk in the sun again."*

I share "Here to There" with my father after dinner. I rest my elbow on his shoulder as he sits in his office chair. Perhaps I'm too old to hold his hand, yet I've forged a new bond with my parents these past months, a connection rooted in confusion and struggle and survival. Now it's my turn to hum, and I'm surprised by the thousands of hits the song has accumulated. As he watches, I consider his cluttered desk, the red clay pencil holder I made for him in kindergarten, his notes on the fallout's effect on the spring buds, measurements and sketches and charts. The song ends, and the girl who's no longer a stranger approaches the camera, her hand swallowing the frame. "Goodbye all." The screen goes dark.

"That's lovely," my father says. A pause, and in his gaze, a judgment. "Do you want to see what I've been working on?"

He pulls up his faculty page and clicks. I've heard about The Movement. Online whispers at first, posts and tweets from musicians and artists. At its birth, The Movement had only one message—the invitation to all mankind to take pause. To reflect before stepping back into the light. To wrestle with the responsibility of living in a world teetering upon the brink. Here, amid tragedy, waited the gift of a second chance, the opportunity to redefine ourselves. We could end hunger, nationalism, militarism. We could look upon every child as the gift of a single, beautiful tribe. The Movement's message countered by the government's talking points, and the state-controlled airwaves reverberate with buzzwords and shadings and repeated slights. *Intellectuals. Elitists. The ones who sold the toil and blood of the common man to socialists and international cabals.*

My father leaves to fix us tea, and I page through his blog's entries. His expertise of roots and soils abandoned but not his tone or his lens of structure and reason. I read an entry pleading for clear thought from a species with the unique power to both save and destroy itself. I read another on the ballet of genetics and the mechanical wonder of organs, the deep seas of commonalities waiting beneath the wrapping of skin. All of us brother and sisters. All of us evolution's most beautiful blooms.

He returns with a pair of steaming mugs. He dunks the bag until my water turns orange then transfers the bag to his cup. Tea another rationed item and I wonder if it's really tea at all. Another click, the blog's stat counter. "You've got a lot of views."

"Less than a percent of your song."

"It's more than just your normal geeky professor types." I lift the cup and let the warmth rise over my face.

"There's a lot of people writing all over the world." He dunks the tea bag, his water's pale hue. "Guess we all have a lot of time on our hands."

"Fran's dad said The Movement is a bunch of naïve people manipulated by communists."

"What do you think of that?"

I blow the steam from my cup. "He's always been a bit of an alarmist. But before he limited it to refs and people who drove too slow."

"Stakes are higher now. Unfortunately."

I picture the redness in Fran's father's face, the dinner table silent until Fran's mother joked about the latest ration decree.

I set down my mug. "He said they want to close all the churches."

"Do you see any evidence of that?"

"Fran's dad thinks there is. Although I'm not sure you and your peer-review crowd would approve of his sources."

"Suggesting a reexamination of religion's role in the current political landscape is a far cry from calling for the closing of churches." He sips. "Do you think we're naïve?"

"Perhaps, but I don't see a better option."

He puts his arm around me. "These blogs, your song—they're all asking for the same thing, I think. We can follow the same path—or we can find a new one."

"Have a plan," I say.

He nods. "A new plan because the old one's nearly killed us all."

I lean against him. "Fran's right. Normal will be weird after all this." I click out of his blog. "Want to hear the song again?"

"Sure."

* * *

The Shut-In ends on a cool June morning. A presidential declaration and the ringing of church bells. There are stipulations—the RAD count will be monitored for the foreseeable future, and fishing is banned until further notice. Infants, the infirm, and the elderly are advised to keep their daily outdoor exposure to under three hours. None of these restrictions cloud my mind as I wait on Fran's steps. She appears at the window, a welcoming wave from me on the outside, a squeal from within. I can't recall being either more excited or more nervous, the fretfulness of a dreamed-of reunion. A toe-dipping into a new normal.

We walk through the neighborhood. Our masks off, my breath unsoured, and the breeze on our faces. My strides, free from my deep-sea-diver's larval shell, stretch across the sidewalk. My gaze lifts in hopes of catching the birds whose calls my father taught me during the Shut-In. Fran and I knot our sweatshirts around our waists and let the sun warm our skin. We reach Main Street, its open shops and shade-giving sycamores suddenly exotic, and I take Fran's hand, wanting only to anchor myself, the fear I may drift into the sudden expanse.

We walk until our feet ache, rest, then walk some more. The warmth, the smells, and I think of my father's words. This world of small miracles and a new beginning. We reach the park and share a bench. Others join us. Missy and the Wolf Pack girls pass a cigarette by the tennis court fence. Children shout, their sneakers a blur across the grass. The adults watch, but their smiles are different, the understanding of how fragile this all is. On the second day, Fran and I bike to the river, an adventure and the sense of wilderness. We claim perches atop

57

the shore's smooth boulders. A packed lunch and the confessions of young women—boys, our dreams and fears. The sun-kissed flow splashes against the rocks, and we're entertained by the flights of dragonflies and a low-flying crane. The third day a Saturday. Another bike ride, the campus rally my father's organized. We're wary of every passing car, the lookout for Fran's father's sedan. "If I got grounded after being cooped up for so long, I swear I'd fucking burst."

We sit along the quad's fountain. My father hangs the podium's breeze-swelling banner as Dr. Klein wrestles one of the fluttering ends. Her son is walking now, clumsy steps across the clover surrounding the fountain, and his little hands clutch the soap bubbles his sitter blows. Students fill the quad, more people than I've seen in months, and in me, an unexpected welling. All these faces, all these stories. Sunbathers in the grass, the shirtless boys who toss Frisbees and footballs. There's almost too much to look at, and I fight the urge to close my eyes, the fear of being overwhelmed. My father stands before the microphone, his hands raised. The guitar strummers and football throwers join the crowd.

"Welcome. Welcome all," my father says, the words barely out of his mouth before he's interrupted by a handful of counter-protestors pushing toward the stage.

"Leftists!" A stocky man presses a megaphone to his lips, his words distorted but his tone unmistakable. The counter-protestors in white T-shirts and sunglasses, many with faces masked by red bandannas. Their voices raised, a rough tide as they force their way forward. Scuffles break out, the white shirts retaliating, their bulk and menace. A bearish man waves a flag that snaps on the breeze. The red circle and white cross.

The students on the quad lurch forward, but their taunts are cut short by my father. The voice that read me a library of picture books echoes off the library's brownstone. "Please,

please! Haven't we learned anything? Step aside and let them through." The students draw back, a clear path carved to the stage where my father extends a hand. "My friends, I invite one of you step forward. You may speak first. We will all hear you out."

The men in white look at one another, their flag raised but no longer waving. They huddle, conversations muffled by bandannas, then a retreat. The crowd pulls back again. One of the guitar players strums a few chords and by the time he reaches the refrain, the quad is awash in song. Fran and I stand atop the fountain's rim, laughing as the white shirts' pace quickens, and we offer our voices to the chorus. *We will walk in the sun / You and I, you and I / We'll walk in the sun again.*

* * *

My father and I debate as we take Chestnut on his evening walk—do the discoveries of scientists like Wegener and Franklin and Kepler that went unappreciated in their lifetimes turn their stories tragic? I think yes, but my father proposes they, like all who are fortunate enough to have discovered a passion, were probably more interested in the process, in the meaning one finds in a lifetime of work. I offer a compromise—maybe they died disappointed but not bitter.

"Perhaps," my father says. "Life offers no guarantees, does it?"

"Unfortunately."

We pause as Chestnut lifts his leg. Walking an old dog, especially one fond of sniffing and marking, requires patience. "His way of being social," my father once said, explaining a dog's sense of smell, its ability to reach into the past. Each sniff and dribble a memory rejoined, a delve into a relation beyond the shackles of linear time.

Our house in sight, and our pace slows as Chestnut runs his nose along the base of our neighbor's light post. Slater on his porch, a whining drill in hand. I give the leash a tug. I indulge the dog, yes, but I want nothing to do with Slater tonight. His peevish observations, his proudly displayed flag of white and red. His new gaze, the look I receive from men and boys, a stare with a hitch and unwelcome heat.

My father pauses. "Hello!"

Slater pulls up his goggles, his shirt white with chalky dust. The drill winds down. "What?"

"Hello," my father repeats. "Beautiful night."

Slater glances up. "Hmmm."

My father steps forward. "Your bit." His tone hesitant,

apologetic. Let's add Mendel to that list of unappreciated scientists, and allow me to use his once-scorned theories to propose that I am both my father and mother's child. Imagine my feelings about Slater as alleles on a Punnett square—my mother's open disdain, my father's willingness to believe the best in others—and me a mix of the two, my distance kept but my judgment, for the moment, reserved. "Don't know if you've got the right bit for that," my father says.

Slater wipes dust from his chest. At his feet, a gold-plated mailbox. The sun through the trees casts a glint on the box's lid. *Slater* embossed in the metal. I follow my father up the walk.

"I've got a special bit for mortar."

Slater calls to me: "Don't let the dog go on my flowerbeds." A pause. "Please."

Chestnut's nose in the daylilies, only a few blooms this year. I tug the leash. My father turns. "Will you fetch my toolbox? The one with the red lid?"

Inside the foyer, I unhook Chestnut's harness. My mother on the couch with a book. The dog ambles to the kitchen and laps his water bowl. My mother lowers her book to her lap. "Where's your father?"

"Talking to Mr. Personality." I go to the basement and retrieve the toolbox. The concrete floor scuffed, my roller-blade circlings. Upstairs, I join my mother by the living room window. Skater's red and white flag lifts on the wind, masking then revealing my father, Slater, and the golden mailbox.

"What're they doing?" my mother asks.

"Slater's putting up a mailbox. Only he's doing it wrong." I shift the toolbox to my other hand. "Dad's going to help."

My mother sighs. "Even kind men can be trying."

"Think he's too nice?"

"No."

"Too trusting?"

She lets go of the pulled-aside curtain. "I guess there are worse things."

I leave my sandals in the foyer. The grass cool under my bare feet, and the toolbox bumps against my thigh. My father and Slater fall silent as I approach.

"Thanks, sweetheart." My father balances the toolbox on the porch railing. His fingers scour its depths, and the clatter of metal accentuates the stillness. The breeze brings the scent of just-cut grass, and the flag brushes my father's face. When I reach to pull it away, my hand collides with Slater's. He grips the flag's corner, the material held back, and we consider each other. My father urges me to humanize those I dislike, to consider the history beneath a prickly surface, and I should be able to use my gift of vision to see Slater in a kinder light. A childless man who, on my spyings over his backyard fence, I've caught kissing his dog. A man who's filled his empty spaces with uniforms and flags and shiny mailboxes. I should be able to do this, but for the moment, I'm distinctly my mother's daughter, and in my gut, a churning mistrust for this grown-up bullyboy.

My father hands Slater a drill bit. "This should work." He secures the box's latch.

"I'll return it when I'm done."

"No rush." We descended the porch steps. "Hope it helps."

When we reach the sidewalk, I lean close and whisper. "Mom says you're too kind."

He laughs. "There are worse things."

"She said that too."

We climb our front stoop. Chestnut on his hind legs, his snout and perked ears blurred by the screen. Welcoming barks for the creatures of his pack.

* * *

I toss Chestnut's ball, a game of backyard fetch. Another evening's red fade, colors out of a child's crayon box. The science of refraction and reflection balanced by the Internet's folklore. The red the blood of millions, a river of ghosts haunting the cusp of dark and light. Last summer, I sat with my father on the open second floor, the taste of ice cream, the roof beams and sky above. He raised his hand and pointed out the constellations, and in me now, a softening, an appreciation for man's penchant to craft narratives to explain the unexplainable.

I was inside earlier, but I can't take any more of the TV and its reports of sit-ins and general strikes. The protests peaceful at first but in this past week, a change. The police in riot gear and the spread of martial law. Molotov cocktails. Protestors shot and trampled. Running battles in the streets of Milan and Rio. The right's warnings that The Movement's been hijacked by Communists. Two of the Movement's leaders pulled from their houses and murdered, the victims either patriots or thugs, depending on the narrative one believes. The unrest also close to home, and I've seen the online videos of the protests outside the capital's assembly chambers, the smashed windows, the cars set ablaze. The governor's declared a curfew, and as the stars came out last night, Fran and I hurried home from practice. Last week my father staked a placard in our lawn, The Movement's slogan—NEVER AGAIN, the sign gone by the second day, and I'm unsure who to blame—Slater, who, since the Shut-In ended, has blared patriotic music on his patio as he smokes his evening cigar—or my mother, who now watches the nightly news in silence, her hand often covering her mouth.

I toss Chestnut's ball, and he half-runs, half-walks through the grass. August, a month of Sundays, lazy afternoons and sleep-in mornings. Chestnut returns, tail wagging, and drops the ball near my feet. My father's garden, groomed and tended, flanks the lawn and its flagstone path. The rabbits kept away by the clatter of aluminum pie tins hung on stakes, the soft breeze colored with thoughtless notes and silver glimmers. Higher up, arranged on crates and end tables rescued from flea markets, the more exotic strains in pots painted by my mother and me.

I pick up the ball. Its skin gnarled and bitten. I throw it again, but Chestnut abandons his chase near the garden's brick border. He buries his nose deep in the grass, and as I near, I spot the mound of black feathers. I pick up Chestnut, the bird at my feet. The dog twists, looking down, drawn by instincts. "Dad?" I call. "Dad!"

The bird's beak points skyward, its wing crooked, a pose that reminds me of a broken and forgotten toy. This is the second bird we've found in our yard. More in town, reports up and down the coast, some struck in midflight, gravity-driven plummets that have caused accidents and broken windows. The government sources unable—or unwilling—to identify a cause.

My father steps on the porch. "Kay?"

I walk away, trying to calm Chestnut. "Another bird."

He goes inside and returns with gloves and a plastic freezer bag. He kneels, a gentle handling, the gardener's pose I've seen him in a hundred times. He seals the bird in the bag, a specimen destined to join the others in his campus lab's freezer. I set Chestnut down and he follows my father inside. I walk the flagstone path. Sirens wail in the distance. A spider web breaks against my arm, a dewy whisper. At the yard's rear, I flex my legs, leap, and latch onto the oak's lowest limb.

I swing up my legs. The earth's sure touch gone, and the bark rubs rough against my thighs. I pull myself up and set upon the familiar path of footing and grip. I climbed the oak the day I first walked across this empty lot. I climbed it last Christmas Eve with my older cousin Mark, a race to the top and me the winner. I climbed it dozens of times in between. The tree has grown with me, and here, in the shaded labyrinth beneath the leaves, I know the tree better than I do from my bedroom window view. Twigs bristle as I work around the trunk, and I'm surrounded by shadows and red-hued slivers. Above, the flutter of a robin's brood, a nest tucked in the thinnest branches.

Higher, and I come to the climb's first challenging step. A balanced moment, a pose that stretches every centimeter from my body. Bark scrapes against my fingers. I push aside a branch and peer over Slater's high fence. The grill he rarely uses, the patio stones he soaks with herbicide, a yard as empty as it is neat. Slater sits with his feet up on a lounge chair as his stereo plays songs that sound like country hymns, God and nation and the might of a patriotic heart. He wears a white T-shirt and his blue work pants, dark socks, one with a hole for his big toe. He reaches down and pulls his panting pug onto his lap. Slater coos baby talk, his T-shirt wet with the pug's drool.

I twist around the trunk. A new perch brings the sag of weaker limbs. The mother robin protests, and I go no further. Another view here, the house across the alley with a sticker-bush hedge. The strange woman who lives alone. Her front porch dark on Halloween, no visiting cars for Thanksgiving or Christmas. The woman drags a trashcan to the alley. On her way back, she picks up a soccer ball and tosses it over the hedge. The neighborhood kids weave their stories. The money she's buried in her yard. An ex-con who poisoned her husband. A witch.

Our screen door shuts. Chestnut scoots through the grass. My father close behind, a pot and trowel in hand, and around him, a frame of branches and leaves. "Kayla?"

The distance between us, this perspective of dreams, and I try to see him as others might. His plants. His campus speeches. His dream of brotherhood and the stone's-throw reality of fences and hedges and locked doors. He calls me again, and the worry in his voice lures me down. Chestnut waits in the shade, front paws scraping the trunk. The return journey with its own challenges.

My father scoops up the dog. I sit on the lowest branch, my feet hanging at the level of her father's shoulders. "Dad?"

"Yes?"

"Sometimes I think about all those people, you know? The ones who died. But then I can't because it's too much. And then I feel selfish and small because I can't."

"We can't help but be numbed by something so horrible. Either that or it drives us mad."

I lower myself and drop to the ground. "But that doesn't feel right." I brush off my shirt. "I feel like I owe them more than numb or mad."

My father sets Chestnut down. The dog sniffs my feet. "So do I. At the very least."

* * *

A count of three, and Fran and I jump into the pool's deep end. The first leap's chill long gone, and as we sink, my hair rises in the diving well's deep blue. We near the bottom, and our lips move with silent confessions, bubbles that carry the names of the boys we'd like to kiss. *Todd* for Fran. *Billy* for me. We surface, laughing and gasping, a reunion with voices and splashes and the lifeguard's whistle. We cling to the side, and I'm content just to be, my body tired, an hour of swimming following an afternoon practice, the scene today normal like the normal I once knew. The diving board twangs. A boy pumps a plastic tube, a watery arc that glistens in the sun. Yet throughout the afternoon, we hear sirens. Rumors overheard at the snack stand, the mobs and fires in the capital, the governor's call up of the National Guard.

The pool crowded today, an afternoon hotter than most and everyone trying to squeeze in a last bit of summer. I adjust my shoulder strap. I missed the pool's delayed opening, my old bathing suit obscene, the tight elastic and pinched flesh. I'm wearing my mother's bikini, my first, and I'm self-conscious— my breasts, of which Fran says she is now officially jealous; the muscled shoulders that could pass for a boy's. We have to leave, and Fran proposes a final race to shallow end. She gets a head start, but I catch her as the pool's bottom angles up to us. The water chops, my windmilling stroke. We cross into the shallows, and I'm breathing, my face turned, when I collide with a body in my path. I stand and rub my eyes. Before me, a silhouette in the chlorine-stung haze, an older boy. "Sorry," I say, the word barely out of my mouth before he touches my bare skin beneath the surface. When I try to pull back, he grabs my wrist and forces my hand against his suit's bulge. I twist away and swim, kicking hard. Fran's waiting at the ladder by the time I reach the edge.

We gather our towels and bags. I shiver in the warmth, unable to speak, knowing if I tell Fran there will be a scene, a fight or a call to the police, but all I want to do is go. I walk ahead, wet footprints on the concrete for Fran to follow. The pool set to close within the hour, and on the water, the evening sheen. I wrap my towel around my neck and clench a corner between my teeth. In the pool's glistening middle, the boy who touched me. A shadow's wave before he submerges, and I curse myself for my indecision and late-surfacing rage.

We pass the snack stand. Soft pretzels in the toaster oven. Yellow jackets circle the trashcan. Outside the pool's gate, the high school boys kick up the volleyball court's sand. With the pool out of sight, I breathe easier. I grip Fran's arm, her Todd on the far court, my shirtless Billy on the near. The ball bounces beyond the sand and when it rolls to us, I kick it back. The boy's deep voices carry in the humid air. My mother's car curbside, and Fran and I tease each other as we climb in. Swooning pantomimes and dreamy whispers. Kisses blown from pursed lips. All of it real, yet also an act, my thoughts lost in the feel of the boy's grip, the touch of his swimsuit.

"I'm guessing you had a good time," my mother says. I turn from the front seat, another kissy face, and Fran snorts. An arched eyebrow or curled tongue are the only weapons we need to make the other crumble. In history last fall, we entertained ourselves by tallying our teacher's coffee slurps, and on the sunny morning he doubled his record, we choked on swallowed laughter. Our teacher heightened the absurdity with his demands to know what was so *gosh darn funny* as he continued to swig from his **Number 1 Dad** mug. My answers barely a sputter. Fran's mouth clamped with both hands, her eyes tearing and bright. Being ordered to the principal—a first for us both—a salvation. In the hallway we collapsed against the lockers and slid to the floor, my chest a riot of spams and gasps, control beyond me. The coil wrapped my lungs, then dizziness, and for a moment, the day's colors faded to ash. Fran guided my head between my raised knees and patted my back. "Don't die on me, sister."

My mother exits the pool lot, a final view of the sandy court. The ball high in the air. "Billy Stafford," Fran says.

"Todd Abbot," I say. I turn and smile. "Mrs. Fran Abbot."

On the ride through town, we speak in haughty tones about the charity functions and black-tie galas awaiting the future Mrs. Stafford and Mrs. Abbot. Our mansions' square footage, our cabanas and guesthouses. The names of our polo ponies and perfect, perfect children.

The car slows. My mother reaches out, her hand on my arm. There's a fire engine, its red lights flashing, yet its firemen sit on the rear bumper. The mob surges forward, choking the street and overflowing onto the sidewalks and lawns. The fire engine and its crew as still as boulders in the flow. Drums—two, three, more—and my pulse lifts with the scruffy beat. Men in hardhats sprint up the sidewalk. One with a sledgehammer, another with a wrench as long as his forearm, their expressions a loveless mix of yearning and ecstasy. Smoke drifts through our opened windows. "What's going on?" Fran asks.

"Stay in the car." My mother's words sharp. A motor's whir, and the windows seal. I turn back. Fran's eyes jittery, a hand on her chest. The grill of the pickup behind us fills the rear window. Smoke dulls the sunlight, a low veil over the street's chaos. "A fire," I say, a dreamer's observation, sluggish and obvious.

Fran shakes her head. "Then why are the firemen just standing around?"

My mother anchors her palm on the horn, a single, bleating

note. "Damn it, damn it," she repeats, hushed then louder. Her rage escalates, and the truck behind us joins in, its horn deafening. All of it a nightmare, but none of its images are as upsetting as the sinew straining in my mother's neck. "Move, damn it!"

A fireman rises from the engine's bumper. He wears boots and suspendered pants, but his hands are empty and his head bare. My mother lowers her window. The smoke pushes in, pungent, a stench beyond wood. The drums louder, faster. My mother's hand on the horn until the fireman reaches her door. Tears on her cheeks yet she speaks clearly and forcefully. "If you're not going to do anything, at least get us through!" She shuts the window before he can answer and stares straight ahead, her knuckles white upon the wheel.

Fran's voice from the backseat: "I'm scared."

The fireman waves to his crewmates. They fan out before us, a phalanx of linked elbows as they wade into the crowd. The mob inches aside. My mother lifts her foot from the brake and we roll forward. The firemen close to our bumper. My mother's jaw quivers, and I fear a step too hard or a confusion of pedals. Awareness finds me, and with it, a murderous fear—not for our safety but for the current that has swallowed us. Faces just outside our windows, some looking in. Boys barely older than me. A girl with a red bandanna around her neck. The haze thickens.

Fran's words undercut by the drums: "They have guns." I see them too—a shotgun, pistols and rifles. Others with bats. A little boy, his hair and swimsuit still wet, with stones in each hand. The crowd pushes closer, and when our car reaches the engine's front, the remaining firemen join their brothers. Some in the crowd shove back. Taunts, shouts. A stone bounces off our roof, and the three of us cower.

"Get down!" my mother barks. "Both of you!"

A rock, I understand, meant for our escorts, the ones qualified to put out the blaze. The tires' slow creep, and I swear I can feel every stone and speck of gravel beneath the rubber, swear I can hear every voice, see every red, puffed face with eyes alight. I'm the princess and the fucking pea, only my senses are open floodgates and the seas that rush over me run evil and deep. A scuffle erupts outside, and a man, half his face hidden by a bandanna, crashes against my door. I cry out, the shock echoed by the pickup's rear-end collision, the breaking of plastic lights. My mother mute, her focus forward and unflinching. She shifts into neutral and guns the accelerator. The engine roars, and the firemen look back. The man plastered against my door rights himself. His palm print, wide and thick, lingers on the glass. A sweaty impression, a fortune-teller's map. A shotgun blast, and Fran screams.

A break at the crowd's center, an open space where the firemen take longer strides, and to my left, I'm allowed a clear view of the house. Flames and cords of smoke twist from the second-story windows. At the edge of the clearing, a tattooed man waves flag of red and white. The drummers' sticks a blur. The little boy in the wet bathing suit steps into the open and throws a rock. A shattered window brings cheers from the mob.

We move faster against the crowd's tide, and by the next intersection, we're free. The firemen step aside, the slowest nearly clipped by our bumper, an accelerator stomp and a blur of houses. In me, the crash of momentum and inertia, adrenaline's woozy ebb. A girl on a bike darts between two parked cars, and when my mother slams the brakes, the belt snaps hard against my chest.

The car still. The late sun highlights the windshield's grime. The girl pedals past, her focus on a bike too big, a wrestling of handlebars, the front tire wobbling. My mother buries her face in her hands.

"Mom?" I rub her heaving shoulder. "Mom?"

* * *

I step outside, and the first gust steals my breath, my eyes squinted against the kicked-up dirt. My hair blows into and from my face. Branches clatter, smothering clouds and static all around. Our town over a hundred fifty miles from the ocean, yet I woke to a seagull in our yard. "Not a good sign," my father said. We watched the news last night. A storm churning up the coast, a web of tight isobars, coastal evacuations from North Carolina to New York. My goodbye hugs tempered with contingency plans and reminders of a distant cousin who drowned in a flash flood. I make promises to text, and we establish rendezvous points, just in case.

On my shoulders, a pack waiting for the weight of books. I'm both exhausted and anxious. A night of fitful sleep and restless dreams. A new school year, nine months since my last class. Two hundred seventy-three days; six thousand, five hundred fifty-two hours. Some hours tedious, some maddening, all tinged with the Shut-In's pale fear. A day like today so often dreamed of, a reunion with what I'd lost, but in my heart, a sputtering. The fear when yearning transcends into reality. A fear rooted in fragility and violence and my inability to shake the images of a house on fire or a ghost walking through the rubble.

I take the alley. Basketball backboards waver, and around me, the flight of leaves. I lift Fran's back-gate latch, a moment's glance for the garage's side-door windows. Inside, shadows and dust and the old muscle car Fran's father's been restoring one junkyard trip at a time. Growing opposite the garage's door, a dwarf maple, its umbrella branches trembling in the wind. The thin limbs hang down, their tips tracing the grass, and beneath, a shaded patch, the hiding spot Fran and I chose during

72

summer games of kick-the-can. A refuge often kept after calls of *Ollie-ollie-oxen-free*, our conversations and secrets more compelling than any chase.

I knock on the back door. Fran's mother at the stove, and she waves for me to enter. The door shut quickly against the wind's howl. Fran's mother is a kindergarten teacher at the elementary school, and a child couldn't ask for a kinder guide for the first leg of their long, weird journey. She turns and says, "Let's try again," and we repeat the back-to-back pose we struck in this very spot last week. I feel the hand she's rested atop her head brush my hair. She steps back, a smile, her gaze angling up. "Still can't believe it," she says. She puts on a mitt, opens the oven door, and removes a tray of cookies. She sets the tray on the stovetop and hugs me. Her hand in a mitt and the oven's warmth on her dress's front.

"You didn't blow away?"

"It's pretty crazy."

"You look pretty, honey." She ducks into the dining room, her voice raised. "Kayla's here. Let's hustle, Fran." Then to me: "First day. Always those jitters."

"Fran?"

"Less Fran and more me."

"You? Still?"

"Still. Especially this year."

"I can see that. I wonder what the kids will have to say."

"I've been around long enough to know I can't predict it. All I hope is they don't make me cry." She smiles. "At least not on the first day."

Her spatula scrapes the tray. The cookies pile on the plate. "Tell your mom I'll bring her blender over tonight."

Fran enters. She wears her field hockey sweatshirt but beneath waits the sleeveless, low-cut blouse her mother's forbidden, a secret trusted to me alone. Fran's mother kisses her daughter's cheek and stuffs a rolled-up poncho into her backpack. "You'll thank me later," she says. The local weatherman on the portable TV. New warnings, the predicted crests of creeks. In the capital, sandbags along Front Street. Fran's mother places a napkin and warm cookie into each of our palms.

"You've been doing this for the first day since nursery school." Fran adjusts her backpack. "I'm not a baby anymore."

"So you don't want it?"

Fran takes a bite. "Didn't say that."

Her mother kisses us both. "Be good, OK?"

A hug from Fran. "They're lucky to have you, mom."

Her mother places a hand over her heart. "That's very kind, baby."

"Don't get used to it." Fran takes another bite. "It's probably the hormones talking."

Our route almost a mile, and we talk about the strangeness of return to a life interrupted. I turn silent as I eat my cookie, lost in the drift of being claimed by neither the past nor the future. I'm familiar with the high school's side entrance and the stairwell climb to my old math class, and while I haven't explored much beyond that, I have spent the last week studying the website's floor map. My routes and a dozen variants planned, the periods I can stop at my locker noted and the hope none of my wanderings will cross my path with Missy Blough's. Fran in my Spanish and English classes—and lunch, thank goodness.

Closer now, the school in sight. The wind stronger, and on it, the first drops, a sting upon my bare arms. Fran holds her hands over her ears and cries as she turns around and around, "Auntie Em! Auntie Em!" The clouds ripple and turn upon themselves, a coiling that lends the illusion of life, the constriction of bowels and serpents. The pressure drop an ache in my sinuses and gut. For a moment, the hint of smoke, a scent quickly lost, and I wonder if Fran's as haunted by the other day as I am. The guns. The firemen who didn't put out fires. A little boy throwing stones. The murdered man an agitator fond of confrontations and street-corner diatribes, the distributor of radical pamphlets, a man my father had clashed with after barring him from speaking at his campus rally. "He wasn't well," my father said. "A poor soul sick in his heart and mind." The man a stranger but in the mob, faces I'd seen in the supermarket and church. All of them neighbors.

We cross the open playing fields. The rain picks up. The wind unblocked and the seagulls huddle on the soccer field's midline. Dirt swirls off the baseball diamond, and my shielding hand can't keep the grit from my eyes. We break into a jog. The wind whistles against the courtyard's brick. The napkin that held my cookie lifts from my grasp, and the paper joins the other tumbling scraps, some catching in trees and bushes, the others scurrying out of sight. I wouldn't look up if not for the snap of fabric and the grommets' spastic clank. A new flag flies beneath the old, a red circle and white cross. The clouds unleash, our final fifty yards a sprint that can't save us from getting soaked.

Inside, a gauntlet of lanyard-wearing teachers, ID badges, photos of younger selves. We shake out our hair, and Fran takes off her sweatshirt. "Hot," I say. The crammed space echoes with the teachers' uncoordinated refrain—the herding of all students directly to the auditorium. "Like lambs to the slaughter," Fran says, her "Baaa!" met by a gym teacher's hard glare. The secretaries and teachers point the way, a series of hallways, and my studied map melts into the reality of trophy cases and slammed lockers and a hundred overlapping conversations. We pass beneath a hand-painted banner—GO WILDCATS! The air thick with humidity and the press of bodies, a popping in my ears, the noise, the storm's dropping pressure. More teachers gather outside the gym doors, and I return the wave from my math teacher. Freshmen and sophomores are directed to one side, juniors and seniors to the other. I'm careful on the trembling bleachers, the mortification of starting high school with a public pratfall. I was here at the end of 7th grade—a runner-up in the county science fair, soil studies and a red ribbon. We find a seat, and I look around. Girders beneath the curved ceiling and championship banners on the walls. The lights shine in blinding puddles on the hardwood. Two men in suits gather at center court, each with a clipboard, walkie-talkies secured to their belts. A wide, white screen obscures one of the backboards. The bleachers fill, and around me, voices and shouts. Older boys, and I consider the faces, and although I recognize none of them from the mob, all are suspect. The rain heavier, gusts and bursts, a drumming above our heads.

Teachers line the walls along either entrance, and I fall into a daydream—their division into categories. The ex-athletes, their fondest memories rooted on the courts and fields of their youth. The jaded ones who count the years to retirement, the dispensers of packets and word searches and multiple-choice tests. Then the ones like my father. The ones who come home with stuffed briefcases, who nurture their craft and have patience for all. The ones who remember the pain of adolescence and the rawness of first loves and broken hearts.

A cord snakes across the hardwood and rises to a microphone held by one of the suit-wearing men. He raises his hand, a call for silence. His shoes shined, sharp creases in his pants. A woman on the floor near us raises a finger to her lips. The gym teacher who stared down Fran offers a sharp blast of the whistle lassoed around his neck. The principal speaks, a moment of feedback then a greeting. Wishes for all to have a good year.

He draws a deep breath, and I'm reminded of the little boys at the pool, the gathering of self before their first leap. "We've been through a lot these past few months. In the world as a whole and in our little corner of it. Coming back today is a big step for all of us." The rain falls harder, and the skylights blur with runoff. The principal raises his voice. "We're going to start with the Pledge of Allegiance." He motions and the lights dim. A laptop and projector sit atop a cafeteria table, an image brought into focus on the wide screen, blue letters on a white background—*I pledge allegiance to the flag.* "Over the week-end, Congress approved a new phrase be added to the Pledge." He fiddles with the laptop, an inadvertent click to the next slide before he scrolls back. "So if you'll stand and join me, we'll go through it line by line."

Fran and I stand with the others. The scuffle of shoes, tremors in the wood. The moment's silence undercut by the rain and wind, and from one of the skylights, a slow drip. The assistant principal waves, and a custodian rolls out a garbage can. Inside the plastic, a new rhythm, steady as a heartbeat. The principal clicks through the slides, the gym filled with mumbled responses and dull echoes. "And to the Republic, for which it stands. One nation, under God . . ." The next slide appears, the blue print now red. The principal holds the micro-phone closer to his lips, " . . . chosen and elect and true . . ."

In me, a hitch, a moment of separation, a divorce from the familiar. The new words like pebbles in my mouth, my stumble righted with the next slide. "With liberty and justice for all."

My hand slides from my chest. A look from Fran, and the wordless understanding of best friends. The fire. The mob's cries. A shotgun's blast. A meaty palm pressed upon my window.

The drip's pace quickens. The principal and his assistant and the custodian looking up as the students exit the gym.

* * *

The storm dominates the first week back, two days missed due to flooding, our hockey field a swamp, practices held in the puddled parking lot. Afterward, Fran and I walked through scarred neighborhoods. Downed branches, scattered shingles, couches and rugs pulled from flooded basements and left to dry in the sun. In my backyard, the robin's nest blown from the oak. Come Friday, the pledge's new words still stuck in my throat. My father sighed when he heard the news, an evening talk about the subtext of "chosen and elect." Other dispatches from my first week—my initial log-ins to my online calc 3 course through MIT. Missy Blough's locker nowhere near mine and the rumor she's already been suspended for smoking in the girls' lav.

Saturday evening finds my mother and I preparing salad in the kitchen. Our first lettuce in months, and I trim the leaves' brown edges. I call into the TV room. "Who's on now?"

"Reporters," my father says.

The TV special is carried on all the major networks. *A Healing Gala.* A concert in Philadelphia, commercial cutaways of the Liberty Bell and Independence Hall. The First Lady the master of ceremonies, the show a cavalcade of country music stars and athletes and megachurch pastors. The hour filled with sing-along tunes and appeals to the nation for reconciliation and a return to God. Prayers offered for all true Americans.

I sit between my parents and pull Chestnut onto my lap. My father with a spatula in hand, the burgers on the grill just turned. Chestnut sniffs the smoke on his shirt. I lean against my mother, happy to be here, this warm center, the Shut-In's claustrophobia fading. On TV, the First Lady commands center stage. She's willowy and thin, a college track star, a lawyer famous for her struggle to reinstate school prayer. She flips back her blond hair. The lights gleam, and she gleams in return, her hair, her smile, her jewelry. She paces the stage, and in her eyes, another kind of gleam, the shine of a true believer. She praises her husband's initiative to alter the Pledge of Allegiance and prays for the Golden Age that awaits a united America. Eyes closed, she raises a hand to the heavens, her voice honeyed with bliss and rapture. "Praise be."

I stroke Chestnut's head, his ears folded back. "She's full of shit," I say. "Seriously, really?"

"One never knows." The TV light plays on my father's glasses. "She may surprise us."

"Or she could be full of shit," my mother says. "Like all-the-way-to-the-top full."

My father grins. "More probably that. Still, let's hope for a surprise."

Chestnut rolls onto his side and offers me his belly. The First Lady speaks of a new dawn. Her image looms behind her, a close-up thirty feet tall. She calls out the nation's enemies—the anarchists and communists, the atheists and one-worlders—and the crowd boos each more than the last. She cites the wave of house burnings and lynchings, the violence regrettable, the motivation understandable. The necessity of cleansing a nation's soul, and just as Christ bled for us, so, too, must we bleed for Him. Tears on her cheeks now, and her voice trembles: "This great country has been *chosen*. We are the *elect*. Our survival and greatness waits in our surrender to the highest power—"

The signal dies, blips then darkness. My father clicks the remote. A cooking show, a baseball game—but on the major channels, only black screens. Finally, a flustered anchor, his words strained, and then the cut-away. Distant shots of a roiling mushroom cloud.

My mother silent. My father pale. I am made of stone. We are a family of stone. My chest dry and deep, a hollowness beneath my ribs that leaves me gasping. Static on TV and static between my ears. More shaky images. The horrible plume and the gasps of witnesses. A dozen different angles, nauseating jumpcuts as my father clicks the remote. The room vibrates—or is it just me—my awareness swimming in the overlap of images and voices. The scene over a hundred miles away, but I feel its impact right outside our door, and I know this is no good for any of us. I cross my arms and rock, a shaking off of haze and static, and in me, a stone's sinking in deep water. The lack of oxygen and pressure all around. The rocking forces my lungs to work, the physics of bellows and madmen.

Chestnut lifts his head and sniffs. My father springs to his feet. "The burgers."

I stand, my muscles commandeered by fidgets and short circuits. A chill swirls beneath my ribs. A heartbeat of cold, fluttering wings.

The den's window looks upon the backyard. My father lifts the grill's lid and disappears into a smoky chuff. His arm waves as he scoops the burgers.

My mother offers cereal, but none of us are hungry. The burgers' least burnt bits salvaged for Chestnut's bowl. We're sickened yet mesmerized by the TV reports, and facts soon yield to speculation. Angry pundits declare the rules of war no longer apply, and the radicals and their ilk deserve what they have coming. The First Lady, the country's brightest stars. Preachers who lived only to spread the word. Children and families who'd gathered for peace. Here are our nation's martyrs. Here are the innocents owed justice and revenge.

Hours pass, darkness, and finally we eat, toast for me, warm with melted butter, a simple comfort and with the taste on my tongue comes the night's first tears. First from my father, then my mother and me. On TV, reports from Jacksonville and Cleveland and Des Moines. Bloodshed in the streets. The homes of dissidents set ablaze. The patriots' flag of red and white waves before charging crowds. Then the crash from the living room.

Chestnut leaps from the couch, hackles raised. The click of nails and a barking charge into the living room. My father and mother close behind. A single lamp shines, and across the floor, a constellation of glass shards. Chestnut sniffs the brick upon the carpet. The streetlight slants through the shattered window. The curtain snares on the jagged aperture, and through the opening, voices from the dark. The brick with a crude design, white paint, a cross within a circle. I step forward to pick up Chestnut, then the stab in my bare foot. I hobble to the steps and cross my ankle over my opposite knee. Blood trickles down my arch and heel. My mother close, soothing words as she pulls the sliver. I bite my lip, the pain sharp then gone, the bloody shard cradled in my mother's palm. My father stands on the porch, the door flung open. "We're your neighbors! We're not your enemy!"

* * *

I walk through the late afternoon sun to my father's campus. Actually, I'm walking *back* a block, my attention unmoored, a turn I've made a hundred times ignored. I readjust my backpack, its load heavier, the last of my texts assigned, and in my stride, a painless hitch, the snug-sneaker fit of my bandaged foot. My thoughts wandering from the could-have-been ghosts of quantum mechanics to the yin-yang of equilibrium studies, and as I missed my turn, I was picturing a tightrope walker above me, spangled and beautiful, another ghost, the balancer of a thousand fulcrums—light and dark, warmth and cold, sated and starving. The forces in equilibrium systems are changelings, dependent one moment, independent the next, an ever-fluid dance of position and power. I feel these forces crowding me these last four days. The stares as I walk to school or with Chestnut. My stares in return, the wondering who threw the brick and who nodded in approval when they heard the news.

I make my delayed crossing onto campus. The day's plan—a rendezvous with my father after practice, an excursion to the gym's new climbing wall. Wide lawns spread before me, open areas anchored by buildings of brownstone and ivy and trees that date back over a century. The newer buildings radiate out, structures of brick and glass, and surrounding me, the company of ghosts. The natatorium where I learned the breaststroke. The faculty parking lot where my father ran beside me and my wobbly two-wheeler. The observatory where I watched the earth's shadow cross the moon. The field where I cheered my father in the annual faculty softball game.

The quad close but still out of sight. I love this walk, the shadows and flowerbeds, the brick and stone that rise like cavern walls. Black-eyed Susans tangle at the base of the founder's statue. Chapel bells peal the hour. Ahead, the only elm within thirty miles, the survivor of disease, the gnarled trunk and spreading shade, and just beyond, my father's office window.

Four years, and if we survive McNally and the world doesn't devour itself, I'll be here. I'll envelop myself in theory and thought. A math major, perhaps science. Perhaps both. Perhaps neither, my mind burning with a passion I've yet to discover. I'll walk these sidewalks with my books, and I wonder if I'll feel as gown up as I once imagined college girls to be. I'll make time to meet my father for lunch. Sometimes I worry that we've drifted—just a breath but enough. The Shut-In's tensions, the things I can only tell my mother, the lost days of how easy it had once been to reach out and hold his hand. "Love you," I said before stepping out this morning. A reassurance, an apology. A thanking for the space he's always given me.

I emerge from the chapel's shadow. The quad opens before me but my steps slow. Across the grass, hundreds of students. All sitting, all silent, so many bodies and so little sound, a disconnect, the physics of dreams. The students face the police gathered along the quad's east end. The police three-deep, identical in their riot gear, the dull sun reflected on their helmets and visors. In front, German shepherds that whine and pull at their leads. I hurry behind the police line and slip into a side entrance in my father's building.

Tall windows line the stairwell, and through them, slants of milky light. The stairs steep, and I grab the handrail. A woman hurries down, the box she carries overflowing, a fluttering of papers in her wake. I retrieve the nearest, a typed page, a circle graph—but by the time I stand, the woman's reached the bottom landing. A push of her hip opens the door, and the stairwell fills with echoes. Barking dogs. A megaphone's blared commands.

I hurry up the last flights, and I'm out of breath by the time I reach my father's floor. Dimmer here, the floor's dark tiles, the wainscoted walls. I slow as I pass the lit diorama of riverside life. A stuffed otter perches on a log and, in the reeds, a fox and her kit. As a child, the diorama fascinated and unnerved me, perhaps because it embodied the trickiest tightrope walk of them all. A balance of artifice and reality. A sense of frozen time. A pantomime of life and death.

The diorama's stillness radiates, a greater stillness I recognize all around me, an incongruity with the building's normal bustle, a stillness that threatens to claim me until I break into a jog. I enter my father's office. Papers cover the department secretary's usually immaculate desk, her computer and phone left behind, the framed pictures of her cocker spaniels gone. My pace quicker as I enter the narrow hallway lined with professors' offices. I pass a choked bulletin board, announcements for plays and lectures, the other offices vacant, their doors open, the only sign of life coming from the clatter at the hallway's end.

I near the last open door. "Dad?"

He stops. A potted plant in his hands, his fingers lost beneath delicate tendrils, a look of confusion, a pause amid the chaos of open filing cabinets and a paper-strewn floor. "What're you doing here?" The large window behind him, the elm on one side, a glimpse of Old Main's clock on the other. My father the balance between the two.

"The climbing wall. After practice, right? I wouldn't have come if—"

"I'm sorry." He sets the plant in a cardboard box. "I should have remembered. You shouldn't be here." He hands me the box. Inside, wedged arrays of green, his bred strains. He grabs two stacked boxes. A collective cry rises from the quad, and we draw to the window. Arcs of smoke trace the autumn blue, and when the canisters land, the students scatter, coughing, their mouths covered. Many lost in the fog. A few hurl the canisters back toward the onrushing line of blue. The police's helmets replaced by gas masks, their faces hidden beneath curved insect eyes.

"Come on," my father says. Screams fill the quad. The police batons slash through the smoke, and before them, a stumbling stampede.

My father behind me: "We need to go, honey. Please."

Our steps hurry through the light spilled from the riverside diorama. My reflection flashes in the otter's glass eyes. My father leads us down the back stairwell, this one narrower, windowless, the clatter of pots from our boxes. We step outside, and in the building's shadow, the tiny faculty lot and my father's truck. Students sprint past, many coughing, tears on their cheeks. A girl clutches a grimacing boy, his face streaked with blood. My father places his boxes in the truck's bed and opens the passenger-side door. "Just hold onto it," he says.

I gaze into the box balanced atop my lap. In me, a sudden sympathy for the readers of tealeaves and crystal balls, for written in the tangled stems and vines waits the truth—my father is in trouble. Plants and speeches about brotherhood. Neighbors who live behind fences and hedges. The human clouds overhead all these months, and I've been blind not to see it all before. I speak as he turns the key. "We need to leave."

More students stream around the building. The faster ones pull the injured and dazed, a tugging of arms. A girl with swollen eyes. A boy limping, his jeans torn. The police dogs close behind, their handlers pulled forward, batons raised. The girl with the swollen eyes trips, and one of the dogs pounces. Its front paws upon her chest, its snapping jaws inches from her covered face.

My father jerks the gearshift. The truck, always moody, sputters forward, the jostle of failing engine mounts, the rusted bed that hauled tons in the building of our home. The gas filters around the building, a low haze, and I feel its sting in my throat and eyes. I cover my mouth. "Daddy," I say, fighting the tightness in windpipe, "we need to leave."

"We are, don't worry." He cuts the wheel and shifts again. I lurch as the front tire bounces over a curb. Another pack of students scrambles across the lot. My father stops and yells, and they climb into the bed. Two boys and a girl, all of them urging the fourth, a heavy boy, his eyes streaming with tears, and my father waits until they're able to haul his bulk over the gate. The police close in. The fastest strikes the gate with his baton, and the blow reverberates through the cab. My father tromps the gas. A cough of exhaust and the commotion fades behind us. A half-mile later, we drop the students off. A goodbye in a narrow alley, an urging for them to be safe before driving off.

I dab my stinging eyes. A sandpaper-catch in my throat and the pain of speaking. "We need to go."

He manages a smile. "We're OK now."

"That's not what I mean." I clear my throat, but my voice remains whittled, and I force myself to be heard above the truck's rumble. "We need to leave. Today. Tonight. Uncle Bill's hunting cabin or grandma's place." Tears now, ones that owe nothing to the gas. "Nothing good will happen if we stay here."

My father works the gearshift. "We'll be OK. And if it comes to it, we'll go if we have to." He wrangles the gear shift. "Don't worry, OK?"

The cab quiet for the rest of the ride. Looking down, I realize one of the pots inside my box has broken. A spilling of soil and exposed roots.

* * *

I babysit as my parents help Dr. Klein load her minivan. The crib broken down, diaper boxes and packed suitcases, clothes on hangers. I play with the baby in the backyard. The little boy charges on chubby legs, and I'm close behind, my hands near, ready to catch him. He's always bringing me gifts— blooms and stones, the delicate shells of cicadas. The boy sits, a plop onto his cushioned behind. He rips handfuls of grass, and holds them out to me, the blades lifted and released, a tumbling into my outstretched palm.

My father opens the backdoor. "She's ready."

I pick up the baby. A sniff of his head, the scent of lotion, and I think of a boy not much older than him and the rocks he threw at a burning house, and I wonder about this life's paths, the ones we choose and the ones we're shown. I carry him around the house's side, past the flowerbeds with their last blooms and wilted stalks. The child wiggles until he faces forward. His hands outstretched as we near his mother. Dr. Klein straps him into the car seat and shuts the van's door.

A pause on the sidewalk. My parents and Dr. Klein have already discussed her leaving, a conversation kept among adults but which I understood without overhearing the specifics. The campus shut down until further notice. Windshield fliers decrying godless liberals. The neighbors who no longer talk to us and a brick through Dr. Klein's window, as well. The fear for her child's safety.

Dr. Klein hugs me then my mother. Her embrace for my father longer, her eyes closed as she speaks. "Don't think me a coward."

"I don't."

"If it weren't for the baby—"

87

He steps back, her hands held in his. "We'll all be back together when this settles down."

The baby cries as the van pulls from the curb. We cross the street. Slater on his porch, a closing of his golden mailbox's lid, and I wonder how long he's been watching. His stare open and cold, my father's wave unreturned.

* * *

Three days pass. The college remains closed, and in my school, rumors it won't reopen anytime soon. The news is spread with a kind of glee, a victory proclaimed by the diehard locals who've latched onto McNally's hatred of intellectuals, and in the hallways, a new power structure emerges. The boys who roam in packs and prop their boots up on desks, who openly curse and mock their teachers' attempts at discipline. They're small-town boys, and they have no better representatives of McNally's hated elites than their teachers, men in ties who gush over books, women keen on decorum and following rules. I'm not their target, yet when we pass in the hall, their gazes slip my way. Missy Blough and her boyfriend, a senior louder and more brazen than most, the two of them slowing as I pass. The math freak. The daughter of a poet and professor. The hidden forces that have always fascinated me ooze from their stares, tides fetid and ugly and anxious to settle a score they believe long overdue.

A reprieve comes at dinner where the laughter of my father's visiting grad students brings a welcome light. We share simple meals, the post Shut-In reality of shortages and rations. Discussions of politics give way to academics, the love of science and life overcoming the world's upheaval, their visits usually ending with a garden tour. Another batch of students is due later for a Sunday lunch, but for now, my father takes me out in his truck. What we discuss on the ride—field hockey and the nuances of graphing discrete functions. What we don't discuss—the argument he and mom had earlier about his opinion piece in the morning paper. His condemnation of violence, his appeal to unity. The Movement unmentioned but its ideals extolled. My mother's voice lowered, but still I heard. "Things are different now. Don't you see that?"

Oaks and sycamores line the river road, patches of sun and shade. On the shoulder, a dead groundhog, and the flies stir as our truck rattles by. The caterpillars' nests high in the branches, sunshine captured in the spun tangles. Chestnut on my lap. His snout twitches, his front paws on the door's armrest. The window down and his ears matted by the wind.

We near our destination. Further up river, the shuttered steel mill, a miles-long stretch of crumbling brick and broken windows. A few more miles to the capital. The legislature suspended and sent home, their chambers empty, guarded checkpoints on every major road into town.

My father flips the blinker, and I smile—the road to ourselves and how like him. A believer in the common good, the user of turn signals on deserted roads. He veers onto a dirt spur and stops. "Ready?"

"Yep."

He climbs out, and I slide over. The engine's shudder cuts even deeper when I grip the wheel. I lean forward, my back lifted from the seat. My father settles beside me. Chestnut sniffs me then him.

"Remember how it all works?"

My first lesson a year ago. This very spot, the trees gold and red, a world so different, my father's encouragement and three stalls in a row. "Uh-huh."

"Imagine your footwork. Nice and easy."

I let out the clutch, a lurch harder than expected. The finches gathered in the lane's ruts scatter. My father's tone gentle. "You're good."

I stop at the rail bed. A veil of dirt, golden in the sun, swirls around us. I look north then south. The rails narrow and twist with the river's slow turns. I cross, bucking over the rails, and rejoin the dirt road. The trees closer here, and the lowest branches scrape the roof. An opossum slides into the shadows. I stop when we reach the clearing.

The river opens before us, a wide stretch to the opposite shore. Sunlight slivers on the flow. My father wades into the brush, trowel in hand. The search for a rare autumn bloom, a name in Latin that crumbles on my tongue.

I walk a shoreline of silt and rock. I look for carp in the shallows but see none. Upstream, the steel mill's smokestacks, the city's south-side bridge. Before me, a small island halfway across the river. I've been coming to this spot with my parents for years. Picnics. Explorations. June's mayflies. February's ice. I once daydreamed about the island, a tangle of vines and scrub no larger than our house's lot. On the island, I pictured a house and life all my own. A refuge. A kingdom. My fantasy snuffed with the view from the south-side bridge after a week-long rain. The island lost, its tallest trees barely visible above the flow.

My grid appears, and the vista dissolves into its components. The water's reach. The current's purr. The fog's slow burn. I crouch and cup a cool handful and let the water trickle between my fingers. These drops unique but the flow no different than last year. Ten years ago. A hundred. A thousand. The river a witness to it all. I'll return next spring. Older. A better driver. My father will look for a new plant. My mother will sit on a boulder, her notebook on her lap. Time, so often the blurred axis of my grid, for once in focus. Time will heal us. I pick up a stick and hurl it into the water. The stick visible for a moment, then gone.

A rustle behind me. The sway of lanky reeds. Chestnut bolts from my side. I find my father kneeling in the brush. A small leaf on his shoulder and his glasses crooked. "This is it?" I ask.

"It is." His trowel bites into the earth and claims a small

circle. He lifts, two hands cupping the dirt. Chestnut sniffs the dangling roots. The plant a tangle of green and a single, dime-sized, red flower. He closes his eyes and sniffs the bloom. He looks at me. "Its seed can travel for miles before it takes root, and there might not be another one like it for as far as we can see. It survives the cold and snow then flowers in autumn. A year goes by, maybe two, before it blooms again."

"For our backyard?"

He stands. "Sound like a good plan?"

"Yes." I reach out, a hand to help him over a rotting log. "One must always have a plan."

* * *

I'm dreaming. Or perhaps I'm lost in the white expanse between consciousness and sleep. My limbs distant yet in my thoughts, I run, a deer's strides, only I'm beneath the river. Around me, stones and fish and sunken boats. The miracle of air in my lungs.

Chestnut barks and the river evaporates. Voices mesh with the air conditioner's drone. My bed shakes. *Earthquake*—my first stab at lucid thought, but that's impossible, isn't it? The rumble focused, the front door, and I picture my uncles' hammers. I picture elephants, Fourth of July explosions. Chestnut with hackles raised, his alarmed bark. A disconnect in my head, what's real and what isn't. The stairwell just outside my door, a throat that rises from downstairs' gut and in it, the horrible pulse. Kicks and screams. My mother's voice pierces the din. "Run, damn it! Run!"

I stand, wobbly, this border of real and not. Bare feet on hard wood, and the violence rides into me. The pulse frantic, dark. Chestnut turns from the door to me and back again. My legs like smoke, and I fumble into my flip-flops. I'm halfway down the steps when the front door bursts from its hinges.

Three men flood into the foyer. Their boots crunch over wood and glass, the men all bluster and menace. One topples a lamp, a spill of light, the illumination of shoes. The first man grips a shotgun. Another with a sledgehammer. All with sweaty faces and heat in their eyes. The mob outside and a drum's pulsing beat.

Slater's the last to enter, a pistol in hand. Chestnut lurches past me and scuttles whiplash circles, barking and growling and fearless, a dance around the men who've grabbed my father's arms. I'm in my panties, braless and a white T-shirt, my hand tight on the railing, Slater's stare cut short by my father's cries. A bullish man delivers a blow that snaps my father's glasses. My mouth opens, but I can't scream, my voice consumed by my father's gasp, his pained breath. He struggles to gather himself. "Slater, tell them . . . tell them." Words that bring a different pain. The exposure of my father's trusting heart. His child's belief in good. His faith that his neighbor is his savior.

A stomach punch and my father crumples. My body thick and distant. I picture my hockey stick, the duffle's give, the physics of weight and force. The men holding my father let go, then the stomps and kicks, the smack of leather, and the grunts of my father and his attackers join with Chestnut's barks. The din crowds my brain. I try to scream, but my throat is choked—the silt of dreams, the dust of fear. The bear who broke my father's glasses drags his limp body to the foyer.

My mother charges. Empty handed, screaming. A punch for the bear before another man hurls her against the wall. The smack of her skull, and she slides down, a melting of will and muscle before she collapses into a heap. A mirror falls beside her, and the glass sprays across the wood, an explosion in the river of skewed light. Slater straddles my mother and slams his pistol against her head.

He points to my father. "Get him to the street!" His breath short. The glow of exertion on his round cheeks. Sweat stains mark the armpits of his dark blue uniform. The men holding my father's arms step over my mother. Chestnut leaps across the debris and latches onto Slater's cuff. Slater curses, and with a twist of his round middle, he kicks the dog across the hardwood.

I leap from the stairs. A reflex and a thudding collision with Slater's broad back. My arm locks around his throat. His policeman's cap tumbles. I breathe in his stink of sweat and cigars and whiskey, his hair gel slick against my cheek. I wrap my legs around his thick gut and pull until his curses whittle to gasps, until I feel the lurch of his Adam's apple against my forearm and his throat's shallow gasps. Our pulses join, and the rhythm fuels me, a sensation as if his strength is becoming mine. A single grid fills my mind—the intersection of my forearm and a windpipe struggling to draw air. I grind my teeth, my body twisted, a cruel leverage. Slater reels a spastic dance that kicks over another lamp. Chestnut circles us, barking, barking.

Slater turns and rams his back into the wall, once, then again. Shock rides my spine, my nose flattened against the back of his skull, and in my head, a flash of black light. With a squeeze and a twist, he pulls my arm from his throat. He sucks a greedy breath and casts me to the floor. The black light fades, and I scramble to my feet, but before I can straighten myself, he punches me in the mouth. In seventh grade, I caught a stick to the chin, and I drifted through a chain of unclaimed moments before surfacing back onto the field, but this shock runs deeper, a rumble in my bones. I stagger back then trip. My hair over my eyes. The metallic taste of blood on my tongue.

I lie on the floor, my legs twisted beneath me, my body slowly rising through hazy states of understanding. I push back my hair to see my father being dragged outside. The lamp's skewed shine like a stream of light, and in the stream, over-turned chairs, books knocked from their shelves, the glitter of a broken mirror. My mother draws her knees beneath her, a balancing hand on the wall. Half her face masked in blood. She pulls me to my feet. I see her moving lips, register her volume, but I can't understand her, my ears flooded. Chestnut's barks. The mob's cries. The drum's ratcheting beat.

Our arms draped around each other, my mother and I stagger to the foyer. Another skewed view, the front door off its hinges and the circling wolves on our lawn. Around my feet, broken glass, wooden splinters. My mother pushes back my hair, and I finally hear her voice. "Oh, baby," she says, her fingers tender on my numb lip, her touch mirrored by mine, a stroke of her cheek, her blood slick and warm.

By the time we reach the lawn, we're running, graceless, hand-in-hand. The mob fills the street, and above their heads, a waved flag of red and white. Possessed faces flock beneath the streetlight. The drummer at the light's fringe, an unrelenting *rat-a-tat-tat*. The heat in his eyes too, his hands a blur. My father's head hangs, his chin coated in blood. The men who burst down our door grasp his elbows. Slater commands the group's center. The streetlight shimmers on the chrome of his raised gun. He yells along with the crowd.

"Traitor!"

"Elitist!"

A bare-chested man steps into the light. His tattooed arm swings a series of giant circles before he tosses a rope over the streetlamp's arm. The crowd erupts. "Traitor! Traitor!"

My mother pulls me from the crowd's fringe and into the shadows alongside the house. "Go to Uncle Bill's. Wait for me there."

I don't move. My eyes on the street.

"Go! Now!" A hard push, and I stagger. She's never used a rough hand, and for a moment, we stare at each other before falling into an embrace, her lips near my ear, a stroke of my long hair. Her tears and blood warm against my cheek. "I'm sorry, baby, but you have to go. For all of us."

"But—"

"I'm not going to leave him." She pushes herself back, still clutching my shoulders. "But I need you to be safe. Right now. Go to your uncle's. Wait there until I come get you."

She starts across the yard, turning once. "Go!" she cries.

She pushes through the crowd. A parting of bodies and the noose around my father's neck. My father speaks. *Brothers*, he calls them. His words slurred, a gagging on his own blood. *Friends*. His appeal cut short by a kick to the gut.

I crouch behind one of the azaleas I helped plant, bushes my father said would one day be taller than me. Chestnut barks at the crowd's edge. I call him, imitating my father's whistle, but the dog is lost in the frenzy. Bent double, I scuttle across the grass.

Closer, and through the crowd, I see my parents. My mother stands in front of my father, her finger poking chests as she points out the men who've borrowed her husband's tools, the ones whose wives she's babysat for in a pinch. She chides Slater. A big man who hit a mother and daughter, the one who never picks up his dog's shit. A preening bureaucrat who couldn't be bothered by his neighbors on the Shut-In's distribution days. I kneel in the cool grass and scoop up the dog. Chestnut squirms but I hold tight. My father lifts his head and turns my way. One eye swollen shut, the other clear. *Go*.

I back up, cautious steps, fighting the pull to stay, to somehow help make it all right. Slater pushes my mother aside and addresses the others. They live in a new world now, he declares. My father sealed his own fate, his campus rallies and traitorous blog all the evidence they need. "One America!" he cries.

The mob responds: "Holy America!"

Slater lifts his arm, and the shirtless man yanks the rope. Another man rushes forward and grips the rope, then another. My father rises, an imitation of flight. His hands claw the noose, the spastic kick of his feet, the rope's wild sway. My mother lunges at the men grasping the rope. The large man who broke my father's glasses grabs her from behind and lifts, her legs kicking, the soles of her feet blackened by the macadam. Slater fires his pistol, a celebratory shot. The drumbeat wild, feverish, ecstatic. I'm about to scream when a hand clamps over my mouth.

"Come with me, girl." A woman's voice. Her other hand firm on my arm, and I'm pulled away from the crowd. I squirm, but the woman holds tight and wrestles me back into the shadows.

II.

* * *

You wake to a chickadee. A high-pitched *feebee, feebee*. One near, another far. A call and response your father taught you. You picture the chickadees' tufted heads, their nervous glances. A bird you and your parents sought on winter trails. The three of you as still as the surrounding forest. A survey of naked limbs. The steam from your mouths. The birds so small. Melodies sung for you alone in the hush of brown and white. A new image rises in the trees. Your father lifted on a rope. His legs kicking, then not.

Your hands lift to your throat, the panic of being underwater, and your blinking brings no focus, and from the trees comes your father's voice, his advice if you were ever lost in the woods. Stop. Be calm. Take inventory.

You shut your eyes and breathe.

The water and trees evaporate and you emerge into a small room. White walls. A single bed. The sun snared in flimsy curtains. A crucifix above the door. Your father at the periphery of your vision no matter where you look—there, and with a blink, gone. A guest room, although you have a feeling you're the room's first visitor. Empty shelves and unadorned walls. A sterility flavored with the scents of another life. Soaps and lotions. Kitchen spices. You stand on the back of a ship, all connections severed and the only shore you've ever known fading.

A wince when you touch your swollen jaw, and here's a connection you haven't lost, the presence and memory of pain. Close your eyes, and in the dark, your mother joins your father, both hoisted from the earth. Your father above, his heels' fading twitch, his blue cheeks. Your mother in a brute's lassoing embrace. Your mother curses her attacker, curses them all. Her

101

elbows swing. Her blackened soles and the drum's remorseless beat. Slater and the others push closer, their eyes alight. The pictures leave and return, a short-circuiting horror movie. Your breathing suddenly difficult. You're drowning again, your boat capsized, the sea cold and dark. A series of gasps, but the act's simple mechanics lie beyond your grasp. The movie projector operates on its own power, and you rock in time with the film's shudder through sprockets and cogs. You open your mouth, trying to force air into your throat—if not that, then to scream— but you're capable of neither. The movie shifts to the azaleas' shadows. The slow-motion movement of your mother's mouth. A silent pantomime. *Go!*

Open your eyes and the movie stops. Chestnut stretches and yawns. He lurches over the blanket's folds and licks your cheek. He alone remains unchanged—the short hair between his ears, the droop of dewy eyes. You should be crying, but that place waits far from your heart. You could close your eyes and return to your movie, but with your eyes open, you can only think in facts. In simple, declarative sentences. You're in a strange room. Your mother isn't waiting downstairs. You have your dog. Your father's noose was knotted by people who are now waking up all around you. Men going to work and kissing their children goodbye. Your rocking slows, and in its place, an icy coating. If only you could remain here, this bed, this claimed sliver of certainty. Your hand on Chestnut's side, the breathing of life in him. If only you could keep this balance and remain still forever. Nothing to gain or lose and no one else to die.

The sound of feet on the stairs. Chestnut barks. The ice thickens, and you hug your knees to your chest, a drawing inward, and if you could swallow yourself and disappear, you would. The door eases open.

A woman enters. You know her—in a way—but again,

connection fails you. She carries a glass of milk, a plate with toast and sausage and a sandwich. Chestnut's teeth bared, a low growl. The woman arranges the offerings on the nightstand and pulls a chair to the bedside.

You shrug off the ice and the distance closes between you. Here is the witch. The poisoner who's sheltered herself behind locked doors and a sticker-bush hedge. She's round in her face and hips, a frame stout and strong enough to have wrestled you across the yard and alley. You bit the fleshy palm clamped over your mouth, the taste of sweat and dirt, and this morning, your teeth marks lay wrapped in gauze. You've only glimpsed her in passing or from high in the oak. Up close, the witch loses her menace. Middle aged, gray strands in her coarse, black hair. Pale, weary eyes.

The woman cuts a tip from a sausage link. Chestnut's barking replaced by a twitching snout. "Can he have some? I don't have dog food." Her soft words not what you'd imagined.

Chestnut snatches her offering, inhaling more than chewing. A half smile lifts the witch's round face. She cuts another piece. "He's a nice dog. I never had a dog." She considers you, and you understand the expression you first took for weariness is really concern. "I'm Helen. And I know you're Kayla."

You pick up a piece of toast then set it back down. The thought of eating too complicated, the act of chewing and swallowing belonging to the likes of acrobats. Helen leans forward and Chestnut licks her fingers. She looks at you again. "No one's going to hurt you while you're here." She stands. "Got you a sandwich for later. The bathroom's across the hall. I have to go to work." She scratches Chestnut's head. "And I'll get some dog food." She picks him up. "Let's see if I can let him do his business in the backyard and then bring him back. He's not the running-away type, is he?"

You manage to shake your head. Or at least you think you do.

Helen places her nose between the dog's ears. Her voice softened by fur. "I didn't think so."

The window beside the bed overlooks the backyard. You pull back the curtain. Helen stands, fists planted on her hips. Chestnut sniffs the perimeter of sticker-bushes. A neighbor appears on the hedge's other side. Helen and the neighbor talk. The dog's origins, you guess. Or perhaps the things they heard about last night. The college professor, the noose slung over a streetlamp, whispers of who was involved and who might be next.

Helen returns, setting down both Chestnut and a bowl of water. Another smile. "He's a good boy, isn't he?"

Words spin in your head, but you can't coax them onto your tongue.

"Stay inside today. Don't answer the door, not for anyone. Tonight, we'll get in touch with your people." Helen pauses in the doorway. "I'm sorry. I really am."

The front door shuts. The lock's click. Chestnut sits close, watching. He knows. His pack dwindling and his hopes with you. Yet his black eyes look through you because you're smoke. You're nothing. A stiff wind could scuttle you and you'd never be seen again. Lie back. The ceiling above, its white backdrop a screen, and the movie no longer waits for you to close your eyes. Your father smiling at the riverside, a plant in his hands, the roots and dirt. Your mother's face in the shadows. *Go!*

The sunlight creeps across the bed, the brightness in your eyes then slipping away. You don't move. Can't move. Perhaps you've fallen from the top of the oak, every bone broken. You struggle to determine if you're filled with moonlight or lead. When the last patch of sun slips from the covers, you muster the strength to sit. You pick up a piece of toast. The bread crumbling and cold. A mouthful you force halfway down then hack back onto the plate.

Swing your feet onto the floor. Chestnut lifts his head. You stand and reach across the thousand miles that separate you from the doorknob. This threshold you have no memory of crossing and a single, testing step into the hall. Vertigo bubbles as you look down the stairs. Everything after Helen grabbed you hazy, your memories reduced to flashes and gasps. The hallway tiny, and you cross it as you would a balance beam, heel-toe, your hands outstretched, the fear of falling. In the bathroom, a long piss and the lull of splashing water. You take inventory, but none of the variables add up. The bobby pins and tweezers on the windowsill. The sink's toothpaste and creams. A tub in need of scrubbing. The ship sails on. The shore recedes and the captain nowhere in sight.

Lift a slat in the window's blind. The yard below, a three-row garden surrounded by a rabbit fence. The alley's ribbon of cracked macadam. On the other side, your oak. Sun on the green, the leaves' breezy sway. Hidden and not, the pots and paths of your father's garden. His new plant from the riverside and a single red bloom. Your house, and in you, the amputee's pull of what was and would never be again.

In the bedroom you lie with your face away from the window. Pull the dog close and hug the pillow. You wonder when you will cry—and when you finally do, you wonder if you'll be able to stop. All you have now is emptiness. You are the queen of emptiness, of stretching skies and howling winds, of a horizon that bleeds into a single, meshed hue. You are a little girl alone on a little boat surrounded by an endless sea. The projector sputters to life, and the movie plays.

* * *

Chestnut barks. Hesitation at the bed's edge, ears back and tail wagging, the distance judged then a leap. Your heart wild. Another rousting and these hours of drift, the dreamless sleep of unplugged machines. Now consciousness, sudden and jolting. Your mother at the foot of the bed. *Go!*

The door opens and Helen peeks in. Your mother disappears. "I'd knock but my hands are full."

You mutter through twitching lips. "It's OK." Your voice of rust.

Chestnut abandons his bark to sniff Helen's shoe. Helen sits at the edge of the bed and lays down her offerings. A toothbrush and a bag of dog treats. A plate of takeout chicken, macaroni and cheese. A can of soda. A plastic bag, and inside, a pair of jeans, Helen apologizing, hoping she got the size right. Helen picks up Chestnut. "There's chicken for you too." You pick up a drumstick. Grease on your fingers then panic, the revulsion of flesh on your tongue. You set the drumstick back in its Styrofoam tray, and not seeing a napkin, you let Chestnut lick your fingers.

Helen places a clock radio on the nightstand and sets the time. The radio old, and she apologizes for the poor reception as she twists the knob. Static, a fading pop tune, and you think of your mother's kitchen songs. The only clear station the news channel at the dial's end. The movement of troops, the price of oil. Helen turns it off. A shrug. "It's there if you need it."

Helen offers another piece of chicken to Chestnut and hands over her phone. "Call your people. We'll get you wherever you need to go. Tonight, tomorrow—whatever they need, we'll do."

You study the screen. The ice over you, the distance

beneath. The phone a relic from another world, and for a moment, you can't remember how it works, and you stare, stupid and transfixed. When memory finds you, you enter the number and hold the phone to your ear. A man answers. You whisper. "Uncle Bill?"

"Kayla?" A pause. "Kayla, where are you?"

You look at Helen, Chestnut on her lap. "I'm safe." You shift the phone from the swollen side of your face.

"Are you with the police?"

"No."

"Where are you?"

"With a friend."

The dead air an ocean, and you fear nothing more than saying the words that will make the nightmare real. "We're so sorry."

Chestnut rolls onto his side and offers Helen his belly. His ears pinned back, a gurgle from his throat. "They took mom."

"We're trying to find out what happened to her." Another pause. "The police have been here. They tore through everything. They took your Uncle Alex. They're holding him in the city. At least that's what we think. They've rounded up lots of people. Don't worry. We'll find him and your mom. And we'll get the people who did this." Your aunt's voice in the background, an overheard conversation—the police car that keeps circling their block. Your uncle returns: "Tell me where you are. We'll come get you."

You pause. "I have to go. I'm safe, don't worry."

"Kayla?"

"I love you."

You hang up. Speaking has left you weary. The phone a boulder in your hand. "They have my Uncle Alex. He said they've arrested lots of people."

"I've heard the ones they can't fit in jail they're keeping in the stadium."

You picture the city stadium, a building slated for demolition before the Shut-In. Its leaky roof, the wooden seats cut for a slimmer generation. You went to the circus there, and now you see the tightrope walker captured in a web of light, the starshine reflection of sequins, a beautiful, floating vision above the darkness where your mother might wait.

The phone rings. Helen studies the screen. "Your uncle."

"Don't." Another ring. "The police are watching him."

Helen turns off the phone. She sets Chestnut back on the bed. Her hand reaches out, but you recoil, a reflex, the memory of Slater's fist and the black light that waits on the other side of consciousness. Helen with a heavy smile before patting the bedspread. "Don't worry. We'll figure it all out."

* * *

You lie in bed and stare until the clock's red digits vibrate, an electric pulse, a hum that fills your body. The Earth has almost completed its rotation since the mob burst through your door, and here is your new midnight. You clutch the pillow, your legs tucked against your chest. The movie resumes, and the images now breathe and stretch their legs, and you accept the hallucinations for they seem no less real than anything else. The pictures random, their lack of narrative atoned for in their vibrancy. Your mother crumpled on the living room floor. Your father at the grill, a veil of smoke. Your mother turning as she runs barefoot across the yard. *Go!*

11:34—the minute expands, swallowing you. Close your eyes. Images of your parents tumble over you, and you're reminded of a November day they buried you beneath the backyard leaves, deepening layers, one after the other. Snapshots from last night and a thousand days before. The spasms come, a rocking you can no more stop than a hiccup or sneeze. A reflex rooted in synapses and a truth beyond language. The bedsprings twang, and the headboard nudges the wall. This rhythm your own, the darkness all around, and as long as you keep moving, you can push away the worst pictures, the ones that fight to consume you. A coordinate plane rises from the dark sea, the headboard's thump a crest, the spring's squeak a trough, and your body dissolves into a wave, a thin line rising and falling until the sky bleeds from black to gray.

Exhausted, your skin shining with sweat, you speak to your parents because you feel them near. "I'm OK. I'm OK."

The chickadee calls as you drift. *Feebee, feebee.*

* * *

"I have to go to work." Helen on the bed's edge. Blink away your dreams. Your house the summer it was built. Uncle Bill nailing a crooked stairwell, his insistence the twisted runners were necessary to keep the house from falling apart. You look up. Crows on the exposed roof beams. The birds silent save their feathers' thick ruffle.

"I have to go to work."

The room's dark washes away. The movie spins back into your head. Morning sun in the curtains. You're humbled by the room's lit reality, its modest dimensions and tight corners. Last night you swore this bed was a raft upon a wild sea, swore you'd drown if you tried to escape. Helen sets a plate on the nightstand. A peanut-butter-and-jelly sandwich. "You need to eat," Helen says.

You clear your throat. "I will."

"The chicken's in the fridge. And there's more bread for sandwiches." She strokes Chestnut's side. "He and I already went to the backyard. He's a good boy, isn't he?"

"Yes."

"Maybe I'll get a dog. He's got me thinking that." Her phone rings. She checks the number. "Your uncle again. He's been calling all night."

"I'm sorry."

"He won't know where we are. At least I don't think he can find out." She presses a button and the screen goes blank. She stands. "We can call him tonight if you want. Or later." She gestures to the nightstand. "I picked up some magazines from the break room. Can't say there's anything a young girl would like, but you never know."

A goodbye. A final scratch behind Chestnut's ear. Two

110

windows in the room. The one by the bed faces the alley. You rise and stand at the edge of the other window. The curtain pulled back, a sliver of street. An elementary-school boy on the sidewalk. Flannel sleeves and jeans, a backpack that reminds you of a turtle's shell. He whips the air with a stick. Your cheek against the cool plaster until the boy disappears.

The day passes. You dream—a wooden balcony outside your bedroom window, a structure unnoticed before. Below, your field hockey team scrimmages in your father's garden. Their cleats tear up plants, his pots smashed by balls and sticks. Above you, balanced on skeletal beams, your father and uncles. You call them, but your voice fades beneath their hammer blows. Looking down, you realize your foot is broken and set not in a cast but in a small tree trunk. Snow falls. The hockey game and hammering continue. On the bare wood, eddies of white join the sawdust, the rhythm of waves.

You pick up the sandwich then return it to the plate. You stay awake until dawn then sleep through the day—you don't eat—the rhythms of your life turned inside out. You have stopped being yourself and become your shadow. You switch on the radio to hear a voice beyond the one in your head, dispatches from a world that's continued to turn without you. The weather and traffic. An increase in heating oil supplies, good news for the coming winter. The manhunt for dissident leaders. Campus libraries burned. A turn of a knob and the voice falls silent. Let the world spin without you. You pick up the magazines, drawn by their publication dates, the months before the Shut-In. You flip the pages, scents of stale perfume, then read first paragraphs—dorm-room fashions and exercises for slimmer waists. Lie down and shut your eyes and allow the weight to drag you back into the dark.

Evening and Helen warms leftovers on the stove and takes Chestnut for a walk, a leash fashioned from a length of clothesline. In their absence, you feel small, consumed by the house and its emptiness, and when they return, you rush to greet them but then freeze halfway down the stairs. The angling perspective, the waiting living room. The nightmare you woke into the other night. You are a high diver upon the board, and below, a pool drained of water. "I can't."

Helen dims the lights and draws the curtains. She approaches you, her hand out. She gives a light tug, but you're frozen, and she comes to stand beside you. "I'm right here." Together, you navigate shuffling steps to the table. Helen guiding, her hand on yours. "You're safe here, darling. You're OK."

Silence as Helen finishes in the kitchen and brings your plates. She sits and bows her head, a silent grace, and you follow her lead, wondering if you, too, should pray. Helen talks —the troubles in the capital. The checkpoints and fires and roving gangs. The stadium's new perimeter of fencing and concrete barriers. The dog packs, abandoned animals, their owners missing or dead. A child mauled on her way to school.

Her tone sharper as she describes her job. A windowless cubicle, but a view unlike any other. Her access to the emails of the police, the mayor and his staff. The secrets she knows, the hypocrites and petty crooks. Men and women she could expose with a few clicks. She rails against Slater. "We've had our runins. He's a nobody. He knows it, and he knows I know it, and it galls him." Chestnut in her lap, a strip of chicken held for him to eat. "It's a crime what happened to your family. He's the one who should be locked up. Tomorrow I'll start looking into the stadium files. We'll find out where your uncle is."

Your first and only bite of meat like putty on your tongue. You brace yourself and swallow. A hand on your throat and the fear of choking. You sip your water. "And my mother."

"And your mother." Helen finishes her last forkful. "You're not hungry?"

"No."

She stands, the dog in her arms. "Come with me."

The basement door just off the kitchen. Helen in front. The steps creak, the shine of naked bulbs. A concrete floor and a silent furnace. Cobwebs and thin, black pipes tucked between the rafters. Along the walls, shelves of metal and plastic, stacked boxes, their sides labeled with magic marker. Tools hung from a pegboard, and in the corner, a bike on flat tires. Helen sets Chestnut down, and he sniffs the floor's rusted drain. She leads you to the room's far corner. Here, another set of shelves. Helen moves a stack of boxes, a wooden chair missing an arm. Her feet planted wide, she grabs the shelving unit's side. "Step back."

The shelves swing out. The groan of hinges, the exposure of a hidden room, and you're taken back by the intersection of reality and your dreams' warped architectures. Chestnut steps forward then halts, front paw raised, snout twitching. The scent strikes you as well, damp and stale. Helen crosses the threshold and dissolves into the dark. A cord pulled, a harsh light, a framing in a room barely large enough for her to turn around. You step forward. Shelves on one wall. Canned food. A lantern. Unmarked boxes. Against the other wall, a folded cot. You slide one of the door's heavy locking bars.

"The kids think I'm crazy, don't they?"

"No."

"You're lying." She tiptoes, a quick peak onto the highest shelf. "They think it because their parents tell them. Only a crazy woman would have a secret room like this."

"My parents never said anything like that."

Helen nods. "No, I'd bet they didn't." She swipes a cobweb from the light. "Truth is this room was here when I bought the house. I bolted the shelves to the door, but that's it. Can't say I mind having it. Even if someone knew you were in here, they wouldn't be able to get you out. Not without a blowtorch." She pulls the bulb's dangling cord, and you step back into the light. She swings the door and shelving unit back into place. "If something happened while I was gone, you could hide in here. No one would find you."

Another night. The digits on the nightstand clock. A march forward, and your past crumbling. Tonight you are not smoke. Tonight you are pure weight. The weight pins you, your heart smothered. The weight not of stone but of memories and fear. Your brain alight with haywire images. The projector's bony clatter. A thousand moments, beautiful and mundane. Then your father's broken glasses on the floor. Your mother lifted in another man's arms. The movies have a hundred thousand beginnings but only one end. You close your eyes and rock. You struggle to bury your thoughts, to overflow them with distractions, the reciting of theorems and formulas and statistics. A thicket of graphs. Trajectories beautiful and elegant. All of it true. All of it undeniable. Sleep coming only when the chickadees wake and greet the sun.

* * *

A note waits on the nightstand.

I already let the dog out. There's some food here—and more downstairs. Please eat something if you're ready. There's a towel and cloth on the sink if you want to shower. Don't answer the door. I will be home as soon as I can.

A water bottle beside the note, a plate with a fresh sandwich. The dog's snout nudges your hand. You lie still, listening. A truck in the alley. The roll of wheels. A squawk of breaks and a tumbling din. Trash day, you think. Wednesday.

Your hair matted. The sheets sour with your smell. You cry as you step into the shower. Your first cry. The vulnerability of nakedness, the shower's masking drum. You leave the bathroom door open, the curtain pulled back, a view into the empty hallway. *Let them come*, you think, the men with their ropes and guns. *Let them come.* You lower yourself, and your hip strikes the tub's side. Suds circle the drain. Let them come. You're so tired. Tired in body, in mind. Tired of being adrift. Tired of the horror movies that have taken the place of dreams. You lift your chin. The water stings your face. Your vision blurs. Water mixes with your tears, all of it running down the drain. You say your mother's name, your father's. They're just sounds, syllables uttered to feel them upon your tongue, to hear them spoken in a world that shouldn't be allowed to forget them.

You turn off the water. The shower curtain drawn, the

space dim. A lingering of warmth. You pull the towel over your shoulders and curl up. Echoes in the porcelain. Your breath. The drain's gurgle. You close your eyes and fade into the white noise.

* * *

The call of sirens rises from the pipes. You sit, kinks and pain. Your neck stiff. Pull aside the shower curtain. A spray of drops and the clank of metal rings. Chestnut waits on the mat. Your first steps awkward. You latch onto the sink, the door. Your legs dead. An ungainly navigation back to the guest room and a flop onto the bed.

You bring Chestnut to your side. The sirens swell, overlap, fade, swell again. You turn on the radio. The heralding of arrests in the capital and beyond. The infiltration of terrorist cells, conspiracies squashed. Repeated urgings to tune in to the Civil Defense Network's twenty-four-hour loop of wanted radicals. Right-thinking citizens called upon to band together and police their neighborhoods. With a click, you snuff the voice.

You tear the crust off the nightstand's sandwich and feed it to Chestnut. Your lack of hunger surprises you, and nestled in the shadows of your belly, a tiny, scintillating ember. Your body operating on a kind of internal starshine. The consumption of reserves, a private and pure cannibalism. You alone in control.

You drift. Dreams, consciousness, and their gray borders. The movement of sunlit patches across the bed and floor. You hold the dog to your chest and try to visualize your existence in component pieces but you're vexed by the blank spaces. You try to think ahead, but the world beyond this house seems impossible. Dusk comes, and you wait for the click of the lock's key. An hour passes beyond Helen's usual return. Then another hour. A quiet radiates through the rooms, and you imagine the stillness rising from the basement's rusted drain. The hush of broken watches and seized motors and gaping, breathless mouths. A poke from Chestnut's wet snout, a whimper, and you wish the dog would just go. You can live with the scent of urine, but not his pleas. When you can take no more, you pick him up and tiptoe down the stairs.

"Helen?"

The dog frantic, whines of thanks and urgency. A glance out the front window. The driveway empty and no one on the street. All the porch lights out. More sirens. Chestnut yelps. You hurry through the unlit rooms, apologies, calm whispers. "You're OK. You're OK."

You kneel on the back porch and let the dog go. Chestnut fades into the dark. The night pulses with sirens and crickets. You wait then grow worried. You call the dog, a harsh whisper as you creep down the porch stairs, the concrete cool on your bare feet. "Chestnut?" Your oak tree across the alley, a rising as tall as a ship's mast, and its leaves sway beneath the hazy moon. "Chestnut?" Panic now. The fear the dog has wormed beneath the gate, the instinct of return. The fear of losing the last thing you love. Then the jangle of his tags, his jerky stride. A reappearance from the night.

You pick him up and hold him close. "Don't scare me. Please don't scare me again."

* * *

The small hours beyond midnight. Helen no doubt caught at work, stranded by the nightly curfew and the capital's checkpoints. She'll return by morning. You repeat this. At first to yourself, then out loud. "Helen will be back soon." You throw back the covers and pace. Upstairs and down and up again. Your eyes adjust to the dark, and you're cast into a diorama, a mistake amid the scenes of stillness. Helen will come back with supplies and a gruff story that will make you smile, her adventures, your relief. You repeat the words, you voice a lonely wave in the quiet. "Helen will be back soon."

You return to the guest room. Your body's rhythms twisted. Day for night. Your empty stomach and loss of hunger. Your fear of loneliness and your fear of the mob. Your fear of the life you can no longer imagine waiting beyond Helen's front door. The feeling of home in a stranger's house. On the radio, an interview. A local patriot leader, talk of the freedom of submission that awaits a Godly nation.

You open the window beside your bed. A sliver, and you bring your nose close. Fresh air. The world's greens and your father's garden. The crickets' thrum. The radio announcer lost in ecstasy, a tirade your mother would have chided. A playing to fear and hatred of the other. The mistaking of volume for truth. "This is a rebirth! A new beginning for us all and a glorious—" Frayed wires circle your gut, a thorny current. A current you surrender to, and you rock in time. Tremors in the box spring. The clock's digits the bright red of your father's riverside bloom, his hands cupped beneath the plant, tender, careful. "Victory is ours. The shining city on the hill awaits—"

You yank the plug. Silence. A black display. You lie down

120

and hug your knees, a child's pose, your fist at your mouth, your knuckles bitten. Close your eyes, and in the dark, images as clear as photographs. The projector hums. The pictures cup your heart. The pictures rip your spine.

* * *

Morning. A vigil by the bedroom window. This narrow view. Minutes of nothing but sidewalk and street. Then a passing car. A boy on a bike, a lazy pace, his backpack sagging from his shoulders. You think of school—bells and the cafeteria's din. You imagine your empty seat in a half dozen classes and wonder if your teachers still call your name. You imagine voices and drama and the cold morning you punched Missy Blough in the mouth. All of it slipping away, notes in a larger fading. What is and what was and what's lost forever.

Downstairs and you open the backdoor, checking for neighbors before letting Chestnut out. "Don't be long," you whisper, a kiss between his ears, his favorite spot. Chestnut sniffs his way around the rabbit fence and shed. His funny stride, a mystery of his stray's life, a secret you'll never know. The air cooler, autumn's chilled dew. The next-door neighbor backs his car from the garage. Chestnut bolts to the back gate, barking, hackles raised. You crouch, your voice hoarse and low. "Chestnut! Come!" The car hesitates then rolls off. Chestnut returns, tail wagging, a meandering route. A gimpy ascension of the porch stairs.

A turned knob and the bolt slides into its sleeve. The note a period, an ending. Helen's not coming back. The notion sudden. Obvious. She isn't coming back—at best, not soon. Perhaps never. The things she knows, the people she could expose. Then another understanding—you have to leave. Mail will pile in the box. The man next door will wonder about Helen's new dog. A boy will tiptoe through the gate to retrieve his football. Neighbors will notice the empty driveway and uncut grass. A knock will come. A good Samaritan. A busybody. Slater. The door will push open, and the

122

world will flood in, and you'll be powerless to halt the tide. *Have a plan.*

You take inventory—the offerings of the refrigerator and pantry, the understanding that even if you're not hungry, your journey will require fuel. Chestnut on your heels. Eyes of watery black, patient, intent. Your search extends to other rooms, and you sift through drawers and cabinets. A new vision, one keen to appreciate the overlooked and forgotten. Calculations of a hundred different futures. You fill your pockets—a Swiss Army knife, matches, a pen flashlight, a compass. Bookending this, another perspective, and you pause before framed pictures and run a hand over upholstery, pick up the shelves' knickknacks and puff away the dust. You think of a life interrupted. *We are all energy*—your father's words. All sunlight. All stardust. All conjured from a single handful of elements. You wonder what happens to a candle snuffed so quickly. Wonder if its energy simply leaves or if it lingers, making its peace with this world before moving on. You know which answer you think is true and speak out loud, "Thank you, Helen."

You climb the stairs. The weight in you. You'll eat later. You'll push aside your throat's gag and refuel. You enter Helen's room and set the dog on the unmade bed. Chestnut sniffs, a tightening circle until he burrows beneath the blankets. A dresser, a drawer open, a tangle of bras. Socks on the floor, a pair of jeans. Atop the bureau, hand cream and moisturizer. A crumpled receipt. A shopping list. Two more framed pictures. Helen and another woman sitting in a sidewalk café. An older photo, its color faded, two children in white gloves and Easter bonnets. The window's shade drawn, and from its side, a sunlit sliver stretches across the rumpled bed.

You lie next to Chestnut. The sunlight cuts across your belly, and you surrender to the drift. Numbness claims your toes, your legs. Vines of sleep climb from your pelvis and into your chest. Your fingers on Chestnut's side, and the rise and fall of his breath meets yours. You think again of Helen, her disappearance and the stillness left in her wake. You think of your mother and how all that matters now is to find her. Your hand slips from Chestnut's side and reaches out, a slow glide over the covers. You'll rest now, and when you wake, there'll be work to do.

***

The pool frozen, and you're skating, the slash of metal beneath you, but it feels like flying. Or perhaps you're flying, just a bit. You're chasing a man, his back to you, a winter coat and old-fashioned hat, but as you near, your right arm grows so long it drags beside you, and the ice beneath begins to fissure and the groans fill your ears. You skate harder, escaping the cracks that threaten to swallow you. You skate and skate and skate yourself right out of your dream to discover Chestnut licking your hand. The sun gone from the window. You consider the bedside clock and wonder if your team has a game today. The tap of the ball on your stick, the sun lower and your shadow stretching, the grass crisper as the season goes on—you yearn for these yet no longer feel their claim. Your playing, one of the cornerstones of your days, just another element of your abandoned life. And around you, Helen's abandoned life, a shell you inhabit, and you think of your father's stories of interloper species. The hermit crab. The cuckoo. The poor magpie.

Downstairs, and you make peanut butter on crackers. Mouthfuls forced down, a gagging you temper with sips of milk. The food a betrayal, an acceptance of all that's happened. Yet you need fuel. You need to get to work. The basement next. Chestnut sniffs the silent furnace. You open boxes, scour shelves. Your take gathered in a canvas shopping bag. A length of clothesline. A box cutter. A long screwdriver.

You latch onto the safe room's shelving unit, and with feet planted wide, pull. The door heavier than you imagined, a strain in your shoulders. The shelves inch back and with it, a breath of must. You cross the threshold. An inside handle makes the door easier to close. Chestnut's nails scrape as he tries to stay ahead of the door's swing. His eyes on you until the eclipsing slam of metal and wood.

Darkness. Not even a doorjamb sliver. Your feet and hands lost. You picture the room, a locked box within a locked box. You picture the twists of the hermit crab's shell. You listen to your breath, and in this blackness, who's to say the space before you isn't a thousand-mile vista or a rooftop's ledge.

Chestnut's barks muffled, his frightened call. "It's OK, it's OK," you say. You open the door, and Chestnut squeezes through. A welcoming rub against your shins. You pull the light cord and scan the shelves. A set of keys, a fire extinguisher coated with dust and cobwebs. You tiptoe to reach a rusted tin can on the top shelf, and inside, an envelope stuffed with cash, bills limp and faded. Behind the can, a plastic shopping bag. The bag weighty, and you realize it isn't a single bag but many. You peel away layer after layer. The plastic flutters down, and Chestnut sniffs the soft pile at your feet. A flutter in your chest. The object's buried weight growing more certain until the final bag drops.

* * *

You'll leave at midnight. This is your plan, but the in-between hours twist in your brain. You pace, visualizing your excursion's stages yet the details fade in uncertainty. Connection proves elusive, and you veer between the things on which you need to focus and the nightmares you're desperate to forget. You talk to yourself, mutterings like the mad woman you thought Helen to be. You punch your sternum, a hard smack. *Focus*, you scold. Focus on the horizon's distant light. A light of control. Of having a say in this madness. You check the clock again. You'd scream if you weren't afraid of waking the neighbors. Your fists clench and release. The checking and rechecking of your provisions. 11:25, and another moment inside will tear you in half. You prop open the basement door with an old paint can and step outside.

Three times Chestnut follows you up the well's steps. Three times you pick him up and bring him back. Three times you fight the desire to nuzzle him, to whisper assurances. If something happens to you, you don't want him trapped, starvation, abandonment's slow death. You put him down and speak sternly. "Stay." Your finger held up until he sits and you back away. "Stay."

Pause at the yard's edge. Shadows all around, and you remember what it was like to step out after the Shut-In, the sensation of losing yourself beneath a suddenly open sky. You make a final check for Chestnut, his whimper tempered by the crickets. With your first step onto the alley's macadam, you become a diver knifing into deep water. A plunge. A new reality. A new identity. You carry a black trash bag, your steps hurried, a cool breeze. You strain to picture the moment beyond the moment and the moment beyond that. The jeans Helen bought for you a size too small, and with each stride comes the nudge of the pistol tucked into your waistband.

The earth soft beneath your old oak. The years of shade and dropped leaves. Your grill missing, its cover a formless pile. The shed doors flung open, and on the lawn, a broken rake, your first two-wheeler. A rabbit picks amid the garden's toppled pots. The half-moon shines on the house's unbroken windows. The picnic bench strewn with a trowel, gloves, and bag of soil, and in a pot, the riverside's closed red bloom. Your flip-flops slap, the flagstone path you could walk blindfolded.

Dogs bark, and you think of Helen's stories, the city's roaming packs. For you, in this one and only moment of quantum possibilities, reunion and the paralyzing confluence of memory. The baking weeks you watched this house rise. Your scrambles down these back steps and the door's thoughtless slam. A thousand moments as preserved as the bio department's riverside diorama, scenes ready to step into and reinhabit. But the girl from those memories doesn't feel real tonight, and in you, the discomfort of being lost in the place you know best.

Four concrete stairs. The porch's elevation allows a glance over Slater's fence. His house quiet. The haze of return fades, and you slip into a moment vivid and real. His brow's sweaty sheen. His booming commands in a living room where voices were seldom raised. The drum's beat fueled your grip, and you rub your forearm, the place where your pulses met, and if only you'd held on, been stronger. A trading of your father's pained face for Slater's. A trading of fates and the wish you would have choked the life out of his dark, greasy heart.

Your father's voice next and the image fades. *Have a plan—* and you recount the list of what you've come to claim. Clothes, boots, food. A set of car keys. In ten minutes you'll be on the road. Moonlight on the trees. Chestnut by your side, the passenger window lowered, his snout testing the country air. You'll find your way to your grandmother's house in the country, the route pieced together from years of backseat memories. You'll fall asleep at dawn and wake to the call of woodland birds. You'll help your grandmother can her garden harvest. You'll catch fish in the stream, thankful for the squeamish memories of your uncles and their gutting knives. You'll cry as you tell her about the mob. And at the end of every thought, your mother. A waiting reunion, each of you poised to save the other.

The door swings back, the mudroom, then the kitchen. The penlight's thin halo ripples over the floor's broken dishes. Chestnut's bowls overturned. Scattered silverware. The air still and hot. Flies, the buzzing near then far then near. You cover your mouth, the garbage, the windowsill's rotting tomatoes. The refrigerator and stove gone, gap-toothed spaces your mind keeps filling, hallucinations of reflex and memory. The family room next. The TV ripped from the wall. The stereo gone. The bookshelves toppled, their falls arrested by the mounds of spilled books that didn't interest the looters. Volumes on flora and fauna, some books kicked into far corners, others splayed open and trampled and creased, the intricate drawings that had once fascinated you. You lift the penlight's tip. Red spray paint on the wall, a cross within a circle.

The dining room next then the foyer. Uneven footsteps. The path cluttered, papers, books, chairs. The front door askew, its top hinge yanked from its mooring. Glass fragments capture the penlight's shine. The car and truck keys gone from their hooks. A peek out the door's crooked window. The curbside and driveway empty. Just the streetlight and its cone of white. Your pulse spikes. *Have a plan.*

A steadying grip on the stairwell handrail. The past a mist that breaks over you with every step. Voices so clear it seems impossible you're alone. You reach your room, the window allowing its angle of streetlight. The looters here too, and you pick through the mess. The plastic bag whispers as you gather your wardrobe's remains. Your laptop and phone and jewelry box gone, your dream journal left behind. You kick off your flip-flops and slide into socks and sneakers. Your parents fading and now strangers all around, and you shudder in their presence. You change into jeans and a black, long sleeved T-shirt. Your hair tied back. The gun tucked back in your waistband.

The doorway of your parents' room, and you think of Lot's poor wife and the price of looking back. The penlight's shaft sweeps across the clothes and upturned drawers. The bedframe smashed, the mattress tossed aside. A glimmer by your feet, and you stoop and pick up the necklace your mother sometimes wore. A silver cross barely an inch long. A piece of jewelry she received on her confirmation, a delicate chain with hints of tarnish. You slide your hands beneath your hair, secure the clasp, and as you do, you feel the touch of her hands, the braids she wove, the intimate talks where your eyes never met. You lift the cross. The metal a breath against your fingers.

The stairs, and the cross taps the base of your neck. A pause at the steps' bottom. From outside, a dog's deep bark. You don't belong here, not anymore, and in you, a reversing of poles, the pull of home now a revulsion. You fall in your scramble to leave, the floor's littered mess and a hard strike to the knee. Your hand finds a broken vase. Dirt on your palm, a fern your father wanted to transplant before the first frost. You right yourself and kick through the debris. You picture the room's shards and flotsam swelling in your wake, the shattered mess rising. A tide destined to swallow you if you stay.

Catch your breath at the picnic table. The house's unbroken windows dull eyes upon you. You walked those floors when the sky stretched blue and wide between the roof's first beams. You helped your uncles mix mortar. You woke in the comfort of your room, your parents' voices nearby. Miracles you didn't appreciate. All of it gone. You pause at the alley trashcan and open your bag. Your dream journal held for a moment, a palm gliding over its cover, before you let it drop.

Then the drums. A sudden springing to life, one, then another. Voices from the street. Sirens. You hide your bag beneath the picnic table and crouch behind the azaleas. A fire engine passes, a sluggish turn of wheels. Red lights, bloody swaths across the faces of men and boys hurrying in the same direction.

You wait until the street empties. Then a dash between houses. A backyard path. A ducking of clotheslines and low branches. A landscape of shadows. Sidesteps around a sandbox, a forgotten wheelbarrow. Gather yourself beside a paint-peeling garage. The drums louder. The earthy scent of September gardens. The sting of smoke.

The alley meets the road, and the flow masses at the next intersection. You press yourself to the garage's side. In the street, boys you recognize from church and school. Todd Abbot and Billy Stafford with their lingering pool tans. The boys joined by men, everyone charging forward. The drumbeat in the garage's wood, and the throb calls you to witness. Beside you, a tall trashcan. You sit upon the can's lid and pull your feet beneath you. A steadying breath and a straightening of legs, a measured extension until you stand upright. A reach, a grasp of the roof's ledge. With a scape and a grunt, you lift your leg. Your heel finds purchase, and you pull yourself onto the roof.

My little monkey.

I don't think I want to be called monkey anymore.

A twelve-by-twenty tarpaper patch. You move on hands and knees, and beneath you, the crunch of leaves and cicada shells. You squat behind the front's small peak. The tarpaper against your palms gritty and warm. From here, a clear view of the intersection and the mob's circling of the opposite corner. A house with its second floor ablaze, and how many times have you passed, never noticing the porch's loveseat swing, the silver wind chimes? The first flames poke through the roof's shingles. The crowd roars.

The drumbeat faster. You hunker down, your eyes just above the peak. A brick flies. Gunshots and the shatter of glass. A fire engine eases forward. The engine's horn bleats, and the mob shuffles back. Knotted flames from the upstairs windows, more holes through the roof. Gutters warp and sink in long frowns. Smoky torrents darker than the night. Showers of sparks. The firemen turn their hoses on a neighboring roof. Flags wave, the circle and cross. Strobes and firelight flicker over the mob. Most with their backs to you, others with faces that balance shadow and light. Their cries build with the drums' beat. "Come out or burn! Come out or burn!"

A new commotion in the yard beside the garage. A girl screams. You shift, belly pressed against the tarpaper. The yard dark, a border of shrubs. Two men, bald and muscular, their hands on a writhing girl, pulling, wrestling. The girl jerks free, a kick to one man's shin, a scrambling escape. The chains of a child's swing set rattle, and the three of them stumble and grope until they collapse in a heap. Tangled limbs and curses. Her top rips, their hands on her breasts, her short skirt pulled to her knees. You gasp, and one of the men turns. You draw away and roll onto your back. A hand over your mouth. The gouge in your spine. You arch onto your shoulders and slide out the gun. Your insides a wasteland wider than the stars' reach. A two-handed grip on the gun. The butt hard against your chest. Firelight on the chrome, the trembling barrel aimed at a sky of coiled smoke. You lie still, the occupier of a plane parallel to the girl in the yard. You strain to hear but can't above the voices and sirens. You're fearful you'll be betrayed by the mechanics of lungs and pulse, by a cough, the smoke fouled with burnt plastic and foam. The fire cut from view but not its sparks. Orange flecks, orphans on a current that rises then fades. Cinders fall, ashed flurries still warm to the touch. You aim the gun toward the roof's edge, waiting for a face, a horizon's horrible moon. Everything louder, the mob's screams and chants, the drums. You rest a finger on the trigger, and you wonder if firing it is as simple as it looks in the movies. You want to help the girl but you're afraid, not just of the men but of the violent tide that's claimed so much of your life and spit you into this nightmare.

A new cry from the yard. Barking dogs, the men shouting. You roll onto your side. The girl still and naked in the grass. Legs spread, arms outstretched, the pose of a fallen star. Her face turned and hidden by a mask of hair. A dark strip of cloth around her neck. The girl's body a border—the men on her left, one fumbling into his shorts—and to her right, a Rottweiler and a mutt no larger than Chestnut. The small dog yips, charges forward and back, nimble leaps over the girl's legs. The Rottweiler's throat curdles, guttural threats before it charges with a jangle of tags. The men's half-stumbling escape around the house's side and then the dog's silent return, its snout prodding the girl's shoulder and hair. The Rottweiler licks her arm then makes his way to the alley. The mutt on its heels then scuttling ahead. You're transfixed by the girl's tranquility. By the moonlight shine of her breasts and pelvis. By the sober understanding that here is a new reel for your horror film.

You crawl back and crouch behind the roof's peak. The flames have spread, the porch roof, the downstairs windows. The fire a living thing. Its draw of oxygen. Its consumption of wood and wire and plaster. Its groan of split beams and shattered glass. The crowd steps back, the closest shielding their faces. You're distant, yet the heat reaches you, and you pull its warmth into your lungs.

The front door flings open. A stillness in the mob. The drums slow. The fire rumbles and moans. A man and a woman stagger onto the porch. Towels over their mouths. Their eyes blinking away the soot. The man the first to descend the stairs, the woman's hand in his. She swoons and he catches her, and her weight brings him to his knees. An embrace, silhouettes before the flames. A reprieve before the crowd remembers itself and rushes forward. Makeshift weapons raised—bats and rakes and shovels. The couple consumed.

You turn, your back resting against the roof's peak. *Go!* You have no other plan. *Go*—back to Helen's, to Chestnut, an extraction from this horror. You slide the gun back into your waistband and lower yourself from the roof. A trembling perch atop the trashcan then an easing onto solid ground. You move through the yard's dim rhythms, the greater currents of smoke and clamor flowing above. *Go* but a deeper tide draws you to the body. You circle the girl, the path of a curious dog, observant yet distant. Your father taught you about dogs, their markings and sniffs divining the past's ghosts, a hidden dimension you now understand for the act's violence and terror lingers. You crouch, the grass cool. With a delicate touch, you brush the hair from the girl's face.

Missy Blough's eyes, watery and blank, consider you. A gaze from the bridge between worlds. The skin around her red bandanna pinched and blue. Her open mouth stuffed with white panties. With a delicate pinch, you pull the panties. The elastic catches a tooth. A snag, and with it, a lift of her jaw, a sigh as if she were struggling to utter a last word.

You back away. The panties fall to the grass. Your feet tangle with a soccer ball. The alley and you try to run, but your knees betray you, each step a spastic lurch. The macadam lists, left to right and back again. You place your hands against a garage, seeking balance as flecks of paint rub against your palm. Your head hung and the calliope of images spins behind your shut eyes. The vomit a surprise, warm, gagging. The bile of an empty stomach. You wipe your mouth and stagger forward. The waiting cross street recedes, an illogical geometry, and you think of the monkey you once saw in a dream. A beast with backward feet. Coming and going, going and coming.

A growl, close and low and deep. *Go!* but you can't move. The desert inside you. The Rottweiler at the alley's edge. The dog waist-tall and thick with muscle. A silky step from a car's shadow. The faintest shimmer in its coal eyes, and the fear and unsteadiness drain from your body. This dog and you linked. Both of you castaways. Both of you silent by the side of a dead girl. You reach out, your hand steady, and the dog's growl calms. Tail down, the Rottweiler steps forward. Its black snout twitches, its wetness on your fingers.

A shotgun blast echoes along the alley's cars and garages. You cower then find your legs, and you and the dog scramble in opposite directions. Another gun, two quick shots. Your frantic backyard path, the obstacles rising from the dark, a trip over a hose. More gunfire, and you crouch under a tree, the smoke thick beneath the leaves. You retrieve the gun and lay the barrel against your cheek. They've lost their minds. All of them. The mob. The world. You.

You run. Your block, and you skirt the shine beneath the pole that held the rope. Your father lifted. The mouth that had only offered kindnesses reduced to gasps. His face pale then blue. His spastic feet. You slow and consider the light's circling of moths. The moment's peace and the violence of memory. His shadow passes over you.

You sit at the backyard picnic table. Your heart jagged but settling. The garbage bag retrieved. You pause and delicately lift the closed, riverside bloom. You consider the house, and in you, the sting of exile. A severing that's left you invisible.

Invisible, and you rise above your body's meat, above this yard and the night's terror, and your machine—for you're now a machine, have to be a machine to survive—moves with efficiency, its tremors shed. You cross the alley, upright, almost unafraid. The bag pulls at your hand, plastic whispers against your thigh. Helen's yard, the sticker-bush hedge, and a whiff of smoke as you descend the basement stairwell. Chestnut barks, a warning then his welcome. You set aside the paint can propping the door. Chestnut waits, but when you kneel, he pauses before accepting your embrace. He circles you, his snout poking your jeans and shirt. Your scent carrying your story.

* * *

Y ou wake with a gasp and your hand on your throat. A dream of the scarf you and your mother knitted. The blurred margin of real and not. Your heart thudding as you clench the cross of your mother's necklace.

Swing your feet to the floor. The fire's stink on your clothes, your hair and skin. You lean against the wall and peer out the side window. A passing van. An empty patch of sidewalk, and in the yard, the sycamore's first dropped leaves. A woman jogs by, her dog on a long leash. You can imagine school and practice but not your place in them. You think of your house. Your parents. Of a branch you tossed into the swollen river, the stick visible then not. Gone.

The garbage bag beside the bed, its top weighted with Helen's gun. You go downstairs. Chestnut on your heels. You rub your temples. The past has expelled you, and you need to envision a new future in order to make it real. You need to shut down your skull's sputtering movies. Your mother and father. Missy. Your mother taught you about Occam's razor, but all the easy solutions have been stolen. Staying here. Going home. A car to steal. Refuge in an upstate cabin. The film hiccups, and you flinch at the sight of your mother's blackened soles, at the strips of Missy's milk-white skin. Your hand returns to your throat. Your pulse quickens. A phantom burn and the squeezing of your lungs. A riot in your heart but all else paralyzed. *Breathe,* a long inhale, a longer exhale, but the rhythm escapes you. The cross grasped tight. Silver sparks across your eyes. Flashes as bright as the magnesium strips you watched your father burn in a darkened lecture hall.

In the bathroom, you cup your hands beneath the spigot's flow, but your focus unravels in the water's tumble. You see the

137

river, and if only you could fold yourself into the current and escape the body that's become your prison and curse. You splash water over your face, calmly at first, then faster. Your shirt wet, drops on the floor, but you can't wash away the smoke or the images that play behind your shut eyes. Dry your face then kneel on the linoleum and stroke Chestnut's back. You'll leave. Tonight. Possibilities are a luxury of the quantum plane, and all you're left with is a dim, singular hope. One way or another, dawn will find you far away.

A knock at the front door, and you freeze. Another knock. A polite tone, one without venom but with the same promise to bring the outside crashing in. Chestnut in a frenzy, and each bark a betrayal. The dog scampers down the steps, you close behind, whispering, "It's OK, boy. Come here. Come here."

You move through the downstairs, bent double, aware of windows and spying eyes. You sit on the dining room floor with your back against the wall. Whispers. "Please, Chestnut. Please." The knocking stops, and after a final, preening bark, the dog returns. You scoop him up and whisper soft assurances. Then the back door. The knocking louder this time, and in each successive rattle, you think of murder—fire—a used girl left beneath the smoke. Your grasp on Chestnut so sure you fear you'll hurt him. Your words a mantra of all the jittery calm you can muster. "It's OK. It's OK."

The knocking ceases, and with the dog in your arms, you retreat to the basement. You'll barricade yourself in Helen's safe room. The tremor of the sliding metal bar. A shut door, a starless dark. You'll stave off the world until the threat passes then you'll leave and never return. This house. This town. You're halfway down the steps when a man's voice joins you in the basement. "Hello?"

You slump onto the stairs. The basement door left unlocked —last night's frightened return, your right-thinking undone by nerves, by Missy Blough's unblinking eyes. The man's voice again: "Hello?" A voice that belongs to the knock. Apologetic, wanting to help, a voice that fades amid the basement clutter, and for you, a hesitation. The weighing of whether to speak, to step forward and throw yourself up to the merciful world in which your father believed. You remain silent.

Chestnut twists, a yipping escape. A flop onto the stair and you succeed in righting but not catching him. The dog's labored descent, a stair and a bark at a time. He reaches the bottom and charges. You clamp a hand over your mouth. Captured breath, the taste of your Shut-In mask, and beneath your ribs, a keening pressure. The wind-sprint heave of your lungs. Your cartwheeling heart.

No line of vision connects the door to the steps. The man's voice gentle, inviting: "Hey, boy. Hey there, boy. I was wondering about you." The dog's nails scratch over concrete. The basements smells of must and mildew. Chestnut's yipping bark. You bite your knuckle, fighting off the spasms and the tears. You picture the neighbor you've seen talking to Helen and wonder if he belonged to the mob. Chestnut's frenzy eases. The man's voice softer: "Come here. Come on now."

The barks stop. "You're a good boy, aren't you?" the man coos. The screen door shuts. Remove your fist from your mouth. A gasp, a greedy breath and an understanding of drowning. Tears on your cheeks. Tears for your dog and for the silence that muffles your heart. Tears for the all of it and for the nothing you have left.

You rock, movements rooted in brainstem, as automatic as breathing. Fold your arms across your belly, your fingers digging into your sides. You rock to stay atop the current. You rock to push aside your gut's hollow rot. You rock to prove you're more than dust. A flowerpot shakes on the step below your feet. The clank of terracotta, and the note rises from the pot's open mouth, a tone that lifts and warbles until the pot falls, an end-over-end tumble, and shatters on the concrete.

You need to go. Before the vandals come to ransack the house. Before the police. You stand, but your knees buckle. The dust swirls inside you, the hiss and static of your broken machine. A grip on the handrail, a step-at-a-time climb. The first floor—kitchen, dining room. This shell, its human parts flowing out as surely as blood. The next flight of steps harder. Your perception melts, the house's plumb lines warped. You're alone. You own nothing beyond the items you can carry. You lie down and think of the heartbeat that separates the living and the dead, the cusp of knowledge and the abandonment of the body. You close your eyes and drift. Then, in your emptiness, a filament. Dull at first then waxing brighter. You'll find her. You will.

* * *

Your packing like a geometry problem, questions of volume and space. The room illuminated by disparate sources. The streetlamp. The moon and stars. When necessity dictates, you flick on the pen flashlight. The beam pans across your problem's variables. What you'll wear—jeans, a black long-sleeved top, hiking boots. What you'll pack—a poncho, a sweatshirt, black thermals, sneakers, a hat and gloves. What you'll eat—a bag of peanut butter sandwiches, some crackers and pretzels. Then the rest—Helen's money, a knife, twine, tampons. The gun. You fill and empty the backpack, your equation without balance until you begin to subtract. You stuff your pockets—the money and knife. The laces of your sneakers tied to the pack's bottom. You put on the sweatshirt and slide the gun into the front pocket. The bag's remaining contents pushed and stuffed, a fight with the zipper.

Lie on the downstairs couch, the pack hugged against your chest. The pack's weight your anchor, the tide all around. *Have a plan.* You could steal a car, but beyond finding a set of keys, you have no idea how to go about that. You could steal a bike, navigate the alleys across town to your uncle's house, but you fear the sharing of your own bad luck. The neighbors fond of snooping from pulled-back curtains. Judases eager to prove their loyalty.

3:35 on the stove display. Cool, blue digits. You pause in the doorway, a look back. A goodbye to the shelter of locked doors and a roof before you cast yourself back into the tide. A breeze in the backyard. The oak's leaves still green. The black-eyed Susans' fading blooms. The sycamores have already paled, and their dropped leaves scuttle on the wind, a crisp snagging around hedges and garages. You enter your backyard. Rhythmic taps to your back and belly, the dangling sneakers, the gun. You study the house next door and think about Chestnut. Then your father's garden and memories everywhere. His spirit not in the broken pots but in stems and roots. You pause by the back stoop. Inside, everything broken, the little that remains violated by the mob's sweat and curses. But here in the dark garden, your father waits. These wonders of adaptation and evolution. The beauty of a single, red bloom.

You crouch behind the azalea bush and listen for cars and dogs but only the crickets answer. You flush a rabbit, a bounding path, a melting white tail. The grass tall in Dr. Klein's backyard. Spider webs break over your face. You run the final alley stretch.

A sidewalk leads from the alley to Fran's back stoop. To your right, their small garage, cinderblock, swinging wood doors and dirty windows. To your left, the dwarf maple and its veil of drooping branches. You push aside the branches and settle into the space beneath, a return to hideaways and summer games. You slide off your pack and use it for a pillow. Around you, the scent of earth and must, and no matter how you curl, you can't keep your boots from sticking out from beneath the branches.

Have a plan. Your father urged you to see beyond the moment, but the fog of the past days has claimed you, and the luxury of making everything right feels more and more like a fairy tale. Reunion, salvation, happy endings—they hang about you, as flimsy as the daydreams you and Fran once shared in this damp space. You lie across the dirt and tuck your knees to your chest. This much you know—you want to be safe. You want to sleep in a bed. You want to talk to Fran, and in time, tell her the things you've seen. You want a hug from Fran's mother. You want to start the work of finding your mother. You want to be loved and recognized and counted among the living.

You want to be unafraid of the night. You want to cry for your father.

You open your eyes, unsure if you've slept. The predawn gray ebbs between the leaves, and above the lawn, a white fog. The sun low, and its haze outlines the trees and houses. In the neighbor's yard, an apple tree, windfalls in the grass. Fran's house splintered by the hanging branches. A car rumbles down the alley. The maple's branches rustle, a sprinkle of dew. You wait. The sun inches higher. A squirrel gathers acorns. In the distance, the whir of a power saw, the clatter of metal. A pair of boys from your grade walk the alley, backpacks over their shoulders and their sneakers kicking stones. You're relieved, your grasp of time fractured, your fear today might be a weekend. You turn your attention to the house and wait for the back door to open.

You hear Fran first. A goodbye to her mother, a promise to call if practice is rained out. The door shuts, Fran's slow walk, one hand plugging in an earbud, the other bud dangling around her neck. Her thoughts no doubt on school, tests and papers. Your coach. Todd Abbott. You remain still and consider staying tucked beneath the leaves. An excuse of not wanting to startle your friend; the truth that you're afraid of setting in motion what you can't control. Afraid of a world that's left you behind. Afraid the people you've lost and that the horrors you've witnessed are masked by a face that hasn't changed—and beneath that face waits a heart that can never be the same. Indeed, nothing can be the same. This neighborhood. These people and their belief in God and country. A picture—your feet and hands taking root. Your mouth sewn with vines. A lapse into a dormant state, a claiming by the soil. The freedom to never speak again.

"Fran?"

Fran pauses. Her hair cut since the last time you saw her.

She pauses, looks behind her, the earbud removed, the music a faint crackle. "Fran?" You sit up. Your cloak of leaves trembles. You push aside a branch and squint in the slanting light.

Fran's expression blank as she steps closer. She kneels in the grass. "Shit." A slow smile. Then one hand over her mouth, the other reaching out, a tender tracing of your swollen jaw. She grips your fingers, loose at first, then tight. "I thought—"

"I know." Another car in the alley, the crunch of tires over gravel. "Pretend you're tying your shoe."

Fran sets her bag aside and rests her chin on her knee. She pulls her sneaker's lace and reties. Her head down as she speaks. "Where have you been?"

"Not far."

"Your dad—"

"Don't. Not now."

"And your mom."

"They have her. Somewhere."

Fran glances back to her house and unties her other sneaker. "I'm sorry. I'm so fucking sorry. I fucking hate all this."

"Who else is missing?"

Fran lists classmates and teachers. Some arrested, others simply gone, their cars packed in the dead of night. A few murdered. "That crazy lady behind your house, too," Fran said. "And just up the street two nights ago, like that day after the pool."

"I was there. I saw it."

"Do you think they're after you?"

"I don't think so. But they're not going to just let me stay. They'll take me away."

Fran unzips her backpack and sticks her lunch bag between the branches. "Don't say no. The cafeteria ladies are still making food like everyone's still around. They were giving it away yesterday at the end of the period." She rises. "Wait there." She glances toward the house then tests the knob of the garage's side door. She waves. Hunched and stiff, you step from beneath the bush. The leaves brush wet against your hair.

Fran closes the door behind you. Sun filters through the dirty windows, and an earthy haze wraps Fran's father's prized Impala. The same model he drove as a teenager, a car already a relic by the time he'd inherited the keys. A gearshift on the column and a pushbutton AM radio. You were in the backyard the day the tow truck delivered the car. A bird's nest on the passenger seat. Rust on your palm as you helped Fran and her father push the car into the garage. Fran's mother refusing her husband's invitations to come and get a better look.

"Stay here until I get home." Fran pulls a leaf from your hair. "Look at you." A flutter of her lower lip then an embrace. Fran breathes deep, steps back, and wipes her eyes. "They say it's going to start raining by noon. If we don't have practice I'll come right home." She readjusts her backpack's strap. "Even if we do have practice I'll be right home. But don't go anywhere, OK?"

"I won't."

She strokes your face. "Promise?"

"Hope to die."

Fran's smile crumbles. She begins to cry. "Don't say that. Please."

"Sorry."

She dabs her tears. "Do you remember where we keep the outside key?"

You nod. A fake brick at the end of the house-hugging flowerbed. A secret compartment inside. Another hug before Fran leaves. The promise to be back soon.

You circle the car, a path so narrow you're forced to turn sideways. Your shoulders bent to avoid the hanging ladders and tools. The smell of oil and grease. The front grill inches from the workbench, and you pick through the tools, the boxes and shelves. Switches. Fuses. Glass-jar collections of nuts and bolts and screws. You take nothing, yet the inventory feels vital, your survival hinging on an awareness you're only beginning to appreciate. You step back then rise onto your toes. At the garage's far end, an open loft. A shadowed berth of scrap wood, a door with a ripped screen.

Your heel strikes a box. A rattle, and inside, four shiny hubcaps. When Fran's father drove you to your club tournaments, there was always the chance the ride home would include a junkyard detour. Fran mortified, her eyes rolling with each word from her father's mouth. You quiet yet intrigued. The rusting landscapes. The scurry of mice. The cars' crumpled histories. Their loss of shine and glint a kind of death. The Impala an amalgamation of ancient-decayed and ancient-preserved, gleaming here, tarnished there. Fran's mother full of sighs, the foolishness of it all. You pick up a hubcap. Your distorted reflection slips across the chrome. The quest to restore a car lost in a man's youth. Your desire to play varsity and kiss Billy Stafford. How little it all means.

You settle into the driver's seat. The window crank missing. A new rearview mirror. You open Fran's lunch bag and take a few bites of a sandwich. The act joyless, but a machine needs fuel. A note in the bag's bottom. *We're thinking of you.*

The Impala's steering wheel similar to the one in your father's truck, and you glide your palm over the circumference of hard plastic, the underside's rippled grip. The windshield dirty, and its radiating cracks fragment the workbench's tools and rags. You grip the wheel, your foot on the gas. You imagine acceleration's push, the sinking of your spine into the seat. You imagine the river road, the trees' shadows and the water's radiant flicker. You don't picture a destination, only motion.

In the backseat, you unzip your backpack and place the

gun inside. A blanket covers the ripped upholstery, and when you stretch out, the rough material scratches your neck. You bunch another blanket into a pillow. Around you, scents that remind you of your uncles, their trucks and toolboxes. Fatigue fills you. Close your eyes. The rain comes, a soft rhythm on the roof, and again, you find yourself in a box within a box. Then another box, this one carried deep in your chest. The burial plot for all you've lost.

* * *

Yₒu wake with a cry. Fran by the driver's-side door. She jerks back, hands raised. "Only me, hon." The rain's ragged rhythm echoes. Her shorter hair still a surprise. "Let me see if anyone's home, OK?"

You slip into your boots. The heaviness of sleep crumbles, and you focus on the task at hand. You wrap the gun in a blanket and climb atop the car's hood, eye-level with the loft. The triangular space recedes to darkness. Dust and cobwebs, and atop the scrap wood, more boxes. Sheets of shingles. A roll of linoleum. A chipped sink. You tuck the blanket into a nook between the ceiling's slant and a stripped bike frame.

You've gathered your backpack and laced your boots by the time Fran returns. "Just us. Come on." A dash across the backyard. The rain. The fear of being seen. A thick sky and breeze-jostled trees.

The kitchen. Your sense of time adrift, this step back and the seamless alignment of memory and reality. Everything in its place, but with your next breath, you stand in your old kitchen, its mess and empty spaces, a boneyard of broken dishes and scattered silverware. You grow lightheaded. Disoriented by thirst and the stainless steel's glimmer and the refrigerator's hum. You lay a hand on the counter. All of it so real, so solid—your flesh a breeze destined to evaporate when the others open their eyes.

"Hungry?" Fran asks.

"Water?"

Fran at the spigot. The glass filled, and the flow curdles in you. Both hands on the counter and the fear of collapse. "School sucks without you." The glass handed over. Fran wipes

148

her hands against her jeans. "How about a bath? You can wear my stuff. I'll wash whatever you want."

Fran's cat in the doorway, a look then backwards steps to the dining room. Above, the echo of the filling tub, the push of water through thin pipes. You place your hands under the spigot. The cold water cupped and a splash on your face. The sensation of being awake yet not. On the ledge above the sink, a photo of Fran and her parents. The three of them posed atop a hilltop boulder. You imagine a picture little different next door. And in the neighbors' houses beyond them. And beyond them, a web unbroken until it reaches the edge of town. You think of a thousand snapshot smiles and a mob's rage, and you wonder how a person can contain such extremes. Wonder if you, deep down, are any different.

The water shuts off. "Kay?" Fran calls.

You lug your pack up the stairs. The bag holds all you own, and again, you consider the hermit crab, its house carried on its back. You enter the bathroom, a wall of heat and haze. Fran sets a towel on the sink. "I'll get some clothes."

"Stay," you say. "Please."

Fran sits on the toilet. You peel off your top and unbutton your jeans. Your bra and panties next. In you, the fear of being alone. You bunch back your hair. The touch of your mother's necklace takes you off guard, and you lift the cross and let it drop back to your chest. Naked, you picture Missy. Her pain. The panic of last thoughts. Fog on the medicine cabinet mirror, your face blurred. A toe to test the water, and the heat rises into you, a sensation just shy of pain. You lower yourself. A guarded immersion and a long, settling sigh. The water bleeds gray. The garden's dirt. The tarpaper's rub. The smoke in your hair. You cup a handful and wet your neck and face. The water turns your skin red and your melting continues. Your lungs open, and you breathe deeper than you have for days.

"We'll blow up the air mattress," Fran says.

Your hand moves beneath the water. Lazy circles, swirls of dirt and soap. "I can't stay. Not forever. I don't think it works like that now. The people around us—they're the ones who did this." You rub a bar of soap over your arm. You contemplate telling her about Missy, but you don't think you can without breaking. "They're not going to want to see me walking around, reminding them of what they did. Or who they are."

Fran silent for a minute before she starts percolating with plans. Tomorrow morning she'll leave for school but then join you in the garage until her parents go to work. Her parents both carpooling, a necessity dictated by eight-dollar-a-gallon gas. There'd be a car and you'll drive to the stadium. Fran has over a hundred dollars, and you have Helen's stash, and surely you could bribe a guard to let you see your mother. If that plan fizzles, you'll just drive. Fran will take you anywhere you want. A new town, and she'll help you find an apartment. You'll get a job and Fran will send what she can. You'll lay low until the world either comes to its senses or forgets about you.

You half-listen, then not at all. Fran's words withered by the steam, by their improbability once they meet the cold air on the other side of the bathroom door. You turn the spigot and lose yourself in the splash and heat, a drift shattered by the front door's closing and a call up the steps. "Fran?"

Fran stands. "Let me talk to her first."

The door opens and closes. A moment's cool draft. You listen to the rain. You hug your legs, your chin resting on raised knees, your hair wet and dripping across your back.

Footsteps. An odd rhythm—trepidation, eagerness. A knock on the door. "Kayla?"

The door eases back, a silent asking of permission. Fran's mother's smile weaker than her tears. Her work clothes—a white blouse and tan skirt. Stockings but no shoes. Magic marker streaks on her fingers—purple and orange. She kneels by the tub. Her hand shakes as she touches your cheek. "I'm sorry, honey." Her touch crumbles into an embrace. The dampness on her blouse, and the material clings to your chest. "I'm so sorry, baby."

Fran's mother sits back upon her heels. Her eyes ringed with black. Her hair and blouse wet. Again, the wavering smile. Her hand on the tub's side, and you place your hand on top, the press of her wedding ring into your palm. Then a repositioning, your fingers laced. Welcome in her mother's eyes, yet beneath, another look. A mirror's gaze. The reflection of what could be.

"Have you heard anything about my mom?"

"No, honey." She stands. "I'll start dinner. You take your time." Her palms smooth her skirt. A pause at the door. "I'm glad you're here, Kay. We were so worried."

Let the water drain. A gray whirlpool. The chill spreads across your back. A towel that smells of the backyard line, sun and trees and grass. You dry off. The mirror slick against your palm as you wipe a swath. Your eyes stare back, the puff and bruise of your jaw. The rest of you lost.

Draped in a towel, you stand in front of Fran's closet. "Take whatever you want." Fran at her desk, her homework out. Her pencil tapping. She lists the people she's heard were at last night's fire. Neighbors. Coaches. Todd Abbott and Billy Stafford. "I hate them all," Fran says.

You dress. Sweatpants, your travel team's T-shirt. You wrap your hair in a towel and slide a book from Fran's backpack. A seat on the bed and a propping against the wall. A pillow's soft luxury. This year's science text. The stretching universe, the living Earth. The formation of fossils. A gap near the end, thirty-some pages ripped out. A glimpse to the index—Darwin and his finches and *The Origin of Species*.

"Fuck it." Fran pushes her papers aside. "I can't think about school. Fucking Todd Abbott. Fucking Billy Stafford. Fucking all of them."

"Can I have your phone and buds? I'll listen to some music while you work."

"And fuck my work, Kay."

You smile. A slipping into old roles, you the one who encouraged Fran to study. "Get your work done and we'll have time to hang." *Hang*—the word catches in your throat, and you glance down.

"I may need some help." Fran hands over her phone and earbuds. Her words normal but you detect a hitch, the artifice of playing a role. Of not addressing what you're both thinking about. "Math is a bitch this year."

"I'm all yours if you need me."

You hold the phone, the earbuds secure, the screen cupped and hidden. A YouTube clip you watch five times in a row. An instructional video, a gun like Helen's, the basics of loading and firing. When you're done, you clear the history and pick up Fran's field hockey stick. You flick your wrists, the heel turned in and out. You hear your mother calling from the sidelines. Fran talks. Her homework forsaken for the weaving of ever-more elaborate plans. Perhaps, Fran says, you'll run away together, just the two of you. Schemes questionable at best, others outright criminal.

You wonder when Fran will feel the emptiness between you. A chasm sudden and deep and glaring. The foundations you shared eroding with every breath. You drift on the flow and each hour takes you further from what you shared. Fran's words—and her reality—lost beneath the current.

The front door opens. A man's voice. Fran saddles up to the door, her ear to the opened crack. The downstairs conversation quickly masked by the radio. Fran's father works for the Transportation Department. A desk job in the capital, a start twenty-five years before on a road crew. His voice the sideline's loudest at their field hockey games. Admonishments for Fran to hustle or focus; exasperation with the refs, tirades that earned him a season-long ban during your eighth-grade season. His heavy footsteps. Fran sits on the bed and holds your hand. A knock on the door.

He wears a loosened tie and unbuttoned collar, rolled-up sleeves. The cat twines between his scuffed shoes. Fran and your mother the best of friends, your fathers polite but never clicking. Their politics, your father's ignorance of sports. Carried in Fran's father's wake, music and kitchen smells. You stand and embrace. A whisper, "I'm sorry, Kay." He steps back. "Come on down for dinner."

An extra plate at the table. The spot you think of as yours. Your history of dinners, of peanut butter-and-jelly lunches and breakfasts after a sleepover. Chicken stew, steam from your bowl. You nibble bites between answered questions. Slater's role in your father's murder. Your rescue and Helen's disappearance. The fate of Chestnut. Your plan of finding your mother among the stadium's detainees, an explanation abandoned after a sidelong glance from Fran's father.

Fran's mother delivers seconds to her husband's plate. "Kayla, you've hardly eaten. Is it OK?"

You speak into your lifted fork. "It's good. Thanks."

An itch on your skin. Fran has yet to recognize your incongruity, but her parents are more perceptive. Her father's stares. The pauses before her mother speaks, the sentences cut short. Each an acknowledgment that you're a wrong note in their harmony. A reminder of what could be lost and what they're anxious to preserve. A fugitive, even one of a lesser degree, is bound to be noted by the neighbors who walk the right path. You're no longer their child's teammate, her partner in back-yard cartwheels or winter sledding. You're the daughter of dissidents. A feral creature, dirty and unclaimed. A girl who would, sooner or later, have to be answered for.

Fran's father silent by meal's end. Fran's mother flustered, a nervous bubbling, stories about the girls' playing days, their pool summers. Her voice whittled by the time it reaches your ears, the acoustics of pipes and seashells. In the place of words, a rise of the room's undertones. Clattering silverware and gnashing teeth. The slurp from glasses. The rattling breath through Fran's father's nose and the squish of your pulse. Eat, you think. Fuel. But with your next forced mouthful, your throat closes, and you crumble into a coughing fit. Fran and her parents turn to you. The room swims, their voices lost beneath your hacking. The vibrations within and the tears in your eyes. A sip from your glass, and the water slops down your chin. "I'm OK," you say. Your napkin held to your mouth. The certainty you'll collapse beneath their stares. The understanding you no longer belong here and how blind you'd been not to see it. Your mother's face. *Go!*

You and Fran return to her room. The rain steady on the roof. Fran's parents clear the table. A discussion in the kitchen, and you and Fran sink to your knees, your ears pressed to the floor. Then the rush of water, the dishwasher's hum. Fran returns to her desk. You go to the bathroom and sit on the tub's side. Your heart fidgety. Your breath unable to sink deeper than your throat.

You rub your temples. Perhaps tonight you'll sleep. You're so tired. Tired in body. Tired in mind. Tired of failed plans and foolish hope. You made a mistake coming here. The proof on Fran's father's face and in your gut's woozy crawl. You can't sit through another awkward dinner. *Have a plan.* Eyes closed, you stand outside your skin and see yourself projected into a movie. A girl who does things. Who overcomes. Who walked unafraid as a sixth grader into a high school math class. Who, with stick in hand, returned as many elbows as she received. Who punched poor Missy Blough in the mouth. You watch the movie-you wait until the others have fallen asleep. You'll slip out, take Fran's bike, and pedal through the rain. *Have a plan*, and with your uncles' houses under surveillance, you'll go to your grandmother's. Forty minutes by car, and if you pedal all night and don't get lost, perhaps you can be there by morning. Your grandmother still healthy but fading. Her hearing, her refusal to drive after dark. Your mother's worries during the Shut-In, the invitations for her mother to come live with you, an old country house too much for a widow with failing knees, the winter snows and her reliance on a neighbor older than her to plow her lane. Come dawn, you'll appear at her door, the sun low and the wet night behind you. A place for you to stay far from the history you're anxious to escape. You'll cut wood and tend to the fireplace and stove. You've driven your father's truck— and with a lesson or two, you could plow the lanes of your grandmother and her neighbor. You step from the bathroom as Fran's father calls up the stairwell.

"Get yourself ready for your piano lesson."

Fran meets you in the hallway. "That's tomorrow."

"Your teacher changed nights, remember? We walked about it last week."

Fran's expression blank. "I forgot."

"Grab your music. You know how she is about being late."

You join Fran in her bedroom. "I'll never get to my homework." She unearths a slim packet amid her desk's clutter. "I've barely practiced this week. I try to lie about it, but she sees right through me. She's weird like that." A smile. "How about you do my math? But leave a few mistakes so my teacher doesn't get suspicious."

Fran's mother enters. Coat on, keys in hand. "Come on,

honey. We need to go." A turn halfway out the door, a hug for you, a wordless goodbye.

You sit at Fran's desk. The cat leaps onto the bed. The cat sits, sleepy eyes watching as you page through the math book. Formulas, graphs. Concepts you grasped years ago but which tonight bring the comfort of certainty. You close the book. Music from downstairs. The rain softer now, and you're thankful you packed your poncho. A smile as you imagine your long ride through the night. You, a modern Huck Finn, a story your grandmother read you years before. *Before*, you slow at the word. Before.

The cat lifts its head, a twitch of his black tail. The front door opens, and you picture Fran, rushed and frantic, a piece of music forgotten. Men's voices—or is it the radio?

"Kayla?" Fran's father's voice. "Kayla, can you come down for a moment?"

You stop halfway down the steps. Fran's father steps aside. A pair of policemen crowd the foyer. Their hats and jackets slick with rain. Fran's father looks away but not the policemen. Their wide jaws. Their holstered guns. One slips a pair of handcuffs from his belt. The other beckons with a twitch of his fingers. "Come with us, please."

III.

* * *

The awkwardness of her shackled hands. The pinch of metal. Cool rain on her hair. The policeman's beefy grip, and the numbness radiates down her arm. The walk to the waiting cruiser. A dog barks. The scent of wet grass and fallen leaves. The sensation of eyes upon her from behind shut doors. "My backpack," she says, as if its possession were the key to keeping everything from falling apart. "My things—"

The policeman holding her arm guides her into the cruiser's backseat. His other hand on the back of her head. The door slams shut. The seat smooth and hard, and the space stinks like her gym teacher's office—disinfectants and burnt coffee. The smudged partition behind the front seat warps the dash's orange lights. The radio's terse chatter, addresses, numbered codes. A shotgun secured to the dash. The policemen climb into the front seat. The squeak of plastic and springs, the rattle of gear. Kayla looks back. A rain-streaked window. Fran's father pauses then shuts the door. The porch light snuffed.

She wriggles, the stifled instinct to push her wet hair from her eyes. The handcuffs dig into her wrists, and the twisted posture strains her shoulders. The driver puts the car into gear. The one who cuffed her speaks into his shoulder microphone. The car rolls beneath a streetlamp, its wash of light a snapshot. The partition's array of handprints captured then fading back into the dark. "My clothes," Kayla says. Her throat constricted. Her words lost beneath the radio voices, the cruiser's muscled prowl.

Her neighborhood glides past. The lit bedroom windows of girls from her team. Streets where she rode her bike. The husk of the house she watched burn. The playground where she broke her index finger. The high school's fields, the empty

159

hockey cages. All she knows turning liquid, the distancing flow she felt at dinner now a riptide. Coherent thought, the movement of her body—all of it beyond her. The cruiser reaches the river road and turns north. Neither policeman speaks. The dark deeper here, town's streetlights replaced by overhanging willows. Wet leaves on the shoulder. Her panic a seed at first. An image that burns in eyes both opened and closed. Moonlight on pale breasts. A bandanna's bite against a neck's tender skin. Open eyes staring into hers.

Breathe, but she can only manage shallow clutches. Her panic blossoms. She's drowning, here with the air all around her. Her brain's electric fire. The river's black flow glimpsed between the trees. They'll rape her. They'll rape her and beat her, and when they're spent, they'll cast her into the river. Her wrists bound, the water claiming her. A burial without a witness. She'll fade even in the minds of those who loved her. Questions at first, then less so. The swallowing of time. Even Fran. Even her mother.

She feels the water upon her. Its weight and volume. She holds her breath, a fight to stave the river from claiming her. The pressure builds behind her eyes. Her throat's ache before she surrenders with a gasp. She presses her shoulders into the seat, lifts her knees, and slams the soles of her shoes against the partition. The plastic quivers, ripples of orange light. She kicks and screams, powerless to lift herself above the surface. The water rushes into her lungs. The current cold and black.

The cruiser jerks onto the shoulder. The crunch of gravel, and Kayla tumbles onto her side. Rain on the roof. The radio's indifferent chatter. She rights herself. In the woody strip between the road and the river, a headlamp shines. The light hurtling closer then passing, the rattle of boxcars and tankers. The thunder of wheels in Kayla's chest, and knitted into the din, the life and rhythm of every creature huddled along the riverbank. The cop in the passenger seat turns back. Half his broad face lit, a fire's hues, and in the set of his jaw, she sees the cops who smashed their batons into the faces of the campus protestors. Who sat in their cars as houses burned and the mobs called for blood.

"Fuck you fuck you fuck you!" she curses through scalding tears. The salt on her lips. Her hands bound and useless. Sobs so thick she gags—then gags again when she thinks of a pair of panties stuffed down her throat. She doubles over, coughing, her head between her knees. A spindle of drool hangs from her lips. She speaks into the dark space between her feet. Her words eked between sobs. "Just let someone find me. Don't throw me in the river. Just let them find me."

The policeman's voice breaks over her. "Get up."

She wipes her face against her jeans' leg. The act of sitting impeded by the cuffs, and she thinks of an overturned turtle her father righted on a leaf-strewn trail. Finally, she sits, her lip bit as the policeman considers her through the partition that now bears the imprint of her shoes. In her gut, a shine no larger than a grain of sand yet which grows with each heaving breath. The light an understanding of defiance and strength. Let them do what they want. She'll look them in the eye until it all becomes too horrible. She'll hoard her pain and turn the act upon them, her stare the mirror they'll carry for the rest of their lives, a reflection waiting beneath every moment of joy or content- ment. A gaze waiting for them as they gasp their final breath.

"No one's hurting anyone, kid. But if you kick my seat one more time, I'm hog-tying you, and you wouldn't like that. Understand?"

She says nothing.

He turns back. "Let's go."

The river road empty. Silence after the train's last car. Silence in her thoughts, the stillness echoed as they pass the steel mill. The plant over a mile and a half long. Empty lots where weeds strain between cracked blacktop. Barbwire and snares of windblown trash. A rusty fence cut and patched and cut again. Teetering piles of wooden skids and spools and casings. The smokestack rows, slender towers, and below, the stretching shops of crumbling brick and broken windows. Cranes that sway in thunderstorms and blizzards. Her grandfather and great uncles worked the mill, their fathers before them. The plant now the setting for the town's horror stories. Rat infestations. Shooting galleries. The squatters, men lost and violent. Black Masses and butchered animals. Rumors, and who knows what's true. For Kayla, a final look back. A flicker in one of the long windows, a small flame.

They pass beneath the south-side bridge. Memories amid the shadows—the backseat of her parents' car, raucous school busses. Trips to the museum or the riverside stadium. To Front Street's festivals, the road closed and packed with vendors and food carts. Old town, this neighborhood that keeps an eye on the river's ice jams and high water. The streets quiet tonight, everything the same then not. A burned-out block, a heap of beams and bricks, staircases that strain into empty air. Across the street, untouched homes fly flags of red and white.

The cruiser slows. Three men step from the corner. The cop in the passenger seat lowers his window. The cool air, the heaviness of rain. The men wear ponchos. Their faces shadowed by baseball caps and hoods. Red bands around their arms, rifles over their shoulders. One of the men rests his forearm on the roof. His face lit in the dash's orange. Droplets in his beard, more clinging to his cap's brim. A laugh as he says they're doing "a little night hunting." He considers Kayla. "And where're you taking this pretty thing?"

"Girl's center."

A smile. "If you'd like, we can take her the rest of the way."

"You'd better behave yourselves," the cop says.

The man steps back, his rifle taken off his shoulder and held before him. "Not us you got to worry about behaving right, brother."

The window rolls back up. The man with the beard points at Kayla and winks. The cruiser slinks off. Kayla turns, and the man fades in the dark. How easily men like him have risen in this new order. She'd been naïve before, the belief that people like her parents were the norm. She'd overlooked the world's crueler histories—the crowds who filled the Coliseum or called for the burning of witches, the ones who loaded the trains headed to the gulags and concentration camps. A current that had always churned now free to rise from the rubble and claim its rightful, horrible place.

They turn onto a side street. An unfamiliar neighborhood. A weaving through tightly packed blocks. Kayla tries to align their present with the river road, the Capitol building, but after a few more turns, she loses her bearings. The car slows. Their arrival marked with a tire's scrape of the curb.

* * *

The driver jots notes in a ledger. His partner checks in with dispatch. Kayla rests her forehead against the rain-streaked window. She swallows back her panic. The girl who planned five steps ahead now blind. She forces a series of deep breaths. Take inventory, she tells herself. Try to understand. Outside, a wide sidewalk. A tall fence lined with razor wire, and the drops glisten along the metal loops. Beyond the fence, an old graystone building. A school, she guesses. Tall windows. The building H-shaped, a middle corridor connecting two larger, parallel wings. She cranes her neck to take in all three stories. Between the building and the fence, a blacktop playground. A backboard, a hoop without a net. A swingless swing set. A tall pole, and atop, a pair of limp flags. She commits it all to memory, and the act grounds her.

The policeman in the passenger seat gets out and opens Kayla's door. His callused palm, an impatient yank onto the sidewalk. She shivers, the rain, her clinging T-shirt. A rough handling between the policemen, her hands still cuffed, each now clutching an arm. Numbness in her wrists and shoulders.

The driver pushes the first gate's buzzer. Kayla lifts her gaze. The rain a curtain around the streetlight. A security camera angles toward her. A buzz, and the driver swings back the gate. A small pen next, fences on either side of the walk. At the chute's end, a second gate. Another button pushed, another buzz. The walkway continues, a short stretch to the entrance's stone steps. Puddles cup the building's spilled light. The tall windows caged. Kayla squints back the drops and studies the higher windows. Silhouettes gather behind the glass in both wings. All looking down upon her.

Kayla's feet slosh through the puddles, and if it weren't for

164

the policemen's grip, she might have melted into the entrance's wide steps. A light shines above the double door. Around the light, a hood, and the metal steams in the rain. Another camera bolted to the stone, a teardrop's red eye. She feels the slip of years around her, the class photos taken here, poodle skirts and bell bottoms. The stone smoothed by the elements and the traffic of once-children now old or dead. A pause atop the landing, and the rain relentless. The matted hair she can't pull from her face. Her clinging T-shirt and the handcuffed thrust of her chest. The driver stares, and in Kayla, a chill that has nothing to do with the rain.

The door opens, a spill of light. A woman's hand reaches to prop the door. A scolding for the police. "You can't get her a coat?"

They step inside. Kayla squints. The sudden illumination, the ceiling's fluorescent row. The door shut behind her, and she flinches at the accompanying buzz. A taped line runs down the hallway's center. Kayla pictures the building from outside and aligns that vision with this view then steps beyond, imaging what lies beyond the waiting corridor, the H's link between the two wings. A memory of their old apartment, her father pushing aside the dinner plates and smoothing out their house's blueprints. She blinks water from her eyes and continues her survey, a cataloguing of doors and nameplates and fire escapes.

The woman in the green scrub top stands as tall as Kayla. A thin frame, square shoulders. Her blond hair pulled back, a ponytail that brushes the nape of her neck. Her ears pierced but unadorned. Scuffed white sneakers and a clipboard in hand. Her smile a weary echo of her lanyard's ID. "The rose between two thorns."

The driver lets go of Kayla's arm. "Now you're just being hurtful."

The other policeman holds tight. "We have feelings, you know. But you can make it up to us with a cup of coffee."

"Want me to put some on?"

A crackle over the policemen's shoulder mikes. "Next time," he says.

An understanding for Kayla—this is all routine. That she's the latest delivery in an on-going trade. She pictures the second-floor's gathered silhouettes. The policeman lets go of Kayla's arm, her torso twisted as he unlocks her handcuffs.

"Let's get you out of those wet things, honey," the woman says. She turns to the driver. "Any problems?"

"She's a little shook up."

The other cop loops the cuffs back on his belt. "Thought we were going to dump her in the river."

The woman rests a hand on Kayla's shoulder. "No one's going to hurt you. OK?"

Kayla thinks of Helen and wonders how different their fates are now. She nods and rubs her wrists.

The driver opens the front door. A push of cooler air, the scent of rain. "We'll expect coffee next time."

The other man follows his partner. "A fresh pot. Not that mud you gave us last time."

The woman stands at the door and calls after them. "How about you bring us a bag or two of those good beans I hear the downtown folks keep for their own?"

"We're just the protect and serve guys. We get the same shit coffee you do."

The door closes, another buzz. The nurse with a smile and a check of her clipboard. "Kayla, right? That's all the heads-up I got."

Kayla nods. A young man with a shaved head and pencil-thin beard studies her from behind a window. A slot at the window's bottom, a circle cut in its middle, the design of bank tellers and movie ticket booths. The man also in green scrubs. Behind him, an array of monitors, high angle shots, deserted hallways and stairwells. A darker screen shows the policemen's return to their cruiser. The man behind the glass still staring, a return to his sports magazine after Kayla folds her arms across her chest.

"Doing a bang-up job there, Jimmy," the woman says.

She leads Kayla to a small waiting room. A desk, a few chairs. Posters on the wall—STD symptoms, a fetus in the womb. The woman hands Kayla a towel and an examination gown. Another door, and the woman flips the light. A white, windowless space. Cabinets along one wall. Half-filled jars on a long counter, cotton balls and tongue depressors. A stainless steel sink. In the floor's center, an examination table. The crinkle of paper, a roller's spin as the nurse pulls a fresh sheet. "You can leave your underwear and socks on if they're dry."

Kayla strips. A puddle beneath her wet clothes. She pulls the towel around her shoulders, dries off, and slips into the exam gown.

The woman pats the table's edge. "Up here."

Kayla sits. Her knees pressed together, toes dangling above the floor. A glimmer on the table's metal stirrups.

"You hungry?"

Kayla shakes her head.

The woman washes her hands and retrieves a stethoscope from a drawer. "Let me know if you change your mind." She holds the stethoscope's disc under her arm. "Warm it up a bit." She puts in the earbuds and places the disc on Kayla's back. "Deep breath."

She works the stethoscope around Kayla's torso. "Breathe. Deeper. Good." She asks about Kayla's school and hometown.

Kayla's answers one-word whispers. The nurse's hands busy, her routine rehearsed. A rubber mallet's swing. A light shone into Kayla's eyes and ears. A command to keep her head still and let her eyes track the nurse's pencil. More questions, the sports she played. The nurse grins over the mention field hockey and points out the imperfections of her twice-broken nose.

"I'm Ms. Williams." She secures a sleeve around Kayla's arm. The squeeze of a ball, and the sleeve tightens. "The girls call me Nurse Amy." The pressure ebbs, and she removes the sleeve with a rip of Velcro. "Kayla's a pretty name. Is that what they call you? Or Kay?"

"Kayla." She blinks. "Kay, too. Both."

The nurse sits on a wheeled stool, and Kayla thinks of her skates across the basement floor. Paperwork on the nurse's clipboard. More questions. Did she have asthma? Epilepsy? Did she take medications? Had she had surgery? Kayla shakes her head. *No, no, no.*

The nurse slips on a small headlamp. A shine in Kayla's eyes. "Looks like I'm going exploring, doesn't it?" She picks up a comb. "Can you bend your head a bit?"

Kayla tucks her chin to her chest. The nurse forges parts, her touch gentle on Kayla's scalp. "You have beautiful hair. How long since it's been cut?"

Kayla hidden, shadows, her curtain of hair. "A while."

The nurse moves to the Kayla's other side. "You'll find almost all the girls have situations similar to yours. They've lost their parents. Or they have ones that can't take care of—"

Kayla's gaze on her dangling feet. "They have my mother. Somewhere. Maybe at the stadium."

She trembles with the mention of her mother's name. The tightening of springs, spasms in her bowels. The tremors radiate beneath her skin. The nurse removes her headlamp. "You cold?"

Kayla lies. "Yes."

The nurse retrieves a blanket from one of the cabinets and drapes it over Kayla's shoulders. Kayla pulls the blanket's edges tight.

"There are places we can contact," the nurse says. "People we can write. I've helped some girls get in touch with their people."

"Can we do that?"

"I've reached out more times than I've gotten answers, but we can try."

"When?"

"Let's give you a few days to settle in. Then we'll talk. Promise." Her fingers wriggle into an examination glove, the elastic secured with a snap. "I need you to take off your underwear."

Kayla stares.

"It's OK, honey. I'll be quick. When was your last period?"

Kayla tries to think, but she's can't untangle the hours and nights of her recent days. "A week. Maybe two."

"Are you sexually active?" She pulls on the other glove.

"No."

"Good." The nurse turns her headlamp back on. From her tray, she picks up a speculum, and the light shimmers on its chrome bills. "Ready?"

The nurse's eyes patient. Kayla tries to let go of the blanket, but she can't. Her fingers rusted, her spine swaying in time with the room's hidden rhythms. The pulse of electricity. The flow of water. The greater tide of this place's traffic of police and guards and lost girls. Its eye-of-God video streams, and with this perspective, Kayla understands her body, which just the day before she viewed as a machine, is only the latest sacrifice to a greater machine. A machine, she feels it now, the crush of gears and cogs and fates. She hears its heartbeat from behind the walls, sees its redlining circuits and pistons just beneath the nurse's kind face. The machine opens wide, its only desire to consume her.

Her fingers clumsy, a rip of cotton. Her panties balled in her hands, and she thinks of Missy, both of them sisters, fodder to a vast evil. She surrenders and the rocking eases. She obeys the machine's demands. The panties slip from her hand, and with the kiss of cotton and tile, she pulls away from herself. She climbs onto the exam table, the stirrups cool against her heels. The headlamp's light catches beneath her gown. She pulls back her vagina's folds. Her focus on the ceiling. The machine can have her meat and bones. Her skin and face and hair. She'll keep the rest, a claiming of memory and identity. She grits her teeth against the metal's chill and vows to mine a space deeper than the machine's reach, and when she finds it, she'll bolt the door tight behind her.

"Done." The nurse peels off her gloves. "I'm guessing you wear an eight-and-a-half or nine shoe?"

"Nine."

The nurse leaves. Kayla's knees together, her arms folded across her chest. The machine presses down, and Kayla locks her door. Force against force, a problem out of her physics text. A formula with many variables and dwindling constants. The nurse returns. A pile of folded clothes, and on top, a pair of plain, white sneakers. She hands Kayla socks and panties and a bra. "We don't win any fashion awards around here."

Kayla dresses. Gray sweatpants. A long-sleeved white T-shirt. Before she can don the final garment, a maroon scrub top, the nurse lays a hand on her shoulder. "I'll need to take that, honey."

Kayla's palm covers the thin cross. She'd forgotten about

the necklace. Its butterfly weight, a chain as thin as pencil lead. The nurse extends a hand. "I'll keep it safe for you."

A whisper: "It's my mom's."

"Promise I won't let anything happen to it. There's no jewelry inside. It only brings—"

Kayla's hand over the cross. A welding of flesh to flesh, bone to bone. The cross's imprint upon her palm. "It's my mom's."

The machine churns. Its weight, its force, and in her ears, the return of rushing water. The room awash, blurred boundaries, auras of bad electricity. The nurse's words lost beneath the thrash of Kayla's heart. She can't move her hand from her throat. Can't solve the equation that will yield the words to make this all right. Her bones no better than twigs. Her skeleton poised to snap into a hundred pieces.

The nurse slips the maroon scrub top over Kayla's head and guides her limp arms into the short sleeves. Kayla her puppet. "Tell you what. It's late, and I'm guessing you don't want to go through the thousand-question thing with the other girls. I'll fix you up on the break-room couch. And I'll let you keep the necklace for tonight. But I'm taking it tomorrow morning, understand?"

Kayla nods. The nurse's guiding arm around her shoulder. The hallway floors recently washed, a squeak beneath her sneakers. The center's taped line. The room of video monitors, and the guard looks up from his magazine. Another door, another room. A soda machine's lit panel. A small countertop, a sink and microwave. The char of burnt coffee. A bulletin board posted with shift schedules and clipped cartoons. Beneath the bulletin board, a sofa.

"I'll be right back," the nurse says.

Kayla sits. Crumbs on the sofa's cushions. A soda can on one of the tables. A pencil on the other. A small refrigerator beneath the counter. A hand-printed sign above the microwave. *Your mother doesn't work here. Clean your mess.* Kayla rocks, her body struggling to divine a strain of harmony beneath this upheaval. A narrative she can understand. Her motions a wave on a graph that stretches over the city's roofs and into the night.

The nurse returns with sheets and blankets and a pillow. "Still cold?"

Kayla nods.

They make up the couch. A brushing of crumbs. A threadbare sheet over the cushions. A pair of thin blankets, the scent of industrial detergent. Kayla hugs herself, rubs her arms, conscious motions, a disguising of her sway's haywire current. Her body a betrayer. The nurse hands her a water glass and a pill. The glass trembles, a spill of drops. The pill small and oblong and peach-colored.

The nurse steadies Kayla's hand. "Lots of girls take one their first night."

Kayla places the pill on her tongue. A moment of bitterness and a washing down. She slides off her sneakers. This time last night she lay on Helen's couch. She said a goodbye and walked though her sleeping neighborhood. The shelter of a bush she once played beneath. A morning's mist and afternoon's rain. A nap in a garage and a dinner with a family that had called her "daughter number two." A ride in a police car and the fear of sinking beneath the river. The city's burned-out buildings. A man with a gun, his stare and the things he'd do given the chance. A dozen backdrops, a landscape strung together with the logic of dreams. Then a waking in this windowless room. The nurse pulls her chair close as Kayla rests her head upon the pillow.

"The first few days can be rough here."

Kayla pulls the blanket under her chin. The nurse tucks

Kayla's hair behind her ear. "You'll have to make your way. If you need to, you can ask to come see me."

Kayla says nothing.

The nurse stands. "I'm on through tomorrow night, so I'll see you in the morning." She pauses in the doorway. "Try to get some rest, OK?"

"Nurse Amy?"

She flips the switch, her body a shadow against the outer light. "Yes?"

"Can I start that letter tomorrow?"

"Tomorrow's going to be busy. Believe me. But we'll do it soon. I promise."

The door closes. The soda machine panel shines, a candied light. Kayla lies awake, ten minutes, a half hour. Her rocking eases. A drip from the faucet. A red light blinks on the ceiling's smoke detector. The twitchings of the machine that holds her in its belly. A thin bar of light beneath the door, and she thinks of her father, a tennis ball and flashlight. She closes her eyes and feels the tug of stillness. She thinks of the pill and wishes she could have taken two. Her heartbeat softer with each minute. The machine's purr brushes her skin, but she holds tight to the things that are still her own—her pulse and breath and will.

Have a plan, but certainty and familiarity have abandoned her, and all she can do is struggle to keep her head above the tide. To keep her mouth shut and her eyes and ears open. To think beyond the moment and the moment beyond that. To have hope even after all her other hopes have turned to ash. She closes her eyes. Hope. She needs hope. She touches her necklace. Nurse Amy. A letter. A mask she'll wear and the workings of her mind. She has these . . .

She wakes, brushing her cheek. A touch or a dream, she can't be sure. A man's silhouette eclipses the soda machine's red light. The man backs up, a collision with a chair. Kayla unsure if she's seeing his front or back. She opens her mouth, but can't summon the coordination to speak. The door opens, a flood of light, then darkness when it shuts. She closes her eyes and sinks back into the sea.

* * *

Kayla considers the break room's textured ceiling tiles. She thinks about a world awash in currents seen and not and all the forces that have landed her on this strange shore. Her mother waits on another shore, one perhaps only miles away, but the distance between them stretches as wide as any ocean. She'll find her. She'll find her or she'll survive until she's found. But first, Kayla needs to navigate this new reality. She lies still, picturing the building from outside and meshing what she saw last night. 8:35 on the microwave's clock, and she sifts through the machine's morning rhythms. The footsteps overhead. The running water and flushed toilets. She pictures the second-floor windows and the shadows who witnessed her arrival.

She stands, stretches, the kinks worked from her spine, and as she shuffles to the sink, she considers the places she's woken these past days—a car, beneath a dewy bush, this couch. She turns the faucet's handle and cups her hands beneath the flow. A sip for her dry mouth. A cleansing for her face. She dries off, remembering her necklace as she presses the paper towel against her neck.

She drops the bunched towels into the sink. A quick working of the necklace's clasp. Her fumbling reflection in the microwave door's dark glass. The chain slides from her neck, and she hides it in one of the scrub top's wide front pockets. The doorknob turns, Nurse Amy's voice: "Kayla?"

Kayla steps back. She tucks her hair behind her ear. Fiddles with the cuff of her long-sleeved T-shirt. The nurse smiles. A tray balanced on one hand, a plate, toast and sausage. In the other, a small pail, and in it, a washcloth and soap, a boxed toothbrush. She elbows the light switch. A spit of fluorescent, and Kayla squints.

They sit at one of the round tables. Nurse Amy fills a glass at the sink and apologizes for the cold food, the plate wrangled as the cafeteria workers broke down the breakfast line. "It's fine," Kayla says. Tiny forkfuls and a gag with each swallow. The revulsion of the machine's sustenance. A bite of toast, a sprinkle of dry crumbs. She wipes her mouth but quickly returns her hands to the table. The fear of drawing attention. The necklace she can't surrender. Her body a shell offered to the world. The real her waiting beneath, a collection of secrets. Her thoughts turning. Her eyes opened wide.

"I let you sleep in," the nurse says. "The other girls are done with breakfast and morning large-group. We'll take you upstairs after you eat. You'll have morning class then work duty. After lunch there's afternoon class and another work duty, but that's not all the time. Then exercise. Sometimes that's outside, sometimes in. There's chores and free time before dinner. Then evening activities. Craft classes or games. Just reading if you'd like. There's a movie once a week. At 8:30, it's back into your pod and lights out by 9:30. Starts all over again at 7:00 the next morning. 8:00 on weekends."

Kayla imagines the hours on a timeline. The horizontal slots claimed by numbers and empty spaces. All of it waiting to be made real by her witnessing.

The nurse leans forward, her elbows on her knees. She pinches the scrub's sleeve. Kayla's chewing stops. "You're a red," the nurse says. "You're in the east wing. The whites are in the west. You've seen the lines in the hallway?"

Kayla nods.

Nurse Amy's smile weak. "Reds stay on the left. Whites on the right. Same thing in the auditorium and gym."

Kayla sips her water "What's the difference?"

"It's just how things are. The folks who run things don't say it out loud, but it's understood the whites have it better. You're going to have to accept that." Nurse Amy sits back. "It depends where you came from. Your circumstances. The reds have situations like yours. Their parents with The Movement. In holding or . . ." She trails off. "And some of the reds are just girls in trouble, you know? The whites come from families where the parents were lost on the other side of things. They were police or military or with the government. Some were shipped from Philly after the bomb."

A short circuit—a jump cut. Her father swaying. The faces below, glistening with sweat, shouting, smiling. She sets her fork on the plate. "Is it OK if I don't eat anymore?"

"Sure." The nurse slides the bucket across the table. "Why don't you get yourself ready at the sink?" She speaks as Kayla brushes her teeth. "Have you ever switched schools?"

Kayla shakes her head. She spits into the sink and dries her mouth with a paper towel.

"But you've been at school when a new girl came, right?"

"Yes."

"It's not easy being the new kid. Knowing where to fit in when so much is already established. And it's going to be even harder here because there's no home you can return to at the day's end. You can't just shut your door and escape it all."

"What about you?" A pause. "Can I come to you?"

The nurse nods. "Last resort. But it's better if you handle things. Or handle them as much as you can."

A soft knock and the door opens. The girl who enters is a good head shorter than Kayla. A wiry frame lost beneath a maroon top. Thin nose and thin lips and wide, brown eyes. Pale but not sickly. Auburn hair, long and straight. A veined forearm and on her wrist, an India-ink tattoo. A spread-winged bird. She reminds Kayla of the cross-country girls who ran laps around the playing fields, a pace Kayla could hold for a half mile at best. Then she could see this girl leaving her, fading. Her stride as steady as a clock and not a glance back.

"Kayla," the nurse says, "this is Heather. She's going to show you around the first few days."

The nurse recounts Heather's duties. They've obviously done this before, Kayla the latest link in a sad chain. Heather silent, nodding. A matter-of-fact intentness. A memory for Kayla—the Chinese restaurant her mother loved, the waiters who never wrote their orders.

"You're in Mr. James's class now?"

"Yes." The girl's voice barely a scratch against the machine's hum.

"Then that's where we'll go." The nurse picks up the pail and toothbrush. "We all know how much Mr. James appreciates an interruption."

"He does." A lift at the corner of the girl's mouth.

Kayla follows Heather and the nurse. The entrance hallway brighter, the angling of morning light. The machine's drone rises to Kayla—voices, footsteps, a cart's rolling wheels. A radio song from the room of surveillance monitors. The screens flicker with activity, unaware passings, the guard's seat empty, and she thinks of the man in the break room and waking to a stroke of her cheek, and she wonders if she simply dreamed it all. She anchors her hand in the scrub's pocket. The entrance hallway short, then a right at the longer corridor that connects the two main wings. Heather and Nurse Amy on the left of the hallway's center stripe. Kayla too, only her steps stray closer to the boundary. The tape dirty, scuffed in spots. Every so often, a missed seam, a sloppy angle addressed with a newer patch.

The stairwell wide. Concrete risers. A mid-floor landing, and Kayla glances up. Two girls in white on the stairwell's other side. The one in front Kayla's size. Blond, pretty. A polite greeting for the nurse but her gaze on Kayla. Heather by her side, a whisper over Kayla's shoulder, "Don't let her stare you down." A taller girl behind the blond, a redhead with thick shoulders and a strain of freckles across a broad nose.

"Look right through her or don't look at all," Heather whispers.

Kayla and Heather on the landing, the other girls halfway down the flight. Nurse Amy takes two quick steps toward the girls in white. "What're you doing out of class?"

The blond's smile a veneer of politeness. "Mr. Thomas sent us to the café to get some paper towels."

The nurse: "These aren't the white stairs."

"Does it matter if everyone's in class—"

Nurse Amy points up the stairwell. "Turn around and go down the other side. Now. Didn't the hallway guard stop you?"

"He wasn't there."

The nurse sighs. "Up, up, ladies. And I will check with the guard. And Mr. Thompson."

The girls in white walk back up. The blond pauses at the top's landing. "Have a good day, Nurse Amy." The redhead lumbering in her wake.

Nurse Amy holds the door. Behind her, a hand-painted poster of blue and red and green. *Positivity, Productivity, Community*. "This is the red stairwell," the nurse says. "And on the second floor of this wing are the red pods and classrooms. Each side has a common room for TV and gatherings. Whites can't be on the red side unless they're supervised, just like you need to be if you ever pass the guard's post and venture into the white side." As Heather passes, the nurse asks, "How's Betty this morning?"

"Nothing out of the ordinary," Heather says.

They pause in the wide hallway. To their left and right, long corridors lined with shut doors. From the hall's end, a hesitant piano, a disharmony soothed by children's voices, one of the patriotic anthems Kayla heard blaring from Slater's porch. Kayla arranges the layout in her head. The east wing. The red stairs. A shorter hallway before them, its center marked by a pair of sawhorses and a metal desk. A man in a green scrub top settles behind the desk. His hands readjust his belt, a newspaper beneath his arm. The nurse turns to Kayla. "Betty's going to test you a little, I imagine. She's in your classes. And your pod. It takes her a while to get used to new things. Stand up for yourself but give her a little room. She usually warms up in time." They pause outside a classroom's shut door. "Think that's good advice, Heather?"

Heather purses her lips. A moment of pause then, "Yes."

The nurse knocks. Kayla looks through the door's small window. A middle-aged man strides from his podium and opens the door. A lanyard and a dangling ID, a loosened tie and rolled-up sleeves. A mustache and thinning hair.

He opens the door and sighs. "Another one?"

"Her name's Kayla," the nurse says.

He steps aside. The whispers behind him. "Come on in. Not like we're doing anything important."

Heather's faint smile. "Nurse Amy said you wouldn't mind the interruption."

"Did she?"

Kayla the last to enter. Nurse Amy and Mr. James huddle behind the desk. Notes on the chalkboard—*fur trade, Mississippi*. The east-facing windows tall and yellowed. The city's grit, the soot of fires. An avalanche of dirtied sun. The girls sitting near the windows reduced to shadows. Her hands clasped before her, Heather drifts to the window just beyond the teacher's desk. Her thin frame at first a silhouette, then consumed by the glare.

A rippling of whispers. The words *new girl* repeated. The

weight of stares upon Kayla. She lifts her gaze. The voices fade, and she studies the dust motes' sun-lit dance. Their journeys random, yet in them, she discerns the loops and dips of her graphs. Testaments to hidden forces and random beauty. Her father told her each recognition of beauty was an invitation, and Kayla trades her body's anchoring physics for a place amid the swirl. A memory. Fifth grade, the riverside. Summer blue and the sun bright upon the water. Kayla blew dandelion seeds, her cheeks wet with tears. A black dress for her and her mother. Her father in his coat and tie, bare feet and rolled-up pants. Her mother braided Kayla's hair as they sat on a boulder. The water lapped the rock, a lullaby's rhythm. The dandelion seeds lifted on the breeze. A moment taken to regroup after Kayla's grandfather's funeral.

"You don't think he's in heaven, do you?" In her, the exhaustion of tears allowed to run dry. A trance woven by the water, by the tug of her mother's hands.

"I like to think of him on a journey." He lifted a smooth stone from the water's edge and cupped it in his palm. "One I'm not wise enough to understand. And I'm sure for a guy like your grandpa, it's a wonderful and amazing trip."

"But it's not the him we know that's doing that."

He threw the stone, a small splash, and joined them on the boulder. He slid his unknotted tie through his collar. "His body is on its own journey, the type of journey this world takes. The tangible things. The things we can see." He wrapped the tie around her neck and secured a knot. "The things that made grandpa the guy we loved, they're not the kinds of gifts we can hold in our hands. That's the part I think is on the journey. Maybe heaven. Or someplace like it." He smiled. "I like to think it's all a mystery, which is pretty cool."

"In Mass they talk about the mystery of faith."

"There are a lot of good things we can learn from Mass."

Kayla smiled. "Like you ever go."

He nodded. "I should. I will. More at least."

A crane flew past, wings outstretched, a glide inches above the water's surface. "What do you think happens?"

"I have no idea."

"What do you want to happen?"

"I'd like to think that when we go, we're released into the all and everything of this life. The oceans and the clouds, the forests and cities. All of it and us just tumbling through."

A sharp voice shatters her drift. "Are you deaf, girl?"

Kayla blinks and struggles to pinpoint the voice amid the shadows and glare.

Mr. James steps from behind his desk. "That's enough, Betty."

"I'm just asking where she's from, Mr. J." The girl's tone jarring after Kayla's drift. "I asked twice, and she's just staring into space." Laughter from the others. "I'm worried she's deaf. Maybe deaf and dumb. Maybe both kinds of dumb."

"I assure you she's not," Mr. James says. "Although there are some mornings I wish I was."

"Oakmont." Kayla's voice dry, still lost amid the river's purr.

"What's that, girl?"

"Oakmont," Kayla says. She takes a breath. "I'm from Oakmont."

"Oakmont? Like south along the river? Isn't that fancy. Most Oakmont girls get to wear white. Who's slumming it now, Miss Oakmont?"

More laughter. The nurse, her clipboard tucked beneath her arm, rests a hand on Kayla's shoulder. "Not a girl here I didn't check in. Not one of you who didn't come in a bit shook up, no matter where you're from or how tough you thought you were. In that way, there aren't any of you who're different than the rest."

"That's the truth, Nurse Amy." Kayla still unable to see Betty's face. "And now tell us another truth—you like us better than them snooty whites. Just a little bit, right?"

The nurse smiles. "You know I don't love one color more than the other. Being fair to all is the only kind of love I'm dishing here."

"I was thinking about coming with you, Nurse Amy," Betty says. "If it's OK with Mr. James."

Mr. James returns to his podium. "That would be agreeable with me."

"And what ails you, Betty?"

"Stomach ache." She groans. "Did you see breakfast today?"

"You know the rules for getting out of class," the nurse says.

Other girls join Betty, a lilting chorus: "Fever. Blood. Vomit."

"Very good." The nurse offers a final squeeze for Kayla's shoulder.

Betty calls out: "I still love you, Nurse Amy!"

A wave as she exits. "And I love you, too."

The class's laughter cut short when Mr. James asks Heather to escort Kayla to Carolyn's desk. Heather steps from the window, a lifting from the light. She leads them down a narrow aisle. A science fact—a hydrogen atom is over 99.9999% empty space, and as she walks, Kayla imagines herself in the same way. Her heart her nucleus, her will and awareness a spinning electron. The machine free to claim the empty space she's left hollow. She squints against the light, but with each step, more comes into focus. Girls in maroon scrub tops. Betty with arms folded and an unapologetic stare. A scrutiny mirrored by the others. Kayla both the new girl and an echo of their stories. Five rows, five desks each, only a few empty seats. Heather motions to the desk behind hers.

The desks old. Hinged wooden lids, varnished and nicked. Kayla's with a pair of etched initials—*cj*. Mr. James at the class's front. "Let's get back to the business at hand, people. Page 88."

Heather turns. She holds up her book. A blue cover. A painting of the Founding Fathers. Men in frilly shirts and leggings and powdered wigs. "In your desk," Heather whispers.

Kayla lifts the lid. A whine of hinges. Inside, a slim metal ledge, a broken pencil. Kayla unrolls a balled paper scrap. A girl's handwriting, a passed note, a smear of ink. The page torn, its message lost. Kayla slides out the blue-covered book and sets it on the desktop.

Mr. James speaks. The roots of the French and Indian War. The book's binding loose. Inside the cover, a twenty-year string of previous owners. Over the names, a red stamp— DISCARDED. Kayla turns the pages, a parade of pictures and maps. New World explorers. The Columbian Exchange. The Pilgrims and the hardship of New England winters. All of it old news. Mr. James lectures about a young George Washington's military exploits at Fort Necessity. Kayla studies Washington's dashing portrait on page 88 and imagines the truths unwritten. Genocide. Smallpox. The brutality of the Middle Passage. Her father's voice: "The victors write the history books. The rest of us have to be smart enough to read between the lines."

Kayla looks up from the book. The girl beside Heather turns in her seat. Her hair short and oddly shorn. Her stare blank and unashamed.

* * *

History ends at 9:00. The French defeated, the Revolution brewing. Math next, a switching of texts. Betty's desk lid slams. A mumbled apology. Her head down fifteen minutes later and her arms folded on her unopened book. The plotting and graphing of lines, the linear relations Kayla learned in second grade. Mr. James walks the aisles. He lets Betty sleep and crouches beside the girl with the cropped hair. A red pencil from his shirt pocket, a line sketched as he explains the connection between equation and graph. A sigh when he stands, a rub of his knee. He picks up Kayla's worksheet and sets it back down. "Very nice," he says.

Betty lifts her head and twirls her finger. A tone sarcastic and bored. "Yeah, Oakmont."

The class dismisses at 10:30, and the girls file out for their morning work shifts. "You're with me," Heather says.

Betty's shoulder bumps Kayla's. Betty shuffling, her eyes half closed, but open enough to know what she's doing. Anger flares in Kayla's hollowed space. She endured Missy Blough's barbs for months before uttering a word, but she's shed that version of herself. She thinks again of a tennis ball and a flashlight, the notion of shared yet opposite worlds, and she wonders how she can be both dead on the inside yet so raw. Betty mumbles, "Watch where you're going, Oakmont."

Before Kayla can respond, Heather tugs her arm and leads her down their wing's stairwell. They keep to the line's left even though they're alone. Heather opens the door and allows Kayla to pass. They walk the downstairs hallway and pass the side corridor that leads to the main entrance and nurse's office. Kayla committing it all to memory. Steps and doors, windows and hallways. Her footsteps a path marked in red. Her eyes open, a dovetailing of the visual and physical. A map of her own. Her desires to know and analyze ramped from the conceptual to the imperative of survival.

"They limit the passing time between us and the whites," Heather says. "Their classes end five minutes earlier. They eat before us. We'll see them after meals and in Large Group after breakfast. Outside that, they like to keep us apart."

A push through the cafeteria's swinging doors. A tiled floor. White walls and beneath the high ceiling lights, the fog of dishwashers and boiling pots. The serving line to their left. Stainless steel, a runner for trays, glass shields and empty warming wells. The kitchen entrances behind, and from them, the clatter of trays slid in and out of ovens. The call of women's voices. A radio and the warm scent of dough. The floor claimed by circular tables, each with eight bolted seats. Caged windows along the far wall. A sturdy woman in a hairnet and blue rubber gloves stacks trays and silverware in the line's cart.

Heather leads Kayla to a nook in the cafeteria's rear. "Wait here," she says and slips inside a supply closet. The closet opposite an alarmed door. The door's window looks out on a dumpster and small loading dock. Next to the closet, another door marked *Staff Only*. Kayla steps into the nook's cramped space, the cafeteria cut from sight, and glances out the door's window. Beyond the loading dock, the schoolyard macadam. The razorwire fence. Beyond the fence, a line of row homes where life, she assumes, goes on uninterrupted.

Heather closes the closet with a nudge of her hip. In her hands, spray bottles and white cloths. She hands one of each to Kayla. She nods to each door. "That's the loading dock. And that's the back stairwell. We're not supposed to use that unless we're with a guard."

The girls work together, each taking half a table, the

surfaces sprayed and wiped. "Do you usually do this on your own?" Kayla asks.

"Carolyn used to help me." She pulls back her hair and tucks it beneath her collar.

"Where did she go?"

"Away. That's all we know. That's all we ever know. She and Betty were pretty tight. At least when they weren't fighting." Heather's rubbing harder when she hits a stubborn spot. The bolted chairs tremble. The veins in her arms strain blue. "Cafeteria's not bad. There's worse places." She grins. "Maybe not, but still, it isn't bad, considering."

The last table, and they return to the supply closet. Heather takes Kayla's rag and bottle and emerges with a pair of wide dust mops. They start at the cafeteria's back. The mop heads silent and gliding, a twisting to reach beneath the tables.

Women in hairnets settle serving trays into the line's wells. Their mitted hands lift the trays' lids. Rising steam, their faces veiled. Rice, a pale mix of corn and beans, squares of white fish in a buttery sauce. Dirt collects along the twined fringes of Kayla's mop, and in her, the sense of rift. The desire to claim her body for herself. Her fear the machine's sustenance also carries its seed. Balancing this, her pocketed necklace. Scant grams yet a connection as heavy as chains. A woman in a stained apron lifts another lid, more fish. The fish's stink, the woman's fogged glasses. Kayla nudges her dirt pile and studies the food. She'll accept the machine's offerings and spit out the seeds. She'll keep herself strong. She'll put together the pieces and recognize her deliverance when it stands before her.

The woman with the fogged glasses speaks. "Wake up, you."

Kayla guides her mop's pile to meet Heather's. The girls crouch. Heather sweeps the dirt, Kayla holding the dustpan.

A guard enters. A young man, a key-jangling belt. More

adornments around his straining belly—a walkie-talkie, a set of zip ties, a baton. He calls to the women behind the serving line. "Ready for round one?"

Kayla dumps the last scoop into the garbage can and wipes her palms on her sweatpants. She rolls the trashcan to the cafeteria's rear and waits as Heather returns their things to the supply closet. She follows Heather back to the entrance. Behind the guard, the doorway glass and a lineup of girls in white. In front, the blond girl from the steps. Behind her, the hulking redhead and a frowning brute who could only be her twin. All three with their eyes fixed on Kayla.

Heather turns. Her tone passive yet clear. "Don't let them stare you down."

The fog's faded from the line worker's glasses. She raises a spatula. "Send them in."

The entrance composed of two swinging doors. The girls in white behind the right door, a single file on their side of the hall. The guard waves Heather and Kayla through the left door. Another guard, this one stoop-shouldered and grandfatherly, straddles the taped center at the end of the white line. A murmur from the hall's other side. *New girl. New girl.*

Heather unflinching, a forward gaze, balance-beam steps. Kayla glances back. The girls in white staring. One with a raised middle finger. Another drags a thumb across her throat. Heather and Kayla reach the stairwell. The slanting bank of sun. Heather squinting, her pearl-shine skin. Her reedy voice. "Told you not to look at them."

"I know, but—"

"Heather?"

The girls pause. Nurse Amy at the stair's bottom. Her words echo up the well's concrete and cinderblock. "Take Kayla to your pod. She'll take Carolyn's bunk. I'll bring her towel and linens."

Heather climbs the stairs. In Kayla, a shifting of memory and vision, new lines for her map. As she stepped from the police car, she blinked away the rain and saw another floor, its windows smaller and unlit. None of the stairwells she's seen reach beyond the second. Perhaps she was mistaken, fooled by fear and the night.

Mr. James's class, then down the red wing to another door. Their sneakers' light squeak across the tile. Inside, a narrow hallway and walls of unadorned plywood nailed to vertical beams. Kayla pictures her morning classroom cut in half. Five bunks. At the end of each bunk, a footlocker and small set of shelves. Along one wall, a long desk, mismatched chairs. The bunk in the near corner stripped. A footlocker with a yawning lid.

Betty sits by the window. A vigil fixed on the schoolyard below. She turns once. Her chiding tone replaced by indifference. "You're not in Kansas anymore, Oakmont."

Two girls sit cross-legged on opposite ends of a bunk. Playing cards in their hands, rummy runs and triplets and a long discard pile on the pilled blanket. The nearest girl the one with the oddly cropped hair. The other girl obviously her sister, the shared configurations of noses and eyes and chins.

Heather gestures toward the girls. "That's Linda and Chris."

"I'm Linda," says the one with short hair. She offers a wave.

The other girl lays down three kings. "I'm Chris."

"And you kind of know Betty," Heather says. "Everyone, this is Kayla."

Linda picks a card from the deck. She and her sister speak in near unison. "Hi, Kayla."

"I'm sticking with Oakmont until I change my mind to say otherwise," Betty says. "What're they dishing out down there today?"

"Fish," Heather says.

"Blah." Betty sticks out her tongue and turns back to the window. "Doubt it's even real fish anyway."

"Nurse Amy!" Chris says.

The nurse enters. She hands Kayla the pail with its soap and toothbrush and washrag. Kayla's name printed on the side in black marker, another girl's name scribbled out. She sets the folded sheets and blankets on the bed, but before she turns, Linda embraces her. A hug, a wordless history. Linda steps back, a squeeze of the nurse's hand before returning to her card game.

The nurse speaks to Kayla. "The others will help you out. Just follow their lead. They're a good bunch."

Betty keeps her attention on the window. "I'm not rolling out the welcome mat for anyone."

The nurse touches Kayla's shoulder. "Betty will warm up."

"All I got to say is Oakmont better not be a chatty one. I can't stand another running mouth in my life."

Kayla follows the nurse to the door. Her tone soft so the others won't hear. "The letter? If I write it, you'll help me send it off?"

A sigh, the exhaustion of a long shift. A hand on Kayla's shoulder. "Sure. But get yourself settled first. There's a whole new routine to get used to."

Heather takes one end of the sheet and Kayla grabs the other. They each give a snap, the sheet pulled over the corners and tucked in. Betty at the window. "Oakmont's probably used to having her maid do that."

Chris looks up from her cards. "Is Oakmont really nice?"

Kayla circles the bed, the sheet tucked beneath the mattress and the cot's net of metal springs. "It was."

"They got toilets made of gold and . . ." Betty's voice trails.

"Hold up. Hold up." She waves, and the others join her at the window. "Here we go, ladies."

Kayla the last to reach the window. A view of the building's back. The macadam moat. The street and houses beyond the fence. A guard swings back the fence's double gates. A black pickup rolls in, a splash through the macadam's puddles. The guard relocks the gate. The pickup jerks a series of tight turns, its reverse siren chirping. The guard waves until the truck's bumper nears the loading dock directly below the pod's window. The girls press their foreheads against the glass. The driver steps out. A young man, a baseball cap and scruffy goatee. He pulls back the bed's tarp and reaches into a box. A handshake exchange, the cigarette carton slipped beneath the guard's coat.

Betty smiles. "You'd better be coming through for us, Zacky."

"He said he'd bring some pens this time," Linda says. "I hope he does. And paper."

"He'd better be bringing more than that." Betty turns. Kayla at the window's far end. "What're you looking at, Oakmont?"

Kayla considers her, then turns her gaze back outside.

"You'd better not be a talker." Betty rests her cheek against the window, her neck craning.

"I'm less a talker than you seem to be."

"Yeah, well I got a right to talk, Oakmont. I've been here longer than all of you."

The driver carries a pair of stacked boxes into the cafeteria's rear entrance. "My name's Kayla."

"Kayla? Ha!" Betty shakes her head. "I'll bet half the princesses in Oakmont are named Kayla."

"I think Kayla's a pretty name," Chris says.

"Living with you and your sister is like living with fucking Chip and Dale," Betty says.

Chris smiles. "She calls us Chip and Dale sometimes."

A buzz from the intercom. The girls pull back from the window. "Fish," Betty says. "Dried out, foul-ass fish." Heather and the sisters line up at the door. Betty stands on a chair then climbs onto the desk. She raises herself onto her tiptoes. With a stretch and reach, she pushes aside a ceiling tile. "How am I looking?"

Heather at the door. "You're good."

Betty gropes in the black space then returns the tile. She climbs down and tosses a half dozen cigarettes on Kayla's bunk. She smiles. "New girl's got to stash our loosies for a spell until we see what's what."

Heather snaps her fingers. "That mean's Panda Bear's coming to round us up," Betty says. "You'd better hide those cigs or else you'll have some explaining to do."

Betty and the sisters look at her. Betty still smiling but not the sisters. Heather snaps her fingers twice. "Better hustle, Oakmont," Betty says.

The cigarettes' paper smooth against her palm, a loose cradling. Outside, a man barks orders. The voices of the girls from the adjoining pods. Kayla slides her hand into her scrub's pocket. Then the touch of her necklace.

Three quick snaps of Heather's fingers. Kayla looks around. She's only seen this room as a collection of its most basic elements—its windows and beds, desks and chairs—now, a mouse's vision. A hiding place, a crevice beneath the obvious. The guard's voice just outside the door. Kayla picks up her pillow and slides the cigarettes deep into the case.

"They'd better not get crushed," Betty says.

A face at the doorway. The bald guard with the thin beard, the one from her break-room dreams, the smooth-headed silhouette against the soda-machine light. A stain on his green scrub, blood perhaps, faded. He surveys the room before his gaze settles on Kayla. "What's the hold up, ladies?"

Betty in the lead as they file out. "I don't think the new girl's a real quick learner."

The girls lean against the corridor's opposite wall. Betty in front of Kayla, Heather behind. The guard marches up then down, counting as he goes. The alcohol scent of his aftershave wafts over Kayla. He reaches the line's front and waves. "Let's roll, reds."

Kayla turns to Heather. "Panda Bear?"

Betty's voice low. A slowing step, the distance increased between her and the guard. "Because one day he drives up and there's this big-ass panda bear in his passenger seat. He bought it for his girl, but she didn't want it."

"Not long after that, she didn't want him," Heather says.

Betty turns back when they reach the stairwell landing. "Can you blame the sister?"

"So he drove around with it in his car," Heather says. "For like a month."

Linda pokes her head over Heather's shoulder. "It was kind of creepy."

"But not as creepy as him and his skinny-ass beard," Betty says.

They claim one of the cafeteria's round tables. Another guard, this one with a wide belly and greasy blond hair, at the entrance. The women in their hairnets clear the serving trays. The door in the cafeteria's rear opens and closes as the pickup driver stacks boxes outside the supply closet. He pauses, a tip of his cap for Betty.

She smiles and speaks softly. "Thataboy, Zacky." Her fork flakes a white-gray sliver from her fish. "You like eating, Oakmont? Because there's some things to learn here. One is there's never seconds for the red lunch. Good news is usually no one wants seconds of this shit."

"It's bad, but it's not super-duper bad," Chris says.

Linda lifts her fork. "It's been worse."

"Shut up, both of you. Jesus." Betty points her fork at Kayla. "But sometimes they have sheet cake or sweet rolls. Somehow they manage not to fuck them up too much."

"That's when there's any left for us," Heather says.

"Don't get me started." Betty turns to Heather. "You done cleaning up down here?"

Heather nods.

"So you'll take care of the closet tomorrow."

"Yep."

"Keep an eye on Oakmont here. Don't want anyone messing up the routine."

Kayla brings another forkful to her mouth. The fish dry and cold and bland. The other girls' conversation littered with codes and established truths. Kayla's plan—shut up and listen, their words more pieces of the puzzle. She washes down the fish with a sip of water. Food and observation—these will be her weapons. She'll keep her eyes open. She'll learn. She'll ignore the wilderness all around and focus on the path. She'll fit in where she can, make herself invisible when she can't, fight when she has to. She'll walk the hallways and stairwells until her map burns vivid as neon. Fish, stews, stale bread, sweet rolls, a bed to sleep in and a roof above—she'll accept the machine's offerings and bide her time. Her focus in the moment. Her destiny waiting, a reunion beyond the fence's razor wire.

"Alright, reds." Panda Bear claps his hands. "Let's move out."

Trays in hand, the girls line up at the dishwashing station's window. The clatter from the window, the warmth and wet steam. Kayla behind Betty. The other guard by the tray drop. A slim cord snakes from beneath his collar, earbuds tucked beneath his greasy hair, his boot tapping. Each girl pauses before him, an inspection and a nod before he waves them on.

Betty turns. "And this one here's Mr. Heavy Metal." They reach the line's front. Betty sets her tray on the window's tiled ledge. She hands over her plate and cup then holds up her fork and knife and spoon. The guard nods and Betty tosses the silverware into the sudsy bin. The utensils rattle, and when Betty steps behind the guard, she raises her hands. A pair of devil horns, her tongue out. "Heavy metal, baby."

* * *

Kayla's first night in the pod. Lights out, the other girls talking. Kayla listens. Her map growing. The cigarettes returned, yet the tobacco scent lingers on her pillow. Betty's tone quieter. A story about her uncle's house, backyard horseshoes, lightning bugs kept in a jar then released in a sparkling fountain. The sisters impossible to distinguish in the dark, their voices like competing halves of an echo. Heather's bunk next to Kayla's. Heather with the least to say, but when she speaks, the others listen.

Silence, the beginning of drift. A reunion with the machine's stripped pulse. The courtyard lights angle up. The ceiling above Kayla dark, but just beyond, a watery shine. She wonders if she'll sleep. The thrum of her heart. The bad electricity in her head, the projector waiting to sputter to life. A floorboard squeaks, a scrape of metal on wood. Kayla turns to see Linda pushing her bunk until it rests against her sister's.

A whisper: "Goodnight, Kayla."

"Night, Heather."

Betty's raspy voice: "Don't you two ever shut up?"

The sisters, curled in their adjoining beds, laugh.

Kayla slides the necklace from her pocket. She turns, holding herself still as she secures the clasp behind her neck. She lies back, her palm resting over the cross, her eyes open. She grows accustomed to the dark, and the ceiling's black and white blend into a field of ash. She fights the urge to rock by clenching and releasing her muscles. Arms, legs, chest—the rigidity of seizures, the release of death. She falls inward; her body pushed back, the squeak of grinding molars, pain in her jaw. The demand comes in waves. Minutes apart, then longer.

She's forgotten the feel of hours—these days of running and hiding—but reason tells her a few have passed. Around her, the machine's purr, the murmur of sleeping breath. She drifts. A surrender, if not to sleep then at least to a floating pool. Her body offered to the ether, to the ceiling's lake of gray.

* * *

She wakes to music on the loudspeaker. The pool in which she'd been drifting evaporates, a delivery from the hallway outside her father's office. Light spilled from the diorama, a shine on floor tile that held like glue to her bare feet. The otter's glassy eyes upon her, and it rose onto its hind legs and spoke even though its mouth didn't move. *This is my home, Kayla . . .*

Linda pushes her bunk back. Heather slides into her flip-flops and drapes a towel over her shoulder. The music soft at first, then louder, a tune Slater played often on his patio. "*My America, I'll fight for you. Holy America, I'll bleed for you.*" Betty still in bed, and when the song swells into its chorus, she pulls her pillow over her face and screams. Kayla follows the others' lead and gathers her towel and pail.

"Morning, Kayla," Linda says. "Morning," her sister adds.

Betty shuffles past. Her eyes slits. "You'd better not be a morning person like Chip and Dale here, Oakmont. Talkers and morning people can all go to hell."

Linda plays with her cropped bangs. "Didn't you sleep well, Betty?"

"Shut up, Linda. Jesus."

The bathroom down the hall. "Oldest pod goes first," Heather says. "That's us." The bathroom tiled in yellow and white. A drain at the center of the floor's gentle slope. A series of stalls along one wall. Opposite, six sinks, and above, a wall-length mirror. The girls line up at the sinks, Kayla taking the empty spot between Heather and Betty.

Kayla's fingers beneath the spigot. A waiting for warmth that doesn't come. The splash of tepid water, a tiny bar of soap. Her eyes covered as she rubs the towel over her cheeks. She slings the towel over her shoulder and is met by the staring reflections of Heather and Betty and the sisters.

"What?" Kayla asks.

Betty reaches out. Her wet hand against Kayla's throat, a lifting of the cross. Her tone quiet. "Shit, Oakmont. You can't wear that around."

Kayla fumbles with the clasp. "I forgot—"

"You need to hide it," Heather says. "At least during the day. They'll take it."

Kayla slides the necklace into her pocket. Panda Bear's gruff call from the hallway: "Let's hustle, pod one. Pod two, get those beds made."

The girls gather their things. "Where'd you get that?" Betty asks.

"It's my mom's."

Chris by Kayla's side as they file into the hallway. "It's pretty."

"It is," Linda adds.

The girls back in their pod. Betty silent as Kayla folds the necklace into a blanket and tucks it into the bottom of her footlocker. Kayla makes her bed and slides into her maroon top. The girls file into the main hallway. Kayla glances down the line and guesses the youngest are six or seven. Babies, their voices high, yet she wonders what hauntings they carry. Betty at the line's front, her shoulders slumped against the wall, head back and eyes closed. Chris behind her then Linda, her hands knotting a loose braid into her sister's hair. Kayla next and Heather behind her.

Panda Bear at the line's end. The fluorescent lights shine on his shaved head. The jangle of his keys as he makes his count. He stops at the line's front. "OK, ladies, let's move."

A single line. Betty setting the pace, shuffling steps and a hummed tune. Kayla looks down the hallway that connects the red and white wings. At the hall's center, a guard at a desk. The dividing sawhorses. Opposite the desk, a central stairwell, and she wonders if these are the stairs that lead to the third floor.

They exit the red stairwell and line up outside the cafeteria's double doors. Betty resumes her wall-leaning pose. Panda Bear marches by, another silent count. On the other side of the doors' glass, the girls in white drop off their trays and form a line of their own. Heavy Metal chews a roll and laughs with one of the cafeteria ladies. The girls in white file past, his silverware-checking duties overlooked. He wipes icing from his mouth. He reaches the line's front and opens the door. The whites march past, and in Kayla, the awareness of stares and whispers. A blond girl with pimpled cheeks flashes a scissor-cutting gesture as she nears Linda.

"Anyone ugly as you shouldn't be drawing attention," Betty snaps. Chris and Linda rub their temples with raised middle fingers.

"Hey, hey." Panda Bear at the line's end, a straddling of the taped line. "Let's keep it civil up there, Betty."

Near the line's end, the blond girl Kayla saw on the steps. Behind her, the hulking redheads. The blond stops in front of Kayla, a glint in her eye. She steps across the line and strokes Kayla's cheek. "She's a cute little thing, isn't she?"

Betty's hand a flash. A smack of flesh, the blond girl's fingers batted away. The blond's fists jerk up, then Betty's. Heavy Metal hustles between them and pushes Betty against the wall. A smile from the blond girl before she moves on.

Betty squirms as Panda Bear latches onto her arm and rousts her across the threshold. "Why're you grabbing me when they're the ones getting all touchy?"

"Just shut up and eat." Panda Bear releases her with a shove. "Too early for you and your attitude."

Betty adjusts her scrub top, her tone lower. The girls at the serving line's head. "Wish I knew if he was more ignorant or stupid. That way I'd know what to hate the most about his ass."

Heather takes a tray and hands one to Kayla. "He sure isn't colorblind."

The women in hairnets scoop out powdered eggs. The serving trays behind the glass less than half full, the steam no longer rising from the wells. Each girl given a sausage slab. "Cold eggs," Betty says. "The breakfast of champions."

The girls claim their table. Kayla's toast crumbles beneath her butter knife. "Forget it, Oakmont," Betty says. "Cold eggs, cold toast." She shoves a forkful into her mouth. "Just shut down those taste buds and swallow." She waves the fork in Kayla's direction. "You've got to stick up for yourself, sister. Can't let a white step to you without setting her back on her heels. Can't let them cross that line. Especially that bitch Donna."

"Donna's kind of their leader," Chris says.

"And Betty's right." Linda ducks a bit and whispers. "She's a real bitch. And the redheads are mean. Super mean."

"Don't forget stupid." Betty takes a bite of sausage. "Lord knows there's enough stupid to go around."

Heather smiles. "They don't smell so hot either."

"Amen," Betty says.

The cafeteria workers break down the line. The trays lifted from their wells. One of the women hums along with the piped-in music. A post Shut-In song, callings to Jesus and America. Betty finishes her milk. "Only thing worse than the food is their goddamn tunes."

The blond girl's touch still on Kayla's cheek. Next time will be different. The girl's hand squeezed, her fingers pulled back until her knees buckle. Kayla's fork scrapes the plate. Fuel. She needs fuel.

Panda Bear cups his hands alongside his mouth. "Let's move out, ladies."

Kayla's table at the line's end. The girls with trays in hand, their pace slowed by Heavy Metal's inspection. The dishwasher's steam thins beneath the high ceiling. Linda and Chris whispering. Heather silent, a calm Kayla envies. Betty stops, and the others bunch behind her.

"What's that?" Betty nods to the circular tray at the serving line's end. The tray covered with a white baking sheet and scattered with crumbs and flecks of icing. "Did they have sweet rolls again?"

The cafeteria lady slides on her rubber gloves. "We did. Earlier."

The dishwasher drop-off waits just beyond the serving line. "And they were good," Heavy Metal says.

"Thanks, hon." The cafeteria lady rests her fist against her hip. "We do our best with what we've got."

Betty not moving. The gap between her and the girl in front of her widens. "What do you mean 'were good'? Like there's none left? Again? Like again like it's been three times in the past two weeks?"

Heavy Metal motions her to move along. "Don't get snitty. I should take you back to the street. Lots of folks are getting by with less than you these days."

Heather steps around Kayla. A rising onto tiptoes, a whisper in Betty's ear. "Forget it. We have other things to take care of."

Betty slams her tray to the floor. Her glass and plate jump. The silverware scatters. Kayla freezes. The sisters draw back. Heather shakes her head, then speaks to Kayla: "Just get out of her way."

"Fuck your fucking sweet rolls!" Betty grabs the baking sheet, and with a grunt and two-handed release, sends it flying.

The tray's paper cover flutters off, a pinwheeling of crumbs. A flash of silver, a whirling flight and an echoing crash. A moment of tranquility, of perfect balance. The cafeteria ladies still as statues, their trays and utensils in hand. The other girls silent. Even the guards frozen, a spell broken when Betty snatches Heather's tray and hurls it above the deserted tables.

Heavy Metal and Panda Bear step forward. Their mouths grim and set. Betty takes Chris's tray, a grunt and a heave toward the serving line. The cafeteria ladies duck and a plate shatters behind them. Kayla's tray next, a single, swift motion, snatch and release.

Heavy Metal pushes forward, his boot stomping Kayla's foot. Betty darts off, avoiding their snares, a passing of the serving line where she topples the tray's rolling cart. Next the silverware, handfuls flung, a dozen pings, odd, metal notes. Panda Bear slips on a clump of eggs, cursing as he scrambles to his feet then slipping again. The floor littered with broken plates and spilled juice. Heather slides a fork into her scrub pocket. Linda stoops, the cuff of her sweat pant lifted and a knife slid into her sock. The chase escalates, Betty cursing and weaving between tables until she stops in an open space near the entrance doors. She stands, panting, hands raised. "OK, OK. I'm done."

Panda Bear the first to reach her. He snatches her wrist and wrenches her arm behind her back. Betty's body arches, a grimace but no cry for mercy. Heavy Metal latches onto her other arm, his free hand grabbing her neck, her head pushed until she's bent double. "Fuck you," she snorts. Her wriggling only bringing a rougher handling.

"She's not fighting, you fucking goons!" A cry from Heather, a tone Kayla finds more jolting than the guards' violence.

Panda Bear turns. "You're next if you don't shut up!"

"She's not fighting!" Heather's cries picked up by Linda and Chris then the rest of the girls. The cafeteria echoes with their voices.

The guards on either side of Betty, her arms pinned behind her, a duck walk across the scattered trays and silverware. Betty turns as they push her through the cafeteria doors. "You take care of things, Heather. You hear me?"

Nurse Amy leads the reds down the center hallway and through a set of double doors. Kayla's map morphs, the absorption of details, an acquiring of depth. This new space a combination gym and auditorium. The white pods, she believes, overhead, just as theirs are over the cafeteria. At the gym's far end, a backboard, a painted basketball key on a pinewood floor. The walls lined with mats. Cages over the windows and lights. At the near end, four steps lead to a wooden stage, its recesses cloaked by tall green curtains. A podium in front of the stage. The taped centerline runs between neat rows of folding chairs, the right section already claimed by the whites. Donna in an aisle seat. Her voice rises as Kayla and Heather pass, "Sweet rolls were good this morning. Too bad some people missed out."

Kayla follows Heather to the last row. They sit, the sisters beside them. Beneath their sneakers, more lines, ones painted years before the floor's center divide, boundaries for hopscotch and four-square and volleyball. The smallest reds claim the front seats, Nurse Amy rubbing their heads as they pass. A tall man strides to the podium. The hinging of his knees and elbows slightly off-kilter, an ungainly stride offset by his focus, his air of command. A black suit, a reverend's white collar. An armband of red and white. A face that reminds Kayla of her uncles', one that knew the sun and hard work. His hair short and curled, black fading to gray. Kayla guesses he's nearly six-and-a-half feet tall, a frame more comfortable beneath the other end's backboard. He sets down a Bible bristling with bookmarks, grips the podium's sides, and looks over his audience.

Chris taps Kayla's shoulder. "That's Reverend Blake."

"We just call him the Deacon," whispers Linda. "He kind of runs things."

"Nurse Amy really runs things," Chris says.

"Yeah," Linda says, "but the Deacon's the big-wig type."

"We do this every day after breakfast." Chris rolls her eyes. "Sometimes it's a drag."

Heather crosses her arms. "Sometimes?"

Chris nods. "Well I guess sometimes suck more than others. All depends on how long the Deacon wants to talk."

"Or what's up his ass," Linda says.

The Deacon slides a pair of glasses from his pocket. Nurse Amy approaches him, a huddled conversation. He nods as he flips the Bible's thin pages. Kayla leans toward Heather. The auditorium thick with chatter yet she still whispers, "What's going to happen to Betty?"

"I'm guessing isolation for a few days."

"This isn't her first time," Linda says.

"I'm worried," Chris says. "What if they—"

Heather cuts her off. "They won't. She'll be back in a few days."

Panda Bear and Heavy Metal enter and join the podium's gathering. Heavy Metal's hair disheveled, Panda Bear busy adjusting his belt and tucking in his shirt. The Deacon slides his glasses up his nose. The guards retreat, Heavy Metal by the door, Panda Bear behind the folding chairs. Nurse Amy leaves but not before a final wave to the youngest girls in the front rows.

The Deacon raises his hands, his palms up and shoulder-high. A pose that reminds Kayla of the cranes she's seen skimming over the calm river. The girls stand, Kayla a moment behind.

"Lord, thank you for this day and its blessings." His eyes closed now, a wide smile. An expression as though he's imagining himself as Kayla's crane, soaring flight and the kiss of wind. His voice a baritone of ice and stone. The girls with their hands clasped before them. All with their heads bowed save Kayla and Heavy Metal and Donna. "Please, Lord, help us to use Your bounty to serve. Let us follow Your light along the righteous path. Amen."

A brief scuffing of chairs. The Deacon waits until all are still, then another pause that adds to the room's heaviness. He adjusts his glasses then latches onto his coat's lapels. Another beaming smile. "It's a good day for the Lord, isn't it, ladies?"

Calls of *yes* and *amen* from the whites. A silver sheen eases into the Deacon's words. "I understand there was some unpleasantness during second breakfast." Smiles among the whites. "Which is unfortunate because we live in a time of great need. The scriptures are full of passages about the power of humility and grace. So many have so little these days that we must remind ourselves that despite our sufferings, we are never truly lost, not as long as we have faith, which is just as vital as food and shelter and the clothes on our backs. So with this in mind, let us pray for ourselves and for the young lady who couldn't be with us this morning." He lowers his head and draws a deep breath. "Dear Lord, hear our prayer. We ask for Your guidance in these difficult times. We thank You for Your abundant gifts, and we ask for the wisdom to use these gifts for Your greater glory."

Kayla bows her head. She thinks about praying but stops short. Not here. Not with strangers. Maybe later, her bed, beneath the protection of the dark and the silence of a sleeping room. A glance to her side. Heather's clasped hands, the cuff of her long-sleeved T-shirt pulled up just enough to reveal her wrist's crude tattoo. Her thin lips moving, her eyes squeezed shut.

* * *

History quieter without Betty. Kayla believes even Mr. James misses her, his lesson on the Revolution limping along, no one in the mood to raise their hands. Then math, Kayla's worksheet finished in three minutes. Mr. James busy with the youngest girls and his stack of homemade flash cards.

Kayla sets her sheet aside. A delicate tug, a page torn from her thin notebook. She balks, a blank moment, a reckoning of the white space and all that brims within. She steadies herself and her pencil scratches over the paper.

Dear Mom,

When this finds you, please know that I am well. I'm living in the city in a school for girls. One of the girls says we're on Forster Street, but I'm not sure. There is food and I have a bed. I miss you, and when I think of your hands holding this letter, I feel less alone. I'm dreaming about the day we can be together again—and the belief that this will happen soon and the knowing that you are waiting for me is enough to see me through whatever awaits.

She looks over what she's written. She hears voices—hers and her mother's—words that evaporate into the morning light. She brings her pencil back to the paper.

"Kayla," Linda whispers.

The voices fade. Mr. James stands behind her. She slides her math worksheet over her letter and sits up straight.

A moment's pause. "Very good," he says and moves on.

Kayla folds the letter, in half then in half again. The creases crisp and straight. The paper slid into her scrub top's pocket.

***

Heather in the cafeteria supply closet. Their spray bottles and rags returned. Kayla outside, not wanting to look until she's invited. She gazes through the dirty glass of the loading dock door. An alarm on the door, and beyond, a small patch of raised concrete, a few steps to the playground's macadam. Trash on the blacktop, papers on the breeze, a rolling cup. On the other side of the locked gate, a girl on a bicycle, her knees pumping. A flash between parked cars.

Heather hands Kayla a pair of dust mops. "When we're done, we've got to take back what Zach's dropped off. You good with that?"

"Yes."

"Good." She turns off the closet light and shuts the door. Kayla leans a mop's long handle toward Heather. "No," Heather says, "the other one."

The glide of Kayla's mop reminds her of sawdust-littered floors. Her uncles. Her father. She closes her eyes and sees his face, the sun's glint on his glasses. She can still be his daughter, the girl he took to see the riverside's wonders. They can take away everything in the moment but not her past.

"You OK?"

Scents from the kitchen—soup, grilled cheese. Kayla yearns to lie down. Here, now. Yearns to fold her body into the earth and never rise again. Yearns to both never think of her father and forever be with him. She opens her eyes. "Yeah."

"You look kind of pale."

"I'm good. Thanks."

Heather slides her hand from the top of her broom's handle. "Mine's the one with the nicks." She releases her grip to show three small grooves carved into the wood, scars of natural grain beneath the varnish. She closes her hand and returns to sweeping. The cafeteria ladies bring their trays. The clamor of metal, the open space's watery acoustics. The kitchen's radio and voices. "One's for my mom. One's for my dad. One's for my sister."

Kayla's dust pile grows. "Maybe you can tell me about them sometime."

"Maybe."

And if Kayla stays long enough, maybe she'll tell Heather about the botanist strung up on the mob's vine. The poet who melted into the night. The girls kneel and sweep their piles into a dustpan.

They return to the supply closet. Heather hands Kayla her mop and nods to the door. "Keep an eye out, OK?"

Kayla at the closet's threshold. Her attention split. The cafeteria ladies' final preparations, the tying of aprons, the grabbing of spatulas and ladles. The whites line up outside the entry doors. Kayla steps back. The closet cramped. Walls lined with shelves, shadows beneath a naked bulb and the memory of Helen's secret room. Heather crouches and slides out a box marked with a red dot. "It's light. Betty's going to be pissed."

Heather pulls out wads of brown wrapping. Inside, a tube of hand lotion. A disposable lighter. A cigarette pack and a pint of whiskey. She returns the paper and slides the box back onto the shelf. She stands. "How do we look?"

Kayla checks the cafeteria. The whites approach the serving line. Panda Bear with his back to Kayla. Donna and the redheads staring. "We're OK."

"Here." Heather hands Kayla the cigarettes. Kayla slides them into her scrub pocket. "No, like this."

Heather lifts her top, the hem of her T-shirt clenched between her teeth. Her belly exposed and her sweatpants lowered. She slides the pint and lotion beneath her underwear's elastic. She knots her sweatpants' tie and lowers her T-shirt and scrub. She smiles. "The baggy style isn't all bad. Just hold your hands in front of you and walk slow."

The cigarettes in Kayla's underwear. The tug of elastic, the box's corners hard against her belly. Heather shuts the closet, and they step back into the alcove. Donna and the redheads glance over their shoulders. Kayla imitates Heather's posture. Her hands grasped in front of her, an anchoring of the pack against her belly. In Kayla, the charge of contrasting currents, one fearful, the chance of being caught, of the guards' hands upon her—and beneath, another current, the freedom of giving over, of sisterhood and placing herself outside the machine. Her lot balanced upon this tightrope walk past Panda Bear and the whites.

Donna doesn't look up as they pass her table. Her sandwich held near her lips. "Our box better not be light, cunts."

* * *

D ays pass. Kayla the only one tall enough to take Betty's place in stashing their take above the ceiling tiles, the others voting to wait for Betty's return to sample the goods. In Kayla, a growing appreciation of the surrounding tides. The exchange of magazines, the bartering of favors and chores. The running feuds between the whites and reds. The guard who spikes his thermos coffee. The crackers and rolls the cafeteria ladies sneak out in their purses. The flow of rumors from beyond the fence. Whispers of unrest. Predictions for a harsh winter. Looming food shortages. Kayla listens—in the cafeteria and bathroom and common area. She imagines the children's game of telephone, the butchered messages passed down the line, yet beneath—perhaps—a glint of truth. Today's rumor— morning's tirade between Betty and the Deacon. Betty given an extra day in isolation for complaining about the third floor's mice, the Deacon's prayers drowned by her curses.

History class—the surrender at Yorktown and the Louisiana Purchase. In math, Kayla takes the end-of-the-year exam. A perfect score followed by a hallway conversation. Kayla's partial confession of the courses she's taken, Mr. James's promise to track down a more challenging text. Until then, they strike a deal. Kayla the tutor for her pod-mates while he works with the younger girls. Kayla unsure at first, but her hesitance is no match for the sisters' enthusiasm. Their desks pushed together, Kayla illustrates the rules for multiplying and dividing exponents, for finding equations of lines and parabolas. Linda leans close and whispers, "You explain it better than Mr. James."

"A lot better," Chris says. "Nothing against Mr. James."

Linda's quick echo: "No, nothing against Mr. James."

Heather nods. "But true nonetheless."

After lunch, forty-five minutes of outdoor rec. The red section of macadam in the building's rear, their pod's windows above. Monkey bars and the swingless swing set. A kickball diamond's painted bases. The delivery gate and its thick padlock. The cafeteria's loading platform, and in its nook of brick and concrete, swirls of wind-swept trash. Kayla stands at the cusp of the building's shadow. A small row of windows runs above their pod, the glass reflecting the clouds and weak sun. Kayla waves just in case Betty is looking down.

A backboard and hoop on the white side. A ball's dribbling twang, the clank of iron. Another rumor—the Deacon's plans for a three-on-three tournament. His playing days in high school and Bible College. His belief in the morality of sport and the purity of toil, metaphors he extolls in his morning talks. His office door open as Kayla and the others pass—shelved trophies, framed photographs and yellowed newspaper clippings. Whites against reds, the rumors claim, three age groups. Heather and Kayla lean against the fence just beyond the younger girls' kickball game. Linda and Chris playing too, the little ones begging until the sisters joined them. "You ever play basketball?" Heather asks.

"Some. A CYO league for a couple years." She picks up the underinflated kickball that's bounced their way, an underhand toss that Linda juggles and drops.

"Good," Heather says.

The guards corral the reds after rec. A meeting in the cafeteria and the assigning of new, temporary chores, tasks assumed as the whites work on a project for the Deacon, banners and posters completed in the secrecy of their upstairs wing. Grumbles from some, but Kayla enjoys her chores' mindlessness. Their invitations to daydream. The opportunity to move, to investigate. Panda Bear calls her name and Heather's. "You two are with me."

They sweep the white and center stairwells. When they're done, he leads them to the cafeteria's alcove and opens the staff-only staircase. A trudge up, these stairs steeper, narrower. No security cameras, no dividing line. No windows, a single light on each landing. Rising echoes. The second floor and here, finally, the stairs continue, a climb to a locked door.

Panda Bear sits on the top stair. He plugs in his earbuds. His cheeks milky blue in the shine of his cupped phone. His thumbs tap, the girls left to sweep, a spiraling return to the cafeteria's alcove. Heather's words softer than the whisk of their brooms. Kayla listens, and her map expands beyond the physical. The history of Betty and Zach, the school's delivery driver a friend of Betty's cousin, the two men petty players in the black market. Heather speaks of the whites' ambush of Linda, a reprisal for a coughing fit during Donna's Sunday service solo. Linda held down; her hair smeared with rubber cement. The redheads one of the school's first occupants, Philadelphia girls, their parents vaporized. Donna's mother a suicide during the Shut-In's long winter, her father a cop—maybe crooked, maybe not—gunned down in their driveway. On the first-floor landing, Heather pulls up her T-shirt's cuff and explains her tattoo—an outline of a dove, smaller than a quarter, the beak pointing up if she raised her hand. The work done with smuggled ink, Betty and the sisters huddled close as Carolyn worked the needle. The others planned to get their tattoos the next night but then Carolyn's removal, the ink discovered in her footlocker along with cigarettes and a toothbrush handle melted and filed to point.

"She never told us about the shiv." Heather returns to sweeping. "But I guess she felt she needed it."

Morning convocation. The Deacon at his podium. Rapture in his voice. The sanctity of work and the gift of new beginnings. A describing of the love that pours from God's outstretched arms, the invitation to a woman's glorious role in the new society. The return to tradition. To family. To holiness. His believer's flush, his hands raised. He asks the girls to stand and pray. The whites adopt his pose, their arms lifted, palms up. Some of the younger reds do the same, but in the back, Kayla and Heather and the sisters stand still. Their hands clasped before them. The sisters with their heads bowed. Heather's gaze fixed on the Deacon, her expression today blank and cool.

"Hear us, Lord." The Deacon louder now, his voice rumbling through the auditorium's wide spaces. "Hear the prayers of your humble servants."

* * *

Betty returns ten minutes before lights out. Old John her escort. Old John usually on the night shift, silver beard and weathered face. A thermos of spiked coffee. A heavy right leg, his boot heel worn. A crook in his hip and a sigh when he settles behind the guard's desk that separates the red wing from the white. Kayla hears them first—Betty's laugh then Old John's. Kayla sets down the magazine she's borrowed from the common area. Some of the pages torn, none of them stiff. "The whites get them first," Linda explained.

Betty pauses in the doorway. An arcing wave. "Howdy, campers."

The sisters run forward. Their card game abandoned; hugs that knock Betty back a step. She turns to the guard. "You on all night, John?"

"Yep."

Betty smiles. "I feel safer, then."

"Lights out soon, ladies." He shuffles out. The scrape of his heel, the keychain's jangle. He turns. "I'm sure you'll want to catch up some, but keep it hush-hush, OK?"

Betty holds a finger to her lips. "Hush-hush, A-OK."

The door shuts. A hug from Heather then again from Linda and Chris. Betty silent, her eyes shut for each embrace, a slap for Heather's back. Betty nods at Kayla. "How's old Oakmont working out?"

"She's really good at math," Linda says.

Then Chris: "Mr. James says she knows more than him. Like a lot more."

Betty sits on her cot, and her palm smooths the blanket. "I'll bet old Mr. James missed me, at least in his own tight-ass way."

"She's doing OK," Heather says. "Helped sneak up our stuff."

Betty grins. "Oakmont's joined the panty brigade." She offers a fist, and Kayla's knuckles meet hers. "Bet none of your crew back home can say that."

The lights flicker. Old John's voice from the hallway. "Lights out, ladies! Lights out!"

"He's on all night." Betty raises an invisible bottle to her lips.

Another flicker, the last warning, and within a minute, darkness. The girls settle into their cots. *Goodnight. Goodnight.* Kayla pulls up her blanket. The ceiling with its fields of white and black and gray, a horizon like the water's surface seen from far below. The machine's hum lifts from the floorboards and into her cot's frame. A mechanical heartbeat that knits itself into hers.

Another rhythm—the carousel that turns behind her shut her eyes. A lifetime that comes and goes, random and buzzing. The spin of memories, the gift and curse of being unable to forget. The scratch of her mother's pen, the scent of her steeping tea. Her father's boots stepping across mud and scrap wood. A gnarled ball dropped from Chestnut's mouth. Then the scenes that fall like boulders, the carousel stopped and Kayla pinned beneath their weight. The catch of panties on a tooth. The blackened soles of her mother's feet. The reflection of light from her father's broken glasses.

Heather slips past Kayla's bed. Silent and barefoot, a glance into the hallway and the door pulled shut. A hushed click. "Clear," she whispers.

Betty stands atop the desk and rises into the courtyard's angled light. She pushes aside the ceiling tile and retrieves the cigarette pack and pint bottle. The sisters each take a side of the wide window, a whispered count. The wood's budge and sigh and the sudden push of cool air. Heather wedges a rolled-up towel beneath the door and joins the sisters as they settle onto the floor beneath the window. Betty, a cigarette between her lips, leans against the sill. A lighter's spark, a new illumination for her face. A deep inhale, a savoring before she blows a plume through the window's metal grate. "Shit, Oakmont, you need an invitation?"

Kayla sits at the semicircle's end. Her shoulder rests against the cold radiator. The city's stirrings through the opened window—a truck's honk, the rattle of the riverside train. Betty savors another puff and balances the cigarette on the sill. Heather takes her place, her skin the color of bone in the slanting light. A drag and the cigarette's tip glows across her cheeks.

Betty sifts through the items arranged on the floor. "This is it, huh?"

"We got some hand lotion," Linda whispers. "And lip balm. They smell good."

"But no magazines," Chris says. "And no gum."

"No pens," Linda says.

Heather takes another puff. The smoke blown out but yet some swirls inside. "Second time our box has been light."

Chris next at the window. Delicate inhales, a stifled cough. "The whites have gum. Lots of it, I think." She hands the cigarette to Linda. "They chew it right in front of the guards. Even in front of the Deacon. Don't know how they don't see it."

"Fuck if they don't see it," Betty says. "I need to talk to my cousin. Although I'm sure as shit not paying Zach the way Donna is."

Linda flicks ash onto her palm and blows it out the window. She rests the cigarette on the sill and returns to the floor. "You really think she does that?"

"That choirgirl act is as old as time itself," Betty says. She turns to Kayla. "Well Oakmont, you going to partake?" Betty raises her hand, a haughty gesture. "Or do you require a cigarette holder like your girl Cruella?"

Kayla stands. A gray ribbon from the cigarette's tip weaves the window's mesh. She pinches the cigarette's end and brings the filter to her mouth. She's always been repulsed by the habit. The knots she passed outside movie theaters, the skating rink's tough boys. Missy and the Wolf Pack girls. She inhales. The ashy taste in her mouth, the expanse of her lungs. A moment of dizziness. Her lips brush the metal grate and she exhales. The plume captured in the light then gone. In any other circumstances, she would have declined. Tonight, she takes another drag. The scratch and heat the bread of this communion. A connection to this place and these girls and their shared lot. Another exhale. In the distance, the bays of abandoned dogs.

She hands the cigarette to Betty. A brush of fingers, Betty sucking a final draw then a careful grinding of the tip against the windowsill, the snuffed cigarette returned to the pack. She takes her place in the floor's semicircle. The pint's cap snaps with her twist. The dark flavored with the whiskey's sharp scent. "Thanks for waiting for me, ladies," Betty says.

"We wouldn't do it without you," Chris says.

Linda rubs her palms together. A child's grin. "But now I can't wait a second longer."

Betty holds the bottle. The pint a heart of captured light. "Just a swig. Not sure when we'll get another." She sips, the bottle eased from her lips and a deep inhale. She closes her eyes and smiles. "Now that, my sisters, is something to tell your grandma about."

Linda next. A grimace, the shudder of a rouge current. An identical reaction from her sister. Heather pauses before her sip, the opening held beneath her nose. She drinks. A lift in her chest and a long, steady exhale between pursed lips. A smile as she hands the bottle to Kayla.

"Deacon says there'll be a basketball tournament next week," Chris says. "Did you hear that up there, Betty?"

Linda chimes in. "Donna and the twins have been practicing outside."

"No, I didn't hear," Betty says. "And no, I don't want to talk about the fucking Deacon tonight." She sticks out her tongue. "We had ourselves a go-round in iso. The fucking creep had me hold his hand while we prayed, then when he was done, he gave me an extra day, the fucker."

"That hand-holding part is gross." Chris says. "Eww."

"Like holding hands with a crocodile," Betty says.

Linda's expression serious. "Crocodiles don't have hands, do they? They're more like paws or something."

"Shut up. Jesus," Betty says. She nods to Kayla. "You holding that thing all night?"

The glass cool against Kayla's palm. She lifts the bottle, the scent cutting. A smell that lingered in the living room's glasses last New Year's morning. That other life's final moments. All of it gone. She guides the bottle to her lips. The warmth on her tongue, her throat's burn. The night's second communion. A shared transgression. A claiming of independence. A shudder she can't hide and tears in her eyes. A cough stifled with the back of her hand.

Betty takes the bottle. "Look at our gal Oakmont. Getting down with us plain folks."

Linda hugs herself. "I'll bet you're good at basketball, Kayla."

Kayla blinks and catches her breath. She bunches back her hair and pulls it over her shoulder. Her hands stroke the length of her ponytail. A tug at her scalp and the memory of the braids her mother wove. "It's not my sport, but I'm OK."

"You could play with Heather and Betty in the tournament," Chris says. "Linda and I aren't too good at sports."

"Ain't that the truth." Betty holds up the bottle. "What do you say, sisters? Is this a two-swig night?"

Linda offers a soft clap. "Yes."

* * *

A few younger whites claimed the hallway outside the cafeteria. A long banner of crinkling paper, the smell of paint. The girls kneel, brushes in hand. One girl looks up, unsmiling and observant, as Panda Bear leads Heather and Kayla into the cafeteria. The ovens' warmth, fish again. The radio's patriotic tunes. The dishwasher's humid current.

They stop outside the supply closet. These past days of double-duty, the whites excused from all chores as they paint banners and rehearse songs. The Deacon smiled during morning convocation, a wink to the whites and the promise the reds would soon appreciate the fruits of their sisters' labors. Panda Bear's phone tucked against his shoulder as he fumbles through the supply closet. A woman's shrill complaint. Panda Bear agitated, sighs and eye rolls. "No, no. That ain't right!" The caged window on the loading dock door. Rain again, soft and steady, and Kayla pictures the earth's patterns. The change of seasons, the cooler mornings and longer nights. The swirling clouds and their cleansings of water and wind, a picture from one of her father's science books, and Kayla a child again on his lap. Their house full of books and music and light. The scent of Chestnut's wet fur. Her mother's pen hovering above the page as she searched for the right word. Her father kneeling in his garden. A thousand memories and a thousand on top of them, her own book and its pages of comfort and sorrow.

Panda Bear hands each a broom and leads them into the back stairwell. Panda Bear's scent sharper here. Cigarettes, cheap aftershave. The stairs navigated with a finger's belt-loop tug of his sagging jeans. His lanyard's glossy ID catches the light as he turns the second-floor landing, and his agitated voice echoes up the stairwell's concrete throat. "Prove it then! Prove it!" He presses the phone against his chest and speaks to the girls. "You get up and start working your way down. I'll be back." He hurries off. His voice rising in his wake. "If I'm a goddamned liar then goddamn prove it already!"

Kayla leans over the railing. The stairwell's hollowed core. A corkscrewing perspective that takes her back to her yard's oak. The weave of branches, the solid earth below. Panda Bear's curses fade, and with the slam of the cafeteria alcove door, they disappear.

"Poor girl," Heather says.

A final flight to the top landing. Kayla's broom makes its first sweep. Heather's hand on the door's latch. She pulls and the door swings back. "Sometimes they don't lock it if there's no one in trouble."

Heather's broom lies across the threshold, a bar to keep the door from closing. The space lit by the dreary spill through rows of small, dirty windows. The scrape of tiny claws across the hardwood, the mice Kayla's heard as she lies in bed, the machine's faintest notes. The roof's angles, bare boards and beams. The rain's patter just above their heads. The sour of mildew and stale air. A floor of wide planks, and Kayla imagines her footsteps' echo in their empty pod below. Before her, four stripped cots. A sink. A toilet without a door. A few overhead lights. In the space above the wings' connecting hallway, a wall of desks and chairs and cardboard boxes. Rusted sinks and broken toilets. Filing cabinets, their sides dented, their drawers scattered.

Kayla and Heather stand by the windows near the cots. Below, a steeper perspective than the one Kayla's used to, the building's front, the entrance's fenced chute, but beyond razor wire, a wider scope. The tarpaper roofs of the neighborhood's row homes. A church's white steeple. The slope toward the river. The trees that have lost their leaves. The south end's railroad bridge. The veins in Heather's arms strain, Kayla helping until they raise a window. The wood warped but finally giving, and with the sash's lift, a dislodging of paint flecks and a flight of roosting pigeons. No cages here, and the girls stick their heads outside, breathing in the cold and damp. Kayla closes her eyes, listening. The traffic's drone. The thinned shouts of playing children.

They shake the rain from their hair as they walk back to the door. "Have you been up here before?" Kayla asks.

"Once." Heather picks up her broom. The door eases shut, a kiss and a whisper. "Betty and I snuck up to see Carolyn. Nurse Amy let us come with her."

They start sweeping. A stirred haze in the light's shine. "So no one knows where Carolyn is now?"

"Not really. But there're places worse than this. At least that's what they tell us. I don't believe much, but I do believe that."

They turn the first landing. Below, a door closes. Panda Bear with a soda can. "This is all you got done?" He pushes between them and sits on the step just outside the iso door. His thumbs tap across his phone's screen. "Pick up the pace, ladies."

He remains there as the girls work their way down. A pleasant tightness in Kayla's back and arms. She's started doing planks again before bed. The others joining in, the girls counting, the sisters the first to crumple, then Betty. Heather and Kayla the last, their arms trembling, the others urging them on.

On the first floor, they sweep up their piles and return the brooms to the supply closet. Kayla wipes her hands against her sweatpants as they exit the alcove. A sneeze from the stairwell dust. At the cafeteria's other end, the Deacon directs the redheaded twins in the hanging of a long banner. The paper crinkles as they lift and pull the banner straight. The revealing of a declaration in large, white letters—PURITY.

*   *   *

Kayla with the other reds, a single file into the auditorium. Another new girl at the line's front, and upstairs, the maintenance crew's busy cadence, hammers and saws and deep voices as they prepare a new pod in the wing's last unused classroom. The new girl quiet, her eyes dull and downcast. Also new, a swirl of rumors, whispers in the hallways and cafeteria. Claims fueled by the flier Heather picked from the courtyard's wind-blown trash. The brewing insurrection. Armed clashes and the bombing of government buildings. Pirate broadcasts and the promise that The Movement isn't dead.

The Deacon at his podium. A smile for each girl as she passes. "Good morning, Kayla." Kayla usually studies her shuffling feet, but today she returns the Deacon's gaze. His large hands grip the podium's sides, a smile, but perhaps, Kayla thinks, an expression less joyous than normal. The rumors, cracks in his believer's world. Kayla turns up the center aisle. The whites already seated. Betty kicks the foot Donna's stuck into the aisle.

The reds settle in. A few of the younger girls cough, the windows closed and the sharing of germs. The Deacon pauses and allows the silence to lengthen. Make them wait, a showman's trick. In another life, he might have been a theater professor, a colleague of her father. The Deacon's voice a tool of his craft, the volume that rises and ebbs. The hands that lift from the podium and cradle his holy book, gestures to the heavens, a finger pointed at his audience, a palm planted over his thankful and humbled heart.

"We'd like to welcome our latest arrival today. Samantha

will be in red pod three, but as soon as the workmen are done, she and a few other young girls will be moving to a new pod." He smiles at Samantha who sits with Nurse Amy in the first row. Nurse Amy's hand rubs the girl's thin shoulders. "Our family continues to grow, and we're happy to welcome another soul to our flock. Remember—my door is always open."

Betty whispers, "And my mind is always closed." Linda and Chris cover their mouths.

The Deacon continues. "I'd like to take a moment to thank the white pods for their volunteering to help with the banners and posters we've been hanging around the school."

"Next he's going to thank us for volunteering to do their chores," Betty leans back and crosses her arms. "You just wait. This sister has faith."

The Deacon glances over the glasses that have slid down his nose. "The banners say 'purity.' And that's the focus of the government's kickoff campaign from the new Bureau of Culture and Tradition." His chest swells, and he breathes a muscular vitality into his words. "Purity of actions. Purity of thought. Purity of faith. And here's the beauty of this gift I'm offering—all of you have the chance to claim it." He holds out his upturned palm and draws his fingers together. "Even if you've lost it, you can still take it back—"

Betty fakes a cough, her fist covering her mouth. "That's good news for Donna."

Heather lowers her head and hides behind a curtain of hair.

"—we can reclaim purity as individuals. We can reclaim purity as a society. In the coming weeks, I urge you to ponder the notion of purity. I want you to find where it resides in you, and when you do, I want you to nurture it. Together, we'll help each other on the journey. We'll find its wellspring within us. Together, we'll drink from its waters."

Another fake cough from Betty. "Or we can drink some booze, thank you."

"Let us bow our heads."

* * *

Morning classes. The Monroe Doctrine. Manifest Destiny. Kayla guides her podmates through quadratic factoring. Betty shakes her head. "We might just start calling you Einstein instead of Oakmont."

"We don't really call her Oakmont," Linda says. "We call her Kay—"

"Shut up," Betty snaps. "Jesus."

Lunch. Whispers of a sheet cake for the whites, the scent of baked sugar. Crumbs on Heavy Metal's shirt. Kayla and her podmates tense, but not a peep from Betty, her exit made with a wave and a parting call to the guards and cafeteria ladies: "Have a nice day, lunch friends." Her animation saved for outdoor rec. The wind's sting, and the girls shiver in their thin coats. The sisters coax the new girl to join the kickball game. Kayla and Heather and Betty with a kickball of their own. The Deacon laughs as he shoots basketball with Donna and the redheads on the playground's sunny end. The younger whites gather, goading until the Deacon agrees to dunk. The rim rattles. The girls cheer. The board's quaking shadow flickers over him as he bows.

"That's pretty pure." Betty produces a stub of white chalk from her pocket. "Pure motherfucking shit." Bent double, she sketches a rectangle on the macadam. The chalk flakes, and Betty speaks as she draws. "You think you're as good at ball as you are with numbers?"

"Probably not," Kayla says. "Definitely not."

Kayla's hands in her pockets. A shuffling to keep warm. Her jacket pinches her chest, and the buttons' strain makes her self-conscious. Stares from Heavy Metal and Panda Bear, even the Deacon. "I played a couple winters. I was a forward." She

229

doesn't mention she only signed up because of Fran's cajoling or that their team lost more than they won. Doesn't confess she found the game claustrophobic, a surrounding of wood and walls that made her yearn for a green field and the sun's warmth.

Heather dribbles the kickball. Side-to-side, between her legs, feats made difficult by the ball's airy bounce. She dribbles one-handed as she tucks her hair beneath her collar. Then a return to her stunts, a spin move around Kayla, a few strands already escaping, frames for the widest smiles Kayla has seen her wear.

Betty stands in the rectangle's center. "Here's the paint." She walks to the rectangle's top. "And here's the foul line." She paces ten steps to the fence. "And here's where the basket would be." She stands with a foot on the outline's edge. "I'm low post. You're high post. Heather's going to work the perimeter." She points the chalk's tiny nub at Kayla. "You know how to set a pick?"

"Yes," Kayla says.

"Better plant your feet wide and cup your crotch. Those redheads aren't ballerinas."

Heather dribbles behind her back. "That's the truth."

"So here's the plan," Betty says. "Oakmont, you're high post. You'll go side to side and set picks for Heather. Donna's going to guard her, so make sure you throw a good elbow for me."

"And me," Heather adds.

"But keep it close." Betty holds her arm as if it were in a sling, her elbow pointed just beyond her side. "Like this, then a short pop."

Heather dribbles between her legs. "But a good pop."

"Fuck yeah," Betty says. "Now after you poke that bitch, Heather will either kick it out down to me or drive the paint. If she does that, you step out to the clear side. She'll take it to the rim or if she gets doubled, she'll pass it off to the open man, which will probably be you more than me. Got it?"

They practice. Betty calls out the partnerless dance, announcing double teams and switches. The ball fed inside, a feigned shot or a kick out to Kayla. Heather's skills sharp. The ball an extension of her body. Betty helps Kayla find her place. A step out to screen. A dash to the weak side. The movements come back to Kayla. The footwork of pivots and block outs. The memories waiting in muscle and bone.

Panda Bear blows his whistle. The whites wild as the Deacon dunks once more, a smile afterward, his arms raised, the pose of his beseeching prayer. "Pure," Betty says. "Pure motherfucking assholes."

* * *

The Saturday morning of the basketball tournament. The chairs folded up or pushed aside. Kayla and Heather and Betty allowed a five-minute shoot-around after Donna and the redheads are done. The Deacon stretches on the sidelines, his hands unable to reach his toes, the hanging sway of his lassoed whistle. Theirs the tournament's final game. The youngest reds losing by one, a marathon of air balls and beneath-the-basket scrums. The middle reds falling by five after the Deacon benched their best player for saying, "Goddamn."

Linda braided Kayla's hair as the younger girls played. The braid thick and tight, the way Kayla liked it. "Thanks."

"You have nice hair," Linda said. "Bet you've heard that before."

Two balls for the shoot around. Heather claims one, jab steps and feints. The ball's rapid twang, Donna and the redheads watching. Kayla and Betty work the high-low, kick outs and bounce passes. Betty practices her spins to the hoop, her turn-around jumper. Kayla hears her old coach's words —*line up, follow through, position.* She divides the floor, a chessboard's squares. She steps out, a pass across the paint. A twinge as she crosses the center's red-white divide.

The younger reds sit cross-legged on the floor. The clapping originates with them, two pine-board slaps, a quick clap. The standing reds join in, the slaps replaced by foot-stomps, the vibration building until the Deacon blows his whistle. He turns to Kayla and her teammates. "One minute."

Nurse Amy chats with the youngest on both sides of the divide. Yesterday she told Kayla she delivered the letter to her stadium contact. "I can't promise anything," she said, a squeeze of Kyla's hand. Kayla hearing only this: there was hope. Hope,

232

headier than a whiskey sip, a pinprick of starlight in this gloom. Last night, the girls shared a cigarette and swigged the pint's last offerings, and when they were done, they huddled to the lighter's flame and reread the pamphlet Chris had plucked from the Deacon's trash. The Movement's promise to overthrow the theocracy. The return of freedom of the press and speech. The release of jailed dissidents, and the mobs' murderers brought to justice. Threats, vengeance—currents Kayla knew her father would have disavowed but which buoyed her here in this place where she felt so raw and lost.

The Deacon blows his whistle. "Game time, ladies."

Kayla and Betty and Heather huddle at the top of the key. Heather tucks her ponytail beneath her scrub's back collar. She lifts Kayla's braid and does the same. "Gives them less to pull on."

"I'm betting these bitches don't play the polite CYO ball you're used to, Oakmont." Betty puts her hand in the center, and Kayla and Heather pile on. "Let's light these fuckers up."

The Deacon calls the teams to the foul line. The armpits and collar of his *USA* T-shirt already sweat-darkened. Betty and Heather pick up their heels, the soles of their sneakers brushed. They crane their necks and wring their shoulders, their hard gazes returned by Donna and the redheads.

The Deacon holds the ball. "Game's to eleven, win by two. Missed shots have to be taken back past the foul line. Three fouls and you're out." He rests the ball against his hip and pulls a coin from his sweatpants pocket. "Heads or tails?"

"Heads," Donna says.

"Figures," Betty says.

"What do you mean by that?"

Betty raises her eyebrows, her tongue poking the inside of her cheek.

"Cut it out, both of you." The Deacon flips the coin, Donna

glaring as he catches it and slaps it on the back of his wrist. "Heads it is. White ball. Let's have a clean game, ladies."

Donna handles for the whites. Her eyes alert, deft crossovers and the squeak of sneakers. She changes direction, lowers her shoulder. Heather half-a-step quicker, her hands raised, her body blocking Donna's path. Donna steps back and calls a reset. Ashley on Kayla, or so Kayla gleans from the chatter, the twins still indistinguishable to her. Ashley pushes off with her backside. Kayla counters her deficits in height and weight with quicker feet and a hip check of her own.

Donna drives. Ashley steps to the top of the key, a hard pick and a groan from Heather. Donna pulls up. Kayla jumps with her, the shot deflected and snagged by Betty. "That's my girl, Oakmont!"

The first point comes when Betty puts back her own miss. The second when Donna threads a bounce pass to Amanda in the post. Heather with a long rainbow. Donna with a shot fake and a drive down the lane. Kayla takes a ten-foot jumper that bounces off the front rim. Ashley pushes off, her forearm hard against Kayla's back, her hand grabbing her shirt when they're close. Curses under her breath. Kayla's first basket less satisfying than Ashley's cold stare-down.

The game tied at five and again at seven. The red cheers raucous, the youngest girls dancing with each basket, a display snuffed by the Deacon's threat to send them back to their pods. The Deacon's whistle silent for the whites but put to use for a hand check against Heather, a charge on Kayla. A timeout for the whites, a respite followed by a choreographed play. Donna drives the lane, the way cleared by Ashley's jersey tug and the sharp elbow Amanda delivers to Betty's gut.

Betty holds her stomach. "Damn, Deacon, open those eyes the Lord gave you."

He blows his whistle, his hands gesturing an emphatic T. "Next foul and you're gone, Betty."

"Foul for what?" she demands.

"Your attitude." He takes the ball. "And your blasphemy."

"Are you kidding? Je—"

Heather clamps a hand over Betty's mouth. "We're good, Deacon. How about we take our last timeout now?"

The girls huddle, their arms around each other's shoulders. Their voices low and the gym awash with chants. "We're not going to get any whistles here," Betty says. Sweat glistens on her brow. "We've got to win this on the floor." Betty puts her hand in the circle's middle. "Time for a little purity of our own, ladies."

They break. Heather waits for a ball check at the foul line, but the Deacon waves her off. "Possession changes on a technical."

"What?" Betty cries. "Are you just making this up as you go along?"

He hands the ball to Donna. "It's called sportsmanship, Betty."

Betty turns to Heather, then Kayla. "On the floor, ladies. No other way to take this."

Donna dribbles at the top of the key. A scrum in the high post, Kayla returning Ashley's jabs and holds. Donna's jumper clanks off the back iron, and the ricochet sails over Betty and Amanda's outstretched hands. Kayla breaks away, Ashley still holding her shirt, and Kayla's collar pulls against her throat. She bends down and cradles the ball, a shielding from the twins' gropes and whacks. Donna in front, a reach in and a poke in the eye. Kayla curses and shoots up, a rising that kindles sparks around the room's lights and faces, a flush of blood. Her poked eye shut and teary. She raises her arms with the hope of kicking the ball out to Heather. Then the bony smack against her elbow.

Stillness. Gasps. The cheers swallowed back and the swatting hands gone. Kayla with one, watering eye, an imperfect witnessing. The Deacon pushes Betty aside, the shrill call of his lip-clenched whistle. The numbness in Kayla's elbow radiates to her fingers. She drops the ball, and it bounces, unclaimed, until it rolls to a stop.

Nurse Amy runs onto the court. A muffled moan behind Kayla. The Deacon calls, "My child, dear lord." Nurse Amy fishes gauze from her pack. Ashley holds a hand over her nose. Blood runs down her chin and between her fingers. Blood streaks on her white top. On the floor, a growing constellation of red stars.

Nurse Amy grips Ashley's wrist and eases her hand from her face. A blood bubble fills and pops beneath her nostril. The blood on her cheek mixes with her tears. "It's broken." Her words cast through a pained filter. "That bitch broke it."

Amanda turns from her sister. A dullard's fire in her eyes, yellow and red and tinged with bile. A squinting rage that distorts her freckled cheeks. A step forward, her fists balled. Her momentum snuffed when Betty steps in front of Kayla. A bumping of chests. Betty holds her ground. "Easy there, big fella."

The Deacon snags Betty's arm. Donna by his side, a finger jabbing the space between them. "That was deliberate! You need to throw her ass out!"

Kayla's jaw slack. Her injured eye blinks. In her, the numb awareness of the dentist's chair, the distance between her and the others blurred. She wants to apologize, to say she didn't mean to hurt anyone, but she's both mesmerized and unashamed by the sight of blood and the guilt that ties her to its flow. Nurse Amy's arm around Ashley's waist. A towel held over her nose and a splotched trail over the hardwood as they shuffle to the exit. The Deacon scoops up the ball and orders the guards to take the reds back to their pods.

"What about the game?" Betty says. "They can substitute. We can finish two-on-two. Or—"

"Game's over," the Deacon says.

"Then we should be the winners," Donna says. "If she hit—"

"Fuck that!" Betty snaps.

"No one wins." The Deacon points to the exiting reds. "You three join the others."

Betty turns, a backward walk, a final taunt. "We had you, pretty girl." Her finger wags. "We had you and you know it."

Panda Bear grabs her, a hard push back into line.

"No need to get all huffy, big man." Betty straightens her shirt and rests a hand on Kayla's shoulder. "Seeing that cow bleed might have been better than winning anyway. Maybe I've underestimated you, Oakmont."

Kayla stands guard outside the cafeteria supply closet. Delivery day, Heather inside taking inventory. Three days since the basketball game. Whispers each morning as the reds file into convocation. Donna pointing at Kayla and nodding. Ashley's swollen nose topped with a pair of black eyes. "The raccoon," Betty said, "Panda Bear's ugliest woodland cousin." They laughed, but beneath, the understanding there was a score to settle. Kayla hadn't meant to hurt anyone, all of them bent low and scrambling, a scrum's close focus. Part of her wants to apologize—not so much for her elbow's wild swing as for the backstories that have rendered them more alike than different. All of them damaged. All left to cobble together families among the misfits and strays.

Kayla steps from the alcove when she hears the clatter of wheels on tile. Donna and the twins and two other whites. A trio of rolling mop buckets. The girls' jaws work mouthfuls of gum. Heavy Metal their escort, but he abandons the girls for his customary visit with the lunch ladies. His voice carries as he steps into the kitchen. "I'm smelling something good today!"

Kayla glances into the closet. Heather kneels before the box with the red dot, its top opened, crinkled paper on the floor. "Donna's coming. Her crew, too."

Heather slides the pint bottle and cigarettes into her panties. "Guards?"

"He peeled off. A kitchen stop." The rolling wheels closer. The pop of gum bubbles.

Donna stops short of the alcove. A glance back before approaching. She holds a spray bottle and a dirty rag. The twins flanking her. Ashley with her black eyes, her sister's dull stare. The other whites behind them, their mop handles gripped tight. Donna blows another bubble and nods to the supply closet. The alcove sugary with the gum's scent. "Heather in there?"

"Maybe."

Ashley's bubble the largest, her broken nose eclipsed. The bubble pops, and her thick tongue licks the pink from her lips. Donna speaks: "Our box in there?"

"I don't know." Kayla unsure where to focus, her grid overflowing with white shirts and hard stares.

One of the girls pushes her mop bucket toward the closet door. Donna twirls her cleaning rag. "Too bad you don't seem to be getting any gum. Doesn't seem fair, does it?"

Kayla leans back. "Let's go, Heather."

A hug from behind lifts Kayla from her feet. Freckled hands lock across her belly, a jerk that forces the air from her lungs. Amanda's growl in her ear. "Fucking bitch." Kayla twists and kicks. Amanda holds tight, her bulk overpowering. Her sister shuts the supply closet door and leans into it, pushing back Heather's attempts to escape. Heather's fist pounds from inside, her voice muffled. "Kayla!"

Donna shoves the rag into Kayla's mouth. Kayla gags, the foulness of detergent and soot, and beneath, a deeper panic. The panties she pulled from Missy's mouth. The pull of a tooth on the elastic, the head jerking, an imitation of life. Donna holds the spray bottle to Kayla's face and pulls the trigger, and Kayla's eyes burns in the dark. One of the girls slaps her head, the pull and tug of tangled gum. The others quickly upon her, their sticky hands slapping then yanking chunks of hair. Kayla twists, powerless to escape or scream. She opens her eyes only to be sprayed again. She thrashes, wild and mute. Amanda's grip tightens, their bodies caught in a lurching dance, Kayla's screams forced back down her throat. The tugs and rips of her hair give way to punches. Blows to the jaw. The nose. Her chest and gut.

Amanda hurls Kayla to the floor. A final kick, a last wad of gum spit into Kayla's hair and ground in with the pulled-up collar of Kayla's scrub. Kayla on her side. The cool floor, writhing and gagging as she pulls the rag from her mouth. She wipes her eyes, but all she can discern are watery shapes. Heather by her side. The outline of the pint bottle beneath her top. The whites jog off, and Donna calls back in her sugary tone. "Thanks for putting our stuff away, guys."

Heather pushes the hair from Kayla's eyes. "Shit, babe. Shit." The gum and hair stuck to her palm. Kayla winces with the tug. "Stand up, girl. Come on now."

Heather cups Kayla's elbow, a guiding hand on her back. A righting on shaky legs. Kayla spits, the chemical bitterness, the cloth's strands on her tongue. Everything blurry, the lights caught in watery prisms. Her pulse in her jaw. Gum on her hand when she pushes back her hair, a yank on her scalp. Long strands dangle from her fingers. Her words a whisper. "Are they lining up for lunch?"

Heather steps from the alcove and returns. "Yeah."

"I won't walk past them like this."

"Sure." Another check of the cafeteria, and Heather returns to the closet, the last of their delivery plunged into her pockets. She opens the back stairwell door and reaches for Kayla's hand.

The steps, and Kayla rises in spite of herself. Movements no more than imprinted rhythms, stumbles and the memory of putting one foot in front of another. Pain, yes, humiliation, but stronger than these is the desire to return to her pod. To collect herself in a place where she'll be safe. To rob the whites of the opportunity to see her broken. The second floor, an entrance to the red hallway. The other reds returning from morning chores. Gasps from the bathroom's line. "Kayla?" a young girl calls.

"Not now," Heather says.

Kayla with her head down. The shock recedes, and in its place—tremors. A skull shrouded in mist. The budding resolve to keep her tears private. Betty turns from the window. The sisters run, their cards tumbling off their cot. Heather guides Kayla onto her bunk.

"Jesus, girl," Betty says. A touch of Kayla's shoulder before she clenches her fists and screams. "I'm going to fucking kill them!"

Linda runs out, stopping only to shoo away the gathered crowd before closing the door behind her. Chris sits on the bunk, her hand rubbing Kayla's shoulder. Heather returns with a washcloth and wipes Kayla's eyes, and the faces of her gathered friends lift from the fog. Stands of loose hair in her fingers, her body's dull ache of punches and kicks—and just as it had in Helen's house, the ice forms over her. And beneath its chill, a new perspective, a clear, beatific logic.

Betty paces from the window to the door. Cursing, the spitting of threats and vows of revenge. Chris lists the treatments they tried on Linda's hair—peanut butter, ice, Vaseline. Heather silent, Kayla's hand held in hers. A tight grip given and returned; their knuckles white.

"Don't worry," Kayla says, calm words slurred by a jaw she can't totally shut. "It's going to be OK."

The pod door opens. Linda first, Nurse Amy close behind. She pulls a chair in front of Kayla and opens her first-aid kit. "Oh, sweetie. Who did this?"

The night she arrived, Kayla collapsed into the nurse's arms. She's stronger now. She sits straight and owns her pain. She swallows it and keeps it in the dark of her belly. The pain will become stone, an alchemy of scars and unshed tears. When the time comes, she'll grip the stone tight and remember this moment. She lowers her chin, not wanting to look at the nurse as she lies. "I don't know. It happened so fast."

A pause. "You know you can't do anything foolish. Not with the way things are around here." She looks around and addresses them all. "Promise me you'll see me before anything like that goes down. Do that and I'll make sure the Deacon isn't up here asking too many questions."

"Fuck that," Betty snaps. "We're going to—"

Nurse Amy cuts her off. "Open your eyes, Betty. You don't think he'd like an excuse to get rid of you? Only person who's going to do anything is me and that's only happening if Kayla wants to tell me about it."

Kayla whispers from behind her hair. "It happened so fast."

"I understand." She reaches into her bag. "It'll take some doing, but we'll be able to get most of this—"

"Cut it," Kayla says.

"Oh, honey," the nurse says. "Your hair is so—"

Kayla's gaze on her lap. Heather's hand in hers, Chris taking the other. "Cut it. Please. Cut it all. It's OK."

Betty pulls a chair to the room's center. Linda drapes a towel over Kayla's shoulders, another over her lap. A voice from the hallway—Panda Bear calling the reds for lunch. He sticks his head inside the pod's door. "Lunch. Let's line up."

"We're staying," Betty says.

"Like hell you are." He steps into the room. "What happened here?"

Betty plants a fist on her hip. "If some folks around here kept their eyes opened, they'd know what's going on."

"Or if they got off their phone once in a while," Heather says.

"Or maybe they knew all along and let it happen," Linda says.

"Listen, you little bitches. I don't need your—"

Nurse Amy interrupts. "They can stay if they want. Tell them to leave out some lunch. I'll bring the girls down when we're done."

Panda Bear scowls. "I'm not promising nothing—"

"They'll do it if you say it's for me." Nurse Amy retrieves her scissors. "And if I ever hear you call any girl here a bitch again, I will personally see to it your ass is gone."

Panda Bear huffs but says nothing. An exit, the door slammed.

"Thanks, Nurse Amy," Chris says.

"Yeah," Linda says. "Thanks."

The girls stake a circle around Kayla, seats on their cots and drawn-close chairs. Kayla's head bowed. The snip of scissors, and on the floor and her lap, clumps of hair mottled and tangled in pink. Much of the gum pressed hard against her scalp, falling strands longer than her arm, and in the jumbled mass, a picture of a life that's no longer hers. Her last haircut at the salon her mother went to. Music on the radio. The scent of shampoo. The hairdresser cooing about her hair's shine. Kayla's mother looking up from her magazine, a smile on her face. Almost two years ago. Another world. Another life.

The strands grow shorter. Nurse Amy pauses, stepping back then returning to work. Apologizing again and again as she promises to do her best to even it out.

"It's all right," Kayla says. She blows snippets off her lip. The feel already different. A coolness on her scalp and neck. The other girls intent, tight-lipped smiles when Kayla looks their way.

Linda runs a hand over her own head. "It grows back quick, Kayla. Really."

***

Night, the girls arranged in a semicircle, the icy floor. One by one, they take their turn at the open window. A week has passed, and in the morning mirror, Kayla's tightly cropped hair is a surprise but no longer a shock, the reflection not her so much as a new her. The girl in the glass stronger. Less willing to blink or look away. Strands still show up—on her pillow, whisked against the baseboard. Her hand often rubbing her scalp. The hair's bristle, her exposed neck and the hardness of her skull. When her turn comes, she rises into the window's grainy light. She sucks a drag, and the cherry's burn nears the filter. She places her lips near the grate and exhales. The pleasant mix in her throat, the smoke's warmth, the biting cold. She considers the world beyond the schoolyard fence. The dark houses. A passing car. The bay of lost dogs.

She rests the cigarette on the ledge. Before rejoining the others, she lowers herself into the day's final plank, two minutes counted under her breath. The quiver in her arms as she sits beside Chris.

"You're so good at that," Linda whispers.

"You're getting better too," Kayla says.

"Yeah, but not like you." Linda picks up the hammer sitting in the circle's center. She stands, the hammer held high, a choppy swing. The head flashes in the gray light. She found the hammer behind a hallway trashcan before lights-out, the tool misplaced by the crew partitioning the new pod. "It's heavy." She taps the hammer against her palm. "But not too heavy."

Betty sucks the cigarette's last puff. She grinds the tip against the windowsill and strips the filter, the paper and cottony strips slid through the wire mesh. Below, the courtyard's trashy swirl. She closes the window. The breeze snuffed but the cold lingers.

Chris gasps the hammer's head and holds the rubbed-coated handle near her mouth. "For my next song, I'd like to sing a tune you all know and love."

"We've all heard you sing." Betty takes the hammer. "And it ain't pretty."

"Should I put it back?" Linda asks. "They'll be looking for it."

"This isn't a charity, girl." Betty climbs atop the desk and hides the hammer, cigarette pack, and lighter. The space behind the ceiling tile blacker than the sky. "If there's any that deserve a little charity, it's us."

The girls return to their cots. Kayla kneels, the squeak of her locker's hinges. The necklace retrieved. She secures the clasp and slides beneath the blankets. The chain's touch different without her hair. She lies still, her gaze upon the ceiling, the white and black and gray. She rubs her scalp. She passed the Deacon at morning convocation, a moment's glance before he returned to his Bible. Donna and the redheads smirked at first. They snapped their gum and smoothed their palms over their heads, gestures Kayla answered with the stare she'd practiced in the bathroom mirror and the cold grin that's taken her by surprise. A smile because she now looks right through them. The understanding that she's taken their worst and now it's their turn to wonder how she'll settle the score.

A snag in her drift. The scrape of metal on wood. Kayla confused—she already heard the sisters push their beds together. A tremor, a bump of metal, the docking of Heather's cot. "Do you mind?"

"No."

Heather settles in and lies on her side facing Kayla. "I'm freezing."

"I wonder what winter will be like here."

"We'll be the first to find out, I guess." Heather smiles. "Can I look at your necklace?"

"Sure." Kayla reaches for the clasp.

"Don't." She cups the cross in her palm, the back of her fingers against Kayla's throat. Her breath tasting of smoke and toothpaste. "It's so delicate." She pulls back and clutches the covers beneath her chin. "I should push my cot back."

Kayla opens her mouth and the machine's heartbeat fades. "You don't have to."

* * *

Outdoor rec. The sky clear. The blue startling, these overcast months. A cold sun. The younger girls busy with their kickball game. All of them jumping in place or hugging themselves. A breathy fog above their heads. The whites inside, a meeting with the Deacon. Rumors—they were being moved to the country, the busses on the way—or perhaps just the whites were going somewhere where the heat worked and the playgrounds had grass.

Kayla and her podmates at the monkey bars. A sharing of mismatched gloves. Turns taken grasping the last metal rung, their chins above their bar until their strength gave. As they wait their turn, the girls read the flier Chris found in the guard's break room. The paper passes hand-to-hand, their backs to the windows. The rebellion spreading. Whole neighborhoods taken in Baltimore and Pittsburgh and Brooklyn. Mass defections from the National Guard. Armories raided and emptied. The Movement's weekly report the internet's most downloaded podcast. Or so the pamphlet claims.

Cries from the kickball game. The twang of rubber, and the red ball sails over outstretched hands. The hustle on the base paths. Kayla slides on the gloves. One black and tight, the other blue wool. She grasps the bar and pulls herself up. Cold radiates from the metal. The breeze light yet sharp, a wetness in her eyes. This new perspective. The kickball game given depth, the tops of her friends' heads. The sisters huddle as they read the flier. Heather and Betty's sneakers scrape the macadam, a stone kicked back and forth. Kayla's arms tighten, the pain in her back. The pitcher rolls the ball, and a runner strays from second base. A police cruiser approaches, sirens and flashes of red and blue, a halt in the game as it passes. Kayla closes her eyes, and the strobes color her darkness. She slips into herself, then slips deeper still. Until her body's complaints melt. Until she grows deaf to everything beyond her breath's seashell hum.

Her grip gives and she drops to the macadam. "You were up there forever," Linda says.

Heavy Metal opens the school door. "Inside, everybody! Right to the auditorium!" The kickball game abandoned. The younger girls run, the promise of warmth. Kayla folds the pamphlet and slides it and the gloves into her pocket. Heavy Metal shivers as he holds the door at the top of the concrete steps. "Let's go. Don't ask to go to your pod. Don't ask to use the bathroom. Do not pass Go. Deacon's waiting!"

Kayla flexes her fingers, her sleeve rubbed under her runny nose. They walk beneath a long banner. *PURITY*. The whites just leaving the auditorium, each in a new winter coat, hats and gloves. The younger whites excited, their sleeved arms held up as they compare colors and styles. Donna at the line's end. A flip of her blond hair over her jacket's furry collar. A smile as she passes Betty. "Might be a few left that aren't too shitty."

Heavy Metal leads the way to the auditorium. The echoes deeper here, the high ceiling and open space. Just off the stage steps, a picked-over pile of coats. Atop the stage, a jumble of hats and gloves. The Deacon gestures to the pile. "Take your pick, girls. The local charities were kind enough to supply us with enough for all. We had the smaller sizes on the left, but it looks as if our order has been lost. Still, help yourselves."

The younger girls' voices bright. The thrill of a gift, a distraction. Betty and the sisters at the pile's other end. Betty holds up a man's trench coat, a frayed sleeve, a gash at its elbow. "Are you serious?"

"It has a nice lining," the Deacon says. "Warmth is more important than fashion."

"So it's all about warmth?"

The Deacon smiles. "Yes."

"So you made sure the whites had the best looking and warmest coats?" She drops the trench coat and retrieves one of the handful of army jackets. "Didn't see any of them walking out like G.I. Joe."

"Vanity isn't pretty, Betty."

She drops the army jacket. "Then vanity's got a lot in common with what's left here."

"That's enough," Panda Bear says. "Pick a coat and be done with it."

Betty turns, her tongue out, her words low and mocking. *"Pick a coat and be done with it."*

Kayla and Heather sift through the hats and gloves. An orange knit cap for Kayla. A pair of thin, leather gloves, and she tosses her old mismatched pair onto the pile. Heather flicks the hat's fluffy pompom. "Nice."

The auditorium doors open. "Hold on, everybody." Nurse Amy's steps hindered by a trio of bulging trash bags. A strained smile as she passes the Deacon. She drops the bags at the pile's edge. She opens one, then the other, and shakes out a soft jumble of coats. "Forgot to put these out earlier." She shrugs toward the Deacon and empties her last bag onto the stage's pile of hats and gloves. "Guess I was distracted by all the commotion."

Linda and Chris take off the jackets they picked, try on new ones, then switch. The younger girls in an impromptu fashion show, a catwalk alongside the center's taped divide. Betty leans into Nurse Amy, a nudge of her shoulder. "You can never leave us, you know that, right?"

Clad in her hat and gloves, Kayla takes a seat on the stage's edge. She smiles, cheered by the younger girls' laughter, their shiny voices. New coats and new gloves. A revived sense of justice. The gift of breaking even, and she thinks of her father and the world of small miracles. Linda nears. She holds out her arms, admiring her coat's sleeves. "What do you think?"

"It's nice."

Betty and Chris further down the stage, the trying on of gloves. "I like your hat," Linda says.

"My head's going to need some cover this winter."

"Aren't you going to get a coat?"

Kayla slides off the stage. "Guess I should, huh?"

She's the last to pick. She holds up Betty's trench coat. The hem past her knees, a surprising weight, a ticket stub in the pocket. The trench coat slung over her arm, she sifts through the pile's layers. Then the flash of blue and a furry cuff. She slides the coat from the pile and holds it by pinched shoulders. A coat identical to the one she'd worn the last two winters. Same fake trim. Same deep blue. This one with a patched elbow, a gray stain on the collar. She slides her arms into the sleeves. The zipper full of catches. The lapel held to her nose, the smell of smoke. A size too small, and the zipper pushes against her chest. She runs her hand over the front and hears the whisper of sleet against the smooth material. She sees the pellets cradled in the blue folds. She rubs the collar's fur against her neck and steps back onto the riverside path. Her father by her side as he shared the beauty of ice. The shelved alcoves. The teardrop coatings of fallen branches. The shore-to-shore stretches that moaned as the current pushed beneath.

Linda in an aviator's hat, earflaps secured with a tie beneath her chin. "Is that the one you're going with?"

Kayla steps back, a pose struck. "What do you think?"

"Oh, it's nice," Chris says.

"Very," Linda says.

* * *

The sisters' beds pushed together. Betty tossing and pillow-punching before her snoring drift. All with their new coats laid atop their blankets, the room colder by the night. Kayla's gaze upon the ceiling. The windows' reaching light and the darkness above. The warp of hours and the tangle of unmoored thoughts. Her eyes closed. The machine's purr a stream, a tide to the worlds she's left behind. Her team. Fran. Chestnut. Her mother. Her father. She conjures their faces. Dresses them like paper dolls and arranges them in storybook settings. Her body floating, then falling like a stone. The horrors she can't stop seeing. The drift evaporates into panic. Kayla desperate not to be a witness. Not again.

Sirens, the frequencies with which she's become familiar. The police cruisers' wail, the fire engines' bleat. The ruckus approaches, but unlike other nights, the calls don't fade. Kayla opens her eyes. Stabs of red and blue across the ceiling. The flicker of orange. Kayla whispers: "Heather?"

"I see it."

Kayla slips on her coat. Her socked feet, the cold floor. Pulses of red and blue in the windows' dirty glass. The cage's webbed shadow. The sirens louder than morning's piped-in music, and beneath, the faint thread of drums. Kayla passes the sisters' beds. Linda's sleepy voice: "Kayla?"

Chris sits. "Kayla?"

Betty and Kayla reach the window together. The sisters next. Flames shoot from the second-floor windows of the brick double at the corner of the first cross street. The police block the intersection, their cruisers like boulders, and around them, the crowd's push, a flow bristling with rifles and bats and waved flags. The mob chants. Bricks smash the house's windows. A

251

man climbs atop a mailbox and twirls a noose over his head. Ash on the breeze. Old John and the Deacon in the courtyard. Their fingers twine the fence, a conversation with the policeman on the other side.

"Fuckers," Betty says.

Then the bursts from the house's first floor windows. Blossoms of starshine. Glass shards tumble to the sidewalk. The *pop-pop-pop* of the firecracker strings Kayla's uncles lit at summer barbecues. The girls flinch, Linda and Chris in an instinctual embrace. The Deacon and Old John scramble to the loading dock.

The burning house's front door flings open. Two men and one woman, figures lit by fire and strobes. They rush forward, rifles leveled, their *pop-pop-pop* sharper. Kayla and the others with their heads just above the sill. The crowd turns upon itself, the motion of a wave pushed back from a sea wall, the drums replaced by screams and cries for help. The mob's fringes melt into alleys and shadows. Bodies in the intersection. A cop. The man atop the mailbox who held a noose now face-down. The men and woman on the corner, guns blazing, the police and crowd returning fire as they stagger back. In Kayla, the recognition of justice. The satisfaction of blood from the blood-seekers.

One man from the house falls, then the other. The woman still squeezing off rounds as she lies bleeding on the sidewalk before a shot rips off the top of her head. The police step forward, guns raised. A spasm in one of the men's hands, and the police respond with a barrage. The fire pokes through the roof. A torrent of sparks and smoke.

"Fucking hell." Betty rests her elbows on the sill. "If I get my hands on a piece, that's how I'm going out if it comes to it. The fuckers."

She remains at the window. The sisters return to their

pushed-together beds. Kayla sits on the edge of her cot. Heather still beneath the covers. Her back to the window. Her body curled, a child's pose. Kayla crouches by her side. "You OK?"

"I hate them all," she whispers. The shadows not deep enough to mask her glistening cheeks. Kayla picks up her cot and sets it beside Heather's. She piles her blankets and jacket on top of them and waits for the warmth to find her. Heather's eyes closed. Her hand reaches for Kayla's. Her grip tight, as if she's afraid she's about to fall.

Whispers in the common room. Gunfire on the city's north side. Conjectures about the evening's surprise auditorium meeting, the white wing just escorted down, the reds wondering if they'll be next. The younger girls play board games, the missing pieces replaced by pennies and bottle caps. A few read paperbacks with tattered covers. Others watch the wall-mounted TV, a government station they can't change. Pre-Shut-In sitcoms, families with troubles that belong to another time. All the girls in their winter coats. Snow piled on the windowsill. Kayla's pod in the room's corner. Chris and Linda on the floor, facing each other and smiling as they play another round of Rock Paper Scissors. Betty shuffles a deck of cards, cursing to Heather about their dwindling deliveries, her mistrust of Zach and Donna.

Kayla at the couch's end. The cushions sag, the fabric's embedded cigarette stink. The couch, like all of them, with a before-life. Kayla's cheek rests against her fist. Her body tight with a chill that has nothing to do with drafty windows or tepid radiators. She felt fine until dinner. Then a breaking wave, an ache in the meat of her thighs, the veering between chills and sweat. She rubs her palm over her cropped hair and covers her eyes. The room's voices pull away. Kayla on an island, just her and her pain.

Panda Bear strides across the room. The TV light blue on his shaved scalp. "We're heading to the auditorium." He turns off the set and tucks his hands into his sweatshirt pockets. "We've got a visitor. Deacon says you all need to be on your best behavior." He points at Betty. "Especially you."

Betty sticks out her tongue. *"Especially you."*

Kayla pulls herself from the couch. The soreness spreading,

her back and neck. The motion a putrid wave beneath her skin. "You OK?" Linda asks.

Then Chris. "You're really pale."

"Just tired." The girls arrange themselves in a ragged line. The stairs, Kayla's grip tight on the handrail. The first-floor hallway. Betty in front of Kayla, Heather behind. The nurse's office. The PURITY banners. All of it passing like images from a dream, as if she's being pushed on rollerblades through an icy chamber. Panda Bear holds the auditorium door. "Watch your language. Remember we got—"

"We got a visitor," Betty says. "We know, we know."

The whites already seated. The auditorium warmer—or perhaps not—Kayla can no longer tell—hot and cold, shivers and sweat. Old John helps Mr. James push an upright piano to the podium. In Kayla, the vertigo of overlapping voices. The scraping of chairs and shoes. Echoes, discordant notes. Kayla worries she may vomit. Her eyes unable to rest, the room vibrating, undulations of noise and motion. Heavy Metal and Nurse Amy straddle the aisle's center line. "Looks like all hands on deck," Betty says. The Deacon by the flag-flanked podium, his hands clasped before him, a conversation with a squat, broad man in a blue cap and matching uniform. Epaulets on the smaller man's shoulders, a single gold braid. His back to the incoming reds. The Deacon's gaze flits between his visitor and Betty.

Kayla shuffles past, the waiting salvation of slumping into her seat and shutting her eyes. A glance as she passes the Deacon. Then the crumble of recognition. The current carries her; she has no other truth to explain her forward motion. Each step a stumbling miracle. She reaches ahead, an anchoring grip on Betty's shoulder. The current fades, and she enters a balloon, its skin stretched. The distortion of faces and sounds, her struggle to keep on her side of the aisle's taped line. Kayla lost within the balloon. Everything filtered. Everything veiled, a dimming at the edges of her vision. The last row's salvation, and she slumps into her chair. Her gaze on the gym floor. The bellows of her lungs. The balloon's stale air a poison she can't escape. The Deacon speaks, a call to attention. Kayla covers her eyes. She thinks of death, and for the first time, she doesn't imagine fear. Only peace.

Heather touches her thigh. "You OK?"

"Just dizzy." Her mother's voice—*breathe*.

The Deacon speaks, and she opens her eyes. His hands on the podium, his body leaning forward. The pose of a bird of prey eyeing an open field. A few words penetrate Kayla's balloon . . . *duty* . . . *vigilance* . . . *pride*. The rest crumble, and their dust joins the balloon's haze. Kayla's attention on the man beside him.

The cap. The mustache. The preening stance and bully-boy's girth. The shoes that could pass as a child's. His dimpled chin nods through the Deacon's introduction.

"Our guest this evening is Mr. Robert Slater, our sector's newly appointed Director of the Bureau of Culture and Tradition. He's here to talk about the Purity Project, not just about our humble efforts, but also what's going on throughout the sector and state and all across this changing nation." He steps back and offers a sweep of his arm. "So please join me in welcoming Commissioner Robert Slater."

Slater approaches the podium. His swaying arms angle around his girth; his chubby, chopped strides—motions that betray him more than his mustache or glistening brow. Feedback as he adjusts the podium's microphone. Kayla rubs her brow. Her eyes masked, her head hung. A shiver as Slater begins to speak.

"Thank you, Revered Blake." Kayla looks up, a reflex, her movie's most horrible scene. He takes off his hat. In Kayla, a flood of tangled impulses. The yearning to shout. To flee. To storm the podium, grab his fat face, and dig her thumbs into his eyeballs until she feels the orbs' pop. Until his blood warms her hands. A hundred short-circuit cravings. A paralysis of fear and rage and sickness. Each of Slater's sentences falls upon her like a shovelful of dirt. Kayla in the grave, fading, suffocating . . .

" . . . I was your age long ago, almost too long to remember. I was in chemistry class, and we were conducting an experiment. We held a crucible over a flame. The powder inside bubbled and smoked." He chuckles, a pause and smile as premeditated as his comb-over. "The smell wasn't pleasant, but in the end, we were left with a beautiful silver liquid, a substance so shiny it actually glowed. What we'd done was burn off the impurities. The filth. What we were left with was a substance purged of contaminants. A substance that was pure."

The lights glint on Slater's medals and buttons. In the balloon, the rubbery echo of his words, an overlapping until his voice falls a beat behind his lips. He gestures to the surrounding walls. "I see your banners and they fill me with pride. They fill me with hope. This is what our campaign is all about. We are on the journey to a pure society. It's the rarest of opportunities. A new dawn. A new way."

He nods and the guards hand out printed papers. A classroom's rustle. "Starting next spring, a new song will be sung whenever we play the national anthem."

Heavy Metal reaches their row. "You'll need to share."

Heather hands the paper to Kayla, but she shakes her head. "Sure you're OK?"

Kayla nods. A lie she can't live without, the fear an uttered word will break her into a thousand pieces.

Slater blows his nose. A jangle from his medals as he stuffs the handkerchief back into his pocket. "Your Mr. James will play the piano, and I've been told—" He looks at his notes. "—

Donna DiBetto has been practicing for the past week to sing for us tonight."

Donna stands and joins him. Slater's hand rests on her shoulder. "You all know Donna's story. I, myself, was humbled to learn of her family's sufferings and heroics. And she's here, like all of you, making the best of her situation. Improving herself because she knows that soon she'll move on and join the crusade that's changing our nation and the world. She'll bring her sense of purity—"

"Ha!" Betty blurts. The sisters lower their heads, their hands clamped over their mouths. A glare from the Deacon, Slater too, and Kayla ducks, the charade of tying her sneaker. Slater returns to talking, and Kayla sits up. She considers the paper and rubs her eyes. The letters black minnows in a white sea, their sounds and meanings lost within their splash.

The piano's first chords. Mr. James's playing cautious, a prelude before the Deacon gestures for all to stand. The wooziness in Kayla, the sway she felt high in her old oak on a windy day. Her fingers rest on the back of the chair in front of her.

A pause then the piano's opening bar and Donna's accompaniment. Her voice beautiful, startlingly so, full of light and calm. Kayla closes her eyes and stands riverside, mesmerized by the finches, their turns through the gnat swarms. The birds swirl faster, and their calls and the flap of their wings alchemize into Donna's reaching alto . . . *tribulation* . . . *triumph* . . . *purity*. The song finishes only to begin again. The Deacon gestures, imploring all to join. The Deacon with his pulpit's boom. Slater's lack of range countered by his sweating vehemence, his puffed cheeks, his mouth's fishy oval. Kayla cartwheels through the balloon. The solidness of bone fades. Her surroundings dissolve into mist.

"Kayla?" Heather whispers.

Kayla opens her mouth. The balloon bursts. The mist rushes to claim her, a sinking deep in her lungs . . .

. . . the fog upon her. Within her. Time has passed, she understands this, but she can't say whether it's a minute or an hour or a day. She understands her thirst, understands that she's lying down, a bed beneath her, the ceiling above. She understands the rawness in her throat, the ache in her back and legs. The room dim. She closes her eyes and the fog returns. She's safe—Slater and Donna nowhere near—she feels this deeply, a notion as true as her pain. A voice from the fog's edge, her name, soft, concerned. A cool cloth pressed against her forehead. Kayla opens her eyes. A shadowed form leans close.

"Mom?"

* * *

The girls by the window. Winter coats and a passed cigarette. Flurries in the exhaled smoke. The wind puffs back, calm then a gust then calm again. Kayla just returned from the infirmary, two days of fever dreams. A drag on the cigarette and a cough she fights to suppress. Below, the loading dock, the pickup's bed loaded with snow, a plow rigged to the front. Across the street, the burnt house. A husk of collapsed brick. The rubble picked through for wire and pipe.

Betty closes the window, and the girls sit on the floor. A rolled towel under the pod door. The blowback smoke kept in and the hallway light snuffed. Linda and Chris shoulder-to-shoulder. Each holding a side of the assembly's handout. Linda flicks the lighter, and the flame illuminates the paper.

"Don't waste that," Betty says.

Linda lifts her thumb. The flame extinguished. "But we need to remember it for tomorrow. Deacon said—"

"Fuck the Deacon," Betty says.

"Fuck the anthem," Kayla says.

"That's right." Betty snatches the paper and crumples it into a ball. A swat of her palm, an upward tap. Heather next, the paper batted from Linda to Kayla to Chris. Their smiles growing as they keep the wad aloft. Finally, an errant pass, and the paper falls in the circle's center. Betty leans back. "Maybe I'll take a page from Oakmont's book and pass out next time they ask me to sing."

"You're lucky Heather caught you, Kayla," Chris says. "You were going down hard."

Kayla raises her hand. A slap of Heather's palm. "I owe you."

260

Linda hugs her knees to her chest. "Know what I could use tonight? A little sip. Just a taste before bed."

"Zach's coming this week, right Betty?" Chris asks. "At least he brought some pens last time. And a pad."

"He's screwing us," Betty says.

Chris smiles. "Maybe that's because Donna's screwing him." She and her sister giggle into gloved hands.

"Purity, my ass," Betty says.

Heather unwraps the balled paper and rolls it into a thin tube. "Got to admit she has a nice voice."

"Fuck that." Betty shakes her head. "What's gotten into you?"

Silence. The rattle of the window. The wind picking up. "Hard to believe it's almost Thanksgiving," Linda says.

"Nurse Amy said she'd going to bring in Christmas stuff we can hang up," Chris says.

"Christmas in here. I can't even begin to imagine the joy." Betty stands. She rests her elbows on the windowsill, her reflection in the glass. She speaks, her voice softer. "I'm tired of always being scared. Always knowing I'm going to have to make due with less. Always hoping like a fool that tomorrow's going to be different." She turns to the others. "Ain't nothing here that's fair. There's only shit waiting to be taken. Well, I'm tired of being taken from. Tired of getting what's left after the whites have had their say."

A click and spark, a new shine. Heather holds the lighter's flame to the tip of the rolled-up anthem. The flame catches, a wavering light across Heather's face.

"Shit, girl." Betty opens the window. The flame convulses on the current.

Linda waves her hands, the smoke pushed toward the window. "Old John will smell it."

Heather steps to the window. The flame thicker. "Old

John's drunk or asleep. Or both." She sticks the tapered end through the wire. The others draw near. Heather holds the paper, the flame's dance wider. Drips from the metal's ice. A push, and the paper lifts on the breeze. A circling, consuming flight. A yielding to ash. She closes the window, the smoke and cold lingering. "Betty's right. It's time we got first dibs on something around here. And I'm guessing we all know where to start."

* * *

Lunch. The reds lined outside the cafeteria. Betty in front. Kayla and Heather next. Chris and Linda with Panda Bear at the line's end. The whites gather on the door's other side. Stares from Donna and the redheads. Betty and Kayla staring back, and Kayla thinks of zoo animals. The bristle of fur, the coiled muscles. Kayla counts out her steps, a movie in her mind. These past three nights of rehearsing. The go-ahead given after Zach's morning delivery. Kayla conscious of her body and the passing seconds, and she imagines their waiting integration—her body moving, the dance waiting for its moment. She leans against the wall. The crinkle of paper. A banner running from the door to the line's end. *PURITY IS OURS.*

Betty turns. "Ready?"

Kayla nods. Her heartbeat thick. Heather silent, intent. Her hand reaches for Kayla's. Her fingers cold. "It'll be OK," Kayla whispers.

"OK, sisters. Showtime." Betty steps out and straddles the centerline. She waves and yells to Panda Bear. "Hey! I got to go to the bathroom."

He shakes his head. "You can wait—"

"Can't wait." Betty rubs her belly. "I got the flow. Bad. I got to go now. Like right now."

He sighs. "OK. Go in. Just you. Tell them I said it was OK."

A whisper. "Time to shine, ladies." Betty pushes the door, her voice low as Donna steps back. "What're you looking at, bitch?" Heavy Metal at the tray drop-off, Betty calling as she jogs past. "He gave me permission, sir! Got to hit the john!"

Kayla at the front now. A glass pane between her and

263

Donna. An exaggerated chewing of her gum, a flip of her pony-tail. Kayla turns to Heather. "Ready?"

A nod, and with it, Kayla throttles her, a sharp push, a stumble into the girls behind her. Heather's push back weak, still Kayla acts her role. She grabs two fistfuls of Heather's scrub and yanks her across the centerline. Heather bony and bird-like, limp, her hair masking her face. Kayla on her, her left hand an anchoring grip, her right hand raised. The smiles and laughs of their rehearsals replaced by grunts, the smack of flesh. Kayla's blows sharp but careful to strike Heather's neck and shoulders. The other reds circle, the dividing line's authority lost in the upheaval. Donna's palms slap the door's glass. The whites' voices lift in a dog pack's howl. Panda Bear pushes his way forward. "Hey! Hey!"

Heather's eyes dazed, a loose grip on Kayla's shirt. "You can do this," Kayla whispers. Her next slap harder. Heather's head turned, a twirl of hair. "Hit me," Kayla whispers.

Heather springs forward. Kayla crouches. Another prac-ticed move. Kayla hunkered low, Heather striking her shoulders and back. Kayla grabs her waist, and they hit the floor. The wall's banner rips, and the paper droops over them. Heather's initial paralysis atoned for in a series of slaps and shrill cries.

The girls grapple. Turning and clutching moves made to evade Panda Bear's grasps. Then the eruption at the line's other end, and through the forest of legs, a view of another brawl. Linda pulls her sister's hair, Chris bent forward as her arms flail. Panda Bear's hands on Kayla's side, her shirt pushed up, her bra exposed. The cafeteria door bursts open. The reds pushed aside until Heavy Metal reaches the sisters.

The Deacon's voice slices through the din. The reds ordered to sit against the wall, their hands on their heads. The Purity banner torn, and the sections that remain sag over the girls' shoulders. Heather on top of Kayla, their faces flushed, a private tent beneath Heather's hanging hair. Heather smiles. A whisper. "We did it."

"Yeah."

"Sorry."

They roll onto their side. Panda Bear hooks a forearm around Kayla's waist and lifts. Nurse Amy hurries the whites down the hall's other side. Jeers as they pass, laughter. Panda Bear sets Kayla down. The Deacon grabs her, his grip tight on her arm, a rough pushing to the line's end where Heavy Metal struggles to separate the sisters.

"Get them all to my office!" the Deacon snaps. Kayla's pulse against his grip. He pulls her close. His body shakes. "Ungrateful, the lot of you!"

* * *

Their second night in isolation. Kayla now accustomed to the third floor's rattling windows. The ceiling's drip and the scurry of mice beneath her cot.

Dinner behind them. Their food cold by the time Panda Bear brought their plates. The girls ate huddled by the door, eavesdropping on Panda Bear's stairwell phone calls. Linda mouthing the words, *Oh baby, you know it's not like that*. A final, cooing goodbye, and the girls tiptoed their retreat. He stacked their plates on a tray and called from the other side of the door. "Lights out in an hour." But the truth was the third floor never went totally dark. A shaded bulb over the toilet, an anemic and angled light. A room of long shadows.

With Panda Bear gone, the girls kneel above their pod's ceiling hiding place. They rap on the floorboards, a rhythm Betty answers with a hammer's tap. Betty's voice buried beneath the wood: "Goodnight you fucking troublemakers." Next they rearrange their cots. One on each end, nimble steps, the cots set down with a delicate touch of metal on wood. A square formed, and in the center, a salvaged crate. Before settling in, the girls gather by the windows. Winter's early dark, and the sisters breathe on the glass, their names and pictures of suns and sailboats traced in the fog. Kayla's gaze stretching. The lights along the river. The old iron bridge to the other shore.

The door opens. The girls freeze. Rearranged cots would warrant another lecture from the Deacon. Maybe another night in iso. The greater fear they'll be separated, half cast to the other side of the ceiling-to-floor junk pile, but their dread turns to smiles. Nurse Amy, her arms full, blankets, a plastic shopping bag.

"Special delivery." Nurse Amy sets her things on Kayla's cot. She shivers. "Jesus, it's cold."

"You get used to it," Chris says. "Kind of."

"I'll talk to the Deacon. In the meantime, I brought some things." She considers the beds' arrangement. "I like what you've done with the place."

"We move them back before they come up with breakfast," Linda says.

"That's smart." Nurse Amy opens the bag and hands a rubber-banded deck of cards to Linda, a pad and pen to Heather, and two candy bars to Kayla. "Not sure if all the cards are in the deck. I got them from the common room. And hide the wrappers when you're done."

"Thanks," Chris says, the other girls echoing, *thanks, thanks.*

A hug from Heather before she steps back. "Next time bring a mousetrap."

"I'll tell the Deacon about that, too."

Kayla: "Perhaps that isn't the best idea. Telling him, I mean. Don't want to give him an excuse to make another trip up."

Nurse Amy folds her bag. "You're not enjoying your morning prayer sessions?"

"Not saying that." Kayla smiles. "Just that he doesn't have to do anything special for us. We won't be up here too much longer."

"We won't, will we?" Linda asks.

"Shouldn't be." Nurse Amy pauses. "There's a lot of grumbling downstairs, especially among the whites, which doesn't make sense."

The sisters lower their heads. Heather and Kayla silent. Nurse Amy sighs. "Just be smart when you come back, OK?" They follow her to the door. She turns before leaving. "Everyone's going to be keeping an eye on you until whatever you started works itself out. Just don't give them another excuse to put you back up here."

The girls retreat to their bunks. The single light and the windows' dull shine, a room of underwater shadows. The candy bars divided and shared. The chocolate allowed to melt on Kayla's tongue. A luxury, a taste from her childhood. Linda shuffles the cards while Chris explains a game's rules, a variation of rummy, the circulation of unwanted cards, triples and runs laid down and played upon. Linda peeks at Kayla's cards and suggests strategies, the sisters cheering Kayla and Heather when they make a good play. Chris the game's winner, her last cards laid out with a flourish and a soft clap.

A new game, and Linda shuffles. Her smiled wilts. "What if there's a fire? Would they remember us?"

"Linda," Chris says.

Heather picks up her dealt hand. "It's OK. I've thought the same myself."

Gusts shake the windows. Kayla imagines the wind washing over the roof's slope, the shiver of wood and shingles. The light above the toilet shines in the window, dull yet brighter than the night. Kayla thinks of the dollhouse she played with as a child. A roof that swung open. The hours she spent imagining the lives inside.

* * *

Old John leads the girls back to their pod. Ten minutes until lights out, the windows dark. Welcoming voices in the red hallway. The younger girls pause as they file into the bathroom. Kayla and Heather and the sisters in their coats, their hands filled, their toothbrushes and washrags, pillows and blankets. Their procession slowed by Old John's stoop, his right boot's rhythmic scrape.

Betty on her cot, a glance before returning her attention to her magazine. "They still fighting, John? Don't want to find myself in the middle of a riot."

He adjusts his belt. The jangle of keys as he catches his breath. "No, they're all made up, aren't you girls?"

Chris nods. "Yes, sir."

He grins. "You're good kids. You probably don't hear that enough, but you are."

Betty lays her magazine on her cot and stands. She raises her fists, a boxer's stance. "Except when they're duking it out. Then you got to watch yourself." She lowers her hands. "You on all night, John?"

The lights flicker. He coughs. His words choked. "All night."

"You OK?" Linda asks.

"I'm good, thanks." Another cough. "You're good girls. Better get turned in."

Betty winks at Kayla. "Still don't know if I'm comfortable sleeping amidst all this bad blood."

Old John shuts the door halfway. "Just keep it quiet now after lights out, OK?"

Betty calls as he closes the door: "You're a good one, too, John. No one probably tells you that enough either."

Smiles. Betty with a hug for each. "Damn if you gals don't have the whole place talking." She reaches Kayla, a breath-squeezing embrace, a slap on the back. Here, Kayla understands, is her new family. A unit born from the worst of this life, yet, at least for now, stronger than their sufferings, loyal in blood and action and love. Betty steps back. Another flicker, a spasm of dark.

"That means bedtime, ladies," Betty says.

"Wait," Heather says, "did you—"

Old John's voice in the hallway: "Lights out, ladies. Get yourselves tucked in."

Betty settles onto her cot. "You heard the man."

"Come on, Betty," Linda says. "Did you get it or not?"

A final flicker. Betty's voice in the dark. "Did my little chipmunk lose all sense of patience up in iso? Come on, sister, have a little trust in the system."

Kayla stretches out. This cot no different than the one in iso, still she feels better here. She studies the light upon the ceiling. She feels the tug of sleep and is thankful for it. She lays still, the machine's hum comforting tonight. The furnace, the water's flow. The sisters whispering, their cots already pushed together.

"Shh, you two. You're keeping me up," Betty says.

Chris sits up. "How long do we have to wait?"

"It's been like a half hour," Linda says.

Betty laughs. "It's been five minutes. If that."

Linda climbs out of bed. She wraps a blanket around her shoulders and claims a seat beneath the window. "I'm waiting right here." Her sister lifts her blanket from her cot and joins her. The two of them sit cross-legged on the floor. "Me, too," she says.

Betty sits up. "Look at you. Like a pair of mini fucking Gandhis." Betty gets out of bed. She climbs atop a chair, then her desk. The ceiling tile pushed aside. Kayla joins the sisters. Heather slips into her coat, the hood's collar a furry halo, and stands by Betty's desk.

"So?" Linda asks.

The angled light shines upon Betty's smile and cuts into the dark space above the pushed-aside ceiling tile. "Sooooo we did pretty good." She tosses Heather packs of gum. Heather hands the packs to Kayla, and Kayla hands them to Linda who arranges them in the semicircle's center.

Chris claps, a soft meeting of palms. "Yeah."

Betty reaches up and cradles two, three, four cigarette packs in her arm. "And when I say good, I mean like wildest, fucking dreams good."

Heather gives the cigarettes to Kayla. Their pile growing, a hand-to-hand relay of candy, magazines, hand lotion, lip balm.

"This is awesome," Linda says.

"If that's awesome, then tell me what this is." Betty produces two fifths, one brown, one clear. She hands them to Heather then retrieves three pints. The glass shivers in her grip, bony, trilling notes.

"Whoa," Chris says.

Betty climbs down. "Although one of the fifths is peppermint schnapps and two of the cigs are menthols, both of which are gross, if you ask me. Still—"

"Still we did pretty fucking good." Heather holds up one of the pints. The light simmers in the liquid. "It makes it worthwhile. And then some."

Linda holds a bottle in each hand. "And then some more knowing those bitches got nothing."

"I'm thinking it's a three-swig night," Chris says.

"No way, sister," Betty says. "Tomorrow's Sunday. An extra hour of sleep. We're polishing off one of these little fuckers tonight."

"What about the whites?" Heather asks. "What're they saying?"

Betty gropes around the ceiling's opening. "There's some looks, but we got ourselves a little cover due to old Zack getting his sorry ass fired. Which might suck long term, but I'm not even thinking about that tonight. Donna and the rest don't know if he even made a delivery in the first place."

"They catch him and Donna?" Linda asks.

"Worse." Betty replaces the ceiling tile. A smile as she looks upon them. She opens her clenched hand. A ring around her finger, and on the ring, a glimpse of silver. "The stupid fuck lost the pickup keys."

"Whoa," Chris says.

"Whoa is right." Betty climbs down. "Now let's crack a fucking seal. But not on that schnapps." She sticks out her tongue. "Menthols and peppermint schnapps. Those bitches got some bad fucking taste."

***

A waiting room. Slater's uniform on the wall. The gold shoulder cord slithers, a headless snake, a continuous coil. Kayla sits alone. A check-in area, a nurse behind a sliding glass window. The light behind the glass a luminous dust, and the nurse's skin washes away. Music plays, distant, tinny. Just beneath the tune's surface, a one-sided conversation, words she can't understand. A single door beside the glass window, and Kayla is confused—is this the door into the waiting room or the doctor's office? Water flows beneath the door, the tide ankle-deep in moments. Kayla unfazed, the water clean and warm, all of it normal. The water rises. She's happy, incredibly happy. A mirror appears on the opposite wall, and in the glass, her reflection only younger, then older, then younger again. The light from the nurse's window strikes the water, an angle that brings a perfect sheen upon the surface. She reaches down, a cupped handful, the shine of jewels. The water not water but a substance more viscid, a slow melt between her fingers—

—the fire alarm wails. The call knifes into her throat, her blood. The office's furniture and walls dissolve. In their place, the pod's reality. The cold. Her hard mattress. The streetlight's reach across the ceiling.

She sits up. Linda fumbles into her coat, Chris gropes beneath her bunk. Betty's sleep-craggy voice, "The fuck?" The door flings open, an invasion of light. The alarm given depth. Echoes from the hallway. Old John's stooped silhouette. "Fire, girls! Get your shoes and coats. Hurry now!"

The sisters ready first. Betty smears a toothpaste dab onto everyone's finger, mint to cloak the night's whiskey and ciga-rettes. "I don't smell smoke, do you?" Chris asks. Her mouth twisted as she works the toothpaste over her gums.

Kayla licks the toothpaste from her fingers. The taste a harkening to her dream. The doctor's office, yes, but the notion melts beneath the hallway's chorus, the voices sleepy and confused and scared. Kayla zips her coat. Heather motionless at the edge of her cot.

"Come on, babe." Betty kneels and works a sneaker onto Heather's foot. Kayla joins her. Heather's legs limp. The sisters wrap a blanket over her shoulders. The hallway goes black, the only illumination the alarm's silver strobe.

Chris sniffs. "I think I smell smoke now."

Betty grabs Heather's hands. "We're all going together, girl," Betty says.

Old John at the door. His silhouette twitches beneath the strobes. "Hurry, girls. We can't leave anyone behind."

"We're not," Betty says, and with a tug, she pulls Heather up. Kayla on her other side, her arm tight around Heather's waist. "One step at a time, girl," Betty says.

Heather's body rigid at the core, her limbs limp. Betty and Kayla walk, and Heather's sneakers drag over the tile. The hallway, and the sisters look back, the strobe freezing their worried expressions. They file down the red stairwell. The alarms louder here, painful. The younger girls rush ahead, their hands clamped over their ears. The blanket slips from Heather's shoulders. "Leave it," Betty says. Old John waves them on with one hand, the other clutching the handrail, a pause on every step. Heather's expression the only unchanging element in the lights' captured heartbeats. Her eyes hollow, a focus beyond the school's walls and fences. Kayla looks back. A form on the top landing. A flash. A mane of red hair. The figure there then not, and Kayla wonders if she saw anything at all.

Kayla and her podmates atop the final flight. The maw below, the doorway's cramped funneling. Some of the girls crying, others calling names. One screams they're headed toward the fire, that they should go back, they need to go back. Old John gasps and digs a finger beneath his collar. Heather little more than a ragdoll, and only Kayla and Betty's grip saves her from falling. Betty's assurances a steady chant—they'll get through this, all of them together.

The doors' press eases when they enter the first-floor hallway, and in the flickering white, a haze, the smoke not heavy yet strong enough to leave a bite in Kayla's throat. Another jam at the short entrance hallway. The nurse's office. The guard's post with its monitor views of flashing lights and empty hallways. The entrance doors held open, and the cold tempers the smoke. The Deacon props one door, Panda Bear on the other. The girls urged to hurry, hurry.

Betty glances back. "Give me a hand, Linda."

Linda slides next to Heather. Betty doubles back to Old John. His arm on her shoulder. The slump in his walk and the paleness of his cheeks. The two of them the last to exit. The courtyard's moonscape illumination. The wide front steps, the fenced entrance with its chute and double gates. The whites herded to one side, reds on the other, a mingling on the center walk. Nurse Amy runs forward as Betty eases Old John onto the steps.

Kayla and the sisters huddle around Heather. The sisters with their hands pulled into their sleeves. Their steamy exhales in perfect rhythm. Heather blinks, a dazed awakening. Kayla takes off her jacket and slides it over Heather's shoulders.

"No." Heather's voice a whisper.

Kayla zips the front. "We'll share. How's that?" Clouds of breath between them. Heather's face masked then revealed. Kayla's teeth chatter.

Heather opens her mouth. Then the gunfire. The girls flinch, a collective stoop. One burst then another. The shots close enough to pierce the alarm's wail. "Everybody sit! Sit!"

The Deacon rushes down the entrance steps. Arms waving, the desperation of a flightless bird. The girls crouch. The macadam cold, its patches of ice and snow. The sisters hold hands. Heather sits and hugs her knees. Her gaze upon the ground.

A voice behind Kayla. "Pretty exciting, isn't it?"

Donna squats on the center walkway. She scoots closer. Old John on the steps, his exhales filling and collapsing the paper bag Nurse Amy holds over his mouth. Betty still by his side. "I'm sure it's nothing. The fire, I mean." Donna leans forward. "Although your friend seems kind of shook up, doesn't she?"

Panda Bear exits. A sweep of light from the opened door. His grip tight on Ashley's arm and a redirecting shove before he goes back inside. Donna smiles. "Those twins are heavy sleepers." She waves. "Good to see she's OK." She turns to Kayla. A pause, and she reaches out. "Well, lookee here."

Kayla's palm presses her cross against the base of her throat. Another burst of gunfire. One of the younger girls begins to cry.

Donna lets her hand drop. "It's pretty."

Panda Bear steps back outside. In his gloved hand, a smoldering trashcan. He waves away the smoke. A quick conference with the Deacon who then turns to Nurse Amy. More gunfire, closer. The Deacon grabs the trashcan only to drop it. He curses and waves his bare hand. A kick sends the can clattering across the courtyard, a rolling echo, a spill of ash and sparks and smoke.

"Inside!" he yells. He stands atop the steps, the hand he grabbed the can with tucked beneath his opposite armpit. The hallway light spills around him. "Everyone inside! Hurry! Right to your pods!" The smaller girls run ahead. "Hurry, ladies! Hurry, please!"

Donna stands. "A trashcan fire. Weird how that kind of shit can happen."

***

Kayla walks beside Heavy Metal. Glances back as she passes the others. Heather holding their rags and spray bottles. The sisters with their brooms in the main hallway, their work abandoned to trail along until Heavy Metal shoos them away. Stares from the redheads as they carry their week's linens to the white stairwell. Tensions high since the fire, Kayla and the others returning to a ransacked pod. Footlockers opened, upended cots, shelves cleared—but the ceiling tiles untouched. Another party last night after lights out. An extra cigarette, an extra sip. Kayla with her mouth covered, the sisters crying as Betty put on a baboon's face. A hunched circling, an inspection of footlockers, a scratching of her armpits and perplexed head.

Their stash still a secret—and there've been no clashes with the whites—nonevents that make this surprise visit to the Deacon all the more perplexing. Kayla braces herself. The missing hammer. The truck keys. Perhaps the whites have bent the Deacon's ear with rumors of alcohol and cigarettes. Maybe she'll be asked to pee in a cup. She's done it before, her old school's drug policy. A locked door in the nurse's office. The vice principal waiting outside. The awkward positioning of her hand and the stream's splash. Only now she has a truth to hide, and how many times had Fran laughed, calling her "the world's worst liar."

The Deacon's office once the principal's. Or so Kayla assumes. An outer chamber, filing cabinets, a secretary's desk. The stink of coffee left too long in the pot. A wooden door. Heavy Metal's knuckles rap the pebbled glass. The door eases open. The Deacon behind a wide desk, a phone to his ear. A series of waves and a gesture to sit. Another wave to dismiss his guard. He speaks into the phone. Official business, a few questions, terse replies. Figures jotted on a yellow pad. New additions to his coat. Ribbons and medals and pins.

Kayla forces herself to breathe. Measured inhales, the count of three. A thin, decompressing release. Her folded hands on her lap an anchor. She tightens her grip then releases. A diversion from her body's nervous current. She calms herself by looking around, an inventory of the mundane. The desk's framed portraits. A wife shorter than a pair of teen boys, one boy serious, the other with a wide smile, all three in their Sunday best. Framed diplomas on the walls. College, seminary school. A photo of the Deacon shaking hands with the Mayor. Plaques, honors from civic groups. Shelves of binders and thick books. Trophies topped by golden basketball players. Kayla thinks of the principal who once worked here, of the magpie and the cuckoo.

He hangs up. "I apologize for that." He pushes aside his worn-covered Bible and sets a folder on the desk. WHS stamped in red, Kayla's name on the folder's tab. He opens the cover and sifts through the papers. Year-end report cards, citations for sports and volunteer work. The stapled reports from psychologists, many highlighted in yellow, tables and statistics and dry narratives. The little girl who triangulated concepts and experienced them in three dimensions. A gift, the way some could play music by ear. A talent masked by the lack of awkwardness that burdened so many with her condition.

"Forgive me," he says. He licks his fingers and turns another page. "I wanted to reread this section one more time before we spoke."

Kayla sits back. Relief, at least a bit. Her attention on the folder. Glued inside the front cover, a string of picture-day portraits. Nine images, nine years counted back. Kindergarten. Second grade's missing front teeth. Fifth, the dress her grandmother had sewn. Sixth grade's braces. Seventh the year she let her hair grow. Artificial backgrounds, and lost in time, the moments before the bulbs' flash. The shuffling of a long line, the last minute fixing of hair, the photographer's urgings to sit up straight. Then the last picture. The war and Shut-In two months away. Her smile genuine, unknowing. Her eyes yet to witnesses so much. The hermit crab's urge to hollow out that girl and crawl inside. The wish to slip back into the luxury of quantum possibilities.

The Deacon sets down the report. "It takes some time for records to catch up. Yours just came a few days ago. Usually I just meet with girls who have a disciplinary history." He smiles. "But your file, I must admit, is interesting in a very different way."

He pulls one paper aside. "The nurse will need that." He flips through a few more pages. "What do you think about your classes here? Are they too easy?"

She clears her throat. "Yes."

"Mr. James told me as much." He gestures toward the file's papers. "And this confirms it. Are you bored here?"

"Not really. Not overall. I think Mr. James is a good teacher. He tries to help everyone."

"Yes, he's a fine Christian."

Her vertebrae like a string pulled taut then plucked. The Deacon's eyes searching, a mining of spaces she doesn't want him to know. A violation, and the tremors strengthen, the epicenter in her core, in the meat beneath her ribs. The Deacon's voice recedes beneath her temples' squish.

"Are you cold?"

She shakes her head.

"I could turn up the heat."

"No." A pause. "Thank you."

He rises and walks toward her and rests on the desk's edge. A polite distance observed, yet he still looms. The window light blocked, and around him, an eclipse's ragged shine. The leg closest to Kayla crosses over the opposite knee. A pose easy to imagine rehearsed in a bedroom mirror. A grooming of details—the hands clasped on his crossed knee, his fatherly grin. In Kayla, spasms, the urge to rock.

He speaks. Words as practiced as his pose. A speech more intimate than his morning convocations. His delivery punctuated with nods and a wink that makes Kayla shudder. Few words penetrate her fog—*loss* and *empty spaces* and how the ultimate test of character was *the path one chose during difficult times*—yet at the fog's center, a scintillating and mute clarity. The play of his Adam's apple above his white collar. The sway of his new medals. His hands' knuckled ridges, hands at rest but which she sees in a bloodless grip around bats and ropes. Around a naked girl's throat. His tone calm yet beneath, the rumble of screaming men. Of drumbeats. She breathes deep and her tremors ebb into a hardening. A stone in her gut. The weight of hatred.

"I know there are activities I don't see. Some more egregious than others." He uncrosses his leg and returns his foot to the floor. "It's obvious you're a very intelligent young lady. And I see you're different than the others. Your father a professor, your mother a writer." He leans forward, a tone of intimates, of near equals. "I'd like you to be my eyes and ears in the red wing. Not a tattletale or a snitch. But someone who'd give me a heads-up about other things. Important things. The things that could lead to trouble. I don't want any more of my girls to go the way Carolyn did." He smiles. "And of course, I'd make my appreciation known in ways that wouldn't arouse suspicion. Perhaps you could make some phone calls here in my office. Or we could help you send out some letters."

Kayla stares. He's waiting, but she can't leave her clear center and step back into the fog. He leans against his desk.

"Think about it." He clasps his hands. "And in the meantime, let's pray for the strength to make wise decisions."

He lowers his head. His lips move, his eyes closed, and with God on his tongue, and it becomes safe to stare. The cold branches through her, and with it, a revelation. Murder—for the first time, she can justify the spilling of blood. An equation balanced. A quantity discerned. A subtraction deserved.

* * *

The girls outside. Another steely afternoon. Kayla thinks of Eskimos and their words for snow. Her own vocabulary growing for a sunless sky. Gray. Ash. Pencil. Dust. Christmas decorations in a few nearby homes. Light strings in the windows. Cardboard Santas behind fogged glass. The reds shiver alongside the fence. Their shoes tap for warmth. Betty calls out directions as Panda Bear unlocks the first gate and Heavy Metal enters the fenced chute. The girls' football on the other side of the barbed wire, a careless punt, Betty taking blame for the ball's trajectory. "Guess the NFL ain't calling anytime soon," she calls to Heavy Metal as he steps onto the sidewalk. "Over there. Across the street. It rolled behind that car. Maybe under it."

Kayla breaks from the crowd's fringe. Her hands in her pockets and her gaze down, a pose, she hopes, of thoughtless wandering. The macadam by the loading dock deserted. The breeze stiffer here. Heather nearby, hands in her pockets. A nod, and Kayla crouches by the pickup's door. Another pantomime, the tying of her shoe. She glances up. The cafeteria's fogged windows, her pod above. She lifts the door's handle. A click and the door swings back. Her body low, a pained angle, her elbows and chest on the seat. A toolbox on the passenger side. A thermos. A pair of rubber boots. A scent that takes her back to waking in Fran's garage. She slides the key into the ignition. A quarter turn, a guitar's blasting stab. The crackle of blown speakers.

She slides the key back into her pocket. A nod from Heather; the door's shutting click masked by the girls' cheers. The ball retrieved and tossed over the fence. Betty's hands reach above the others. A snag and a return to the younger girls.

282

"Thank you!" Betty cries.

* * *

The girls line up in the entrance hallway. The fluorescent lights above, the furnace-rumble in Kayla's sneakers. The whites in front, the reds behind. Nurse Amy and Panda Bear by the door. Heavy Metal pulling up the rear. The Deacon paces from front to back, lips moving, a final headcount. The younger ones chat; Kayla and the older girls quiet. All anxious. This night of memories. The fear of abandoning the known. The fear of revisiting what was. Kayla rubs her fur collar against her neck. Nurse Amy calls for everyone to don their hats and gloves. The radio predicting single digits. Old John steps from the doorway of the video monitor room and helps a young red pull her hat over her ears. "It's a cold, cold night, sweetie."

The Deacon claims the space between the reds and the whites. His voice fills the hallway. "Two by two! Two by two!" His nerves betrayed by his officious stride, his fretful gaze. "Four blocks and we stay together. No one lags, no one wanders. No one decides to set the pace themselves." He calls ahead. "Ready when you are."

The double doors open. A rush of cold, exclamations from the girls in front. The line inches forward, and is it the wind's sting or are the lights actually dimming, another fade, the building's currents receding before the chill. The papers tacked to the hallway's billboard rustle. "Jesus," Betty says, her words muffled by her wrapped scarf. "I ain't cut out for this shit."

Outside, a backup on the wide steps, a funnel through the fenced chute. Kayla's shoulder brushes Heather's in the narrow passage. The school's floodlights behind and a walk through chain-link shadows. The sidewalk and Heavy Metal locks the gate behind them. Kayla turns. This her first step outside the

284

fence since the warm, rainy night she arrived. A night no longer real. A night they all experienced—red and white. The school's lights shine, the windows' illusion of warmth. The plow fixed to the pickup's bumper, another forecast of snow, and from the kitchen, whispers of shortages—sugar, coffee, rice. The Deacon steps into the street. His gloved hand waves, a stern urging for Kayla and the other stragglers to close ranks. "Only a couple blocks. Let's stay together."

Kayla's seen the church steeple from the common room. The view from iso even prettier, a white pillar above the roofs. A cross against the clouds. The Deacon's surprise dinner announcement—the arrangements he made for the girls to attend a Christmas Eve candlelight service. His wide smile wilted beneath the girls' silence. Their progress slow. The numbing wind, and the girls bow their heads or turn their backs, their scarfs like fluttering banners. The unshoveled sections of sidewalk. The slip of shoes over paths rutted and icy. They pass a window fogged and ringed with lights. Kayla pictures her attic, the cardboard box of ornaments and tangled lights, their globes of red and green, and she wonders if the mob took those too. She slows as she passes the corner's burned house. Glassless windows and collapsed walls. The blurring of snow on charred remains.

They could run, Kayla thinks. The five of them scattered in different directions. The Deacon could outstride her for a block or two, but if she got a head start, he'd never catch her. But they have no plans, no rendezvous point, no beckoning sanctuary. And part of her is frightened. The world suddenly so vast. These caged months, a horizon snuffed by walls and fences. The maze of unfamiliar streets. The canopy of a frigid sky. The sensation of being swallowed whole.

A commotion at the line's front as they turn the next corner. Nurse Amy and the Deacon usher the girls to the far sidewalk. Nurse Amy in the street, her hands outstretched, a crossing guard's pose. "Don't look, don't look," she says, but Kayla can see the whites' upturned faces in the streetlight. The younger girls gasping, the older ones silent. The Deacon's stern admonishments to hurry. To keep their eyes down.

Betty the first to reach the corner. "Holy fuck." The sisters clutch each other's sleeves. Heather's gloved hand seeks Kayla's, a tug as they cross the narrow street.

The church waits at the next corner. On the block in between, a single light pole, and dangling from its branching arm, a man hung from a rope. The lamp's shine close and harsh, the light of Renaissance angels. The man's head slumped to the side, snow in his hair, on his eyelashes and brows. Snow on his shoulders and the folds of his shirt. His socks and shoes taken, his feet as blue as his face. A sign pinned to his chest. *Traitor.* The mob that knotted the rope gone. Below, the dead man's shadow on the street.

"Hurry, children." The Deacon waves his long arms, his face pale and ruddy. Kayla slows, powerless to pick up her pace or divert her gaze. Heather tugs her hand, a whisper: "Come on, baby." The rope angles down, its knotted end secured around a porch railing. "Kayla!" the Deacon cries, and she finds her feet again. A look back as they near the church. The man frozen, belonging to neither the earth nor the stars.

Their sneakers on the church's brownstone steps. Kayla thinks of the old quarries outside town. A watery pit she visited with her father, a perch on a high cliff, their voices and echoes captured in a well of stones. The heavy oak doors close behind them. The girls cram into the dim vestibule. The organ's murmur. The smell of perfume and winter coats and incense. The squeak of sneakers over the floor's stone. The hanged man half a block away, but Kayla brushes her shoulder, feeling his shadow. On a side table, flowers in a vase. Kayla's finger circles a soft petal. A lifetime has passed since she's seen a bloom. Thoughts of her father's garden, and in her, another kind of pull, the knowing that somewhere near, flowers grow. A hothouse carved from the cold, a place of light and warmth and color.

The Deacon's arms outstretched, a silent shepherding. His jacket open and glimpses of his holstered gun. Kayla follows the others down the center aisle. A hush, even for Betty.

At the end of every other pew, a candle burns atop a metal holder. A corridor of soft light. More candles along the outer aisles and lining the altar. The current of passing bodies, and the candles flicker. Kayla's hand brushes the pews' curved wood. All of it beautiful. The girls segregate themselves, the pattern of morning convocation, whites to the right, reds to the left. Nurse Amy waves the girls to fill in the rows. The Deacon behind, his gaze on Betty as she and Kayla and the others from their pod settle into the last pew.

The poet and the biologist didn't believe, at least not in the way others did. Still, Kayla's parents had her baptized. First Holy Communion and Confirmation. "Tradition," her mother told her, "isn't always a bad thing." Her parents seldom spoke of God, but they praised this life's thoughtless beauty. They urged their daughter to do unto others as she would have done unto herself. To know a tree by its fruit. To look into the eyes of another and not see a stranger.

A rustling, the shedding of hats and gloves. The organ plays "Hark the Herald Angels Sing." Kayla's foot topples the kneeler, and with it, a child's mitten slips to the floor. Kayla bends forward. The mitten damp, so small she can only fit a few fingers inside. The vestibule doors open. A push of air, and the candles dance. Christ atop the alter, spasms across his bony ribs, an illusion of breath. The statue white plaster, as large as three men. Another man hung outside the church doors, and what, Kayla thinks, ever changes?

The music stops. The priest ascends the pulpit. The candlelight on his glasses. A white robe and golden sash. He holds out his hands. He speaks of the children's mass that ended an hour before, a smile as he recounts their joy. Their innocence. Kayla balls the mitten in her fist and wonders how many saw the man outside. The priest goes on—the season's power to speak to our sense of wonder, to our common humanity. God's kingdom can be their kingdom. Now. Tonight. All they have to do is open their hearts and accept His blessings.

Heather rests her head against Kayla's shoulder. Kayla the unbeliever soothed by the priest's words. Maybe, she thinks, it's enough to be safe, if just for the moment. And within that moment, if she has food in her stomach and is warm and is among people she's bled for and would bleed for again—then that's all the salvation she needs.

The priest's final words lost in Kayla's daydream. The organ plays a four-bar intro. The priest raises his hands, and the girls stand. Chris hands Kayla a hymnal. A turn of thin pages. The organ pauses, and with the first note, the priest lifts his voice. The Deacon next. Donna's choirgirl show. Kayla joins, surprising herself. "*Oh, little town of Bethlehem . . .*" A reflex, a stumble atop the chasm of what's been. The hopes and fears of all the years.

Tears warm her numb cheeks. She doesn't cry for want. She cries from the swell of fullness, the realization she's been stripped bare, and if the mob wants, they can beat her. Rape her. They can lift her from the ground with their twisted, fucking vine. They can take her last breath, and in return, she'll keep something they can never have. The love she's known. The memories of a little house in a little town.

A smile through her tears. The words on her lips. *How*

silently, how silently, the wondrous gift is given. The sisters crying too. Betty with an arm around Linda. Chris slumps back in the pew. Kayla feels the current among them, a dark energy, the call of lost voices.

A series of pops, a dozen echoes, this neighborhood of brick and narrow streets. The organ fumbles. A collective flinch in the pews. A bullet through the glass, and in the candles' glimmer, the stained-glass spray. An unclaimed moment before the pane tumbles, a jigsaw piece removed from the garden's betrayal. The pane strikes the floor, and what was broken breaks even more. The young whites scream as they push toward the center aisle. Through the gap, the whistle of wind, pinwheeling flurries. Shouts of men, and the gunfire draws near.

The priest on his hands and knees, a scramble from the altar, his Bible tucked to his body. The Deacon stands, arms outstretched, a shadow of his looming savior. "Everyone down! Take cover!"

The girls slide between the pews, a drowning in a wooden sea. Kayla lags, watching it all. Gunfire outside the church, screams inside. An explosion, close enough for the concussion to squeeze her heart. The surviving glass in the garden scene rattles. A gust, and the candle below dies. Heather grabs Kayla's wrist and pulls her down. The five of them in awkward poses. Kayla thinks of her old history text, the trenches of the First World War. The sisters' faces wet but their tears have stopped. All of them wide eyed. The priest bent double on his aisle walk, his white sash dragging. The Deacon and Panda Bear behind. Another explosion, their heads covered, and Kayla relishes their skittishness. Their pale fear.

She doesn't know who's outside. Bandits. Anarchists. Zealots blinded by ideology. They could be the monsters who strangled a girl with her red bandanna beneath a smoke-smudged moon. They could burst through the church doors and gun them down, reds and whites alike, in the next minute. All that less important than Panda Bear's cowering, the Deacon's twitching lips. She turns to the others. The candle-light above, shadows below, their faces like fish beneath the clear shallows. Their smiles reflect hers. She reaches out, a linking of hands. This shared current. She doesn't have to speak. None of them do.

The gunfire recedes. A running battle. Sirens close in. Kayla sticks her head into the aisle. The Deacon in the vestibule. The oak doors open. A peek outside and the push of frigid air. He returns, a crouched scamper. "Come, girls. They're gone, but we need to move quickly." He claps his hands. "Everyone up. Let's move."

The younger girls first. Hunched, their heads covered. A few crying. Nurse Amy among them, calm reassurances and urgings to hurry. The priest in the outer aisle. The long iron pole shakes in his hands, a snuffing of candles, a dark tide. Through the empty pane, the chuff of smoke. Kayla's pew the last to empty. The girls hold hands, a greater gathering in the vestibule. The Deacon steps outside and surveys the street. His gun in hand.

He turns back. The door opened, and framed behind him, the hanged man above his shoulder. "We're going back. Pair up and look out for each other. The bad men are gone, but we're not taking any chances. We're hustling ourselves right back. Everyone has to stay together."

They set off. The Deacon in front. Nurse Amy next, the smaller children gathered around her, a clutching of her coat and hands. "Don't look, honey," an admonishment as they near the light pole. Heavy Metal in the group's middle. Panda Bear the last out the door, but his steps faster as he passes the shell casings. Kayla and her podmates left to bring up the line's end.

"Hurry, hurry!" the Deacon calls, pausing before turning the corner, a moment's wait, the streetlight's glisten on his gun's chrome. Gunfire, and is it closer or just louder here in the street? The smoke heavier. Panda Bear jogging now, the others ordered to keep pace. Kayla lets go of Heather's hand. "Go," Kayla says. "I'll catch up."

Kayla's shadow joins the hanged man's as she crosses the street. She climbs the curb's snow piles. Betty and the sisters pause. Panda Bear already around the corner.

Kayla takes off her gloves. She tugs the rope's frozen knots. The others join her. Betty jumps and grabs the rope, the sisters following, and their weight gives Kayla a breath of slack. The hanged man twists, a puppet's protest. Heather on the knot's other side, their fingers working in unison, pulling here, pushing there.

One loop, two, and with a final tug, the knot gives way, a snake disappearing into itself. The rope uncoils from the porch railing. The tail end slips through the gloved hands of Betty and the sisters. A shifting of weight. The rope rises. The hanged man falls, a plummet and a thud. A stir of snow and cinders. The girls silent, a consideration of the thoughtless heap, the jumbled limbs, the rope's coil. Kayla steps forward, but Betty grabs her arm. "Come on, girl."

The girls run. Chris slips on the ice as they round the corner, Linda helping her to her feet. The five of them catching up by the time the line reaches the front gate. The school's lights blazing. The dark pushed away. The night as cold as any Kayla can remember.

* * *

Christmas morning. The cafeteria crowded. The first shared meal for the whites and reds, separate tables, a boundary marked by the beaming Deacon and the equally glum Panda Bear. "I know it's a day of miracles because my breakfast is finally warm," Betty says. Sausage and sweet rolls for everyone. The dishes cleared. Carols play on the boom box resting atop the serving line counter. *Come on, it's lovely weather for a sleigh ride together with you.* Nurse Amy delivers a shopping bag to each table. Inside, wrapped gifts, her instructions to wait until her say-so. Another surprise—each girl poured a cup of hot chocolate.

Kayla cradles the cup in her palms. The cup warm and her nose held close. The drink watery yet its smell is distinct. Kayla's thoughts cobwebbed with memories and too little sleep. A whiskey headache, extra sips and the serenade of gunfire.

Nurse Amy sets a bag on their table. "Merry Christmas, girls."

"Merry Christmas," the sisters say. Their sleepy unity.

"Sit with us," Betty says.

"For a second." She wedges between Betty and Heather. "Don't think the others can wait much longer to open their things."

"Thank you," Heather says. "For all this."

"You're welcome. The Deacon did—"

"We don't want to thank him," Betty says. "Just you."

"I'm grateful to be here with you." A smile. "All of you."

"What about your family?" Linda asks.

"I'm going back as soon as we're done."

Linda rubs her bloodshot eyes. "Thank them for sharing you."

Heather puts her arm around Kayla's shoulder. "And tell them Merry Christmas from your other family."

Nurse Amy stands, a brittle grin, and in Kayla, an understanding carried on the good scents of chocolate and sugar. Violence, bloodshed—they can't eradicate decency. This woman, these girls—here's a kind of love she's never considered, the kind that grows from pain. A love stronger than hurt. A love that just might wait in the heart of strangers.

Nurse Amy turns down the radio. Her voice raised over the clatter of cafeteria workers breaking down the line. "Thank you for your patience, everyone. And a special thanks to the Deacon for finding the funds in our tight budget to make this little celebration possible. And thank you to the cafeteria workers who took time from their families to make today's breakfast special."

"We love you, Nurse Amy," Betty shouts.

"And I love you. All of you." She pauses. "On your table is a bag, and in it are five wrapped gifts, one for everyone in your pod. When I give the word, select one, but don't open it. Instead, check it out, give it a shake or sniff, and if you want to, swap it with a neighbor. And when everyone's happy, then you can unwrap them. Not to ruin the surprise, but all the bags are the same, but each of the five presents are different. OK, ready?"

She turns the radio back on, and new sounds join the music, the rustle of paper, bright voices. The girls at Kayla's table laughing as they exchange packages, wrappings of blue and red and gold. The sisters trade gifts then trade back. Betty holds each package to her ear and shakes. "Let's just open the damn things," she says. "Everything belongs to all of us anyway."

"Amen," Heather says.

Betty rips her gift's paper. Heather and the sisters more

deliberate, a lifting of taped seams, the paper folded back. The girls smile, their presents held up for all to see. Slippers. A hairbrush. Notebooks and pens. A coffee mug filled with penny candy. For Kayla, hand lotion and lip balm. The gifts passed around, the others laughing when Kayla runs the brush over her cropped hair.

Nurse Amy collects the wrappings. A final goodbye. Heather asks if her children still believe in Santa Claus. "Yes," Nurse Amy said. "Although I'm guessing not for long."

Linda: "I believed in Santa until I was eleven."

Betty rolls her eyes. "Shocker."

The Deacon stands. His hands lifted, a beckoning for silence, his wait longer than normal, the giddiness of sweets and presents. The stillness allowed to linger before he speaks. His tone marches from hushed to impassioned. The miracle of God's son walking among them. The presents the girls opened mere symbols of the Lord's greater gifts—love, salvation. Gifts that outlast any toy. "Let us pray."

Kayla lowers her head, her hairbrush-holding hands folded in her lap. The Deacon's right, the fucker. He needs a fairy tale's lens to see it, but a fairy tale is OK if it works for him. Salvation, love—they know no special day of the year. They're all around her, waiting, begging to be understood. Her parents' words, and today, she understands them better than before. Her drift interrupted as Donna claims one of the table's empty chairs.

"No one asked you to park your skanky ass," Betty hisses.

"Come on, it's Christmas." Donna's voice a whisper. A glance toward the Deacon. "And I'm going to have this smile on the whole time, and I suggest you do the same." She speaks through clenched teeth. "We know you have our shit."

"Amen," the Deacon says.

Donna's smile bright. "Amen."

Betty sips her hot chocolate. "You don't know shit."

"It's in the ceiling." Donna pauses then laughs. "I can see it in your eyes." She points to Linda. "Especially yours. God, you're dull. I didn't know for sure before, but I do now. Ashley should have looked there first during the fire drill, but she's not the smartest one either, is she?"

One of the cafeteria workers turns the radio back on. *I'll have a blue Christmas without you.* Heather's voice low and even. "Go fuck yourself."

"No, go fuck yourselves. You see the twins over there?" Ashley and Amanda stand near the Deacon, a nod when Donna looks their way. "They're waiting for me to give them a little wave so they can share the news." She scratches her chin. "With all that shit, I'm guessing you ladies will be in iso for a week or two. All except you." She smiles at Betty. "I think the Deacon's as tired of your shit as the rest of us. I'm thinking he's just looking for an excuse to kick your ass out of here. Maybe you and Carolyn can hook up and be bunkies again at the girl's center. I hear it's a good idea to have someone there to watch your back."

Betty leans forward, her elbows on the table. "If we were alone, I'd punch your fucking face in."

Donna mirrors her pose. "And I'd slit your fucking throat." She leans back. "And I'd do the same to the rest of you. You know why?" She stands and brushes off her top. "Because every time I look at you, I see the fuckers who killed my father. And I see the fuckers who'd kill me if they had the chance." She turns to Kayla. "You're going to use that big brain of yours to sneak back to your room, get our shit, and stash it on the top landing outside iso. Ten minutes. Don't make me wait."

She turns. A wave for the twins, and the three of them reclaim their seats. Donna's laughter rises. *That's when those blue memories start calling . . .* The joy Kayla felt moments before evaporates, a disappearance that leaves her gutted. Chris breaks the silence. "What're we going to do?"

Betty slumps back and pushes the slippers across the table. "Go ahead, Oakmont. We'll make sure no one but the blond bitch leaves. If they do, we're having it out today. All of it." She turns to Heather and the sisters. "You with me?"

"Yep," Heather says. The sisters nod.

"If the gingers and the others stay, we'll do the same. We'll take our lumps and pull back and regroup. Most of all, we can't lose the truck keys." Betty turns to Kayla. "Get to the stash. Save the good stuff for us. Give them the fucking peppermint schnapps."

"And the menthols," Linda says.

The Deacon sits with the younger whites, their heads lowered, a circle of linked hands. Heavy Metal's attention on unwrapping his present. Kayla's exit deliberate, not a glance back. The cafeteria door closes, the smothering of music and voices. She jogs, and around her, a blur of the hallway's Christmas decorations. The hand-painted banners—**PURITY**. A security camera's unblinking eye. Kayla's pace faster, and she sees herself both in the moment and as a ghost passing across unwatched monitors.

The stairs. Her pod. She works quickly. The chair arranged, a step onto the desk. The trickle of dust from the ceiling tile. A frantic groping—the truck keys and hammer. She raises herself onto her toes, reaching further, items examined and returned, others slid into her pockets—cigarettes, lip balm, gum. The peppermint schnapps, another bottle gripped as she returns the tile. She climbs down. She pulls up her shirt, the first pint slid into her panties. Donna enters and tosses a cardboard box on Heather's bunk.

"In here," she says.

Kayla hands her the bottles and empties her pockets. The

box small enough to be tucked under Donna's arm. She finishes her packing. "That's not enough."

The morning's filtered light. Flurries again. Church bells, and Kayla imagines a Christmas service, wind through a broken window. A child without a mitten. A hanged man lying in the street. "That's all you're getting."

Donna looks up. "Where're you keeping it?"

"Fuck you."

"Oh—one more thing."

Kayla pauses in the doorway. "You're not getting anything more."

"I want that necklace." She tucks the box under her arm and smiles. "You should see yourself. All that tough-girl shit just washed right out of you, didn't it? Give me the fucking necklace or I'm bringing the Deacon up. The beanpole mother-fucker will have no trouble lifting every goddamn tile, and when he finds your shit, I'm guessing you'll be saying goodbye to your girl Betty." She frowns. "That would make you sad, wouldn't it?"

A pained heartbeat. Her throat constricted. White sparks across her eyes. Distance in her limbs as she kneels. The lid's squeaking hinges. Her hand lost in her clothes' soft folds. A cupping of the delicate chain.

Donna holds out her hand. Kayla lets the necklace slip, a coiling of chain then the crucifix. Donna pauses. "I'll give it back if you tell me how your father died."

"They hung him." A desert in Kayla's throat. Her gaze fixed on Donna's hand. "There were twenty of them. Maybe more. All of them cowards." She looks Donna in the eye. Her words deliberate, sturdy, lifted on a rising tide. "Not one of them was half the man my father was. Not one. They beat him. They put a rope around his neck and pulled him up. He choked. He turned white then blue. He fought and kicked. Then he didn't."

Donna silent, and when she speaks, a new tone, even and steely. "I saw half my father's face ripped off. Just like that. I turned my back. He'd just picked me up from practice. He did everything after my mom died. A car drove by. The blast swallowed every other sound—the birds, the kids in the street. I turned, and he was lying in the driveway. I went to hold him and the gray shit of his brain was all over my hands. I still feel it there." She opens her hand and studies the necklace. "His one eye was looking at me. His lips were moving. He didn't know me. He didn't know anything." She sighs. "The fuckers who shot him listened to people like your father, and none of them, your father included, was half the man he was." She tosses the necklace onto Kayla's cot. "Keep it. It's a piece of shit anyway."

Kayla retrieves the necklace. Its weight a whisper after the heaviness of seeing it in Donna's palm.

"I heard you think your mother's alive."

"She is."

"You're fucking naïve for someone who's supposed to be so goddamn smart." Donna brushes past her then turns in the hallway. "Everything from before is dead for us. White, red—it doesn't matter. We wouldn't be here if it weren't."

* * *

The room dark. The girls on the floor by the window. Chris wears the new slippers, the rest of their Christmas take in the circle's center. The window closed, but the cigarette's blowback lingers. Betty holds the whiskey to her lips. A sip then a closing of eyes. "Thanks for making sure those bitches didn't get the good stuff, Oakmont."

"Peppermint schnapps." Linda makes a face. "Yuck."

"They got enough," Heather says. "They should've gotten shit."

Silence. The building's rhythms, water and steam. A train along the riverside tracks. "I wonder where we'll be next Christmas," Chris says.

"Here," Heather says. "Or someplace like it."

"I hope we're still together," Linda says. "Well, I hope you find your mom, Kayla. But the rest of us, I hope we're together."

"I *hope*. I *wish*." Betty climbs atop the desk and pushes aside the ceiling tile. "I'm tired of hoping and wishing just to have a fair fucking shake." She returns the bottle and produces the truck key. She shakes the ring, a faint jingle. "We need to make a plan, just in case shit gets real in a hurry." She replaces the tile and sits with the others. "A bust-out script if they try to split us up."

Chris takes the key. "Does anyone know how to drive?"

"Shit," Betty says. "Driving can't be that hard if those morons do it."

"It's a stick shift," Linda says. "I have no idea how that works."

Kayla holds out her hand and Chris gives her the key. "I've driven stick. On my father's truck. A couple times, not a lot."

Betty smiles. "Well, we've got ourselves a driver. Old

299

Oakmont's going to be *our* chauffer. That makes a sweet deal even sweeter."

Kayla tosses Betty the key. "Didn't say I was any good."

"Better than any of us," Heather says.

"We got us a key and a truck and a driver." Betty pushes up the ceiling tile and returns the key. "The hardest part's already done, right?"

"We could start thinking about the details of how to do it," Linda says.

"One always needs to explore their options." Chris pauses. She reaches out and squeezes her sister's hand. "That's what our mom used to say."

"Have a plan," Kayla says, her voice soft.

"Let's take a week," Heather says. "All of us start looking at things in a new way. And every night, we'll compare notes."

A smile on Chris's face. "It'll be kind of like spying. Like in the movies"

"What about the trash?" Kayla asks. "Heather and I do the cafeteria, and I'll bet there's shit we can use in there, stuff they just throw out." She turns to Linda. "You could do the same with the office trash."

"There's always takeout menus in the guard's break room," Linda says.

"So we breakout and then get some fucking eggrolls?" Betty says.

"A lot of them have little maps on them, you know? We put a few of them together, and we'd have a better idea of where we're going."

Betty puts an arm around Linda's shoulder. "Now that's solid thinking, my sister."

"And the guards throw out old pens sometimes," Chris says. She stabs the circle's empty center. "We could melt the plastic and make a knife-type thingy. Kind of like how Carolyn did."

"See?" Heather says. "There're all kinds of shit we can bring together. Everything we find, everything we see, we'll bring back here."

"We might have to wait until the plow comes off the truck." Chris takes off the slippers and sets them on the circle's pile. "That's pretty conspicuous."

"That's fine," Kayla says. "It's not about going tomorrow or next week or even next month. It's about us making a plan. A good plan that could get us out of here, just in case. All of us."

"All of us," Heather says.

The sister's unison: "All of us."

"Goddamn right, all of us," Betty says.

"Then it's settled," Heather says. "Every night we'll meet and talk. We'll keep notes. When people come and go. When they use the bathroom. When they have lunch. And we'll pocket anything that looks like it could help us. Not one of us who isn't smarter than Heavy Metal and Panda Bear put together. We ought to be able to find any number of fuckups in their routine."

Linda turns to Betty. "You've got to promise not to do anything to get into trouble. I'm afraid what happened to Carolyn will happen to you."

"'Not do anything?' That's pretty vague."

"You know what she means," Chris says.

Betty raises her hand. "I hereby promise not to fuck up. I promise to lead a quiet and peaceful life—"

An explosion shakes the windows. A shock in Kayla's chest. Snow dislodged from the window cage mesh, a breath of gray. Voices and cries from other rooms. The rhythm of Old John's limping run. The concussion lingers, a resonating in Kayla's gut. The girls gather at the window. A plume billows over the rooftops—a half dozen or more blocks away—Kayla shocked by the distance, her assumption the bomb had gone off across the street. "Fucking A," Betty says.

"The police station's somewhere over there," Heather says. "At least I think it is."

"Or was," Betty says.

Sirens wail, and the girls settle back into their cots. Flashes of red on the windows and ceiling. The sisters' beds pushed together. "Can I come over?" Kayla whispers.

"Yes," Heather says.

The floor cold beneath Kayla's socks. Her bed lifted and set near Heather's. A scrape as she pushes the last few inches. Their opened coats on top of them, a final layer of warmth, and beneath the coats, the girls hold hands. More sirens, then gunfire, short bursts. Kayla still, waiting for the next shot.

Linda's voice first. Thin, soft, her inflections muted, her sister joining before the chorus. Kayla hasn't sung "From Here to There" since a sunny day on her father's campus. A life with no claim upon her now. The room's chill on her lips, she sings, the five of them together for the second verse. More a prayer than an anthem.

A lull after they finish. Chris the first to speak. "Goodnight, Betty. Goodnight, Kayla and Heather."

"Night, Betty," Linda says. "Night, Kayla—"

"Can't we just say 'Goodnight, everybody?'" Betty asks. "Like this—goodnight, ladies. I love you all."

"That's nice," Linda says.

"Fucking A," Betty says.

The sisters laugh. Heather whispers, loud enough for only Kayla to hear. "Night, Kayla."

"Goodnight."

* * *

A week passes. A secret thrill for Kayla, for all of them. A new awareness, a perception that pushes aside the drudgery. At night, they hold their meetings. The rationing of cigarettes. Their whiskey down to the last pint. A plastic shopping bag fills with their scourings—twine, plastic silverware, thumbtacks, a nearly depleted roll of duct tape.

Linda and Chris focus on the guards. Their lunch breaks and check-ins. The days they pull the overnight shift. How long Heavy Metal spends in the lav with the morning paper. When Panda Bear texts his girlfriend. Betty feigns a series of migraines. The nurse's office, the cool washrag pulled from her eyes as she notes the front hallway's comings and goings. The teachers and deliverymen. The handful of cafeteria workers who attend the Deacon's after-lunch prayer session.

Heather and Kayla's attention on the pickup, the delivery gate and its lock and the keys that jangle from the guards' rings. The gate swings back for food deliveries and the laundry's weekly drop off. Kayla counts the seconds it takes a guard to exit a running truck, open the gate, and lock it from the other side. She times the minutes needed to secure the plow. They identify the cars parked curbside. Nurse Amy and Mr. James's minivans. The rusting wheel wells and chrome muffler of Panda Bear's low-slung beater. The Deacon's black pickup.

Heather keeps their notes. The tablet they received for Christmas, names replaced with symbols, times recorded in an arithmetic code Kayla taught her. Linda cuts a square for each player. Their identifying symbol in the center. The Deacon's halo. Panda Bear's cellphone. A devil-horn salute for Heavy Metal. The upper right corner for their arrival time. Lower right for departure. Upper left for their schedules' irregulari-

303

ties. Lower left the wild card space. Other squares cut for the cafeteria's schedule, the truck, the front and back gates. The papers laid out across the semicircle's center. The girls arranging and rearranging, Kayla seeking patterns and sharing them with the others. Whispered debates, possibilities headier than whiskey. Should they go on a weekend or weekday? Morning or evening? Bad weather or good? Who should join Kayla in the truck's cab? Should they escape beneath a diversion's cover?

The meetings end. The papers gathered. Their final conversations dreamy conjectures. Kayla's grandmother's house their goal. Five girls in a rattling pickup, the blind navigation of side streets until they reach the river road. The others not interested in Kayla's worries about finding her way; instead, they demand her stories, tales embellished for their entertainment. The haze over morning pastures. Spring's goldenrod. July's fireflies and bullfrogs. The warmth of a December hearth. Her grandmother's garden, as large as a basketball court. The pear and apple trees. The wandering chickens.

The girls back in their cots. The lull before sleep. Betty's voice: "Chickens and bullfrogs. Who'd have thought I'd ever end up in a crazy, fucking place like that?"

* * *

Heather and Kayla nudge their dust piles toward the cafeteria's back alcove. Their brooms' whisper and the cafeteria radio's patriotic songs. A moment's hesitation, the pocketing of a bobby pin before they sweep the pile into a dustpan. They pause by the loading-dock door. Outside, Heavy Metal starts the truck. Haze from the exhaust. The engine running as he pushes back the gate, the ritual repeated once he's pulled into the street. Heather's fingers squeeze the mop handle's notches.

The girls in the utility closet. Their spray bottles and rags shelved. Kayla turns, a step back when she finds Donna leaning in the doorway. In Donna's hands, a stapled packet, a page flipped, then another. She hums the new anthem as her finger runs down the printed list. "Found this in the Deacon's office." She turns another page. The closet's naked bulb behind Kayla, and her shadow falls over the lines of names and addresses. "Guess I should return it before he notices." She smiles at Kayla. "Your last name's Kellerman, right?"

Kayla silent.

"That's what I thought." Donna's finger inches down the list. "These are all the folks who've been processed through holding at the stadium. Must be a few thousand. They sure are busy there." She turns another page. "Kellerman. It's not the most common name, is it? Still, there's a few. But I'm not seeing any women's names—"

Kayla snatches the packet. *Kellerman* and a first name she doesn't know. *Kellerman, Alex* and *Kellerman, William*—her uncles. She sees them in the summer sun, her house's open second floor, the blue sky above. A buckling in her knees, their reduction to ink on paper. Kayla tries to force her mother's

305

name between theirs. Her eyes blinking, the papers flipped as she checks her maiden name. Nothing.

"Makes you wonder, doesn't it?" Donna tugs at her ponytail, a crack of gum. "Where would she be if she never found her way to—"

Her words cut short by the mop handle Heather thrusts into her gut. Donna doubles over and chokes on swallowed gum. Heather grabs Donna's hair and delivers a sharp knee to her face. Donna drops to her knees. Heather rears back, a final, grunting kick to Donna's side. Heather takes the packet and lets it drop. A quick stamp, a page-tearing twist of her sneaker. A dirty imprint. "Explain that to the Deacon, cunt."

Heather exits the closet. Kayla next, Donna moaning as she steps over her. Heather grips Kayla's hand. A leading through the cafeteria. "There's always hope, Kay," she says. "That's all we need to tell ourselves."

* * *

The girls at dinner. The early sunset, the windows dark. Betty and the sisters intent, a hushed retelling of Heather's scrape with Donna. The news radiates out, whispers at the surrounding tables. Heather's tone without pride or vengeance. She pauses then adds: "It was stupid. I shouldn't have. Not with our other plans."

Heavy Metal outside the cafeteria's main doors, his walkie-talkie to his ear. Unsupervised, the girls gather by the back windows. The first snowflakes, a gauzy curtain beneath the loading door light. Snow gathers on Panda Bear's cap, steam from his mouth as he secures the pickup's plow. Kayla tells of watching Heavy Metal earlier in the day, the gate unlocked, passed through, relocked. The truck running the whole time.

Betty rests her forehead against the glass. "You really think you could drive that beast, Oakmont?"

Kayla imagines her sneakered feet, the lineup of pedals. Right foot up and left foot down, the shifter wrestled, the double bump of railroad tracks. "I think I can."

"Then maybe it's time to move," Betty says. "The sooner the better."

"Hey you!" Heavy Metal yells. He stands inside the cafeteria doors. "Away from those windows! The rest of you finish up and drop off your plates. Let's go!"

"Yeah, yeah, yeah." Betty shuffles to the door. Her voice low. "I'm trying to think of things I'll miss about this place, but I'm coming up empty."

"Nurse Amy?" Linda says.

"Old John," Chris adds. "Mr. James."

Betty smiles, an arm around each sister's shoulder. "You two are a pain in the ass, you know that?"

"Knock it off," Heavy Metal barks. "Hands to yourself. Back in line."

Betty raises her hands, a mock surrender, a smile on her face, but Heavy Metal's gaze unnerves Kayla. A new energy in him tonight, his slouch and indifference gone. He remains near on their walk back upstairs, the walkie-talkie by his mouth, a series of check-ins. Kayla fears for Heather, a pang that spikes when the girls find the Deacon and Old John waiting in the upstairs hallway.

The Deacon's voice stern. "Everyone to their rooms. Doors shut and no coming out until I say so." He points to Betty. "You stay where you are."

Betty's arms crossed, the Deacon's stare returned. Old John hobbles past and shoos the younger girls into their pods.

"Don't let anyone out," the Deacon says. He turns back to Betty. "We're going into your room. Sit on your bunks with your hands on your laps. Not a word out of anyone."

Betty tilts her head. "What's going—"

"Not a word!" The Deacon's face red. He extends his long arm and points. "Go!"

The girls sit. The sisters side by side until the Deacon snaps. "On your own damn bunks!" Heavy Metal the last to enter, the door shut behind him. The Deacon plants his fists against his hips. "Does anyone want to come clean?"

Linda raises her hand.

"Well?" the Deacon says.

"Clean about what?"

"Oh, good Lord." He turns to Heavy Metal. "You start there. I'll take this one."

Heavy Metal opens Kayla's footlocker. He reaches in, her underwear and socks and scrubs tossed to the floor. Kayla bites her lip, the dullard's paws, her necklace's delicate chain. The

Deacon turns Linda's footlocker onto its side and kicks through her belongings. Chris's footlocker next.

Linda raises her hand. "Deacon?"

"What?"

"Can I pick up my stuff?"

He kicks through the clothing pile. "No! Just sit until I say otherwise. And no more questions!" He lifts Betty's footlocker. A shower of clothes and towels. A clear pint bottle, the room light captured in the glass, a soft landing in the waiting clothes.

"Hey!" Betty says.

"Shut up!" The Deacon's eyes alight. "I've had enough of your attitude. Your . . . poison!" He crouches and picks up the bottle of peppermint schnapps. At its bottom, a few sips.

"Fuck if that's mine!" Betty says

"Not another word!" The Deacon gathers cigarettes, another empty bottle. He beckons Heavy Metal. "Take her outside and wait for me."

Heavy Metal reaches for Betty's arm, but she shrugs him off. "That's not mine. Everyone here will tell you so." Heavy Metal latches onto her elbow, a twist, Betty desperate to wriggle free. "The only ones who knew that shit was there were the ones who put it there. The same ones who told you it was fucking there."

"Get her out," the Deacon says. "Now!"

Betty kicks Heavy Metal in the shin and breaks free, the two of them locked in a dance, Betty careful to keep a cot between them. "You came here on a rumor. It's a fucking setup, and you know it! But when Linda and Oakmont get jumped, you do shit. You know why?" Heavy Metal leaps over a cot, a stumble when his boot strikes Chris's side, a weighty thud onto the floor. Betty scurries to the room's other side. "You do shit because you're a coward. A lazy, fucking coward—"

The Deacon strides forward. His arms outstretched, a closing off of the narrow space. Betty ducks, but his hand clamps her neck. Betty yelps, fists swinging. The Deacon's arm rigid, and her punches swipe the empty air between them before she clutches his hand. Her eyes shut and pained. Her voice fading. "You're choking me . . ." She gasp. "Stop . . . shit . . . stop . . ."

"Stop it!" Heather screams. "Fucking stop choking her!"

The Deacon lets go, and with a shove, casts her into Heavy Metal's arms. "Cowards, the both of you," Betty says, a whisper, a gasp. She rubs her throat. "Lazy, motherfucking cowards."

The door slams. Kayla and the others still on their cots. Tears on Linda's face.

"Why'd you have to hurt her?"

"She's telling the truth," Chris says. "That's not hers."

The Deacon possessed. His breathing heavy. Grunts as he yanks drawers off their runners, shelves cleared with a sweep of his hand. The girls ordered to sit beneath the windows as he topples their mattresses. A tirade as he strips Betty's sheets and piles up her clothes. "This wasn't a secret. I know that. I see it written on your faces." He stands beneath their ceiling's hiding spot. The sisters lower their heads. The Deacon cinches the sheet's corners, slings the bulging sack over his shoulder, and kicks his way through the floor's clutter.

Chris stands. "It wasn't her fault!"

The Deacon turns. "Whose was it then?"

"You know who," Heather says. Her gaze lifts from the floor and fixes on him. "Betty's right, and you know it. It was the ones who told you it was here."

The Deacon opens the door. "This isn't over yet. I'll be meeting with all of you first thing tomorrow."

Heather follows him into the hallway. Behind her, Kayla and the sisters. "Hey!" Heather yells.

The veins in the Deacon's neck strain above his white collar. Beside him, Heavy Metal, his grip tight on Betty's arm. "Back in your room!" the Deacon snaps.

Heather steps forward. Old John at his desk, the connecting hallway's divide. Beyond him, a gathering of whites. Donna and the twins up front. "How do you think they knew?" Heather points down the hall. "I don't need to tell you because you already know."

A twitch in the Deacon's eye. "I said back in—"

"You want to see something?" Heather's voice carries. Behind her, the opening of pod doors, a red spill into the hallway. "Let me take you to the golden girl's pod. We'll see what her and her ginger apes have stashed!"

Donna whispers, and Ashley pushes her way back through the crowd.

The Deacon calls to Old John. "Do your job and get them back to their rooms!" He turns to Heather. "You, too! All of you! Anyone not in their pod in thirty seconds will spend the rest of the week in isolation!"

"Go on," Betty twists her neck and works her jaw. "Any fool who wears a collar is going to believe what he wants to believe."

The other reds slink back to their rooms. Kayla and the sisters frozen. The Deacon joins Heavy Metal, a grasping of Betty's other arm, Betty duck-walked between them. Heather shouts, "You got the wrong girl, Deacon. You got the wrong girl, and you know it!"

Old John limps toward them. The jangle of keys. The scuff of his heavy leg. His hands outstretched, a gentle guiding. "Come on, girls. I don't want you getting put upstairs." He stands at their door's threshold, his tone soft. The shutting door eclipses his face. "I'll have a prayer or two for your friend tonight."

The latch's click. The room's silence. The sisters pull their mattresses back onto their bunks. Kayla on her knees, her necklace tucked in her towel's folds. Heather paces—the door to the window and back, a path navigating the mess. Her hands on her head. A muttering of curses.

Linda rearranges her blankets. "How long do you think she'll be in iso?"

"A long time." Chris returns her shampoo and toothpaste to her bedside shelf. "Longer than she's been in before, I bet."

"Maybe we all should go to the Deacon," Linda says. "Tell him the stuff belongs to all of us. Zack's already fired. Not like we'd be snitching. We'll say he brought it and that we're all to blame. And that the whites have been doing it too. He can't punish us all, right? At least not as bad as he can punish one person. And if he finds out Donna's involved—"

"Fuck Donna." Heather pauses her pacing to stare out the window.

"Maybe Linda's right." Kayla lies across her cot and studies the ceiling. "We should go down and all take the blame. Stick it out together in iso—either all at once or in shifts or whatever the fuck they give us. And in the meantime, we'll finalize our plans. We'll rehearse. We won't cause any trouble. And when we get our first opportunity, we'll split."

"Shit." Heather struggles to open the window. "Shit. Shit! Shit! Help me!"

Kayla and the sisters run to her. The window stubborn, an opening of fits and budges, the push of icy air. In the courtyard, Heavy Metal fumbles with the gate's lock. A police cruiser on the other side, snow in its headlight beams. Heavy Metal's long shadow. The pickup and plow layered beneath the white. Betty shivers. Her hands clutch her bed-sheet satchel. Steam from her mouth. The Deacon by her side.

The cruiser eases past the gate. A three-point turn, splashes of red across the snow. Heather the first to yell. "Betty! Betty!"

Kayla and the sisters join. Overlapping voices. Saying nothing beyond her name. The breeze through the window's grate, snow on their faces. "Betty!" A disjointed cry, echoes off brownstone walls. In the near distance, a dog pack's answering barks. Betty looks up, a final resisting against the Deacon's push before she disappears into the cruiser's back. The Deacon closes the door, and his hand pats the cruiser's top.

The girls' cries wither, the unsaid words like stones in their throats. The cruiser pulls through the gate. A last look then gone. Heavy Metal secures the padlock. The Deacon climbs the loading dock steps, a shuffle through the snow. His voice tired, his gaze on his feet. "Shut that window. Or leave it open and freeze. I don't care."

***

Heather and Kayla in the cafeteria alcove. Rags and spray bottles in hand. The kitchen clatter, breakfast cleanup, lunch prep. The radio louder than normal. Pop songs. The weather report. Another storm, a half foot, maybe more. The girls linger in the closet. With them, a waste can from the lunch ladies' break room. A sifting, wrappers and apple cores; the things they stick in their pockets—a safety pin, a lanyard with a broken clasp. Their plans intensifying, conversations spurred by Betty's stripped bed, by the room's new hush. They'll go before another girl is put with them. They'll replace their snoopings with a simpler course of action. Night. Trash can fires in the lav and common room, the alarms and their chaos. A bolt down the alcove stairwell, their supplies in-hand. The pickup's plow a battering ram so fuck Heavy Metal's key and the gate's lock. They'll make their way uptown to Heather's old neighborhood. They'll ditch the truck in an alley and lie low amid the backyard shadows while Heather knocks on a door. Her aunt, a woman who once loved her as her own. In her driveway, a car she rarely drives. She'll hand over the keys and report it stolen the next morning. She will. She has to. Kayla's new understanding—hope, outlandish and improbable—shines brightest when it's the only option. "Tonight," Linda whispered at breakfast, and they agreed. Tonight.

Kayla and Heather step from the alcove. The back stairwell door opens and Ashley's head sticks out. "Nurse Amy wants to see Kayla."

"What about?" Kayla asks.

Ashley retreats, speaking as the door sighs shut behind her. "How the fuck should I know. Something about a letter."

Kayla stares at Heather. Their plans for tonight, these last hours. Now a letter, and who else but her mother—or at least word of her mother. In Kayla, a kindling, a stirring of the dead. The sensation heady, disorienting. Her mouth opens but a logjam chokes her throat, the pull of the past and the present and dozen vague futures.

Heather places Kayla's spray bottle on the shelf. "Go already. I'll finish here."

A navigation between the cafeteria tables. A glance back, a bump into a chair. The thought of her mother a rising tide that pushes all else aside. Kayla rubs her head. The hard press of skull. The realization neither she nor her mother will be the same person. They've suffered alone, survived alone. Her steps quicker as she pushes through the cafeteria doors.

The first-floor hallway. The *Purity* banners, taped and rehung after the fight that landed Kayla in iso. Notes from the music room's piano, Mr. James playing, the voices of the youngest girls. "*What a friend we have in Jesus . . .*" Kayla jogging now, a turn into the entrance hallway. The guard's post on the other side, the bank of monitors. The nurse's door shut. A soft knock. A door locked for privacy. Kayla sees her mother inside, perhaps signing papers, a deliverance she hasn't dared dream. Another knock, this one harder. A testing of the handle.

"What're you doing?" Heavy Metal in the doorway across the hall.

"I'm seeing Nurse Amy."

"Nurse ain't in. At least not until noon. She's—"

Her mother. Reunion. Escape. A child's belief in happy endings. The notions crash around her, as fragile as stained glass, a drowning in colored dust. She pictures Heather and Ashley, the supply closet. Kayla turns and runs, each stride bringing speed. The hallway blurs, a tunnel of color and sound. A burst through the cafeteria doors. An apron-clad woman calls, a scolding to sweep up before the whites' lunch. Kayla zigzags between the tables. The stink of her chemical cleaner lingering. The tabletops glisten beneath the lights.

The alcove empty. Outside, the first snow flakes, the pickup speckled in white. Their spray bottles and rags on the supply closet floor, one bottle overturned and leaking from its cap, a trickle seeking the drain. Kayla steps back, a survey of the cafeteria. The tall ceiling, the lights and exposed ductwork. The swell of her heart consumed by the hush and empty tables.

The back stairwell darker than normal, the first landing light out. The steps taken two at a time then a stumble over the broken dust mop. Heather crumpled in the landing's dim corner, her back against the wall, her head hung. By her side, wooden splinters and a foot-long section of the handle's top. Red streaks across her face. Her sweatpants and panties pulled past her knees. Blood between her legs.

"Fuck, baby. Fuck." Kayla kneels and pushes back Heather's blood-matted hair. Heather's eyes slivers of white, lulling passes of brown. Tremors in her thin lips. Blood rivulets in the handle's carved notches. Kayla wipes the wood against her sweatpants and slides the handle into her sock.

"You're going to be OK," Kayla says. Heather limp as Kayla pulls up her underwear and pants. An arm beneath her knees, another around her shoulders, a lift. Her friend no longer human, just another broken thing in this world of broken things. Kayla struggles to open the stairwell door then squints in the cafeteria's bright lights. The weight in her arms evaporates. Her steps quicker, and the handle's jagged tip pokes her leg. Her tears a wetness she can't wipe. The cafeteria ladies with their hairnets and aprons, spatulas and silver trays—all frozen in the dishwasher's dreamy haze as Kayla rushes toward them.

"Help us!" Kayla cries. "For the fucking love of god, help us!"

* * *

Dinner. The ghosts of empty seats. Kayla and the sisters talk of Heather's return. A week in the hospital, but this morning, Linda saw the ambulance. Nurse Amy with an arm around Heather's shoulders, an escort through the entry gates. "She was walking real slow," Linda says.

Kayla the initial suspect, the two of them alone. Blood on Kayla's hands and clothes. An interrogation in the main office. The Deacon and one of the cops who delivered Kayla on a warm, rainy night. The cop asked about the blood, their use of an off-limits stairwell. The Deacon with his own questions— why was Kayla trying to sneak into the nurse's office? His voice lowered—what about the other rumors? Their joined bunks. This attack sadistic and brutal, the kind triggered by jealousy. A lover's rage.

Kayla straight-faced, strengthened by the truth. Yes, they slept with bunks pushed together, their bond something beyond the Deacon's sick mind. Ashley was the one who should be sitting in this chair. Ashley and her sister and Donna. A long stare as she said the Deacon knew the truth as well as she did. Kayla cleared only after Heather regained consciousness. Of course her friend hadn't attacked her. Trouble was, she couldn't say who had. Her memory erased. The building under tighter security, the reds and whites no longer allowed together, not even for morning convocation, but the investigation of the whites had run dry—their unified alibis, the lack of blood on their clothing, the inconclusive surveillance videos.

Nurse Amy enters. She returns a tray to the dishwasher drop-off. Linda and Chris wave her over. "How's she doing?" Chris asks.

Nurse Amy sits. A rearranging of her ponytail. A tug of her lanyard. "She's OK, considering. Tired. A little shaky still."

"Can we see her?" Kayla asks.

The nurse looks over her shoulder. "Sure. But not for long." She stands. Kayla and the sisters return their trays. Nurse Amy raises a hand as they pass Heavy Metal. "They're with me."

The hallway hushed. In Kayla, the sensation of being whittled away. Her parents, her home and dog, and what remains eroded by the day, the machine's grind, the abrasion of oppression and fears and uncertainty. The girls silent, but the message understood. Linda slips a hand into Kayla's, her other already linked with her sister's.

The nurse's office the same as her first night—hygiene posters, glass cylinders of cotton balls and tongue depressors. The scent of Lysol. Two cots wait beyond the examination area. Around each, a retractable curtain, a bit of privacy. "Heather?" Nurse Amy says. She pulls the curtain aside. "You have some visitors."

Heather sits, propped by pillows. Her face's fading bruises. The girls step forward one at a time, tender hugs and whispered welcomes. They claim seats on the bed's edge, the sisters on one side, Kayla on the other. A silent moment before Linda breaks into tears.

"I'm OK." Heather's words slur. She pats Linda's leg.

"Five minutes, OK?" Nurse Amy says. "You can come again tomorrow. I'll arrange it so you can have lunch together." She draws the curtains, a surrounding of white.

"Thank you," Chris says.

"You're welcome." The squeak of retreating sneakers. "Five minutes."

"How're you feeling?" Linda asks.

"I've been sleeping a lot." A pause. "Wish I could share some of my pills."

Kayla whispers: "We're bolting as soon as you're ready. No more waiting."

Chris leans forward. "But we're going to settle up first."

"Who else was with Ashley?" Kayla asks.

"I don't know. I seriously don't. I see bits and pieces, but nothing really fits together. I can't even say if Ashley was there." A weak squeeze for Kayla's hand. "I see you and I know you were carrying me." She falls silent, a disconnect before she continues. "It felt like I was flying."

Linda wipes her cheek. "Then we'll just get Ashley. One for one, at least that."

"Where will that get us?" Heather lets her head sink back into the pillow and closes her eyes. "If we're going to go, let's go. I don't want messing with them to fuck our plans. Let's just focus on what we need to do." She sighs. "I'm tired of all the other stuff. All the hate. It's killing me." She lays a hand over her chest. "I'm done with all of it."

A rumble in the floor. Kayla thinks of the basement's furnace, the riverside train. The shaking builds. The clatter of shelved canisters and vials, tremors in Kayla's teeth. Chris goes to the room's window. "It's the Army. At least I think it is."

The others join her, Kayla with a hand to help Heather to her feet. Heather's pace hobbled, a shuffling of socks over tile. "I have to take it easy. Don't want to tear again."

The window faces the street. The glass trembles. Outside, a clanking procession. Transport trucks, armored cars.

Linda lays a hand on the glass. "Sometimes it feels like someone's picked up one end of the world and just sent all the loose ends tumbling."

Heather leans against Kayla. Kayla's arm around her shoulder. "I'm tired," Heather says. "Help me back to bed."

* * *

The common room. The final hours before lights out. The
sisters play a board game with the younger girls, encouraging and explaining, keeping the peace. Kayla by the window.
The radio report—light snow, plunging temperatures and then
an even colder snap, an arctic blast and warnings of frostbite.
These past nights of fighting outside town. Distant explosions,
concussions echoed in the building's pipes and plaster. A lull
last night, a peace that found Kayla waiting for the crack of
gunfire, the next blast. They had dinner with Heather in the
nurse's office. A whispering of plans—soon, soon—Linda's
desire to join the rebels. Heather full of sighs, her eyelids
drooping, asleep before the others finished eating. The fatigue
she couldn't shake. The stupor of her pills. A confession of the
dreams that felt so real and a waking reality that felt like a
dream.

Cheers erupt at the hallway's other end. The whites'
common room, a game, Kayla guesses. A special snack, some
indulgence that won't find its way to their end of the hall. *Fuck
it*, Kayla thinks. The unfairness. The prejudice. Their board
games' missing pieces and fifty-card deck. The torn magazines
and unshared sweet rolls. Kayla and Heather and the sisters
will leave it all, an abandonment, an erasure. They'll shake this
place up then dissolve into the chaos.

The cheering ebbs into the singing of the new anthem.
Donna's voice distinct even at this distance. The choir-singer's
glint, the trilling notes. These days of passing stares, and in
Kayla, an emotion beyond hatred. The clear-eyed calm of indifference. A stripping of humanity. A body she wouldn't bother
cutting from the hangman's noose.

The Deacon strides into the common room. The board

320

game stops. The Deacon beams. His black blazer pushed back, his hands on his hips, an exposing of his holstered gun. Down the hall, the whites launch into another round of the anthem. "Ladies, ladies," the Deacon says. "I have news. Glorious, glorious news." His smile widens. "The rebels have been broken. Not just in our sector but all over. Their leaders have been captured or killed, and their units are on the run." He turns on the wall-mounted TV. A newscast, video of armored cars and burning buildings. Men with their hands on their heads. Bodies in the streets.

Nurse Amy runs in, Heavy Metal behind her. A hiccup in the Deacon's crooning, and Kayla sits up. A whispered conference and a hurried retreat. The Deacon pauses in the doorway and calls to Old John. "No one leaves this room until I say so." He turns to Kayla. His lips part, but he doesn't speak.

Chris and Linda continue playing with the younger girls, but between rolls of the dice, they exchange glances with Kayla. The news on the TV. Tanks on city streets. Men in camouflage and armbands of red and white. Buildings on fire. Kayla stands. Within her, an unraveling—their plans, the faces in her pod. Her life ebbing from solid to liquid and so much slipping through her grasp. She pauses by the window.

A gathering below. The front courtyard, the floodlights' shine. The Deacon and Nurse Amy and Heavy Metal. Steam from their mouths, the snow all around. None wearing a coat. At first, Kayla believes their gazes are fixed upon her, but then she realizes their focus reaches higher.

She grunts, the window's warped wood. A budge, and her fingers wedge beneath the sash, a touch of snow. She calls the sisters, Chris kicking the board aside in her scramble. The three of them lift, and the window jerks up. An icy blast. Snow through the grate. Nurse Amy's voice the first to reach them. "Heather! Heather, honey, please!"

"Heather, no!" Kayla yells. A teetering moment before the sisters join her, their faces cramming the opened space. The steam of their breath drifts through the floodlights' shine. The younger girls mass behind them, asking questions, some pushing their way to the adjoining windows. Kayla and the sisters' pleas thinned by the courtyard's emptiness, its dark and cold. Kayla screams. A culling of emotion from her hollowed chest, her vocal cords strained. She grips the window cage and shakes, her flesh sticking to the cold metal. "Heather! Heather, don't! Heather—"

A current passes through the courtyard figures. Words cut short. A communal reflex, Nurse Amy and the Deacon and Heavy Metal turning away. A flash outside. A white gown. A trailing of long hair. Her body turned, a pose of surrender, as if she were collapsing into a hammock. A flicker. The darkness possessed for a moment then purged.

A smack below, brief and dull. Macadam and flesh and the fallacy of flight. The sound little more than a gasp but enough to suck the air from Kayla's lungs. The body blocked from view, but Kayla still sees her. The thin arms and legs. The bloodied, limp form she lifted from the stairwell landing.

She pushes through the other girls. The common room's deserted middle, the board game's scattered pieces. On TV, the government's triumphant reports, men waving flags, rifles shot into the air. Kayla collapses onto the couch. Her elbows on her knees, her head hung. Voices around her, none that make sense. The surge of blood and her vision warps. Her pulse's thud heavy in her bones and teeth. She struggles to catch her breath.

Old John at the door. The girls ushered to their pods, the Deacon's orders. The sisters help Kayla to her feet. The three of them mute and pale, arms around each others' waists and shoulders. Old John at their side. His face streaked with tears.

The lights flicker. Old John in the hallway: "Lights out,

girls. Deacon's orders." His voice cracks. "Early bed, everyone go now." The sisters sit on the edge of Linda's bed. Their heads lowered, legs pressed together, four hands united. Shared whisperings, prayers Kayla can't join. The pressure inside too great. A roiling alchemy. Shock giving way to luminous rage. A swell in her chest, a stretching of skin, and she screams—wordless, guttural—if only to save herself from bursting. Another flicker. The lights die.

She paces. Her insides of haywire pumps and jackhammer blows. She crosses her arms, her fingers dug into flesh, a seeking of pain, a delivery from the moment's horror. She passes through shadows and watery light. She screams again, a single, stabbing cry. The sisters look up, their wet faces. Outside, an ambulance's siren, loud and close. Kayla at the window, the front courtyard blocked from view. The red strobe splashes the fence. The loading dock and pickup in the shadows.

"We're leaving," Kayla says. Words yet more. A proclamation, their secrets about to become truth. She digs through her footlocker. She secures her necklace's clasp and slides the silver crucifix beneath her shirt. "We're leaving. Tonight. Now."

She stuffs her pillowcase. The sisters put on their coats and hats. There's nothing left to say, not now. Their plans boiled down to a mad dash, violence over grace. *So be it*, Kayla thinks. She climbs atop the desk and pushes up the ceiling tile. She pockets the lighter and hammer, the broken mop handle. She tucks Heather's notepad under her arm. The truck key last, the metal loop snug around her middle finger, the key clenched in her fist.

Kayla slides on her coat. Her hat pulled over her ears, gloves stuffed into her coat pockets. The sisters wait by the door, their pillowcases filled. Kayla rips pages from the notepad and tosses them into the room's waste can.

"Should we wait until the ambulance is gone?" Linda asks.

At the notepad's end, the stack of loose pages. Heather's handwriting, symbols and codes. Kayla crumples the pages for Heavy Metal and Nurse Amy, Mr. James and the cafeteria ladies. The final page the Deacon's. She twists the sheet into a taper, flicks the lighter, and holds the flame to the paper's end. "I'm going to pull the alarm." The paper catches. The dancing light lifts the girls' faces from the dark. "Get to the back stairwell and meet me at the loading dock." She plunges the burning end into the trashcan. A crackle, smoke. A blossoming light. She tears out more pages and feeds the flame. She twists another taper and sets it to her pillow. The case burns. The pillow and blanket. The smoke grows thick and drifts into the hallway. "Don't let anyone stop you."

Chris covers her mouth. "Where're you going?"

Kayla hands Chris the truck key and her packed pillowcase. "I'll meet you there. Promise. We're getting out of here. The three of us."

She crosses the hallway and rests a hand on the alarm's white lever. Smoke curls from their door, the ceiling lights dimmed. She thinks of the roof's ledge and a step into nothingness. She pulls. The response immediate, the white strobes, the deafening wail. The sisters behind her.

"Fire!" Linda screams. She and Chris run down the hallway, pounding on the pod doors. "Fire! Everyone out!"

Kayla strides the connecting hallway. The commotion of the reds behind her, the whites in front. Old John hobbles past, his nose twitching. "Fire, girls! Fire!"

Kayla crosses the centerline. All sense of boundaries gone now. The girls in white flow past, some staring, the ones in her way pushed aside. Kayla remembers Linda's words, how one end of the world has been lifted, a pull born out in the momentum of her lengthening stride.

The door to Donna's pod cracks open. Kayla pulls the

hammer from her pocket. Her grip locked tight, a molding of flesh and tool and will. She kicks, and the door flings back. The scent of menthols, Ashley reeling, her eyes dull and uncomprehending. Kayla reaches her in a single stride. The hammer raised then swung with the force of Linda's upturned world. The gravity of pain and blood and fury. The hammer's metal flashes in the strobe, a blink before its collision with Ashley's forehead.

The crunch of bone, the hammer's face caught as Kayla jerks the handle. A groan from Ashley's parted lips. Her hand twitches. She slumps to her knees then onto her side. A single motion, as if her skeleton has melted beneath her skin. Kayla steps over her.

Donna's gaze on the bloody hammer. "Fucking bitch," she spits. Words barely audible beneath the alarm's wail. She topples a bunk and tries to run past, but Kayla cuts her off. Donna retreats then charges, a leap onto a bunk, a spring forward, her hands outstretched.

Kayla staggers back. A swing, a duck. The hammer strikes Donna's clavicle, and again, the give of bone. Donna cries out but presses forward. She wraps her arms around Kayla's thighs, clutching tight. With a twist, she sends them both tumbling.

Kayla's chest strikes the side of an upturned cot. The hammer spins across the tile. Kayla reaches, the handle just beyond her grasp. She turns and rolls on top of Donna. Her knees pin her elbows. Her hands tight on her neck. Kayla leans forward, her weight poured into her grip, the pressure in her thumbs, and beneath, the give of Donna's windpipe. An ebbing current. Gasps dwindle to shallow puffs. Donna twitches, her hands on Kayla's wrists.

Kayla glances toward the door. Ashley motionless. The blood puddled around her head, her hair sopped. Kayla turns back to Donna. Each beat of the strobe brings a deeper haze to her eyes. Donna's hold on Kayla's wrists loosens, and her hands slip away.

A warm night. Her father's fingers slipping from a rope. His open eyes no longer seeing. Kayla screams and lifts her hands. She sits back, a slump of spine and shoulders. Donna rolls onto her side, gagging, spitting. Kayla tries to stand, but her legs betray her. Instead she crawls, a child spent and sick, her throat choked with bile. The broken mop handle slips from her cuff. The back stairwell, their plans. The strobe and alarm a short-circuit in her thoughts. She stands on trembling legs. The back stairwell. The truck key. Donna still on her side, her voice, hoarse and pained. "Fuck you. Fuck you and your dead, fucking girlfriend."

Kayla falls back upon her. A knee on her chest, a hand beneath her pretty chin. Kayla's other hand raised. The handle brought down, and the splintered end mashes into Donna's left eye. A twist. Donna's mouth opens, a wordless gasp. The vibration of her breathing meshes into the machine's hum.

Kayla stands, straddling Donna. The handle rolls across the floor. The alarm and voices wash over Kayla, and she lets the tide carry her—half stumbles over Donna then Ashley. The hallway, her strength finding her. She runs. Old John ushers the last of the girls down the center stairwell, a feeble attempt to corral her. Kayla pushes past, knocking him against the wall.

No strobes in the back stairwell. The alarm muffled. A scramble, the steps a blur beneath her. The light still out on the landing where she found Heather. The sisters huddled and waiting at the bottom. "Come on," Kayla says.

Linda doesn't move. "There's blood, Kayla."

Kayla looks down. Splatters on her coat and sleeves, and in her, a dawning awareness.

"It's all over." Chris reaches out to touch Kayla's face but draws back. "Are you OK?"

"It's Donna's. And Ashley's." She takes the truck key from Chris. "Maybe you don't want to be with me now. You can go back. Maybe you should."

Linda looks at Chris. Their silent language. She turns to Kayla. "We're going. All of us."

The cafeteria alcove, a reunion with the alarm and strobes. A push of the loading dock door, and with it, another alarm, a new pitch. The cold sudden and cutting, the blood warm on Kayla's neck and hands. The dock steps slippery, and a thin layer of snow slides off when they open the truck's doors.

The doors close. The dome light snuffed. The girls' frantic breathing. The three of them crowded on the hard seat, Linda at the door, Chris in the middle. The stale stink of cigarettes. The key scratches the dash until Kayla finds the ignition.

A breath. A moment of alignment. Her feet tap the pedals. A hand on the steering wheel, the other on the shifter. Two years ago, she had to wiggle to the edge of the seat in her father's truck, her chin lifted to see above the wheel. Now, she feels him near. His faith. His love, and what would he think of her now.

The key turns. A whir and grind. Chris looks at her. Kayla tries again, her foot heavy on the gas, a sputter and then a catch. The engine rattles. The radio bursts on, the music blaring, Chris turning knobs until the song falls silent. Kayla doing the same until she discovers the wipers. A sweep, a cascade of white. A view of the lights that spill from the courtyard. At the light's fringe, a few reds. The girls bundled in their coats, a silent studying of the truck.

Kayla presses the clutch and shifts. The engine shudders and stalls. She wrenches the key, her fear the metal might snap. One foot down, shift, the other down. The truck lurches. The rattle of the plow's chains. The tires' churn over packed snow. A taller form wades into the gathered reds. His face shadowed.

"Kayla," Linda says.

"I see him."

The truck picks up speed. She has seventeen yards. Betty paced it off. Betty. Fucking Betty. Fucking Heather. Kayla feels them near too, and they're all getting out of here. Tonight. Together in one form or another.

The larger form breaks from the group. The Deacon in the headlights' periphery, Heavy Metal close behind. Kayla reminded of the deer and raccoons as she and her parents drove the river road. An emergence from the brush. Their headlights reflected in squinting eyes.

"Kayla!" Linda says.

The plow strikes the gate. The engine revs. The spin of tires and the back end's slip. Her foot pegs the gas. A progress of centimeters. The groan of metal. Linda screams. The Deacon's commands to stop echo in the cab. Linda slaps the lock but not before the Deacon grabs the handle.

"Pull it!" Kayla says.

Linda latches onto the inside handle. A two-handed grip. Chris grabs the window crank, but they're not strong enough to keep the door closed. One of the gate's hinges pops. Rubbery smoke rises behind them. The passenger door opens, a framing of the Deacon's scowl. The sisters scream. The Deacon snares Linda's coat, the material bunched, his wide hands. Linda halfway out of the cab, her body caught in a tug of war. The Deacon on one side, Chris on the other. Kayla lifts herself from her seat and presses down on her foot. The engine whines. Heavy Metal at her window, a grip on the door's handle, his barked curses.

The gate snaps, and the truck lurches forward. Kayla cuts the wheel, grappling with the truck's fishtailing end. The passenger side rakes the gate's post. The door slams against Linda's body, a whiplash of metal and momentum that rips her from the cab and leaves her and the Deacon wedged against the post. Linda's expulsion violent and sudden, a wordless moan, a gasp of frightened breath squeezed from her lungs.

The truck swerves into the street. Kayla wrestles the wheel. Their backend slams a parked car. The bent gate draped over the plow. The passenger door hangs open, the alignment of a broken wing. The engine howls, Kayla too panicked to shift. The ferocity of it all, the vibrations in the wheel, in her meat. The schoolyard to their right. The girls turn toward them. A few break away, their fingers laced through the fence. An opening in the crowd, a space between the whites and reds. The paramedics and their rolling gurney. A sprawled body beneath the Deacon's coat.

Kayla stops at the corner. Sirens and calling voices, barking dogs. She glances in the rearview. Heavy Metal runs after them, the smack of his boots as he sprints down the street's center.

Chris turns to Kayla. "I have to go back."

"I know." She reaches for Chris's hand. "I can't. Not now."

"I can't leave her. I—"

"I know. Go."

Chris leaps from the cab. Kayla watches, lost in a calculation of her life's subtractions, thoughts snuffed by Heavy Metal's appearance in her window. His fist pounds the glass. "Get out, bitch!"

She wrestles the shifter. The pickup trundles forward, a slow-motion escape. Heavy Metal runs alongside, screaming and cursing, his spit dotting the window, the door handle grasped until Kayla shifts again. A breath, a fall, and he disappears, a tumbling form in the driver's side mirror.

The street a blur. Row homes. Corner stores shuttered for the night. The streetlights' shine ebbs in and out of the truck. A man pushing a small cart stops and stares, the spectacle of her getaway vehicle, the passenger door hanging from its hinges, the plow topped with a section of twisted fence. Another intersection, a stop sign noticed too late, and with her passing onto another block, the realization she has no idea where she's going.

Left at the next intersection. A grinding of gears, a near stall. The fence's bottom rail rakes the macadam, and the shrill cry crowds her thoughts. She imagines the view from the third floor. A few blocks west, and the street begins its gentle slope. West to the river.

A pothole, and with it, the fence buckles. Kayla wrestles the wheel, but she can't save the plow from gouging a row of parked cars. Sparks fly, the clash of metal. The snap of mirrors. Another tug of the wheel, a righting, and ahead, blocks down the street's center, Front Street's lit vein. Beyond, darkness and the river. Sirens behind her. Her bloodied hands tight on the wheel.

A man steps from the curb. She cuts the wheel. A spin on the ice, and the plow broadsides a car along the opposite curb. Her chest slams the steering wheel, and her forehead cracks the windshield. A blank moment until she surfaces into a peculiar stillness. The street seen through the windshield's spiderweb. She stumbles from the cab, a listing stagger down the street's center. The parked car lifted over the curb and wedged against a stoop. Steam from the pickup's crumpled hood.

Darkness. A removal from the continuum of moments, a jump cut and an emergence into the haze. She blinks, desperate to align sight and thought, to comprehend beyond the cacophony of car alarms and barking dogs. A porch light switches on then another. She walks backwards, both watching and distancing herself. A hand on her forehead, the warmth of swelling flesh. A wince, the pain a call to move.

Her run a series of lurches and recoveries. Her knees throbbing, her chest. She blinks the blood from her eyes, her blood, she realizes, its warmth twisting to the corner of her lips. A voice: "Hey! Hey you! Come back here!" She moves faster, a jerking momentum, the street's sinking grade.

She pauses in a building's shadow. Front Street ahead of her—the road lit and empty. She crosses, a discordant note in the stillness. She climbs a fence, the top snaring her sleeve, a fall onto the other side. She scrambles down the long embankment. The snow up to her thighs. Each reeling step dims the city's lights. Relief as the darkness claims her.

IV.

***

You're near. I feel you close. You're beside me in this bone-deep cold, here on this edge of dawn in the river's mist and the fog of my mind. You're here with me on this slope of scrub and trash, the train tracks below and beyond that, the river, its ice and the groan of its hidden current. You're with me, and for that, I'm thankful because I don't want to be alone. Because your presence is the anchor saving me from bleeding into the cold and mist and pain.

Pain, yes, but don't worry, mom. Don't worry, dad. Don't worry because pain is liquid. Pain flows and pain evaporates. The knot on my forehead will recede, the steering wheel's bruise will heal. The maze of my thoughts will surrender its patterns, but while these ailments press close upon me tonight, I'm thankful for you, mom. Thankful for you, dad. Thankful for your light in this fog. For your whispers so close.

Dawn, and remember the ones we witnessed, dad? The low highway sun on the way to a Saturday tournament, the rattle of my gear and the way you'd let me sleep if I wanted, but most often, you let me talk, my nerves, the pregame butterflies I was never able to shake, and behind me now, that same sun, an illumination on Front Street's morning flow, a blinding through grimy windshields. Fifty feet up this bank waits the world that wants to consume me, and here I wait, shivering in the shadows, my spot kicked clear of snow, a woodsman's survival technique, and see, dad, I did listen, I always listened in some form or another. Always, and look how beautiful, mom, the kind of image you wrestled into your poems, the stillness and hardscrabble beauty, and I'm sorry for never taking the time to read all your work, and if I had your book with me now, I'd read it front to back and back to front, just to hear your voice. Just to stand inside your mind. I look across the river, and the same horizon-peeking light that keeps me in the shadows falls on the far shore, the glint of glass and metal, the cottony steam from rooftop vents, and as the sun lifts, the boundary of shadow and light pulls across the river's glistening ice, a demarcation that creeps toward me, that will claim me, a sunrise different from every other because it will put a period on last night, a locking into an unchangeable past and a truth I will never be able to deny. And I'm sorry, dad. Sorry for who I've become. Sorry for swinging that hammer, the blow that shattered both another girl's skull and all the easy stories I'd believed about myself—that I was good and kind and fair. That I wasn't like the mob I so hated.

The sun lifts and the shadow inches closer, and when the light reaches me, I know this long night will be done, Front Street's sirens and flashing lights, the bloody shine in the dark, and me lurking below, still as the river fish half-frozen beneath the ice, and of course the sirens were for me, even the helicopter with its sweeping beam, the eye of God upon the tracks and ice and knotted brambles, but last night, not even God could find me curled into a ball and tucked beneath the slope's branches.

A crusted tarp lifts itself from the dark, and I can't help but believe it's a gift from you, dad; a sign from you, mom—and although I've never believed in such things before, I do now, I must now, because logic and order have abandoned me or perhaps I've abandoned them. I'm concussed, I realize this, and I embrace my mind's haze as a shaman embraces his visions, and I've got to hope that in this fog waits a new logic, one encoded in symbols, none more immediate and true than the tarp I approach on hands and knees in these last shadowed moments. The snap of twigs and the snare of stickers, and I kick away the snow, the material stiff as I fold the tarp lengthwise and then cover it with snow and twigs until the blue disappears. The sun is almost upon me, and a spike enters my dulled rhythms, the fear I'll be betrayed, that God's vision comes not with man's light but with His own, and I slide into the fold, trying to ease my shaking, careful not to disturb my camouflage, and once inside, I pull the edge and seal out the world and bury myself.

The cold heavier here, the frozen earth, the colder touch of my snow-soaked sweatpants and socks, and what I wouldn't give to be sitting in front of our fireplace, dad, its heat and crackle and the knowing all I needed to see you was to turn my head, the knowing you had built our home with your hands and that even if you were at work, you were still always close, a presence as real as the fire's warmth, and I'm sorry for not appreciating these gifts I was given so easily. Sorry for not understanding the scientific truths of decay and reduction that awaited my memories. Sorry for not realizing what was true in the moment wouldn't be true forever.

The sun touches the tarp, slivers of blue, and despite the material's stink of mildew and old leaves and fish, I think of the pool where Fran and I mouthed the names of boys we longed to kiss, boys I'd later hate after seeing them run to watch a fire, anxious to witness the ugliness, and now I'll never get to kiss a boy or go to the prom or do all the pretty things a girl should, yet I've done things, haven't I, and that's why I'm here, isn't it. I grow thirsty, and I reach from my shell to cup a handful of snow. The cold numbs my tongue, and I wince back the pain in my molars until the snow melts. A swallow, and with it, a stab in my throat then relief.

I blow into my reddened palm then cover it with my glove, an awkward wedging of left over right. I see you, mom, your head shaking and a sigh, your loving exasperation for your forgetful daughter. I see the glove and imagine its fate. On the street by a wrecked truck. Caught on the fence atop the river-bank slope or tangled in the brush below. I flex my bare hand, blow, and my breath curls against my palm. I'm sorry, mom, I was always losing something, hats and bags, losing track of time, losing my bearings as I rode my bike, lost in my head's tangle—and I rest my hand over my mouth and understand now there are new hauntings I can never forget, not visual but tactile, a tattooing of muscle and bone, the vibrations carried on my skin and in my flesh. I flex my fingers and feel the body's thud from below as I held the window's wire mesh, feel the buck of a steering wheel and a hammer's bone-breaking impact. No, mom, I can't forget these. I turn my hand one way then the other. I've abandoned my world of theories and become my body, defined by its deeds and limited by its wounds.

The morning sun short-lived, and within a few hours, a light snow. My fog comes and goes. I lie still, the tarp's edge lifted, a slivered view. The brambles a forest. The iced river an ocean. The cold stubborn, and I fight the stiffness by flexing a joint at a time, a progression from fingers to wrists, elbows to shoulders, one arm then the other. Then my legs, only I have trouble when I reach my feet. I can imagine them, can twist and see my sneakers' laces and leather and rubber, but the signal between my toes and brain fades in my body's static.

The breeze picks up, and on it, the radio's predicted freeze. The flakes slant and the dead grasses whisper and the tarp ripples over me, the material anchored beneath my sneakers and shoulders, and I wonder if anyone's noticed my patch of blue, the cars on the bridge, the helicopters. I think of perspective, views close and far, and I think of slim margins and the hours between now and nightfall.

I hear the ruffle first, a flutter like tiny wings, before the plastic bag tumbles into view. The bag catches in the grass, and I reach out, a finger looped through the thin handle. The bag, its fresh white long faded, fills with the breeze, a billowing almost beautiful, and just beneath the plastic's snap, the call of voices, not one voice but many, whispers upon whispers upon whispers. I relax my finger and the bag tumbles, snared for a moment then gone.

The day passes, and I'd trade my remaining glove for a slice of your bread, mom, fresh from the oven and the butter melting and a thick spread of grandma's jam. And what I wouldn't give to trade the cold of the snow against my teeth for the warmth of our kitchen and the chance to hear your songs instead of the tarp's rustle. But I can dream of you, mom, and I do, this glazed sleep, this suspension an awareness from the pool's bottom, a place below the pain's surface. Here I'm with you, but when I reach out, you're gone, and I can no more hold you than I can hold the morning mist, but holding on is all that matters now, and I'll hold on to you with all my might, and I won't go back to the machine because they'll crack me open, my head and ribs and gut. They'll hollow me out, and I'll be laid bare with nowhere to hide you and everything else I love.

Snow piles on the tarp, my cocoon dimmed, the trapped air of the Shut-In's gas mask, and how strange, dad, to see you in your gear, your smile traded for insect eyes and my insect reflection staring back from your mask, and the fears we had then don't matter now, the worry of inhaling poison and future disease. No, dad, the things we needed to fear lived next door. We breathed the same air in the supermarket lines and dark-ened movie theaters. They idled next to us at red-light intersec-tions, their windows rolled up, their radios tuned to preachers of a different truth. What we had to fear wasn't a drifting toxin but the kind of poison that burrows deep into one's heart, and I love you, dad, but how could you not have seen that?

The things I listen for: booted footsteps and leashed dogs, a gun's cocked hammer. What I hear: Front Street's traffic, the honk of passing geese. I slip in and out of the fog before I'm shaken into consciousness. I imagine tanks, wild horses, a thousand marching soldiers. I imagine Linda's edge of the world picked up and all of it rushing toward me, a drowning in steel and brick and bodies. I lift the tarp's edge. Flurries traces the dark I hadn't realized had fallen. The tremors build, a compression of sound, a horn that pains my ears. The headlamp a hurtling star, and with the tracks less than twenty yards away, the gust lifts my tarp. The locomotive streams by, and behind it, a long line of cars, the clatter of steel, the rolling tons. Car after car until the end. The rattle thins and the quiet rushes back.

I lie on my side, the tarp no longer covering me, and I'm sorry, mom, for all the mornings I lingered in bed, ignoring your calls and savoring those extra minutes, the day's waiting crush less real than my inertia, and you outside my door, mom, never cross, understanding, I believe, what school was like for a girl so different, the genius, the freak. I sit, my joints stiff and unwilling. I'm coming, mom, and thank you for the moments you allowed me to lull, and I just need a minute to let my inner tides adjust to a new gravity, to blink back the dizziness that makes standing feel like an acrobat's trick. I scoop another handful of snow into my mouth and wait for the fog to recede.

The sky black, and around me, the blue radiance of ice and fresh snow. The cold takes my breath, a chill so intense I feel as if my heart is beating at the center of a stalled world. I pull down my sweats and crouch, and the pee patters below me. In degrees, I straighten myself. I stand, swaying, the wind, my dizziness. Complaints from my knees to my neck. My spine a pained conduit that lifts my pulse into my skull. I close my eyes, hoping the dark will ease my sway before doubling over and vomiting.

Remember, dad, that Christmas I lost to the flu? How you sat on my bed and explained a fever's war within, a clash of protectors and invaders. I gag and gasp and vomit again, although there's little to come up. My hands on my knees and my throat's raw ache and everything blurred by tears, prisms and halos around the opposite shore's lights. My first steps little more than a shuffle, my sneakers barely lifting, a set of parallel tracks and the crackle of dead grass, and in each step, reverberations of the crash, the physical imprint on my shoulders and knees and every bone in between. Gravity draws me to the tracks then works against me as I stagger up the rail bed.

The tracks stretch, a two-pronged compass of north and south. I turn, a single step, and seal my fate, the frozen river to my right, the tangle-growth embankment to my left, and beyond that, the city, its lights snared in the branches of the tallest trees. Front Street's hum drifts above me, a surface of light and activity, while I plod through the icy depths. A truck honks, the faint call, and Betty, I know you're up there, and I hope you're not as lost and alone as me, and I'll miss never being called Oakmont again, and dad, I know I thought you were naïve, but I guess I was, too, both of us blind to so much.

South, and in the distance, the tracks converge, a study in perspective, a point that pulls away with every step, a trick of the eye that will lead me back. The river's hidden flow and my graceless steps, the wooden ties and the packed snow. Eight miles. We've hiked father than that, mom, a trail along the Appalachian Ridge, a halfway spot where we lunched on boulders as large as our house. Eight miles and I'll be home by sunrise, and in me, the strength of one who has no options left, the liberation from notions of happy endings, the freedom of being whittled to body and will.

South, and mom, when I was four, you told me about Lao Tzu and the journey of a thousand miles, and you laughed when I doubted you, not the concept but the unit of measure, and we researched the li, the Chinese length approximately a third of the English mile, and our private joke that a journey of three hundred thirty-three and a third miles begins with a single step, and ahead of me waits twenty-four li, and who would smile at that but you, mom, and now that's gone too, the li and our thousand other secrets, all of them stolen, and my pace picks up.

The city's south-end bridge looms, towering arches of concrete and stone, a stretch between shores and shadows beneath, and above the occasional lights of passing cars. Each step brings a wince, and I think of the documentaries we watched, dad, the mountain climbers' tales of frostbite, their bodies surviving but their toes, sometimes whole feet, gone, but I accept the pain just as surely as I accept each inhale's frigid pang. I look up, the bridge no closer than it was before, and I have to remind myself I'm still moving, still walking, and when I look up again, I'm beneath the span, my fog, my empty thoughts, graffiti on the walls and a collection of crates and tarps, a circle of stones cradling charred logs, a hobo's village abandoned, and the wind kicks up and turns back on itself, the soot and snow, and for a moment, I'm blinded, a deeper dark, yet I keep moving, shuffling, the ties beneath me, and folded into the dark, the crunch of snow and deeper still, the stone-cast echo of my breath and the river's buried purr, and in the dark, I lose myself, my skin gone and all that is elemental cast into the night, and as I emerge from the arch, I squint, my vision's slow return, and I understand I am nobody. I am gone. And I'm born again, alone and new.

Notions of miles and li prove slippery, and the act of putting one foot in front of the other seems both miraculous and as automatic as my pulse. I switch the glove and tuck my bare hand beneath the opposite armpit. I pause only to eat snow or squat and pee. The brush masses, ragged and bent and sickly. The river falls away, hidden by growth, only to reappear and fall away again. The snow has stopped, yet the breeze stings of ice. I look up, and the clouds are thinning, the coming of this winter's coldest night, and above, the constellations you showed me, dad. Orion and Canis Major. Hunters and their dogs.

Time abandons me, and in the stillness of bare trees and frozen water, I can see the fog I carry, a moat that warps light and sound, yet which, at its heart, shines a slim yet resilient clarity. The singular understanding that I'm going home to a home that no longer exists. The notion illogical yet more true than any postulate or theorem, and what am I but an orphan returning to be with you, mom. With you, dad.

The vines and brambles rustle, and I halt atop the raised track, nearly toppling, my body robbed of grace by exhaustion and hunger and wooden feet. The clatter grows, a wavering in the scrub then the magical alchemy of wood to flesh as not twenty yards ahead, a buck steps into the clearing. The buck's head held high, its majestic rack, and behind him, two doe. The beasts in no hurry, the cold's dulled rhythms, their lack of fear. The buck gone as quickly as he appeared, a melting back into the riverside brush. The first doe close behind, but the second pauses atop the tracks, her head turned, and considers me. I manage a single step, the fragile balance lost, and the doe slips away.

I reach the spot where the deer crossed. I turn toward the river, the undulations in the thick growth, and around me, the deer's musk and fading warmth, and in the next moment, you're with me, mom, and my heart fills. You're right by my side although I don't need to see you, and your words fill me even though all is silent—sight and sound mean nothing for I can feel you just as surely as if I'd jumped in the pool's deep end, feel you on my skin and deeper, hear you in the squeeze of my lungs and pulse. You ask what I'm doing, and as I walk, my lips move, a confession to the trees and river and you, a telling of where I've been and what I've done, and I thank you for not hating me. The dead, you smile, don't judge, yet you worry, the ties of love stronger than this life, the embrace we once shared before my eyes opened. Don't worry, mom, don't worry, and my gloved hand cups my throat as your voice fades.

I push forward, sometimes wondering if I'm moving at all or if the Earth is simply moving beneath me, this unchanging tunnel view, the narrowing tracks, the framing of snow and trees, a perspective of treadmills and the illusion of motion. My feet dead within my cheap sneakers. Each step a stumble averted, each step bringing me closer, and dad, remember that song you taught me on a long hike, the one mom hated and I think you secretly hated too but which you liked to tease her with, and a smile flickers on my snot-frozen lips *and I will walk five hundred miles and I will walk five hundred more . . .*

I stop, realizing I've reached the old mill. Dad, you always laughed at my absentmindedness, my deep-focus daydreams, and here I am again, startled into the moment, the spur's coupling missed, the tangled saplings replaced by a fenced-in expanse.

There are ghosts here, my grandfather and great uncles and their fathers before them, the toil of generations, and I apologize to my ancestors that all their sacrifices, their dreams for their families' future, have brought them to the sight of an abandoned mill and a half-frozen girl, their blood and kin on the run. The fence sags in spots, a topping of barbwire, and beyond, snow-covered acres, small mountains of wooden skids and casings ten, twenty feet high. The smooth bumps of fifty-gallon drums buried in the snow, scrap metal heaps and a toppled crane. A hundred yards back, the mill's smokestacks like soldiers at attention, brick shops, some low and long, others five stories tall. The structures loom, abandoned and hollow, and I am their shadow. Their echo.

Here is my fear: I will miss the dirt spur we drove, dad, the put-in where you found your special bloom. Dazed, I will trudge past, not noticing the break in the trees, lost in the narcotic mist of the half-frozen, lost in the endless loop of my sneakers' shuffling over ties and snow. Come dawn, having realized my blunder, I'll sit to rest, and in time, fall into the sleep from which I'll never wake. I slap myself, one cheek then the other, a scolding to focus.

A smaller building sits halfway between the mill and the fence, its windows gone, and I imagine little boys and their BB guns, the thrill of breaking glass. A drift wedges the building's northern doors open, and from the breach springs a dog pack. The dogs' shadows against the snow, swift, bounding. The big dogs in the lead, a dodging path between the drifts. Behind them, the smaller dogs, their struggles in the snow, their yelps as, one by one, they're left behind, lost among the drifts, and I flash back to the day we picked up Chestnut, mom, and I'm thinking not of him but all the dogs we left behind, their cries and their snouts pressed to their cages' wire, and I hear that cry again, only this time it's evilled by bloodlust and hunger. I twitch, spastic on the cusp of momentum and paralysis. A Rottweiler and shepherd reach the fence, the others large enough to bound through the snow close behind, and against the chain link, a tide of fur and snapping jaws and white teeth, their barks joined by the rattle of wire. I look about for a weapon, a length of pipe or rebar, a concrete slab, but I'm left nothing, and my fingers so stiff I can't even make a fist. The dogs' wail deafening, and the cry rises up, culled from all that is wicked and waiting in the night, some of the beasts so thin their ribs poke beneath their matted fur. I move, purposeful yet trying not to show my fear, and the pack moves along with me, a rolling wave, whinnying and jockeying, some turning on the others, the biting of ears and flanks. I step quickly, my gaze fixed ahead, a survey of the fence, wary of the work of looters and their wire cutters, but in time, the baying calms, and I turn to find the dogs still and silent, watching, seeing me perhaps in a way they hadn't before. Another lost creature. A fellow survivor.

A mile and a half. I say the words out loud, or at least I try to, my face numb, the boundary between thought and action blurred, my chattering teeth, and my attention becomes a liquid thing, flowing from near to far and back again, everywhere and nowhere at once. The stillness and rails and naked trees turn ominous, all notes in a siren's lulling that could lure me past my turnoff and into a never-ending dark.

You're near, dad, in the constellations above, in the fish beneath the ice, your love alive in my understandings of these wonders. You're near, mom, in the grit and the drive that allows me to keep pressing, and I gaze to the branch-fractured sky and ask for a sign with the power to deliver me from being nobody, to have me claimed by the world, to have someone who knows my name. I scoop a handful of snow but spit it out, its metallic soot, the cough that follows a rib-spasm ambush. I bend forward, hands on my knees, a string of spit from my lips and my tears frozen on my cheeks. I straighten and blink, and manage a weak smile, for here is my sign, the recognition I've reached my destination.

Dad, the memory of our time here burns brighter than the cold. My truck-driving adventures, my shifting struggles, the heat and the haze of stirred dirt, the flight of finches and mayflies and the discovery of a single, red bloom, and here is my sign, a set of snowshoe tracks across the unplowed spur, and although I can't imagine summer's warmth through this numbness, I know those days exist, a past as real as the moment encased in my bones, my body a house brimming with memories. I lift my feet high yet I still stumble, a puppet's march through the drifts, and around me, a tunnel of knotted branches, and I fall, once and again, but I get up, pushing back the lure to simply rest—for a minute or an hour or forever. A cinder-crusted mound separates the spur from the river road, and only as I claw to its top and stumble onto the macadam do I realize I've lost my other glove. I touch my nose, my cheeks, feeling only vague pressure. I walk, the macadam iced and slick, the shoulder buried. A car approaches, a sweep of headlights. I cinch my hood, my jaw clenched, the pain and grind of teeth. The light grows, and after my night of darkness, I'm not sure I've seen a brighter illumination, a shine that births me from the darkness, a creature risen from the river and brush only to fade once the car rushes by.

No other cars pass before I reach the road to town. A turn, a final abandonment of the river, a slow, mile-long incline. The houses sparse, unlit windows at the end of long driveways, and you're with me here, mom, with me here, dad, our bike rides, this long coast to the river, the longer pedal back. Those years you'd loop back to ride with me, your smiles and encouragement, your offers to stop if I needed to catch my breath. Then the last years before the Shut-In, my legs strong from our hikes, from practices and tournaments, the rides where I forged ahead then glanced back, proud of the distances I'd put between us. I pause at the hill's crest and catch my breath. The road behind me empty and dark, and perhaps only looking back can one appreciate happiness squandered in the living, breathing moment, a moment crowded with action and reaction, thoughts slipping between what had been and what would be, and if I could, I'd go back and wait for you both here, wait and tell you how happy I was, wait to thank you and say I love you one more time.

Ahead, the first streetlights, the houses' tighter array, and soon, places I know by name, streets named for flowers and trees and girls. Houses I've been inside, birthday parties and sleepovers, ghosts all around. I take the alleys, my body stone one step, mist the next.

The alley behind Fran's house, the snow packed and slick, the first gray in the east, and even a forever-night can't resist the dawn. A journey of a thousand li may well start with a single step, but the final steps, no matter your unit of measure, are the ones that bleed you, their exhaustion and threadbare hope. I shamble to a stop, and my fatigue yields to confusion, Fran's garage missing. I look around, a twisting of terrain. A deliverance a clearer mind would have expected.

Helen's house to my right, the sticker-bush hedge and coal-black windows. The backyard's pristine snow. I rest a hand on the gate, and how far away you seem, Helen. How far away you feel, Heather and Linda and Chris and Betty, my past a lightless pit, my journey upon this bridge of ash that fades beneath my every step. Only you're strong enough to shine in the darkness now, mom. Only you, dad.

I shiver beneath my yard's oak, and my breath rises through the branches I once climbed. I can't claim the girl who monkeyed from perch to perch, she is as pale as steam, but in the pulses of her existence, I see her looking down upon me, each of us unrecognizable to the other. I trudge through the snow until I stumble onto the shoveled walk. Your garden buried on either side of me, dad, even the pots' rounded humps claimed. Our house's smashed windows replaced, and a faint light flicks on in the upstairs bathroom, and in me, a bleeding of identity, a confusion of time.

A snow shovel on the mudroom porch and beside it, a pair of small boots. The path around the house shoveled as well, and I crouch near the leafless branches, this last place I held your hand, mom, your face as you turned back, *Go!*, but I can't, mom, I simply can't. I can only return, again and again, these film-loop months, returns in spirit and memory, in hauntings and consciousness and dreams, and now, the return of my frozen, battered body, and I hurry, as near a jog as I can muster, wary of the street's lit windows, the early risers. I glance back and our front porch pulls away, and my thoughts need a moment to align its new adornments. Its flag of red and white. Its golden mailbox.

I'm out of breath by the time I reach Fran's garage, and in me, the new fear that I've come this far only to be discovered in the breaking light, to be betrayed by a busybody, by the people who didn't balk when they heard what happened to you, dad, who whispered you had it coming. My feet as dead as clubs, I kick back the drift that blocks the garage's side door, wild swings of my leg, the knob's metal painful against my bare hands until I'm finally able to jerk back the door enough to slip inside.

Dark here, the path of memory, the smells of paint and grease, and here is my imperfect salvation, here is my port and manger, the final gasp of this endless night. I'm crying, a different kind of tears than the ones I shed outside, different than the kind I cried alone in my bunk. These are tears for you for having to see what's become of me, mom; for what's become of us, dad, the family you loved so dearly. We died, the three of us, months ago, and I held on, the girl who couldn't believe in Santa buying into a fairy tale every other red and white saw through, and I can't help but feel my singular survival has been a mistake, a glitch in the universe's proper order.

A final act of daring—my balancing atop the car's hood. A fight to find my center, the smooth metal, my damaged body, the uncertainty of wet sneakers and numb feet. A blind man's grope, the overhang's shadow, its dust and loose nails, and finally, the blanket. I wrap the blanket over my shoulders and cup Helen's gun in my hands. A picture—my Communion dress, my hands held in front of me, and I am both that girl and her ghost.

The car's backseat, and I shed my sneakers and socks and rub my toes, a schism of touch and sight, my flesh distant, and I swaddle my feet with the blanket then bury myself beneath the other blankets Fran's father has draped over the ripped upholstery. My breath steams yet I'm saved the wind's bite. The morning sun on the east window, and the grimy illumination reaches into the car. I close my eyes, the gun held over my heart, and fall away. My world turns to weight, the gun and blankets upon my chest, and then the surroundings pile on—the car, the garage, its wooden roof, the hammers and vices. My exhaustion rises to meet the press of these things and in a breath, I'm gone.

. . . I come to slowly, and I think of you, dad, the rainy October Saturday you taught me about the ocean zones, and I rise from the midnight zone's oblivion of narcotic sleep and then the twilight's mingling of light and dark, reality and dreams, and here, mom, you're with me again, if only for a fleeting moment, because in this ocean, we can only sink or surface, and my time with you is short (it always was, wasn't it? and how crushing to only understand that now). Yet I struggle to stay here, to fight the buoyancy, struggle to swim down and sit close to you, those Shut-In days that stretched so long, and although I chafed against the nightmare outside and the boredom within, I always found solace in you, mom, always found peace by your side, and I hope I told you that enough, I hope you knew . . .

. . . the sunlight I push into is frigid and gray, and I lie blinking, a goodbye to you, mom, and an acceptance of the day. The accumulated steam of my breath a haze beneath the car's roof, and I take inventory. A touch of my forehead's knot. The lag and mist of my thoughts. My chest's bruised weight. My mouth parched and thoughts of water. The gun in my hand, and I click the safety on and off. I sit up slowly, the deep-sea bends twisting my gut, and unwrap the blanket covering my feet. The skin pale, last night's numbness now a tingling. My socks too crusted and frozen to put on, and I'm only able to wedge my feet into my sneakers after I loosen the laces and pull out the tongues.

The car door strikes a shelf, the rattle of cans, and I stumble into the narrow aisle, my body wooden and robbed of grace. A weak sun and the shadows of late morning. Stillness, the brutal cold, the neighbors gone to work, others simply gone. I slide the gun into my pocket then nudge the side door. I squint, the snow's blinding sheen, the sky of aching blue. A dog barks, and I crouch, and through the maple's drooping branches, I spot the bundled man up the alley. I close the door and wait, assuring myself that a man walking his dog on a freezing morning will quickly pass, but the dog's agitation rattles me, and I make my way to the alley-side door and tuck myself in the shadows just beyond the row of dirty windows. The man passes not six feet away. He's wrapped in layers, a hat and scarf, and the dog is wild, the leash taut, and in my chest, a welling for here is my Chestnut in an unfamiliar coat, the dog straining, yelping even after he's pulled away, and I'm not sad, Chestnut, because I know you've been saved, your new human caring enough to walk you on a cold morning, to wrap you in a coat heavier than the one I'm wearing, and I lay a hand on the window, a good-bye, a chance to feel you one more time, your barks' vibrations in the glass, a final glimpse of your funny stride as your new master tugs your leash and you disappear from sight.

I return to the side door, counting a minute and listening to the quiet before stepping outside, and how strange, to be moving in the sunlight, moving among the living, this string of backyards, the snowed-under patios and sandboxes. How strange to have emerged from the night, my body a testament to my sufferings, and I limp the backyard path, and have a plan, you said, dad, our little joke but also a plea to think beyond the moment, and last night's hazy plan was to come here and use Fran's hidden key, the one kept in a fake brick at the flowerbed's edge, but my concussion-addled logic hadn't considered the snow or frozen earth, and I slip down the basement well, the steps unshoveled and a balancing hand on the stucco wall, and of course the door is locked, Fran's father's wariness, his mistrust, and in this cramped space, I hear you, mom, your talk of Occam's razor and the beauty of simple solutions as I slide my hand into my hat and shrug off my jacket and cover the window pane nearest the doorknob. And I think of a man at a stoplight punching through a window as I do the same, two, three, four times until I grit my teeth and swing with all my might and the glass shatters.

I tap out the clinging shards, and from inside come the musical notes of glass striking concrete. I reach in, a contortion to twist the deadbolt, a further stretch to reach the knob. The door opens, and inside, a part of me melts, the furnace's warmth, the embracing dark, the ground-level windows buried by snow. A laundry basket rests atop the washing machine, and among the socks and shirts, Fran's basketball jersey. Another season, another team, a trajectory I no longer understand.

I ball my coat to fill the frame's missing glass, and at the stairs' bottom, I slide my sneakers beneath the last step. My bare feet take the risers one at a time, or perhaps I'm watching a movie of my feet, this lost connection, my tally of subtractions now reaching my body. I open the door to the kitchen, a return to light and lingering scents, breads and cookies, and how I loved your kitchen, mom, and the smell takes me back to another home, and I see you, Betty, in all your raging glory, a crumb-spilling tray hurled through the cafeteria, a display of chaos and rebellion and beauty, and I understand my journey isn't just about me, it's about you, Betty, and all our lost sisters. 10:37 on the stove clock, and I try to sync the house's rhythms, Fran with school and practice, her parents at work. I picture a half dozen clocks, calculations of return, the numbers I once juggled so easily now slippery and only the most general estimates glimmer in the fog.

I fill a glass at the tap and drink, but the first swallows only accentuate my thirst. I fill another, only this time, I choke, the water spit over the counter, my eyes tearing. I scarf down the first food I can reach, a hamburger roll, a granola bar, peanuts. The refrigerator next, cheese and milk and a chicken breast. Crumbs on the counter, my jacket, the chicken grease glistening on my fingers, a devouring, and I have to lean against the counter to catch my breath against the tides of exhaustion and euphoria. A red trickle snakes across my palm, and when I push back my sleeve, the rivulet branches around my wrist and a turn of my hand exposes the glass sliver stuck between my knuckles. I wrap my hand in paper towels, and I'm in the moment, yet also with you, mom, the night a brick smashed our window, your delicate touch and calm tone, two distant universes linked by blood and pain. I walk, and the rub of hardwood and carpet barely registers, this diorama's stillness, the tide beneath the silence, voices, this family I thought loved me. The Christmas tree, Fran's mother's insistence it stay up through January, and as I pass, my warped reflection passes across a dozen colored globes. I open the liquor cabinet, the shiver of glass as I claim a half-filled whiskey bottle. I clutch the banister and climb. The cat watching, impassive, its tail twitching.

The bathwater runs, and Fran, I know you won't mind if I

take what I need, we always shared, always thought of each other as the sister we never had, and how I loved your sass and envied your daring. I fill my hands, yoga pants, underwear, jeans, a thermal top and a hoodie, thick socks and boots. The sun slants through the window, then the smells of moisturizer and hair spray, and I hear your voice and mine, Fran, all those nights we stayed up, whispering, complaining, dreaming, and even though that life once-lived is no longer my own, I thank you for being there. Thank you for seeing beyond the daydreaming, number-freak cage the world was so keen to shove me in.

I close the bathroom door and shut off the water and set the clothes and boots on the floor. The fan left off, the need to hear an opened door. I slip off my sweatpants, its bloodstains, the material frozen from the thighs down, and on the floor, flecks of ice and frozen dirt, but I pause after taking off my top, the maroon material bunched and brought to my nose. Goodbye, Chris and Linda. Goodbye, Betty. Goodbye, Heather. I wipe my towel-wrapped hand over the mirror, my image naked and blurred, this battered, crew-cutted girl a different animal than the lost echoes who'd gazed into this glass before. I rub a palm over my belly, a gentle trace of my forehead's lump. This steamy moment is all I can claim. I have no bed, no roof, no food, my past cut off, the possibilities of quantum futures a lie for a girl who's done the things I have. Only the moment counts. Only the moment is real. Only in the moment can I scratch and claw and fight and bleed, and I need to see this for the gift it is.

I set the gun beside the tub, and with a hand clutching the towel rack, I dip a toe into the water. I grit my teeth against the fire that rides up my calf. One foot then the other, and I push back the fear of blacking out with chuffing breaths to counter the throb. In degrees and millimeters, I lower myself until I sit.

In my feet, a mix of numbness and pain, and I cup handfuls of water, splashes for my chest and face. The soggy paper towels slip from my hand, and rosy wisps curl in the water, the room's fog thickened by my body's heat, dew on the toilet and walls. I take a sip of whiskey, my eyes closed and a deep exhale, a reunion with my lost tribe, connections knitted by hardship and circumstance, and no good was to come of our time together, was it, my sisters? Each of us carrying the mark we were too blind to see. Each of us fated to be scattered and consumed by the new order.

In time, the pain eases—or I grow used to it—and I struggle to imagine the hours ahead of me, but all I see are postcards and shadows. I lift the stopper, and the tub drains, the water's pull in my blood, the drain's whirlpool hypnotizing. A ring on the porcelain, the fog all around, and the glisten of condensation on the gun's barrel. I take another swig and savor the barbed warmth, and how tired I am, I could sleep for days, this house of pillows and hot water and soft beds that may as well belong to the clouds. I stand, a rush of wooziness and the cool fire in my feet. The towel plush, another luxury, the white marred by blood. I raid the cabinets—tape, gauze—and dress my cut. I bundle my old clothes in the bloodied towel and shove them in the back of Fran's closet. Her clothes like a new skin after these past months of baggy sweats and scrubs. Another swig then downstairs, a raid of the front closet, a scarf, the black skull cap Fran wore on our winter walks, her father's gloves the only ones big enough to fit over my bandaged hand. The kitchen next, a plastic shopping bag filled, a long knife, a bottle of Gatorade, peanut butter smeared thick on hamburger rolls, the whiskey bottle. I wipe up the crumbs and blood, not wanting to arouse suspicion, my vague plan to return later, the cloud-house still and everyone asleep. The car keys waiting on the foyer hooks and an escape into the dark.

I return to the basement, its warmth, the furnace's hum. I step into the outside stairwell. The cold's flush on my skin, a foxhole's perspective, the looming trees and wind-sculpted snow, a gathering of self before my backward walk to the garage, my shoe bushing away my footprints, my only witnesses the finches tucked in the naked rhododendrons.

The garage, and with its shut door, the relief of return, the knowing this is where I belong, that I'm no longer suited for the luxuries of a cloud-house. I patrol the narrow spaces, gathering rags, a five-gallon gas can, dented metal and nearly full, a hinged lid and the groan of a rusted hatch. The gas's scent, clean and biting, cuts into the cold.

I burrow into the backseat's blankets, a closed door, an animal's nest. I refuel, peanut butter and Gatorade and whiskey. I stretch out, and with the closing of my eyes, I sense the forces trying to claim me, exhaustion and injury, the warmth of the tub and whiskey, the things I've seen and done. I rub my head, the hair just long enough to lose its bristle, the hardness of my skull, and I slide on Fran's black cap, and, dad, I'm glad your heart survived, lovely and hopeful, to the end, glad you didn't have to witness my hardening and descent. Glad you left knowing me as I once was and not what I've become . . .

. . . I lie still. Dark, yet my eyes have adjusted, this faintest of lights, my breath's lingering fog. I listen for the wind, but I don't hear it. In my thoughts, emerging set pieces, the back-drops of the next few hours. The sensation of gliding through the stillness of abandoned rooms. I'm not afraid, at least not yet. Perhaps when I know my time has been whittled to a few breaths, and I think of you, Heather, squeezing out those tiny windows, think of you alone on the ledge, your bare feet in the snow and the hesitation before stepping into nothingness, and what I wouldn't give to have been there with you, just to hold your hand, just to save you from being alone. Here is my only wish—that I won't be forced to linger on the precipice. That I'm not tortured and raped, but even if it comes to that, I will bear it. I will focus on what waits, not the toll of crossing. Flesh and pain are the only currencies that matter now, and I will surrender both in time.

I climb from the car, and in my body, a shifting tide, my pulse thick in my temples. I hold the gun, the awkwardness of my bandaged hand and Fran's father's gloves, my sense of touch removed. I stand by the door. The lights off in Fran's house and the snow's gray shimmer. I sift through my rag pile and twist a dish towel into a snug rope. I unfurl the cloth and fold it, once then again, a square over the can's opening. A gurgle beneath the metal skin when I tip the can, the liquid's cool evaporation on my fingers. I twist the cloth again, droplets on my boots, and force it down the can's nozzle, the rag a dangling tail, the lid's closing incomplete.

Outside and the cold fills me. The stars' distant pulse ripples in these small, hushed hours. I stick to the alleys, my lumbering pace, the can bouncing against my thighs, the liquid's slosh. I high-step through the drifts in Dr. Klein's back-yard, and I hope your little boy grows up in a saner world, one where politics aren't synonymous with murder and professors aren't hung in the street. I tuck myself along the house's side, the brick cold and the house silent, and I think of the view that once waited across the street, a girl with long hair on the open perch of a second floor. Slater's old house across the way, its windows dark. Our house beside it. The white and red flag. The gold mailbox. And I think of the cuckoo and the magpie and the beauty and cruelty of nature.

I leave the shadows and venture across the street. All is quiet, and hush, you sleeping children; hush, you innocents, and breathe in your fantasies and let me breathe in mine, and I skirt the streetlight's glow, a shadow between light and dark, but I can't help but glance up, a reflex and a moment's blindness, and with it, thoughts of you, dad, and how right you were about so much—but not about justice for I've learned the hard lesson that justice is wielded by the powerful, the violence of mobs, the calculated indifference of governments. For the weak, justice, if it ever comes, is stolen, snatched a crumb at a time.

Our porch steps, and here you are, mom, waiting, a smile for your daughter, and here I am, dad, returning for the last time to the house I thought I'd know forever. I wedge the can between the storm and front doors, and the lens of time veers again, and I drift back to the day I turned a cartwheel over rutted grass while Chestnut barked and the tags atop the surveyor's stakes fluttered. I flick the lighter, the shine on the door glass, on my hands. The Stoics gave us Ekpyrosis, the belief our cosmos is destined to be consumed by fire before it enters anew its cycle of rebirth and growth, and so let it be. I hold the flame to the rag's tip, and when it catches, I hurry off the porch. The rag burns, a hiss, a glint on the mailbox's gold. Knots of acrid smoke. I hobble into the backyard shadows.

The explosion loud, but not like the rebels' bombs. A flash that reaches around the house. A sound more like a weight dropped from a great height, a thud, a stealing of air and breath. I clear the snow from the picnic bench's top and sit. A dog barks. Smoke drifts, and I imagine the fire's spread, the doorway. The red and white flag. The foyer.

Upstairs lights flick on, my old bedroom, the hallway. I unscrew the whiskey and pull a sip long and slow, savoring the bite that no longer makes me shudder. The warmth in my throat a balm and a balance. Another brand of light in the downstairs windows, a pulse of orange and yellow, and memories, mom, of the jack-o-lanterns we carved, the candles burning behind their eyes and mouths. The stillness broached by the crackle of wood, by the split of sheetrock, the melting sighs of ductwork and siding, and beneath all of it, the release of voices. My uncles and my own. You, mom. You, dad.

Can I say the sight is beautiful? It is, truly so. The rise and lick of flames, the curtains catching and twittering like ghosts in their own consumption. The fire hungry, blind, and in time, it roars with a voice all its own, and with each exhale, the light and heat grow, a building rumble that reaches a crescendo when the mudroom door swings open and Slater stumbles onto the stoop.

Smoke roils, acrid and black, a massing beneath the overhang before lifting to the stars. Slater in his bathrobe and slippers, his yapping pug tucked beneath an arm, his other hand alternating between swatting away the smoke and holding a phone to his ear. He coughs and I cover my mouth, too. He sets down the pug, and with it, the exposure of his opened robe, his hairy chest and bulging stomach and shriveled penis. Between coughs, he implores the fire company to hurry.

Mom, do you remember how I cried the night before sixth grade started, afraid of my cross-campus trek to the high school? You told me to keep my eyes forward and walk in like I owned the place, and tonight, you'd be proud, my pace upright and brisk, a flow as natural as the river's. Slater's back to me as he yells into the phone, the dog barking, and when the fire's warmth flushes my brow, when my eyes tear from the smoke and I'm close enough to hear Slater's wheeze, I raise my hand and crack the pistol's butt against his skull. We're connected in the moment, our skeletons sharing this vibration, this violence, before he sinks to his knees. But my attack is imperfect, and the gun dislodges from my grip and clatters to the sidewalk beside him.

He snatches the gun and stands on jellied legs, his free

hand cupping his ear, blood between his fingers. A voice calls from the phone that's fallen into the snow. The barrel jerks as he struggles again and again to squeeze the trigger. His back to the fire and his robe open, the shadows not deep enough to hide his confusion and limp sex. The firelight falls upon me, my shadow on the snow. The kitchen window bursts and Slater flinches when the shards rain over him. Licks of flame shoot into the night, the distraction enough for me to kick him in the crotch and wrestle back the gun.

I release the safety. "Look at me." He's bent double but painfully rights himself. I level the barrel to his chest. "Do you know who I am?"

Steam escapes his twitching lips. I rip off my cap. A siren in the distance. "This is my house, and I want you to say my name."

"The girl." He straightens. His dark eyes narrow.

"Kayla," I say.

His lips twitch. "Kayla."

"You murdered my father."

I pull the trigger. A flash and a kick against my palm. The ejected casing catches the light, the fleeting shine of summer fireflies. He reels back and slumps against the stairs. Blood soaks the robe's shoulder. The flames spill into the mudroom. I aim the gun at his face. His bloodied hand reaches forward. "No, no—"

"And you murdered my mother."

I fire again, and his skull unzips, a splattering of bone and blood and steamy gray. He falls forward, his shoulder striking my leg, a weight I escape with a stagger into the snow. I right myself, his blood on my pants, the space that had once held his voice replaced by the barking pug, the fire's crackle and rumble.

"Kayla?"

"Kayla?"

I hear you, mom. I hear you, dad. The way you'd roust me from a daydream, tenderly, the way one would wake a baby or sleepwalker. I hear you. I understand, and my paralysis dissolves and I'm birthed back into the night. I pick up the phone, the operator assuring help is on the way, and I toss it, the screen glowing until it disappears in the snow. I head toward the street but draw back when I see a bundled form crossing beneath the light. "Hey!" he calls. "Hey you!" The sirens closer, and I stagger-run down the back path, turning back when I reach the oak. Slater slumped against the back stairs and fire in the windows and its flicker across the snow-covered garden, and in the air, the char of our history, the smoke of subtraction and reduction. The Slaters of the world have erased us, mom and dad, and it's only right that I've balanced the equation and erased what remained.

Snow begins to fall—or it has been and I'm only just noticing. Fran's house—the foyer keys, the chance to make a run— but the sirens push me back, the cruisers and fire engines, the stabs of red and blue between the houses. I keep to the alleys but in short time, I become confused. All of it familiar yet also fragmented, and I press on, desiring only to distance myself from the commotion and return to the silence. One alley becomes another and another, unlit veins of garages and tire-rutted snow. The smoke fades on the breeze.

I reach a cross street and crouch behind a pickup. Dogs bark, but I can't tell if they're near or far. I check for cars and cross, a glance of an intersection's sign and the realization I'm heading back to the river. My bubble reforms around me. Inside, the clarity of single-mindedness. Outside, the haze of my concussion, a fire's thinning smoke. Inside again, and I'm alone with my breathing, my boot's snowy tromp, and beneath my skin, other echoes. The smack of falling bodies. A gas can's exploding rumble. A gun's kick. The spaces between the houses grow, the snow piling upon the bare branches. I hurry, a jerky stride, the wrestling of heavy feet.

The bubble bursts, and the outside rushes in, and I'm a puppet torn at the seams, and behind me, a sawdust trail. Part of me lost beneath a summer streetlight . . . more in a white pod turned red with blood . . . more in a snowy yard that was once mine. All I can claim is this damaged shell and a clutch of memories and the mechanics of heart and lungs. My skin fades and the little that remains of me melts into the dark.

I'm not afraid, and the certainty of my ending brings peace. Seeing another dawn will be a miracle, yet perhaps I'm wrong, dad, because you always told me miracles were all around, and I believed you and still do. But you never mentioned that statement's inverse, that for every miracle there is a darkness, a cold malevolence, and just as you said with miracles, perhaps so it is with evil—all one has to do is open their eyes to see it all around.

I reach the river road. The bank's scrub and the silent tracks, the expanse of ice beyond. A car approaches, its headlights behind me, and my shadow stretches, my head down and my hand on the gun, the rush of air as the car passes. The taillights recede then flash, and the car stops, and as it begins to turn, its light bar flashes blue and red and white. I scramble over the guardrail's snowbank and slide into the brambles below.

I struggle forward, the branches and thistles like a thousand pulling hands, my steps faltering through the drifts. Scrims of dislodged snow follow me as I flounder among the saplings. The cruiser stops atop the shoulder and is joined by another, and when I squat in a deep thicket, I hear their radios, the slam of doors. Spotlights knife between the branches, a play of wavering shadows. I hunker into myself, my jacket pulled to my mouth, the fear of being betrayed by exhaled breath. Then the tremors, the tracks not twenty yards, and in the distance, a pinprick of white.

A searchlight passes over me, a moment's reprieve before it swings back. My back's turned, and my shadow snares in the brush. The other light finds me, and I turn, blinded, squinting. A man's voice: "Don't move!"

I spring up, not running so much as hurling myself forward, graceless and stumbling. Branches whip my face and chest, the snare of vines. I turn to witness the descent of flailing beams as my pursuers scramble down the embankment. The train closer, my huffing and the snap of twigs swallowed by the metal rattle, the violence of tons that would take a mile to stop. I clamber up the rail bed, the vibration thick in the wood and stone and steel. The train bears down, its distance impossible to determine, the darkness, the engine's speed, my brain's dense clouds. I step over the first rail, the headlamp upon me, the light of angels and burning magnesium, and I dare not look another second for fear of freezing. The second rail and then a stumble on the bed's other side. The train thunders by, the gust upon me, the rush of compressed air. My eyes stinging with grit.

I try to calm myself, but my lungs heave ragged and wild. The wheels flicker, and beyond them, the wavering scrub, the flashlights' wild angles. I hurry to the river. The trees taller here, the oaks and sycamores that shade summer fishermen, the leaves that burn orange and yellow with the frost, their branches now bare, and in one, a snared plastic bag, a pale ghost. I step over the debris washed ashore during last year's flood. Branches and snapped trees, vinyl siding wrapped around a trunk, a rusted barrel. I reach the clearing and collapse on the riverside's stones.

The train churns along, but the engine is already a quarter mile down river, and I know this time the silence following the last car won't be all mine. Flashlights poke between the turning wheels, and I clutch the gun in my bandaged hand, wondering how many bullets I have left (in my thoughts, a YouTube video, Fran's bedroom, the cloud-house, my parents gone and my hair still long), and I wish I'd checked the clip when I had a quiet moment but I'm afraid to do it now, the fear the bullets will clatter to the stones and be lost in the dark. The river stretches before me, the white expanse, the black sky. I unzip my jacket, my left hand grasping the crucifix. With a deep breath, I press the gun's muzzle against my heart. Snow catches along the barrel.

I close my eyes, and I see you, mom, and I cry because I don't want you to worry, because I know there's nothing that hurt you more than my pain. I cry because I see you, dad, because you taught me about the world's wonders, and here I am, prepared to snuff the most wonderful of them all, an insult to God and science, and I picture my heart punctured and bleeding out, the domino-falling goodnight of my systems. I see you, Heather, and I'm right beside you, and it kills me you had to be alone when the fullness of your pain pushed you from the ledge. And I see with your eyes, Heather, and I see with your eyes, dad—your last conscious moments, a perch high above the earth, a carnival ride's perspective. The muzzle taps my sternum, and I scream, my cry meeting the train's rumble, overtaking it. Then silence, and I lower the gun and stand.

There's snow atop the ice, yet with each step, I feel the slickness beneath, the going smooth at first then the ridges and slants, and below me, the churn of the buried current, and you're right beside me, dad, those frigid mornings we came here to marvel at the beauty of ice, its teardrops on weighted branches, the nooks between the stones, and I hear your stories of those who tried to cross to the other shore. "Only a fool tempts nature."

Steam escapes my chapped lips. "Yes, dad."

"I used to be afraid when you climbed our oak."

I smile. "You were proud, too."

"I was."

The train's final car passes, and I hear the shouting and walkie-talkies. My steps battle the slickness, the heaved slabs. The breeze's bite deeper here, the river's openness, this reduction to ice and sky. A glance back. Flashlights sweep the shore and brush. Voices like the bark of dogs. Ahead, a horizon of bare trees, and here on the ice, I belong to neither shore.

A light falls upon me, then another, and I stop. The shine at my back, and although I know it can't be true, I swear the light carries both heat and weight. I think of death and picture it as a moment, a period, and I think of the story that has come before, the richness of love and warmth and the blood that's washed over my gifts and good fortune and my surrender to the horrible tide.

I turn and squint into the starshine glare. Voices call from the light, harsh commands undercut by the wind and the ice's groan. If death is a period, then let me be the one who puts pen to paper. Let me dictate the last flickers of my thoughts and heart. I aim the gun into the brightest light and squeeze off a single shot. The kick in my hand, a ripple of bone and muscle. I breathe, waiting, savoring the night's deep, cold sting.

ABOUT THE AUTHOR

Curtis Smith has published over one hundred stories and essays, and his work has been cited by or included in *The Best American Short Stories, The Best American Mystery Stories, The Best American Spiritual Writing, The Best Small Fictions,* and the Norton anthology *New Micro.* His books include five story collections, two essay collections, and a book of creative nonfiction. *The Magpie's Return* is his fifth novel.

ACKNOWLEDGMENTS

With deep and humble thanks to Peter Wright, for his assistance with the manuscript's edits, and to Lisa Kastner, for giving this story a home.

And as always, with unending love to my wife and son. Nothing would be possible without their inspiration and support.

Past Titles

Running Wild Stories Anthology, Volume 1

Running Wild Anthology of Novellas, Volume 1

Jersey Diner by Lisa Diane Kastner

The Kidnapped by Dwight L. Wilson

Running Wild Stories Anthology, Volume 2

Running Wild Novella Anthology, Volume 2, Part 1 & 2

Running Wild Novella Anthology, Volume 3, Books 1, 2, 3

Running Wild Stories Anthology, Volume 3

Running Wild's Best of 2017, AWP Special Edition

Running Wild's Best of 2018

Build Your Music Career From Scratch, Second Edition by Andrae Alexander

Writers Resist: Anthology 2018 with featured editors Sara Marchant and Kit-Bacon Gressitt

Frontal Matter: Glue Gone Wild by Suzanne Samples

Mickey: The Giveaway Boy by Robert M. Shafer

Dark Corners by Reuben "Tihi" Hayslett

The Resistors by Dwight L. Wilson

Legendary by Amelia Kibbie

Christine, Released by E.a. Burke

Open My Eyes by T. E. Hahn

Turing's Graveyard by Terence Hawkins

Running Wild Anthology of Stories, Volume 4

Upcoming Titles

Running Wild Novella Anthology, Volume 4

Recon: The Anthology by Ben White

Running Wild Press, Best of 2019

The Faith Machine by Tone Milazzo

Tough Love at Mystic Bay by Elizabeth Sowden

Suicide Forest by Sarah Sleeper
Magpie's Return by Curtis Smith

Running Wild Press publishes stories that cross genres with great stories and writing. Our team consists of:

Lisa Diane Kastner, Founder and Executive Editor

Barbara Lockwood, Editor

Cecile Sarruf, Editor

Peter Wright, Editor

Rebecca Dimyan, Editor

Benjamin White, Editor

Andrew DiPrinzio, Editor

Amrita Raman, Operations Manager

Lisa Montagne, Director of Education

Learn more about us and our stories at www.runningwild-press.com

Loved this story and want more? Follow us at www.running-wildpress.com, www.facebook/runningwildpress, on Twitter @lisadkastner @RunWildBooks, Instagram at running.wild.press

CPSIA information can be obtained
at www.ICGtesting.com
Printed in the USA
LVHW041952061120
670968LV00004B/719